SICK MONEY

A GOLD AND COURAGE NOVEL

KAREN S. GORDON

ISBN: 978-1-7336064-9-3 (Ebook)

ISBN: 978-1-954296-00-8 (Print)

ISBN: 978-1-954296-01-5 (Audio)

For my grandfather, a farm boy who put himself through the University of Michigan Medical School in 1922.

1

Tuesday, Morning, Miami, Florida

V ance Courage stuffed a pair of new flip-flops in the pouch of his suitcase, zipped it, then checked the time.

Why did Sherry Rogers ask to meet on such short notice? It wasn't a request, rather a demand, and it had to be urgent for her to catch a last-minute flight from Indianapolis to Miami. At least it wouldn't screw up his travel plans. She'd set the meeting at the Admirals Club at Miami International Airport, giving him enough time to catch his two-hour fight to Belize City.

He stood curbside waiting for the Uber to arrive, staring at the tiny car icon on his phone, two minutes away.

"How you doing?" the driver asked, hopping out and popping the trunk.

He wasn't much in the mood to talk, distracted, obsessing why Rogers had flown in on an emergency basis.

"What airline and terminal?" the driver asked.

"American, North Terminal D."

The driver nodded in the rearview mirror.

It had been less than a month since he'd authorized the wire transfer of five million dollars from his offshore account into HIPP Corp's, a medical records company seeking investors. He'd been looking for ways to legitimize some of his cash hidden in an account in Grand Cayman, and he'd hoped a company teetering on the edge of bankruptcy would ask less questions.

He'd asked his buddy Jake Fleming, a retired investment banker, to look at the prospectus, and when Jake didn't see any red flags, Vance convinced his partner, Lauren Gold, to go in halves with him. When an investor comes in at the last minute to save a company from ruin, he's known in the financial world as a white knight.

Vance Courage, white knight. It had a certain appeal.

Weekend traffic was light and he arrived at Miami International in just under thirty minutes.

He rode the escalator to the Admirals Club, paid $59 at the door to get in, and looked for Rogers. He spotted her sitting in a plush leather chair in a corner with floor-to-ceiling glass windows overlooking the runway. He parked his bag next to the chair opposite her, pulled it closer, then sat.

"It's good to meet you in person, finally, and thanks for doing this on short notice."

Like she'd given him options. "How was your flight?"

"Uneventful. Listen, I hate springing this on you, but we have a problem."

"What kind of a problem?"

"Two of our doctor clients have lost patients over the last two weeks."

"People change doctors. What's that got to do with us or the company?"

"By lost, I mean died."

He tilted his head.

"Our software tracks pharmaceuticals, and since these are drug-related deaths—"

"What are you saying?"

"Both of the doctors whose patients died recently switched over to our platform. They are oncologists whose patients were on chemo."

"I still don't understand what that has to do with us."

"There're rumors that one of the families hired a plaintiff's attorney."

"Ah."

"I remembered your background and I looked at your file again. As a lawyer and an ex-detective, I need you to come to Indianapolis and meet with the doctor. I know I'm ruining your vacation, but if we have an exposure, I need to know. So do you."

She held up one finger, unlocked her phone using facial recognition, then tapped the screen. His buzzed on the low, round tabletop separating them. She shifted her eyes toward it. He opened the link to an American Airlines ticket to Indy leaving in an hour and a half.

He took a deep breath and exhaled slowly.

"It's First Class," she said.

He'd packed for the beach, not for a business trip to the Midwest. "You're sure about the facts?"

"Of course."

What choice did he have? Rogers was good, she'd ambushed him precisely at the right place, at the perfect hour. When she'd asked him about his upcoming trip a couple of days ago, he'd shared his itinerary. Now he wished he hadn't. Lauren was not going to take this well.

"All right," he said, "but I have to make a couple of calls. I'll meet you at the gate."

2

Tuesday, Midmorning
Ambergris Caye
35 Miles East of Belize City

Lauren Gold stepped onto the second-floor balcony of the waterfront resort and shaded her eyes. The Caribbean Sea twinkled clearer and more turquoise than an Olympic swimming pool, and the salt air smelled sweet, like grilled lobster.

The small Belize island of Ambergris Caye had almost no vehicles. People got around on carts and bicycles, and she'd reserved a golf cart for when Vance arrived, and prepaid a local guide with an old panga boat to take him on a private fishing trip.

She'd shopped at the local grocery, discovering the shelves were sparse, meat cost a fortune, dairy had passed the sell-by date, and if she'd been back home, the fruits and vegetables on display would have been tossed in the dumpster. Oddly, there was no seafood for sale.

She'd pored over the website for the Great Blue Hole on the flight from Miami to Belize City, a giant marine sinkhole about forty miles off Ambergris, located near a small atoll. She'd signed up for a day trip and paid five times retail for snorkels and fins at the local dive shop. Both she and Vance deserved a vacation, and they'd agreed on the island. Online it looked perfect, and after she arrived, she was positive he wouldn't be disappointed.

The first few notes of Pink Floyd's "Money" played on her phone, and when she answered, Vance's face came up on video chat. She positioned the screen with the long dock and private tiki bar in the background. He was going faint when he saw the white sand and crystal water in the backdrop.

"Are you at the airport?" She glanced at her reflection in the sliding glass door, smoothing her hair.

"I am. The place looks fantastic," he said.

"It would be a better picture with you in it."

"Aw."

"The French woman on the first floor sunbathes topless."

"I'm a leg man. That's why I'm such a sucker for you."

She grinned at the screen. He'd stayed to take care of some family business for his mother in Miami and was a day behind her. "You're going to love this place."

"Sorry, but I'm not gonna make it."

What? She turned the phone around and enlarged his face. "Why? What's going on?"

"Sherry Rogers wants me to go to Indianapolis."

She furrowed her brow. "Why?"

"There might be a problem."

"What kind of problem?"

"Something legal."

"And you agreed to go?"

He nodded.

"Seriously?"

"Yeah."

"When are you leaving?"

"In about an hour."

She was speechless.

"I'm sorry," he said.

She sighed into the phone loud enough for him to hear it. They'd invested in that medical records startup company that was on the verge of bankruptcy a month ago. That was *after* she'd planned their trip to Belize. "What kind of a legal problem?"

"A couple of patients died and Rogers thinks one of the families hired a lawyer."

"What's that got to do with HIPP Corp?" HIPP Corp—the Health Information Privacy Program Corporation—sold medical records software.

"She's worried we might be sued and wants me to check it out. I'm sure it's precautionary. The oncologist I'm going to see is a new client."

"Why would the family hire a lawyer?"

"The patients died in the office."

"As in more than one?"

"Uh-huh."

"What happened?"

"I don't have any details yet."

She inhaled through her nostrils and held it for a moment. "I'm going home. I'm not staying here by myself."

"I'm sorry."

His expression on video chat proved it. Tiny teepees formed over each eyebrow. He looked like a handsome basset hound. "You sure? You can stay."

"I know. And I'm sure."

"Okay. I'll call you from the road."

He was about to end the call.

"Wait," she said. "Did you say they're cancer patients?"

"Rogers said the doctors are oncologists, so I assume so."

This was close to home for him. His sister, Kathy, was a cancer survivor who'd been diagnosed soon after they'd first met, and he'd gone to great lengths to help her, arranging travel to Switzerland for treatment she couldn't get here.

"There's probably a perfectly reasonable explanation for it," he said.

"I'll see you at home in a couple of days."

He kissed the screen. It didn't have the desired effect, and instead of romance, she got a magnified view of his nostrils and nose hairs.

She flopped into the wicker chair on the balcony over-looking the white sand with two couples sprawled on lounge chairs beneath private, thatched palapas. A middle-aged man with Jay Leno hair rubbed sunblock on his wife's back while the younger couple read books behind their Ray-Bans. Why couldn't she have a normal life?

She checked flights on her smartphone and changed her return to Miami, paying almost double what she'd spent for the original round trip. She'd booked the resort on a non-refundable, weeklong package. Kiss that money goodbye. After she confirmed her seat on the first flight out—non-stop Belize City to Miami, leaving in the morning—she rented a bicycle and toured the island alone.

THAT EVENING she dined at an overpriced waterfront tourist trap. More happy couples.

More reminders Vance wasn't coming. Couldn't someone else from the company meet with the doctor in Indiana?

The hostess seated a man at the table next to her. He looked like a businessman, midfortyish, mildly handsome, probably a real estate prospector who built million-dollar oceanfront crap boxes. On her bike ride, she'd seen the monstrosities shoehorned along the shoreline, blocking the breathtaking natural beauty of the south side of the island. She'd learned to spot shoddy construction in Miami: It always included stucco siding and a flat roof, like the ones going up here.

A red Ferrari crawled by the restaurant, rattling her water glass and the rainbow-colored bottles of booze displayed over the mirrored bar. Who'd import a luxury sports car to an island with a top speed limit of thirty miles per hour? The man sitting near her smiled and shook his head, amused. She flagged down the waiter, asked for the check, left a generous tip and walked back to the resort.

She, Vance, and their partner in crime, Jake Fleming, had salvaged illicit cartel drug money from the bottom of Biscayne Bay, cash that had been stashed decades ago in the hull of an offshore powerboat resting on the seabed. Money different entities believed belonged to them.

More specifically, the US Justice Department thought it belonged to the Treasury.

Relatives of the defunct cartel kingpins believed it was theirs.

Now that the money was in an offshore bank account in Grand Cayman, she'd begun to feel like they'd earned it. She and Vance had been able to invest in HIPP Corp because the company needed cash. When she and Vance first met with Sherry Rogers, Lauren didn't like her. Maybe it was the duck lips and Botox, or the low-cut blouses and heavy perfume. Maybe it was the idea of handing over five million dollars with no guarantee of how it would be managed.

Vance reminded her that as money launderers they'd be better served acting as silent partners. She'd agreed to keep her mouth shut, let him shoot the arrow, and hope for the best. Legitimizing some cash, even if they lost a little principal, would be a good outcome. Heck, her half of seven percent interest on five million dollars was more than she'd ever made producing videos.

Their partner in the money salvage, Jake Fleming, was a retired investment banker with an eye for business deals. They'd asked him to look at the prospectus, and while he thought it looked a little thin on detail, he hadn't seen any red flags.

More importantly, Sherry promised them confidentiality, reassuring them she'd shield them from public disclosures. They'd receive quarterly interest payments, and once the company turned a profit, they'd receive dividends. Their ultimate plan was to deposit income into a US bank, pay taxes, then sell their shares back. The goal wasn't to live high on the hog; rather, it was to legalize some dirty money.

Didn't going to Indianapolis to snoop around put the plan in jeopardy? He should have asked her before he'd agreed to go, but by now, he was already there.

3

Tuesday, Afternoon, Indianapolis, Indiana

The airport was plastered with Indy 500 motifs, mostly black-and-white checkerboard patterns and green and yellow flags. Travelers milled around life-sized cardboard cutouts of race-car drivers Vance had never heard of, some taking selfies, others posing for group photos.

On the way to baggage, he and Rogers passed the *Indy 500 Grill*, the brightly lit 500 number flanked by a pair of enormous golden wings. The open-wheel race car on display outside the restaurant looked nothing like any Honda he'd ever seen.

Banners. Flags. Souvenirs. Sweepstakes. The town sure was enthusiastic about the upcoming race, and the marketeers were out in full force. They headed for the airport rental car counter where Rogers planned to use her status so he could choose any car on the lot, and she'd insisted on putting the charges on her credit card. He selected the Cadillac XTS.

He dropped Rogers at the long-term lot where she'd parked

her car, then headed to the airport hotel she'd suggested and checked in. After he'd settled in, freshened up, and changed into more appropriate attire, he drove to the address Rogers had given him, a concrete-and-glass structure on Michigan Avenue, part of the University of Indiana medical system. The building's dull color and unimaginative architecture reminded him more of a prison than a place for learning. He drove up three levels in the concrete garage and parked in a visitor's spot.

Following the signs to the skyway linking the garage to the professional building, he waited for the elevator, got in, and pushed the button. When he stepped out on the third floor, he looked left, then right, then saw doctors Emery and Shah's names stenciled in bold lettering on the smoked glass double doors.

The waiting room was cozy, with plush floral cushions and oak side tables. He stood in front of the half-open reception window. A thirtyish woman with short black hair greeted him.

"I have an appointment with Dr. Emery."

She handed him the clipboard. "Fill this out and someone'll be right with you."

It was a new patient form. He stuck his head through the opening and kept his voice down. "My name is Vance Courage. I'm from HIPP Corp."

She cocked her head and squinted with one eye.

"The software company," he whispered.

A young blonde-haired woman sitting offside at another desk noticed him. She stood and spoke through the open window. "Have a seat. I'll let her know you're here."

He picked up a *Martha Stewart Living* magazine, sat beneath a flatscreen TV broadcasting HGTV, and leafed through ads for cosmetics and furniture and dog food before closing it and putting it back on the coffee table. He glanced around at the patients—their sallow faces were . . . expressionless. He recalled the day he'd got the news Kathy was diagnosed, precisely where he'd been and what he'd been doing, sitting behind his desk at the converted office bungalow in Miami, mulling the future of his failing law practice. It was the same week his father died.

He'd read more online about oncology on the plane trip from Miami to Indy than he had the entire time his sister was in treatment. When she was sick, all he'd researched were costs, side effects, and her odds of survival. His interest now was more general.

Surgical oncologists cut.

Radiation oncologists burned.

Dr. Emery was the third type, a medical oncologist, meaning she dispensed poisons and experimental drugs.

Those were the choices. Cancer. That bitch.

A gaunt-looking senior man walked into the waiting room, headed to the sliding glass window and stood for more than a minute. When no one answered, he wrote his name on the clipboard, set it back on the counter, and took the open seat next to him.

"How ya doing?"

"Pretty good," Vance said. "And you?"

"My testicles feel like chestnuts roasting on an open fire. My hair's gone, and the missus is enjoying my winker being on the fritz. I feel like I have to pee all the time, even after I pee. Got some new side effects, like a little trouble breathing after the last round, but the doc says chemo plays all kinds of tricks. Other than that, I'm great."

He might've lost his hair but the old goat hadn't lost his sense of humor.

"Got two more rounds of chemo to go, but you know, it's like all marathons. The last miles are the toughest."

The hollow look was from months of chemotherapy. Someday cancer therapy would look as barbaric as medieval bloodletting and leeches with its standard regimen of cut, poison, and burn. The window screeched open. Vance hadn't noticed the toy soldier standing on the sign-in sheet.

"Hello, Mr. Graham. I'll be right with you." The receptionist then rolled her chair away from the window, back to her computer, he figured.

A few long minutes passed and the door to the back offices opened. "Mr. Graham." The blonde in pink scrubs, the one who'd told him to sit, stood in the doorway. "We're ready for you."

Graham hoisted his body up, using the chair arms to balance, walked to the receptionist window, picked up the toy, and stuffed it in his pocket. "I thought she woulda at least asked about it," he said, walking by him, holding the little plastic soldier in his palm. "I always bring him along."

Vance picked up the free *Living with Cancer* brochure and scanned the pages.

Ten minutes later the nurse reappeared in the doorway. "Miss Lancaster." A pale woman with no eyebrows and a scarf covering her head struggled to her feet and hobbled to the doorway. The man accompanying her—her husband, he assumed—followed, forcing a weak smile as he passed.

Why had he agreed to make the trip?

He wasn't a doctor, or a private detective, or even a practicing attorney.

Thirty more minutes passed. What if he bailed out now? This was depressing, watching sick patients disappear into the abyss on the other side of the door. He should've said no to Rogers. What had he been thinking? If he'd simply said no, he'd be on the beach now, listening to waves breaking and seagulls mewling. Just as he stood to leave, the door opened a third time.

"Mr. Courage, Dr. Emery is ready to see you now."

He'd missed his chance.

"Nice name," she said.

"I hear that a lot." He followed her down the brightly lit corridor, passing exam rooms leading to a wide-open area. Rows of privacy curtains were pulled shut; muffled conversations wafted from the other side, mixed with televisions playing softly. "What's your name?"

"Bibbins Beatty. With four Bs."

"Huh. That's unique."

"I hear that a lot."

He chuckled.

Emery's office was more disheveled than his had ever been, which was saying something. The way she waved him in with a landline telephone receiver cradled against her shoulder suggested she had better things to do. She motioned for them both to sit, and he looked around her office, detecting a spider crawling on a medical diploma hanging from the wall. When she noticed him looking at it, she waved to her nurse, pointing at the Kleenex box at the edge of her desk, miming for her to kill it. Bibbins plucked a tissue, squashed the insect against the glass, and dropped the wad in the wastebasket. She pulled another tissue from the box and wiped the glass clean on the University of Michigan diploma.

"God knows how long I'll be on hold," Emery said. "Bibbins, I'd like you to sit in on the meeting."

After Bibbins introduced him to her doctor boss, she sat in the armchair next to him, across from the doctor.

Emery stood, holding the phone to her ear with one hand— the cord tightening—rearranging a tower of paperwork, creating a line of sight to him. He slipped his hand though the gap and handed her his business card. She looked at it, then dropped the mouthpiece and pressed it on her neck. "I'm not sure why HIPP Corp sent a rep from Florida when we have a local one."

"I'm not a rep," he said. "I'm a partner in the company."

That got Emery's attention. "Is there a problem?"

He paused for a two-beat, realizing it was possible Rogers might not have laid the groundwork. "My understanding is that you've lost two patients in less than a month—"

"You're going to have to make this quick. I spend half my time waiting for insurance reps to tell me why tests my patients need aren't approved. I don't want to be rude, but I don't have a lot of time, and as soon as a live person is on the line, I'm going to have to take the call."

He hadn't expected this. What had he expected? That the doctor would be thrilled that the medical records vendor sent another bureaucrat to waste her time? From his days as a plaintiff's attorney, he knew the drill: She carried malpractice insurance so she didn't have to deal with this part of the business. Damn it. He should have bailed when his gut told him to, and reamed Rogers on his way back to the airport.

"I was hoping to find out what happened to your patients, the two that two died in the office."

"Why? What interest does your company have?"

Obviously, Rogers hadn't spoken to Emery. "It's a courtesy visit," he said, cringing inside at the weak premise.

"I can't tell you anything. There're privacy laws. I don't know what happened."

Talk about awkward. "I'm not asking for patient information. I'd like to know who has access to your intranet and how many administrators you have."

Emery leaned back in her chair. "Why?"

Why was a good question since he was making it up as he went. He'd assumed, wrongly, that Emery would want to talk, especially if there was pending litigation. "We've detected some unusual activity in your files."

She crunched her brow. "What kind of unusual activity?"

"It could be a glitch in the software." He needed to get to the point, to the rumor that one of the families had hired a lawyer, but he had to figure out how get there without irritating Emery more than she already was.

"What kind of a glitch?"

"That's why I'm here, trying to figure it out."

"Great," Emery said. "We switched vendors to straighten out the last mess. If we have another issue—"

"I respect your time," he said. "I'm more than happy to work with your staff."

"You could have picked a better time. Today we're busy in the clinic. The software is so complicated, I don't even know how to log on." She looked at her nurse. "Can you help him out?"

Bibbins nodded.

"She understands it a lot more than I do." Emery leaned back behind the files piled on her desk. "My staff prints out what I need to see patients. Lab reports. Radiology results. Prescriptions that need to be signed. Whatever I need to fight the insurance companies." She looked at his card again. "You're based in Miami?"

"You know how it is these days with telecommuting." He forced a smile, thinking about what he'd say to Rogers for putting him in a situation where he was unprepared. Then he had a thought. "My younger sister was diagnosed with pancreatic cancer."

Emery's face softened. "I'm so sorry."

Ordinarily, it was a death sentence.

"Me, too," Bibbins said, frowning.

"Neuroendocrine pancreatic cancer," he said. It was the same type Steve Jobs had, and though Jobs died, it had a better outlook than other types of pancreatic cancer. "She's in remission."

"I'm happy to hear that," Emery said. "They're coming up with new therapies every day."

"She went to Switzerland for treatment."

Emery's eyebrows went up and she cocked her head. "The clinic at Basel?"

"Yes."

"Wow, most people can't afford that. Maybe sometime we'll have more time to talk." Emery glanced at her watch and stood. "I'm not sure what else I can do to help. I have an office full of patients. What should we do about the software? If there's some kind of issue, what are we supposed to do in the meantime?"

Emery had to know it was next to impossible to make a quick change. Even he knew it took months to move records over to a new program; he'd had to do it once when his law office computer was hit with ransomware. "I'm sure it's nothing major. I'd like to look at the records for the two patients. Then we can make a recommendation."

"You know the privacy laws," Emery said with the office phone still resting on her shoulder.

She wasn't exaggerating about the hold times. It should've been the perfect segue to the question he wanted to ask, the one about impending litigation, but Emery preempted him.

"I'm sure you're held to the same standards as us, subject to equal civil and criminal penalties." She looked at Bibbins. "Show him what he wants to see."

4

Vance followed Bibbins toward reception.

"We can work in a back office. I'm sure Dr. Emery would appreciate it if we kept the problem low key," she said.

"How long have you worked for her?"

"Going on five years. It's only my second job since graduating."

"What was your first job?"

"I had a short stint in sales. It's kind of weird. I was in nursing school the same time Dr. Emery was in medical school. My fiancé was in med school, too. Now we all work together."

"Your fiancé's a doctor?"

She narrowed her eyes. "No, Jack's in medical sales. He works for your reseller, Masson Medical. He sold us your software."

Great. Another important detail Rogers should've briefed him on. HIPP Corp was headquartered in Indy, along with a company he'd never heard of, where Emery's nurse's fiancé worked. Why send him when HIPP Corp could've have sent the local reseller? If he'd known that, he wouldn't have floated the fake story about a software glitch.

"So, you all went to the same college?"

"Not Emery. She went to the University of Michigan. Jack and I, we went to Indiana University."

He was clearly not prepared for this meeting, and it had the potential to get worse. What was he going to do, sit next to her and ask questions about a software program his knew nothing about? "Do you mind if I reschedule?"

"What do you mean?"

"Your boss said it's not a good time. Maybe it would be better if I came back tomorrow."

"It's not up to me. You need to ask Dr. Emery."

"Will you ask her?"

"Sure," she said getting up. "But first I should look in on the patients, see how they're doing."

He followed her partway down the hallway and stopped across from an open exam room. It was where vital signs were measured. Blood must have been drawn there, too, and the tall plastic trash container overflowed with plastic tubing. It looked like an octopus family had been murdered and stuffed inside. His stomach lurched at the sight.

Emery's clinic felt like a place he didn't belong. To his right was the infusion center, an open area divided into eight sections using curtains hung from the ceiling, allowing privacy for patients and their friends and family. The sick reclined on greenish-blue chairs, the kind he'd seen in dentists' offices, tethered to infusion bags strung from portable IV poles.

Bibbins stopped to chat with another nurse.

He watched her pull open the curtain shrouding the recliner closest to the wall. He walked a few steps down the hall where he could watch and listen.

"Mr. Graham," she said.

He didn't answer.

She said it louder. "Mr. Graham."

Still nothing. He looked peaceful. Maybe she should let him sleep.

"MR. GRAHAM."

Then a strange feeling came over him. He watched her squeeze his shoulder, then shake it gently. Still no response. "Mr. Graham." She felt for his hand and pressed her fingers on his wrist, then recoiled, taking a step back, pulling the curtains closed, and rushed past him like he wasn't standing there.

He hurried to Emery's office in time to watch Bibbins barge in.

Emery covered the mouthpiece of the landline with her hand. "Is there a problem?"

"It's Mr. Graham," her voice quivered. "I think he's dead."

Emery dropped the phone, pushed the chair back, and grabbed one side of her white lab coat, pulling it tightly across her waist as she stood. "What do you mean you *think* he's dead?"

He stepped away from the doorway, stopping a few feet past Emery's office, staying out of the way. The doctor rushed out, heading the opposite direction, toward the infusion center, heels clicking against the tile. "Where is he?"

Bibbins led the way, gesturing to the curtains still swaying. He slipped into Exam Room 1 where he could observe.

Emery disappeared behind the shroud. Two seconds later she popped her head out and whispered loudly, "Call 9-1-1. Tell them to send an ambulance. Be discreet."

Bibbins hurried past, heading to the front. He stepped into the hallway to listen as she talked to the brunette who'd first greeted him. "Call 9-1-1," she said. "Tell them we have an emergency."

"What for?"

"Just do it. And be discreet."

It would take a couple of minutes for them to arrive. The ER was downstairs, connected to the adjoining hospital.

She hurried back to tell Emery help was on the way, and when she pulled the curtain back, he saw Emery frantically performing chest compressions on Mr. Graham.

"Keep calm," she told Bibbins, grunting between pushes. "Meet the EMTs in the hallway. Don't make a scene, bring them in through the back. Go, go, GO."

How could they be discreet with a clinic full of patients and their supporters? He checked for witnesses, and unnoticed, let himself into the empty waiting room to spy through the glass doors. In less than two minutes the elevator dinged and a woman and a man dressed in blue jumpsuits exited, carrying a gurney. Bibbins met them, then led them to a back door at the end of the hall.

The frosted sliding window to reception was closed. He let himself through the door leading from the waiting room to the clinic in time to see Emery move to the side, making room for the paramedics who flung open the curtains and unfolded the gurney. He took a position close to the emergency.

The female paramedic emerged, shaking her head. "We need to move him. Now."

Her partner, a short guy, said, "Let's go."

He couldn't see what they were doing, but a minute later Mr. Graham lay on the gurney; they had untethered him from the IV and placed a clear plastic mask over his face, his skin now the color of smoke.

Emery stood, shaking her head, and followed them. "He was doing fine. Labs were good. Attitude was great. White blood count up. Tumor markers. All good. I don't understand." She squeezed her hand into a fist and punched down inside her lab coat, tearing the seam in the pocket.

Emery instructed Bibbins to clean up the aftermath. The

equipment had been disconnected in a hurry. Fluids had leaked into pools on the floor, and the toy soldier lay in one, floating facedown. Tubing dangled from the IV stand, and skinny plastic hoses—pink with blood—were strewn across the infusion chair, other strands draped over a stainless rolling cart. Tissues and towels dotted the floor like bloodstained carnations.

Emery approached him, shaking her head. "I have to talk to the families."

Some had noticed the commotion and stood in the hallway looking in the direction where Mr. Graham had been.

Dr. Emery just lost patient number three, guaranteeing he'd have to come back tomorrow. He slipped out through the waiting room and, looking over his shoulder, pressed the elevator button.

5

B ibbins pulled the privacy curtains closed and snapped on a pair of disposable rubber gloves. She kneeled, mopping pools of fluid from the linoleum with paper toweling. She stood and looked at her scrubs.

Her knees were wet.

Plucking an antiseptic towelette from the dispenser, she rolled her pant legs over her kneecaps and wiped her skin. She waddled to the empty exam room across the hall, grabbed a clean cloth towel from the cabinet, wetted it with soapy water, and scrubbed her knees. When she was done, she dropped the towel in the laundry basket, and the disposable gloves and paper toweling into the biohazard trash.

Pulling on a fresh set of latex gloves, she unlocked a cabinet, removed a rectangular plastic container, and emptied the contents into a clean white garbage bag, then went back to the scene. Carefully collecting the debris strewn by the paramedics, she placed the tubes and bloody tissues in the container, then reached up and unhooked the almost empty infusion bag hanging from the top of the IV pole.

The EMTs knew how to disconnect the bag from the port

surgically implanted in Mr. Graham's chest. All the patients had them. It made it much easier for the nurses to infuse chemo drugs directly into a vein with little to no pain to the patients. Emery insisted on it. Having cancer, Emery reminded them daily, was difficult enough, and this was one of the ways to make the treatment as comfortable as possible.

She saw the toy soldier in the corner near a ceramic planter with an artificial fern where she'd mopped up the fluids by hand and wrapped it in a paper towel. Another patient had given it to Mr. Graham as a reminder to stay strong for the fight ahead. She put it in her coat pocket and took three deep breaths before she headed back to the front office.

She'd learned that patients and their families had different ways of passing the time. Some of the sick read until the high dosages of Benadryl—mixed into the IVs to keep allergic reactions at bay—made them too sleepy to concentrate. Others stared at individual television screens hung from the walls. Many had family members and friends who worked on their computers or stared at their cell phones. Mr. Graham always came alone and slept through his five-hour sessions.

Recently, two other patients had died in the same room, the same way. She'd asked Dr. Emery what happened and the doctor confided the autopsies were inconclusive and that toxicology reports had been ordered, but findings could take weeks. Would they be able to figure out what happened and if the deaths were linked? That reminded her: Where was the rep from HIPP Corp?

She headed to her desk where she kept a pair of clean scrubs and planned to ask the receptionist, Rachel, if she'd seen him, when her phone buzzed. A text message from Emery popped up on her screen: My office stat. Medical-speak for "Hurry."

While other oncologists dropped patients who'd lost their Cadillac insurance, or who'd gone through a divorce, or fell into a pre-existing category—where all cancer patients were doomed —her doctor bosses, a husband-and-wife team, treated everyone.

She grabbed clean scrubs and hurried to Emery's office.

Emery saw her standing in the doorway. "Sit," she said, gesturing to the armchair opposite her, the ones where family members often got the bad news. "Are you okay?"

They'd lost two patients in less than two weeks, three now counting Mr. Graham, and the practice was already reeling. She'd heard rumors the hospital planned to launch an investigation. She nodded.

"I know the timing is bad," Emery said, "but I was looking at my calendar, and HIPP Corp has training scheduled on the new software." Emery took a breath so deep Bibbins saw her chest rise. "I can hardly afford to let you take time away from the office, but I need you to go."

"What about what's going on?"

Emery shook her head but didn't answer.

Was it her imagination, or had Emery's temples gone gray overnight? She'd never noticed the crow's feet around her eyes, either. Two weeks ago, Emery had been stopped on the street, mistaken for Halle Berry. She doubted anyone would mistake her for the actress now.

"What about you? Are you okay?"

"We have to carry on, and I I need you to set an example for the others."

"Do you think it's safe? For the patients?"

"What I know," Emery said, holding up her index finger, "is it's not safe to stop their treatment. Mr. Graham could've had a heart attack, or a stroke, or something else. We have to wait and see."

"What about the others?"

"I'm sure there'll be a logical explanation for what happened. But stopping their treatments is not an option."

"I'll go for training. I don't mind."

"Good. The last thing we need is a problem with the new vendor. Speaking of which, where did Mr. Courage go?"

She told Emery that he'd wanted to reschedule, before the crisis with Mr. Graham, and that he must've left on his own. "What day is the training?" The sessions often went late.

"It's not 'til next week."

That worked. The dinner was tomorrow night, Thursday. "Sure."

"I'll email you the details."

A few months back, Jack had asked her to introduce him to her doctor bosses—Emery and Shah. Both docs politely declined. The medical records company they'd used until recently had had a major problem, randomly deleting half their patient files. Though she'd backed up the data on a portable hard drive and the cloud, the vendor was unable to resolve the problem. Her bosses had a change of heart and had asked her to set up a meeting with Jack, after all. He'd landed the deal and sold them their new EMR software, short for electronic medical records.

She headed to a back room to change clothes. Family members of other patients huddling in the hallway stopped her and asked questions about what had happened. She assured them not to worry, the way Emery had asked, then backtracked to the area where the patient died and closed the curtains. Double-checking her work, she wiped down the recliner, silver tray, and IV stand, secured the top on the plastic crate filled with the medical waste she'd collected, and carried it to Exam Room 1. Then she closed the door and put on a fresh set of pink scrubs.

6

Wednesday, Dawn, San Pedro, Ambergris Caye

There were no seats left on Tropic Air—the puddle-jumper airline with the exclusive route from San Pedro to Belize City—leaving Lauren with no choice other than riding the water taxi. The inbound flight from the mainland had been bumpy and she'd been airsick, but it was a short fifteen-minute hop to the island. Guest reviews for the boat ride on TripAdvisor were ominous. It was a ninety-minute ride, and a lot of travelers warned that conditions could be rough.

It was still dark out when she'd ridden the shuttle van from the resort to the taxi service. Arriving thirty minutes early, she was shocked to see the water taxi cabin already packed tight with dozens of passengers. She left her bag on the dock with the others being loaded down below by handlers.

"Good morning, ma'am." The crew member with the island

accent lent a hand and ushered her aboard. "There're no available seats left in the covered area."

She looked at the space between the dock and the boat and wondered how many slipped and fell overboard.

"Here. Put this on. It's going to be a rough ride."

She pulled the yellow slicker over her head. Though the cabin was covered with a canvas top, it was open air, and the seats were white plastic benches mounted on aluminum poles. She climbed aboard near the transom and sat in the corner on a built-in fiberglass block.

As the V-hull pushed off from the dock, the sun peeked over the eastern horizon, revealing three-foot waves and white caps. She huddled beneath the short strip of canvas overhanging from the cabin. The engines roared and the full boat pushed from the dock, gaining speed, jumping waves, the saltwater spray splashing over the gunwales. She pulled the yellow hoodie over her head and clamped it tightly around her neck with one hand to keep it from blowing off, hoping to keep her hair dry.

Her stomach heaved a few minutes later, the rollercoaster ride mixing with the smell of diesel. She'd been seasick before and knew the best way to stave it off was to find the waterline and fix her eyes on it. But visibility was poor, the sea and sky shades of gray that melded, erasing the horizon. Lightning spiked and webbed through the storm clouds, then crackled, followed by a boom that shook her bones.

How would she survive another hour of this nightmare? Jaw clenched, she gripped the metal railing, her torso churning in place, when she heard something over the sloshing of water and the drone of the engines. A man's voice, speaking loudly.

"Are you okay?"

Hunched over, struggling to swallow, she shook her head.

"Here, take this."

The man grabbed her hand, pried her fingers open, and put

two pills in her palm. She held her hand under her nose trying to focus. "What is it?"

"It's for motion sickness. I took one after I checked the weather report. Go on, take it."

He grabbed hold of her other wrist, felt for her palm, placed a bottle of water in it, and closed her fingers around the plastic.

Wishing for a speedy death, she tossed the pills in her mouth, tilted her head back, and chased them with the water. "I feel like I'm going to die."

"Know the feeling. Give it a couple of minutes. Sun's starting to come up. Watch the horizon and breathe through your mouth."

She prayed to God. *Stop the spinning and make the drugs work fast.* Eyes glued on the horizon, she squinted at the yellow orb trying to break through the clouds. A few minutes later her stomach began to settle. "What did you give me?"

"It's OTC, for motion sickness."

She'd have swallowed rat poison if that's what he'd given her.

"You look a little green. Breathe through your mouth."

She filled her lungs with wet, salty air. The urge to retch receded, replaced by a wooziness. As the whirling in her head slowed, she closed her eyes.

"I'd keep them open," the stranger said.

The sun—now an orange arch—cut into the gray skyline. The seas had calmed. Inhaling deeply, feeling better, she thanked him.

When he dropped the yellow rain hood from his head, he looked familiar, but from where? The natural light was too dim and the ride too bumpy to see him clearly. Then it hit her. He was the man she'd pegged as a real estate prospector.

"Didn't I see you at the restaurant last night?"

"Maybe."

"At the Whale Oil Café?"

"That's right. I remember you now. You were dining alone."

"My friend who was supposed to meet me . . . his travel plans changed." She lowered the yellow hoodie from her head and let it hang down over the back of her neck.

"You look better. You had me worried for a moment."

"I feel better. I don't know if there's a worse feeling in the world than being seasick."

"It's right up there," he said.

"Oh my gosh. Look."

His eyes tracked hers. He raised his eyebrows. "At what?"

"The horizon."

"Why?"

"There're a thousand dolphins."

He squinted, studying the waterline. "I'm not seeing it. Uh-oh."

"What?"

"There's a small amount of belladonna in the pills I gave you."

"What's that got to do with the dolphins?"

He paused for a five count. "Some people hallucinate."

"What!"

"Is everything all right here?" It was the young man from the water taxi who'd helped her with her life jacket and rain gear. He held a wide stance and hung onto the railing, letting his knees work like shock absorbers.

The man answered. "She was seasick but she's feeling better now."

"She's not the only one. Half the passengers are sick. I needed some fresh air."

The crewman stood watching the wake break behind the stern for a couple of minutes, then went back inside.

She looked down at her shoes for a moment, then back at

'the horizon. The dolphins were gone. Geez. They'd looked so real.

The stranger stood just as the bow of the boat dipped suddenly, smashing into a wave, rocking it side to side, unbalancing him. The passengers shrieked in concert.

"What the—?" she said, her stomach doing one of those elevator drops that suspends the contents just long enough to make you wonder if your last meal might come up.

He sat down next to her, waiting for the ride to smooth out. "Where you headed?"

She tried running her fingers through her hair, tangled from the wind and saltwater. "Miami."

"What time's your flight?"

"Nine fifteen."

"I'm on the same one. How about I give you a hand getting to the plane?"

I see a thousand dolphins. How demented was that? *A thousand freaking dolphins?* Her brain wasn't working properly. "I'd appreciate it. I think I could use the help."

The airport was a public place; it wasn't like he'd invited her to his hotel room.

7

Wednesday, Morning, Indianapolis, Indiana

Vance peeked out the curtains at another gray day. He'd self-parked the Caddy at the airport hotel last night after he'd stopped at the local gun store and dropped just over $600 on the last Glock 19 in stock and another $150 for fifty rounds of ammo and a shoulder holster. He'd have packed his own, but he'd been headed to Belize, not Indianapolis, and international law disallowed it.

He'd called Sherry Rogers and left a voicemail after his meeting at Emery's office and was surprised she'd returned the call after midnight. He listened to the voicemail, then started the shower. According to Rogers' message, Emery expected him at 9:00 AM.

He redialed Rogers en route to the meeting, but the call went to voicemail. He dictated a text while at a red light: "On my way to the meeting call me back," then pushed the send button.

He didn't care how busy Rogers was, if she had time to fly to

Miami, she had time to call him back. He balanced his cell on his thigh, screen side up, making sure he wouldn't miss the call.

At five minutes to nine, he parked the rental in the garage across from the professional building, pissed off that Rogers hadn't returned his call.

He entered the waiting room; the glass window at reception was open.

Bibbins stuck her head through. "Come on back," she said, hurrying to the door leading to the clinic. "Dr. Emery is ready to see you."

Walking the hallway, she asked, "How could you tell there was a glitch in the software? Should I be looking for something specific?"

He could thank Rogers for not knowing how to answer this. He'd danced on the head of a pin yesterday and lied about a problem with the software. Now he was stuck with the story.

"I'm not sure," he said.

She stopped midstep, and confronted him. "That's not very informative."

"We're still trying to figure it out."

"I hope you do before training next week. Otherwise, what's the point of going?"

Something else he could thank Rogers for. "That's the goal," he said.

What if there was a problem with the chemo drugs? It would explain what happened to Emery's three patients. Rogers' reason for sending him was to evaluate the company's liability, not to investigate the cause of death. His gut said it wasn't possible to consider one without the other.

He and Bibbins sat side-by-side in the same chairs as yesterday, but Emery wasn't at her desk. A minute later the doctor appeared. He stood as she walked around to the other side of her desk and sat. She looked like she'd aged ten years overnight.

"I told Ms. Rogers that I didn't see the point of you coming back."

He gripped the chair handle until his fingers hurt. Screw Rogers. He was going to do this thing his way now. "Could there be an issue with the drugs?"

"What do you mean?" Emery asked.

"What are the odds of three patients dying during infusions?"

"Extremely low," she said.

"Where do you source the meds?"

"I don't handle that part. The office staff does. I don't see what this has to do with our medical records."

"It has to do with liability. I'd like to look, see if there's a pattern."

Emery furrowed her brow. "What qualifies you to do that? Miss Rogers said you're an attorney."

"I am. I worked my way through law school as a homicide detective."

"Homicide?" Emery looked worried. She repeated it, as if in disbelief. "Why didn't she mention this?"

"I'm not jumping to any conclusions and there's probably a logical explanation, but I am qualified to investigate. It's better to let me look at the records before the plaintiff's attorney does. They're gonna request documents during discovery."

She nodded in an "Ah-ha" way. "That's why you're here, covering yourselves."

Truth was, he was beginning to wonder why Rogers sent him. It was true that Emery would have to turn documents over, and he had no doubt the lawyer representing the family—which would likely turn into families—would demand the medical records.

"We're on the same team," he said.

"Bibbins, will you help Mr. Courage?"

He glanced at the nurse.

"I'll show him whatever he wants to see."

He didn't know the first thing about medical records software, but he'd taken on a couple of medical malpractice cases. He'd have to think like the plaintiff's attorney, which would be easy since that's what he used to be.

———

"Who has access to the files?" Vance asked Bibbins on the way to her office.

"To read, or write, or share?"

"All the above."

"It depends."

"On what?"

"On who has the patients' consent and who's authorized to access them. We never know exactly because it's not one-size-fits-all. If one of our patients has surgery, then the files would be shared with the hospital staff and surgeons. Once it's in a hospital system, a lot of people have access."

"Who has access internally?"

"All of us can add notes and update medications, and report vital signs, but we can't prescribe drugs or make a diagnosis. I'm the only one who can access those files, and I only do it when I get orders from the doctors."

Her voice was as rich as a note from a cello, and in profile, her upper lip naturally separated from the lower one, like a pretty goldfish.

He pulled a chair from behind an empty desk and sat next to her. "Can you show me the records for the three patients that died?"

"Sure."

He looked around while she tapped the keys and logged into the program. A big HIPP Corp logo filled the screen.

"What happens to the records if a patient dies?"

"We keep them open until the billing is settled."

"What about after that?"

"Shouldn't you know?"

It was a good point, but she should know, not him. "I assume each practice has its own policy."

"We archive them on the server."

"For how long?"

"Why does that matter?"

"Because you have to adhere to whatever is your standard practice. If you keep them for a year then delete them, then by law you have to preserve the current ones for the same duration. I'd like you to print out the last thirty days of records for the three who died."

"I think I should run it by Dr. Shah first."

"Dr. Shah?" He'd seen the name on the door.

"He's Dr. Emery's husband, and he's the one to ask."

"Is he an oncologist?"

"Yes. He specializes in palliative care."

"Palliative care?"

"It's end-of-life treatment for patients who have six months or less to live. I'll be right back."

"Hang on. Why do you need to ask him?"

"Because he makes decisions about deceased patients."

That made sense. Her computer defaulted into sleep mode and the HIPP Corp logo disappeared, replaced by a full-screen beauty shot of a beach, reminding him how much he'd looked forward to some downtime with Lauren in Belize. He stood to look at a framed photo on the shelf above the monitor.

"Dr. Shah says it's okay to print the files for you but to

remind you that they're confidential." She cocked her head at him: she'd caught him snooping.

"Is that your fiancé?"

"Yes."

"Congratulations. When's the big day?"

She didn't answer. Something had caught her eye. "This is odd. You're right, maybe there is a glitch."

He moved closer to look. "What do you see?"

"The patient, the first one who died? She has an upcoming appointment. That doesn't make sense. Chemo is every three weeks. Her next appointment should have been in May and the one that's set is for late June."

"Maybe it's a clerical error."

"No." She scrolled down looking at the notes. "Appointments are made when patients check out and pay their deductibles. She didn't check out."

"Maybe someone at reception desk made the appointment before treatment started."

"No, the software has an option where we can't schedule a follow-up until the office visit is paid. Look, there's an outstanding balance."

"Check a different one."

She tapped the keys and looked at another file, closed it, and pulled up the file for Robert Graham.

"Look." She touched the screen with an unpolished fingernail. "They're all scheduled for the same date. June twenty-eighth."

Now he had something to go on. "Is there a way to see who entered the data?"

She took a minute, switching between the three different patient records. "No," she finally said. "Can your people see who did it?"

He had no idea and changed the subject. "Will you please print those for me?"

The machine spit out copies.

"Who orders the pharmaceuticals?"

She stapled the first set of documents and handed them to him. "I'm in charge of that."

"Where do you order from?"

"It varies."

"On what?"

"There're different protocols. Some drugs are time-sensitive and have to be mixed and infused right away. Others are powders. Some are liquids."

"Who actually places the orders?"

"I do."

"Who's the supplier?"

"Most of the orders are sent to the hospital pharmacy downstairs."

"Could someone tamper with them? Before they leave the pharmacy?"

She pursed her lips, exaggerating the pucker of her goldfish mouth. "I guess it's possible."

"What about after?"

"After what?"

"After the drugs are delivered."

"You mean here, as in the doctors' office?"

He nodded.

She paused to adjust the thin tortoiseshell headband holding her tidy blond hair. It had the opposite effect and a small tuft of hair sprung into a small arc.

He moved onto the next question. "How are the drugs delivered?"

"You mean from the pharmacy downstairs?"

"Yes."

"They deliver them daily." She reached under her desk and removed more papers from the printer tray, separated and stapled them, then handed the documents to him. "All the nurses are trained to mix and administer the drugs."

"What do you mix them with?"

"It depends on the drug. Some are push, which means they can be infused quickly or given in a single shot. Others are infusions we do here in the office. Some are continuous."

"Continuous?"

"The patient wears a pump."

This was far more complicated than he'd thought. "What do you mix with the drugs?"

"That's complicated. It depends on the drug. It could be saline or drugs to mitigate side effects."

"Gimme an example of what you add to reduce side effects."

"We use Benadryl for allergies. Zofran is for nausea."

"Have you ever had a patient have a bad reaction?"

"A lot of them get loopy from the Benadryl. Some still get nauseous. But if what you're getting at is if anyone's been sick enough to die? The answer is no."

"Could a patient get the wrong chemo?"

"It's possible, but it's never happened."

"None of them seemed sick the day they died?"

"They're all sick, but if any of them couldn't tolerate the drugs or were having too many side effects, Dr. Emery would have postponed the treatment."

He stood and held up the documents. "Thanks. I'll let you know if I have any questions."

"Don't you want to talk to Dr. Emery before you go?"

"I don't want to take up more of her time. Tell her thanks and I'll be in touch." He paused. "One more thing, it's important to preserve the files. It's illegal to delete or alter them, or do anything outside standard protocol."

"What are you suggesting?"

"Nothing. I'm making sure you don't do anything acciden-tally that could hurt the case."

He let himself out, rode the elevator to the lobby, and headed for the cafeteria on the main floor. He spread the three files across the table and studied them while sipping a weak cup of coffee.

The three patients had different cancers. Patient one had breast cancer, patient two lung cancer, and patient three, Mr. Graham, had been diagnosed with prostate cancer. All were being treated with a drug called DTX. He googled it on his phone. DTX was shorthand for a cytotoxin called docetaxel, made from plant alkaloids: the Pacific yew tree, to be exact.

Patient one was a forty-four-year-old white female diag-nosed with breast cancer.

Patient two was a fifty-six-year-old African American male being treated for lung cancer.

Patient three was Mr. Graham. Diagnosis, Stage III prostate cancer with a nine on the Gleason score.

He had to be careful. He wasn't licensed to practice law in Indiana, and he wasn't representing HIPP Corp: He was an investor, which meant he had a conflict. His involvement could jeopardize the case and help the plaintiff's attorney. About the only decent thing about cancer was it gave people time to get their affairs in order, and to say goodbye to their loved ones. When Emery's patients passed unexpectedly, it must've blind-sided everyone. It must've been awful for Dr. Emery, having to tell the families. And now she was being sued.

He couldn't imagine it; the thought of something like that happening to his sister, Kathy, during her treatment punched a hole in his gut.

Was there a way to do an end run around the doctor and get his hands on the autopsy reports? He didn't have any local contacts, and even before the spike in suicides and overdoses, toxicology reports were typically backlogged for weeks, sometimes months, and often inconclusive. He headed to the parking garage, convinced that something untoward had happened to Emery's patients. A pattern had emerged. He got behind the wheel of the Caddy and backed out of the visitor parking spot.

8

Morning, Wednesday
21 Miles Off Shore from Belize City, Belize

The water taxi hit a rogue wave, splashing a bucketful of cold water over the gunwales, waking Lauren with a jolt. She must have dozed off during the second part of the trip and when she came to, was mortified that she'd fallen asleep with her head on the stranger's shoulder. Startled, she sprang to an upright sitting position and apologized.

"No apology needed. I didn't want to wake you. You look like you're feeling better." He held his palm out. "I'm Hunter Grant."

"How long was I like that?"

"Not long. Ten minutes, maybe."

She folded the cuff of the yellow raincoat higher on her right wrist and offered her hand. "I'm Lauren Gold. Nice to officially meet you."

"How are you feeling?"

"A little woozy."

As the boat approached the inlet, the crew dropped white bumpers over the starboard side to protect the fiberglass from the concrete dock. The weather had calmed, and the dull-green harbor water was smooth as split pea soup. Belize City had the sleepy look of a banana republic with single-story buildings, many with loud paint jobs.

The water taxi listed on an angle as the passengers—competing to disembark—crowded along one side. She checked the time on her phone. They had plenty of time, even if they were the last ones off the boat. Dozens of new passengers stood on the bulkhead waiting to board the outbound ferry. Workers on their way to the island, she figured, from the way they were dressed and their lack of baggage.

"Being seasick is the worst," he said.

Her stomach quaked at the smell of rotting fish mixed with exhaust. They'd ferried in on a V-hull vessel now docked ahead of a wider, more stable catamaran. The triple outboard engines on the cat growled as it reversed, creating a wake big enough to rock theirs.

Hunter helped her to her feet. She stepped up onto the dock, her stomach unprepared for the aromas of hot grease and grilled onions coming from the street vendor carts. She held her breath until she was lightheaded.

"You don't look good," he said.

She nodded, swallowing hard.

When they'd departed under darkness of morning, she hadn't noticed the lime-green-and-white paint schemes of the water taxis. The crew unloaded bags from the cargo hold onto the dock where they were transferred to worn-looking hand trollies. She and Hunter headed to the outdoor pickup area where a rustic Luggage Claim sign hung from a listing awning.

Hunter hailed a cab and wild driving unsettled her stomach again. The road trip was short, and in minutes they arrived at

Goldson International Airport in Belize City, where a fiefdom of local workers herded passengers through the doorway like livestock, a cacophony of voices yelling: *Come on, come on. Move it. Let's go.*

Neither had anything to declare nor bags to check and were hurried to a slow-moving security lane.

While their luggage was being hand checked, Hunter walked through the metal detector, setting it off. A heavyset woman working security sent him back through, and the machine buzzed a second time. She watched as two men motioned him out of line where a second woman ran a wand over his body. When his back pants pocket beeped, he removed his wallet and handed it to the one with the wand.

Three airport workers convened to inspect him, then motioned to a more formally dressed agent wearing black pants and a wrinkled white shirt. Lauren stepped out of line and craned her neck to watch and listen.

The most official of the bunch opened the wallet, removed a badge, then showed it to the others. "FBI," he said with an island accent.

"It would be best if you gave that back to me," Hunter said.

The passengers waiting in line quieted.

Hunter lowered his voice. Darn it, she couldn't hear what he was saying. A screener took the badge from the guy in charge and passed it around, letting the others touch it.

The heavyset woman who'd first detected it held her hand out, as if to return it to Hunter, but when he reached for it, she snatched it away and wagged her finger at him. "Ah, ah, ah," she said, eliciting laughter from her fellow workers.

Since her arrival, she'd seen more open palms than palm trees. Shortly after she'd landed, she gave a five-dollar bill to a baggage handler who turned out to be a panhandler who cut and ran. She'd met a guest at the resort who'd warned her about the fake taxes local workers charged and pocketed.

Hunter held his hand out again, signaling he wanted his wallet back. If they planned to shake him down, he needed his billfold. He rubbed his thumb and forefinger together.

They opened the line back up and she breezed through the metal detector, then waited for him on the other side. Five minutes passed and he was still haggling with airport security. She looked away, worrying what might happen if anyone thought they were together. She jumped when he touched her shoulder.

"I can't decide which was worse," he said, "the boat trip or this."

Her hands trembled on the handle of her roller bag walking alongside him to the gate. The airport ground crew herded them out to the tarmac and told them to stand at the base of the portable stairs leading to the cabin door of the passenger jet.

Had the drugs worn off or was this another version of a thousand dolphins? Was the badge real? What were the chances of bumping into him twice in less than twenty-four hours? Now heading to the same city on the same flight?

What if it wasn't a coincidence and he'd been shadowing her? What if he knew about the dark money they'd moved into a Cayman bank? What if he planned to take her into custody in Miami? *Jesus, get a grip.*

They stood on the tarmac and were last to board the plane. Halfway up the stairs, she turned and asked in a low voice, "Are you really FBI or was that left over from your kid's Halloween costume?"

He grinned. "I don't have any kids."

They'd left their bags on the ground near the base of the stairs where handlers tossed them into the belly of the aircraft.

about being gouged by the airline. He promised to make it up to her by taking her clothes shopping for the gala, a promise he was currently fulfilling. Before he'd picked her up, he'd bought an off-the-rack suit for himself at the local mall.

When she walked out of the dressing room, he wolf whistled softly.

"You like it?"

He paused. The whistling should have been a clue but now the question felt loaded. Before he had the chance to screw it up, she twirled in front of the three-sided mirror and reviewed it from every angle, and said, "I like it, and it's on sale."

She twisted her neck like a corkscrew, checking out the back of the dress in the mirror. "What do you think?"

There it was, hanging in the air—the same question.

She didn't wait for his answer. "I'm going to try the other one on, too. Do you mind?"

"Not at all."

Last night, he'd searched Masson Medical on the 'Net and checked out the leadership team on the company website. Sherry had arranged for him to be a guest of the vice president of sales, a middle-aged guy with a fat neck and an uncanny resemblance to a catfish. According to Rogers, the two knew each professionally.

Lauren stepped out of the dressing room, this time wearing a red gown with a slit to her thigh on one side. He was about to say something nice when she turned and hurried toward the storefront, then stopped and stared out the window.

He put the magazine down and went to see what caught her attention. "What are you looking at?"

"I thought I saw someone familiar."

"In Indianapolis?"

"I know it sounds weird, but remember the guy I told you about, the one on the plane?"

"The FBI agent who fed you a hallucinogen?"

She smirked. "Yeah, that one. I could swear I just saw him."

The sidewalk was empty and his rented Caddy was the only car parked out front. "You think you just saw the guy you met on the water taxi? Here, in front of the dress shop? How many dolphins were with him?"

"Very funny. What if it's him?"

"You think he's stalking you?"

"I'm being serious."

The storeowner approached. "Do you need some help?"

"I'll take this one," she said.

"Good choice," the woman said.

"I second that," he said.

What a relief Lauren had been able to make the trip on short notice. He hated salespeople, chitchat, and corporate events of all types, and having her with him would make the evening a lot more tolerable. In his lawyering days, he'd had a colleague who called salespeople mullets. He smiled at the thought he'd be sitting with a catfish surrounded by schools of smaller fish —mullets.

Collectively, he and Lauren plunked down a lot of cash for their interest in the medical records company. Privacy was everything and if word leaked the software had been breached, it would sink their investment. When he pressed Sherry for more details over the phone this morning, all she'd share was that she and Fields had worked hard landing the deal with Masson Medical—the exclusive reseller of their software—and that doctors Emery and Shah were their first clients.

10

Wednesday, Evening, Indianapolis, Indiana

Bibbins' fiancé, Jack, had hired a limousine to drive them to the impending drunk-o-rama disguised as a company sales meeting. When they stopped to pick her up at her apartment, the driver got out and opened the door for her. She cracked the window to let some of Jack's spicy cologne out, and by the time they got to his colleague Taylor's place, Jack was on his second gin and tonic.

Taylor opened the door and apologized for his date, Emily, who had to make a last-minute pit stop in the house.

"Cool, an eight-door Hummer," Taylor said, leaning in. "Hi, Bibbs."

When his date arrived, Taylor opened the door, and Emily sat across from her. "Hi, Bibbins. Hey, Jack."

When Taylor got in, he brushed by her, hunched over, headed to the back, and she pulled her short cocktail dress tightly over her knees. Compared to Emily's attire—stilettos and a micro skirt—Bibbins was dressed like a schoolmarm.

Jack stared out the tinted windows at the rain droplets beginning to smack the glass. "Too bad they can't see us."

"What do you mean?" Bibbins asked.

"You know, us, in a limo. They're all staring. It's too bad they can't see our faces."

Next stop, the tony suburb of Carmel, to pick up Bob and Bob. One of them had tried going by Robert but the Bob-and-Bob thing stuck. Older Bob was a top Indianapolis plastic surgeon. Younger Bob worked with Jack and Taylor at Masson Medical. Bob the Salesman was a preppie who'd known Jack since they were high school freshmen at the exclusive Culver Academy.

Dr. Bob was twenty years older than his live-in boyfriend, and as one of the most sought-after cosmetic surgeons in the greater Indianapolis area, could afford to keep Young Bob in the style he had grown up in. While Old Bob wanted to get married and adopt two children, Young Bob was content living in the palatial brick Tudor with the three black Scottie dogs he'd brought to the relationship: Beam, Me, and Up. While amusing, it had to be confusing.

The duo jaunted down the walkway in matching tuxedos. "Whaddup?" the younger one said on boarding the limo.

Young Bob played bartender, apologizing as he leaned over her with his armpit in her face, rattling the glassware in the cabinet over her seat.

The last stop was to pick up Marie Elizabeth, her BFF. Bibbins texted her from the limo waiting curbside in front of ME's converted warehouse loft/condo in the trendy Broad Ripple district, ranked as one of the hippest in the country. A minute later her friend sailed out of the lobby.

Marie Elizabeth Masson's family was so prominent in Indianapolis that the local media dubbed her Marie Elizabeth *Money*. Bibbs called her ME for short. ME's grandfather founded Masson Medical, the company Jack, Taylor, and Young Bob worked for, and the one hosting tonight's gala.

ME looked stunning. Then again, she could accessorize a hazmat suit and make the cover of *Vogue*.

"Hey, guys," she said, climbing in.

Jack and Taylor watched her every move. The inside joke was that they loved *Money*.

ME crouched, making her way to the corner of the limousine, and sat next to Bibbins. "You look nice."

"You, too," she said. "I'm so glad you're coming with us."

"It's written into the terms of my trust fund."

There were rumors Marie Elizabeth's father had squandered her share of the trust on a gold digger, but Bibbins never asked her about it. Marie Elizabeth was a realtor, representing exclusive properties that weren't listed to the public. She wasn't sure if she worked because she wanted to or because she had to.

"Sorry about what happened at work," ME said. "That must have been awful."

"It was terrible," she said.

"It was in the *Journal*," ME said.

"I read it, too," Jack said. "It was in the financial section, which is weird. The article said there might be a federal investigation into a medical records company but the story didn't name the company. I hope it's not HIPP Corp. That would be bad for business, and if they're sued, I could lose my year-end bonus."

"Jesus, Jack," Senior Bob said. "Have a heart."

"Yeah," Taylor said, squeezing his date on the kneecap. "Show a little compassion."

"Come on everyone, chill out." Jack downed the last half of his third gin and tonic. "I'm just telling you what I read in the paper."

ME asked, "Did you know the patients?"

"Of course," Bibbins said.

"That's so sad."

"I know."

"Do you know what happened?"

"No."

ME fished inside her purse. "I promised my dad I'd go. They think it's important to have someone representing the family. Thank God you're going and let me know you were. Otherwise, I'd be stuck sitting at the head table with the sales executives. I've tried, and it's torture." She swiped a pretty shade of coral lipstick on her mouth.

Bibbins smiled and nodded.

11

Wednesday, Evening, Indianapolis, Indiana

In Vance's opinion, the JW Marriott in downtown Indianapolis was an architectural affront, the kind of unimaginative glass tower that disfigured skylines across America. While the gray sky and light drizzle shrouded the city in a sense of quiet desperation, the ten-door Hummer limousine hogging a lane in front of the hotel did just the opposite.

Waiting behind a line of cars backed up at valet, he stuck his head halfway out of the rental car and looked up. "What do you think about that?"

"I think it's kind of cool," Lauren said with her head out the car window, tilted up, staring at the giant race-car graphics projected onto the mirrored exterior of the skyscraping hotel. "What about you?"

He half smiled and shrugged. "It's interesting. I guess."

The valet motioned him to pull the Caddy forward under the awning to stay dry, then ran around the front bumper and opened Lauren's door, beating him to it. "Enjoy your evening," he said.

Inside the lobby, a group gathered around a life-sized replica of the Borg-Warner trophy, the Indy 500's version of the Stanley Cup. Deeper lines of people milled around two brightly painted race cars, rolling billboards with dozens of corporate logos glued to the bodywork.

He and Lauren hung around for a moment, then headed to the Masson guest registration desk where they picked up their name tags, his pre-printed, hers blank. The woman behind the table apologized, handed her a Sharpie, then pointed to the bank of elevators. "The event is on the third floor. I hope you have a wonderful evening."

He doubted that would happen. Waiting for the elevator, his phone pinged. A message from Sherry Rogers: Another patient death.

He typed quickly. Emery?

No. A Chicago doc. You can drive up tomorrow.

The elevator doors opened and they squeezed in.

"What was that about?" she whispered.

"Nothing."

"I can tell when you're lying."

The elevator stopped one floor up. More people packed in, sardining them in with their backs against the stainless steel. It stopped on the third floor, and when the doors opened, they joined a party that started just outside the elevator, continuing seamlessly into a balcony overlooking the grand lobby. They snaked through the noisy crowd of well-dressed, socially-lubed Masson Medical folks. A woman cackled over the room noise. A group of young men huddling near one of several open bars stared at Lauren, at the thigh-high slit on her dress.

What a bunch of salivating dogs.

Lauren glared at them, then picked up where she'd left off. "Like I was saying, I can tell you're not being forthright."

This was an infinitely more diplomatic way of accusing him of lying. "It was a text from Sherry Rogers. There's been another patient death."

"Are you serious?"

"Yeah." He showed her the message on his phone.

She furrowed her brow. "You're going to Chicago?"

"I didn't say that. Come on, let's go fishing and have a little fun first."

She shook her head.

"I'm going to introduce you to the VP of sales and I want your opinion."

"About what?"

"I want to know if you think he looks like a catfish."

She swiveled her head. "Do you really expect to find anything out here?"

"What? You ready to blow this pop stand already?"

She curled one corner of her upper lip and sneered at him. "Not yet, Daddy-o, but I think the Midwest is having a weird effect on you."

"Come on." He pulled her gently by the elbow. "Let's throw a couple of lines in the water and see what happens. First, let me buy you a club soda. Did I tell you that you look gorgeous?"

"You need to check your hotel room when we get back."

"For what?"

"To see if there's something in the water."

12

L
auren had worked plenty of corporate events and debated in her head whether it was worse to be a guest or a vendor. If she were working, at least she'd be making money and wouldn't have to socialize. She hated producing video at these gigs where you had to spend hours to get ten seconds of useable footage, where someone in the picture wasn't scratching a body part, shoveling food in an open mouth—which no one, including a Victoria's Secret swimsuit model looked good doing—or hamming it up in front of the camera. Drunks had a hard time resisting option three.

Vance waited in line to get their drinks. Guests were stacked ten deep in front of the half dozen open bars set up around the room. Masson Medical had dropped a lot of money and she estimated the crowd size to be about three hundred. Three hundred times a couple of hundred equaled a lot.

A server carrying a platter stopped and offered her a choice of bacon-wrapped shrimp or mini-filet mignon served with a pat of butter. She loaded her plate with both and waited for Vance to return from the bar. The woman standing next to her dressed for the red carpet, guzzled beer directly out of a longneck bottle.

"Don't judge," Vance said, cocking his head at the beer bottle drinker. "It doesn't become you." He handed her the club soda, took a shrimp from the plate, and popped it into his mouth. "Yum. Let's go find our table."

They'd been assigned to a round-top for twelve set near the stage. She scanned the table, looking for her name. Vance had a reserved place setting with his name printed on it. The placard to the left of his read *Guest*.

A short, squat man in a fine Italian suit approached. He had an uncanny resemblance to a freshwater fish.

He read Vance's nametag and introduced himself as Bill Fields.

She was terrible with names and he wasn't wearing a tag. *Bill*. Like *invoice*. That's how she'd remember it.

"I see you two found the bar."

Vance held up his beer. "It was a challenge, but yeah, we found it." The joke landed and Bill laughed.

Bill specialized in small talk. "I see you found our table. Where're you from? Where didja go to school? Where're you staying? You're with HIPP Corp? How long have you been with the company?"

She listened while Vance did all the talking.

When Bill finished with the banter, Vance whispered, "This could be a long night."

"Long, perhaps, but always entertaining," Bill said, wandering off to kiss different ass.

Vance raised his eyebrows and scowled. She could have warned him that sales executives had bat-like hearing. Except Bill would have heard her.

The room was crowded, and while they'd found their table, other guests milled around looking for theirs. A group of drunks stumbled toward them and one bumped Vance's right shoulder hard enough to unbalance him. He turned to see who'd done it.

An attractive young woman who wasn't with the drunks took a few steps back to clear the aisle and let the rowdies through. She'd noticed the girl because she seemed lost, as if looking for her seat.

"Oh, my gosh, Mr. Courage?" the girl asked.

He looked at her, cocked his head and squinted.

"Bibbins Beatty. We met earlier? At Dr. Emery's office?"

"That's right. Of course. You're out of context, I didn't expect to see you here. Bibbins, meet my colleague, Lauren Gold."

"Nice to meet you," the girl said, then turned toward Vance. "What are you doing here?"

She seemed distracted, looking past Vance at the people milling around Fields' table.

"We got an invitation from Masson. And you, what are you doing here?"

She seemed nervous.

"Um, I'm with my fiancé. He works for them."

"For Masson?"

"Uh-huh."

"Small world," he said.

"It was nice seeing you," the girl said, hurrying away.

Lauren stood on tiptoes to see where she was headed. She stopped at a table near the stage. "Bibbins. What kind of name is that?"

"Maybe her mom was a *Lord of the Rings* freak," Bill said, glancing around. "If Bilbo Baggins had a daughter—"

"I get it," Vance said.

Like most corporate climbers, not much got past Fields, whose table was situated near the stage, closest to the podium. As they took their assigned seats, Bill introduced her and Vance to the guests at his table: a doctor, a supplier, a CEO from an ambulance company. The others, mainly spouses and dates, introduced themselves.

Lauren sat quietly, reading the fixed menu, keeping an eye on Bill. She eavesdropped when the server took Bill's drink order. He ordered Coke with lime, no booze. In the sales world, sobriety was a character defect and might explain how a guy as unimpressive as he was could make it to the top of Masson's corporate food chain.

If she was sizing him up correctly, Bill was the kind of sales mercenary that probably encouraged his team to party hearty. Schmoozing could be very good for business. She'd seen it first-hand working with dozens of corporate executives: When people imbibed, it loosened their lips—and their wallets. And sometimes, even zippers. A client might close a deal just to save face.

She leaned over and whispered in Vance's ear. "I need to use the ladies' room."

He stood and pulled out her chair. On the way to the elevator, she asked the server where the restrooms were. The line snaked from just outside the banquet room to the hallway leading to the bathroom. The women standing in the back of the line chatted, comparing their new Louis Vuitton handbags that resembled dark-brown feedbags with an L and V pattern stamped in gold. If her calculations were close, they'd paid about twenty dollars per letter.

She walked to the elevator, looked at the line, glanced up at the small round numbers showing what floor the elevators were on, then headed to the escalator to use the ladies' room located on the lobby floor.

At the base of the first set of moving stairs, she stopped, turned, and was about to step onto the top stair leading to the ground level when she felt someone grab her forearm. She pulled away, grabbing hold of the rubber handrailing to keep her balance. When she saw his face, a jolt of adrenaline surged through her veins.

"Come with me." Hunter descended the stairs two at a time, his paw clamped on her forearm while she struggled to keep up without jamming her skinny heels inside the moving metal parts.

"Don't make a scene," he said at the base, walking purposefully toward the hallway leading to the restrooms on the main level. She trotted nervously alongside him, across the tile, past the race cars on display, toward the softly lit dead-end hallway.

"Let go of me." She jerked her arm away and faced him. "What are you doing here?"

"I could ask you the same thing."

He motioned her to follow him farther down the hall to speak privately.

She rubbed her forearm. "You scared me half to death."

"Listen, if you'd seen me first, you would've said hello. You're here with someone else, and I couldn't risk a chance meeting."

"Why not? Aside from the fact that your being here can't possibly be a coincidence. Can you at least do me the courtesy of telling me why you've been following me?"

"I'm not following you."

"I saw you at the dress shop."

"Yeah, and yesterday you saw a thousand dolphins. I already said all I'm going to say. Let's pretend we didn't see each other. Please don't turn yourself into a problem."

"Me? Turn myself into a problem?" Now she was angry.

"By the way, how are you feeling?"

"I was feeling a lot better before I ran into you, and I'd feel even better if you'd tell me why you're here."

"Not because of you."

"It doesn't look that way."

"Why would I be following you?"

"I read a story about an FBI agent who stalked women."

Hunter chuckled. "I'm not a stalker." He lowered his voice. "I'm ending our little chat."

"Excuse me," a woman said, sneaking up from behind. The smell of alcohol preceded her. She was dressed in jeans and cowboy boots, obviously not part of the conference. Her gait was wobbly. Lauren leaned against the wallpaper to make room for her to pass.

"Whoa, I could smell her before I saw her," Hunter said. "By the way, you clean up nicely."

"I'd still like to know what you're doing here. It can't be a coincidence." Was it a good idea to grill him? What if his badge was real and he was an FBI agent? What if the Bureau was looking into their Cayman account? What if he was telling the truth and he wasn't following *her*? What if he was following the *money*?

"Do yourself a favor and forget you saw me." He pushed the men's room door open and disappeared inside.

It didn't sit right. Her stomach did a backflip, reminding her of the boat ride from San Pedro to the mainland. What were the chances of running into Hunter Grant tonight? What if he was lying and the bank in Cayman released information about the wire transfer they'd sent to HIPP Corp? Did the FBI investigate money crimes? What US laws had they broken when they moved cash to an offshore bank account? Tax evasion? Money laundering? Fraud? All of the above?

Her head throbbed. She went into the ladies' room to freshen up.

Strolling toward the elevator, she looked for Hunter but didn't see him. She watched in her periphery to see if anyone noticed what had happened, the ambush on the escalator. A couple stood at the registration desk, checking in. The conspicuous limousine they'd seen at valet was still parked out front.

The woman in jeans, the drunk, passed by and disappeared inside the busy hotel bar.

A bellman in a maroon uniform and matching brimless cap rolled a loaded garment cart toward the elevator, then pushed the going-up button. She did a U-turn and headed to the escalator. A young couple standing side by side holding hands passed her, riding the moving stairs going the opposite direction, down.

The escalator triggered a memory from the past. When she was a little girl, maybe six or seven, she held her mother's hand as they rode the escalator together at the airport, going up. The space between the handrail and the moving metal stairs was glass and she peered through it like a store window, up toward the top of the terrazzo stairs between the two escalators going opposite directions.

An old woman in a cotton dress and clunky shoes, hosiery rolled loosely over her ankles, hobbled almost sideways down the first two steps. Suddenly, she lost her balance and tumbled. It wasn't like in the movies when people barreled down: It was in slow motion. She thought someone would come to her aid, but the old woman rolled and rolled, moaning louder and louder, "Oh, God, help me. Please someone help me." As she rumbled down, her cheek hit the edge of a stair, smashing her eyeglasses. "Oh, God. Oh, God."

Lauren's eyes were glued to the glass partition. The woman landed in a heap, her plain floral dress yanked above her knotty knees, a shoe missing, a gash on her face. She groaned and moaned and pulled herself to a sitting position, then reached for the hand railing.

Why wasn't anyone helping her?

Why was she alone?

The woman struggled to her knees, then patted her face, feeling for her eyeglasses. When she tried to stand, something went wrong and she lost her balance again and tumbled down the next flight of stairs, faster this time, grunting and moaning. Her mother gasped and reached down, covering her eyes. She tried to brush her mother's hand away but her grip was firm. What could her mom do to help?

She shuddered at the memory. The back of her neck beaded with sweat and she wiped it with her palm, rubbing her hands briskly to keep the perspiration from staining the red dress. She stepped off the escalator and walked toward the elevator, heading to the banquet room.

"Are you okay?"

It was the young woman she'd met—the one who'd recognized Vance—with the unusual name she couldn't recall. She managed a weak smile. "I'm not big on social events."

"I know how you feel," the girl said. "I hate them, too. I'm heading out for some air," she said, stepping onto the elevator going down.

Lauren leaned against the stainless-steel wall, next to the banks of elevators, giving herself a moment to collect her thoughts.

Seeing Hunter at the hotel couldn't be a coincidence.

She inhaled deeply through her nose and stared over the brass railing with a panoramic view of the lobby. The girl she'd just spoken to walked out the main entrance. A man dressed in black stepped out of the Hummer limo and opened the back passenger-side door. Lauren did a double take as the girl with the unusual name got in. She lifted her red gown at the knee and hurried down the escalators to the first floor.

The concierge behind the mahogany stand, whose job it was, noticed her. "May I help you?"

"No. I thought I saw someone I know."

"If we can be of service, please let us know."

She went back to the ladies' room and stood in front of the mirror, dabbing the perspiration from her brow. She needed a few minutes to chill out, plus she was in no hurry to go back the room packed with sales wolves.

She did a double take. Were her eyes playing tricks or did she just see the same girl who'd just left the hotel pass behind her in the mirror? She turned casually to check, but she'd disappeared into the stall. Lauren leaned closer to the mirror, plucked a tissue from the dispenser, and blotted her lipstick.

A moment later the girl stood next to her.

"Hello again," the girl said.

Lauren pumped a dollop of lavender soap in her palm, then waved her hand beneath the faucet. "Is that your limo parked out front?"

"It's not mine. My fiancé thought it would be fun. He invited some work friends to ride along." She rubbed the horizontal creases on her brow with her thumbs, frowned, reached into her purse for a gold compact, then powdered her forehead. "This is awkward," the blond girl said, "but I can't remember your name."

"I'm terrible with names, too." Lauren opened her purse and handed her a business card.

"I'm Bibbins." She looked at the business card and raised her eyebrows, the lines across her forehead deepening. "I didn't realize you're with HIPP Corp. My fiancé sells your software."

"Really."

She wrinkled her nose. "I know it's rude, but I have an early morning and I'm going to wait in the limo. With a little luck I'll take a nap. Enjoy your evening," she said.

"I'll try," she said, following her out to the end of the hall where they parted ways. The line to the elevator had dissipated. She pressed the up arrow and rode alone to the third floor. There was no sign that the foyer had been packed during the cocktail reception, servers wading through the crowds offering a dozen different hors d'oeuvres. The open bars where Masson's salespeople stood ten deep had been dismantled.

She entered the banquet room through the only set of unlocked doors and made her way through the crowded room to the head table where Vance sat with the executives.

"Where did you disappear to?"

"There was a line at the little girls' room. I had to go to the first floor," she said, plunging a blunt fork into a tomato.

She'd arrived just in time for the main attraction. The MC for the evening, an on-air talent from ESPN she didn't recognize, opened with some lame jokes about salespeople and sharks before introducing Bill Fields.

A slideshow played on a big screen behind him: a boring montage of product shots mixed with candid pictures of people she assumed were selfies provided by the sales force.

As Bill Fields walked onto the stage, the screen changed to a PowerPoint presentation, and he opened with a canned speech, the images changing as he talked about sales, growth, profit margins, and quotas before delivering his keynote address.

"One of the biggest challenges we face is staying ahead of regulations," the catfish said, droplets of sweat glistening on his forehead. "The federal government is cracking down on the pharmaceutical companies, and that affects us since, as you know, one of our business units resells software that helps doctors and hospitals comply with the ever-changing rules.

"Recently our government started sounding the alarm about substandard products manufactured in China. Almost ninety percent of all pharmaceutical drugs and the majority of medical supplies we sell are made overseas. Recently, known carcinogens have been found in many of our most commonly prescribed drugs—used to treat everything from high blood pressure to diabetes. The FDA has red-flagged some over-the-counter pain relievers and vitamins.

"There's an ongoing class action lawsuit against a medical-device manufacturer. When there was a shortage of raw materials to make medical mesh products, a Boston-based company ordered them from China, and when patients suffered serious complications, the Boston company covered it up. One of the major oil companies had to ban the sale of a petroleum-based chemical that wasn't approved for medical-grade manufacturing. It was ordered by a Chinese company who lied to the chemical company about the end use. They'd received the shipment over there, repackaged and labeled it, marked it up a thousand percent, and sold it to the Boston outfit as medical grade."

The crowd fell silent.

She and Vance exchanged a glance.

"Health and Human Services is worried that if there's an upset in the supply chain in China, we could run out of everyday medicines, including antibiotics, and that would make our healthcare system very vulnerable. If manufacturing is brought back to the USA, an idea that's being studied now, prices are going to go up."

The audience reaction was a mix of groans and applause.

"But enough about that. Let's get to the heart of why we're here tonight. We're here to honor our top-performing salesman for the quarter. Come on, Jack, come on up here."

Vance elbowed her softly as Jack strutted by, a mixture of eau de booze and cologne wafting in his wake. Vance pulled his chair closer to hers. "He's engaged to Dr. Emery's nurse."

"Who?"

"Bibbins Beatty. The gal I introduced you to earlier."

The one she'd talked to in the ladies' room. "Really? How do you know that?"

"She has a picture of him at her desk."

That was weird. Bibbins' fiancé was being honored this evening and his betrothed had left the party.

"Small world," she said, leaning back in her seat, making room for the waitstaff, who'd descended upon them, swapping empty salad plates for entrees, refilling wine and water glasses. Lauren was the only one at their table who'd ordered the grilled chicken. She picked at her food while Jack adjusted the microphone at the podium.

Bill held one of those six-foot-long checks, the kind the lottery folks and Publisher's Clearing House used as props when someone hit the jackpot. Two women in sequined evening gowns took it from him and stood next to Jack.

"Wow," Jack said off mic, posing for a photo alongside the catfish and the Vanna White duo. He leaned over to the podium and said, "Talk about a *big* bonus." The crowd laughed, and when the room quieted, he continued. "First, I'd like to thank Masson Medical for putting on tonight's event, and for that great, big, beautiful check. And since we're on the subject of China, did you ever notice the shiny plastic stuff they make over there smells like . . . *shit*?"

She chuckled at the off-color joke. *The stuff did smell funny.* She'd bought a plastic toolbox she threw away because it smelled like fertilizer.

The crowd roared and whistled, then applauded.

When the noise died down, he said, "I'm serious. Like they're using recycled dog poop to make *shit*."

The catfish broke into a wide grin. It sounded like a train passing through as the rowdies banged the tabletops with their fists.

Jack proposed a toast. "Here's to burdensome regulations and rising costs."

"Hear, hear," the crowd roared.

"And to not making shit in China."

Whatever plans Vance had had to dig into the patient deaths

wasn't happening tonight. She leaned toward him. "This guy's a cad."

"I was thinking asshole."

The evening couldn't end soon enough.

She was elated when Vance decided they should leave before dessert.

13

"I could tell you couldn't wait to get out of there," Vance said, waiting for valet to bring the Caddy around.

She gestured to the Hummer limo parked out front. "Your new friend travels in style."

"What friend?"

"The nurse. Bibbins."

"What are you talking about?"

"She left the party early, to catch a nap in the stretch. I got the feeling she doesn't like these events."

"You talked to her?"

"Just for a minute."

"When?"

"I bumped into her in the bathroom. She said she had an early day."

He hadn't seen her after their chance encounter at Bill Fields' table, but why would he? The room was crowded. When he saw the rented Cadillac coming up the ramp, he pulled his wallet from his back pocket.

"It'll be twenty-five dollars," the valet said.

He handed him thirty bucks. "Keep the change."

He hadn't told Lauren everything he knew about Emery's dead patients. Bill's talk about the Chinese was enlightening, especially the part about tainted drugs.

"I'm going to Chicago in the morning."

That took her by surprise. "What am I going to do while you're gone?"

"You're going with me." It was time to share a little more intel. "Dr. Emery's patients were being infused with the same cytotoxins."

She crinkled her brow. "What is that?"

"Substances that kill cells."

"Isn't that what chemo drugs are supposed to do?"

"Yes, but all three of Emery's patients were being infused with a drug called docetaxel. It's a plant-based chemo."

She stared out the window at the gloomy night sky. "Plant-based? I'm not following you."

"There're a lot of different chemotherapies. This one comes from plant alkaloids. They call it DTX for short. All three patients were being treated with the same drug but they had different cancers."

"Are you suggesting there's a problem with the chemo?"

"There are different ones to treat different cancers, and in this case, the drug is the common denominator."

"Were any other patients being treated with the same drug?"

"I don't know, but I'd have to guess yes."

"Then why didn't the others die?"

"That's why I'm going to Chicago. To try to find out more, to see if the deaths are linked. Come with me."

She chewed her lower lip. "Let me guess. The doctor in Chicago is an oncologist using HIPP Corp software."

"You're getting good at this. Now it's your turn."

She cocked her head. "To do what?"

"To tell me who that man was you were talking to on the escalator."

"What man?"

"The one I saw you talking to after you left the table."

"You followed me?"

"Not exactly. I excused myself right after you did to go to the little boys' room. The line to the one upstairs was three deep with drunks, and I decided to use the one on the lobby level. I walked over to the balcony waiting for the elevator and I saw you with him."

"You wouldn't believe me if I told you."

"Try me."

14

Wednesday, Late Night
Indianapolis, Indiana

Bibbins dozed in the back of the limousine, and when she awoke, it was almost one o'clock in the morning. How much longer before Jack and the gang were ready to go home? She'd promised to support him by going to the event, and had felt a twinge of guilt about bailing from the table, but this was ridiculous. He'd promised not to make it an all-nighter.

Dr. Emery had warned the staff about not going to work sleep-deprived. Jack and his cohorts didn't have to worry because Masson Medical never expected their employees to show up before noon after a company-sponsored event, if at all.

Five years ago she'd taken a job as a receptionist for a medical-equipment sales group out of Bloomington. She'd barely been a month on the job when she'd been unceremoniously fired; they'd dispatched a pair of managers to her apartment to confiscate her laptop and company car. She'd obsessed about the humiliation for weeks.

When she told Jack about it, he didn't lend a shoulder to cry on. Instead, he'd said, "You hate sales." True, she hated it. But that didn't give them the right to demean her. When she'd asked why she'd been terminated, they'd refused to say. She suspected it was because of the questions she'd asked about the business they ran on the side.

On the third day of her third week on the job, she'd been asked to fill in for the receptionist at the ambulance service they operated out of the same building. After answering calls that day, she'd become suspicious that the company was using the ambulance service as a perk. At home that night she logged onto the Health and Human Services website to read up on the rules and regulations.

Medicare and Medicaid provided taxpayer-funded reimbursement for non-emergency ambulance services for patients who couldn't otherwise travel for certain medical procedures. The website listed examples as patients at nursing homes, and ones on dialysis. But she'd answered a call from a plastic surgeon's office to take a patient home to an address in Noblesville. The satellite image on Google Earth showed a sprawling suburban estate.

She'd asked her boss about it the next day. That Friday, two managers showed up at her apartment at seven in the morning and fired her. They needed two people so one could drive her company car. Like she'd have refused to surrender her laptop and vehicle.

When Jack told her that Masson recently hired a new vice president of sales named Bill Fields, she'd checked the company website to see if it could possibly be her old boss, but there was a placeholder where his picture should have been. His bio didn't mention employment history from the company in Bloomington. She'd googled "Bill Fields Indiana." 228 matches came up for Bill or William Fields. She'd meant to check the Masson website before the event, but with all that had been going on at work, she hadn't thought to.

She and Jack had gotten separated during the reception, and she'd been trying to find their table when she thought she saw her old boss. Was it possible it was the same Bill Fields? Jack's boss? Then guy from HIPP Corp bumped into her. She'd excused herself, found the table, then slipped out during dinner to check the Masson website from the Hummer. It'd been updated and his picture was up. It was definitely him, the crook who'd fired her. Her blood boiled at the thought.

She checked the time: 1:30 AM.

The doors cracked open and the smell of alcohol flooded the limousine. Jack, Bob and Bob, Emily, and Taylor piled in. ME was last, gracefully sliding in and sitting in the corner next to her.

"Hey, babe." Jack clambered over her knees and licked her face like a dog.

"Ew." She recoiled and covered her knees with her purse.

"Look what I got."

He showed her the bonus check, the real-world version, a receipt for an electronic deposit. "I'm gonna take you to Hawaii."

It was for $19,000.

"If you don't want to go with him, I'll go," Young Bob said.

Old Bob frowned.

God, she hated drunks.

ME rolled her eyes.

Jack knocked on the window dividing the front and back seats. The window powered down. "Take us to Broad Ripple."

"Can you take me home first?" Bibbins asked.

"I can wait," ME said. "You can drop me off last."

"We're not going to Broad Ripple to drop you off," Jack said, "we're going out to celebrate."

Bibbins grimaced. "I need to go home."

"Al-righty," Jack said. "But you know what that means?"

Bibbins shrugged.

"It means you're gonna leave me alone with all those single women."

"You won't be alone, you'll be with your friends," she said. "I have to work in the morning."

"I need to call it a night, too," senior Bob said.

"You two are buzz-killers." Jack leaned through the open divider. "Take us to Broad Ripple so we can PAR-TEE. Then drop the lightweights off and come back and wait for us."

Buzz-killers. Senior Bob might not have been saving lives, but he was a surgeon. Those new noses and boobs required steady hands and a clear head.

"Sir," the driver said to Jack in a low tone, "I'm approaching double-overtime on the clock."

"Add it to my credit card. Let's hear it for our expense accounts."

"Hear, hear," Young Bob and Taylor said, stomping their feet on the floor of the limo, rattling the glassware.

Emily looked miserable, but she always did, especially when submitting to her boyfriend, Taylor.

"Sir," the driver said to Jack. "Nothing's open in Broad Ripple. May I suggest Kilroy's? They're open until three a.m."

"Thanks, bro. Kilroy's it is."

The clear-eyed driver gazed at Bibbins in his many mirrors. "It's only a few minutes from here," he said, apologizing to those not going to the late-night pub. "Help yourself to the bar in back."

Jack took him up on the offer, grabbing a shot glass from the cabinet and pouring an ounce of Grand Marnier. "Let's get going." He tilted the orange-scented liqueur down his throat and let out a loud, "*Ah*. What a night, huh? Fuck the Chinese."

"I love the fucking Chinese," Young Bob said. "Their screwups are going to be really good for business."

Bibbins huddled deeper into the corner nearer Marie Elizabeth, making room for Jack and Taylor, who'd decided to arm wrestle on the table in the back of the limo.

Kilroy's on Meridian was only half a mile from the Marriott. If they weren't shitfaced, they could have walked. It would have done them good.

The short drive to the warehouse district was a time warp. The late-night pub with its arched windows and intricate stonework dated to pre-World War I Indianapolis: a reminder of the city's once-upon-a-time power as an industrial and commercial hub. These days, the historic district was a source of city pride, and a bustling bar scene.

Drunks emerged and stood under the black awnings to see who'd arrived in the eight-door Hummer. Maybe they'd catch an Indianapolis Colt or a Pacer out partying. They looked disappointed to see Jack and his pals.

"See you later," Jack said, standing on the sidewalk, waiting for the limo driver to close the car door behind him.

Next stop, Broad Ripple to drop ME off first.

She looked exhausted when the limo stopped in front of her trendy loft. "At least I can sleep in," she said, getting out. "Good night, you two."

The driver watched until ME was inside the building.

By the time they arrived at Dr. Bob's house in Carmel, the old man was asleep and snoring. When the driver stopped outside his mansion, he awakened on his own. Yawning, he said goodnight.

The city slept under a moonless sky as the white Hummer crept toward her cheap apartment. She sat under the overhang on the stoop of her garden apartment and watched as the stretch limo pulled from the curb. Several sets of eyes glowed in the dark: The feral cats she'd been feeding since she'd moved in three years ago. The only tame one rubbed against her bare leg.

"Hey, Tom," she said, scratching his neck as he arched his back. It had taken two years before he'd let her approach, and now if Tom had his druthers, he'd move indoors with her. But Jack was allergic to cats.

Her phone pinged in her purse. She fished it out and looked at the message.

mind your own business if you know whats good for you

What? She didn't recognize the number. What business was she supposedly sticking her nose into? She typed who is this and pushed the send button.

A red UNDELIVERABLE message popped up on the screen.

She grabbed her purse, looked over her shoulder, and hurried inside. It was probably Jack and his buddies, drunk at Kilroy's, pranking her. Their college frat parties were legendary, their initiation practices so wild they'd come under scrutiny by the college Fraternity and Sorority Judicial Board. She opened a bottle of water, changed into her pajamas, and was about to put her phone on charge when she decided to look at the mysterious text again.

That was strange. The message was gone. So was the one she'd written that bounced back. Weird characters popped up and disappeared so fast she hadn't had time to process them. Were they Chinese characters? Darn it. They hadn't been on the screen long enough to be sure. A tingle ran down her back. She powered her phone OFF and put it on charge.

It was almost 2:30 in the morning. She set her alarm for 6:00 and tossed and turned until 4:00.

15

Thursday, Morning, Indianapolis, Indiana

Bibbins Beatty leaned forward in the driver's seat, applying her mascara using the rearview mirror, waiting for the red light to change. The instant it turned green, the driver behind her honked the horn. She raised her fist and shook it.

She was going to be late for work.

She'd been asleep for just over two hours when the alarm clock buzzed at 6:30 AM. Feeling in the dark for the snooze button, she must have pushed the wrong one or slept through the second one. When she awoke, it was almost 7:30. Hurrying, she skipped feeding her feral cats or delivering the newspaper to her elderly neighbor's doorstep.

Recalling the weird text message from last night, she fished inside her purse at the stop light; the driver behind her honked again. *All right, already.* Where was it? At the next light she dumped the contents on the front seat. Had she forgotten her phone, too? The last she remembered she'd put it on charge.

"Morning," she said, hanging her coat on the hook in the break room.

Dr. Emery intercepted her in the hallway. "I've been trying to call you. Come to my office."

A pit formed in her stomach. She'd never been late before; most days, she was a half hour early and opened the office. She followed Emery down the hall to her office where the doctor ushered her in and closed the door.

"I'm really sorry I'm late."

"That's not what this is about," Emery said, sitting behind her desk. "I'd like you to keep what I'm about to tell you between us."

"Of course."

"The optics of last night, you being at the Masson Medical gala, it doesn't look good right now."

"I'm not sure I understand."

"There was a process server at the door when I arrived this morning."

"A process server?"

"To serve legal papers."

"For what?"

"We're being sued by a second family."

"I don't understand. If I wasn't late, you wouldn't have been served?"

"No. Of course not."

Bibbins was so exhausted her brain wasn't working. "What are you being sued for?"

"The toxicology report is back for the first patient."

"What does it say?"

"I don't know yet, but apparently the family does. Now the same attorney is representing Mr. Graham's kids."

"Two families are suing you?" She rubbed her eyes. "I don't understand. What does this have to do with me being at the dinner?"

"Masson is also named in the suit. Your fiancé works for them and he reps our account."

"You didn't do anything wrong. Neither did Jack."

Emery held up a manila envelope. "I skimmed it. If I'm reading it right, they're suing us for negligence, and they're going after Masson for the equipment."

"What equipment?"

"The infusion bags. They're suing the pharmacy, too, and the drug manufacturer. The person I spoke to at the insurance company this morning says it's typical to name everyone. It's a legal theory called 'Deep Pocket' that takes aim at anyone and everyone who can pay."

"How were we negligent?"

"We weren't. It's why I have malpractice insurance. God knows I pay enough for it."

"But we weren't negligent."

"When people lose family members, emotions run high. It's easy for the personal-injury lawyers to exploit them; it's natural to look for someone to blame. They're suggesting there was a toxic substance found in the decedent's blood."

"They're accusing us of poisoning patients?"

"I'm letting the insurance lawyers handle it. I imagine there'll be an investigation of some kind and the lawyers'll settle out of court."

"Why would you settle?"

"It's not up to me. It's cheaper than litigation."

"You shouldn't settle."

Emery came from behind her paper-filled desk and sat on the edge, facing her. "I don't want you to worry about this, I want you to focus on the patients. No one else in the office needs to know about it. Okay?"

"Okay."

"One more thing. It's a good idea not to attend any more Masson functions for now."

"Why not?"

"The families are suing them, too."

"They're blaming Masson because they sold the infusion bags?"

"I told you, they name everyone. Let's let the insurance company handle it. That's what they do. Let's focus on the patients. These kinds of lawsuits usually drag out. It's best if you don't go to their events just until this thing is settled."

"I wish we knew what was in the toxicology report."

"I'm sure we'll find out." Emery's expression softened. "You might want to check your makeup."

———

BIBBINS DETOURED to the restroom and looked in the mirror. She looked like a raccoon where she'd rubbed her eyes and smudged her mascara. She plucked a tissue from the dispenser, wet it, and wiped the shadows from under her eyes.

She wet her palms, smoothed her hair, then straightened and adjusted the tortoiseshell hairband behind her ears. She looked at herself closely in the mirror. The dark circles under her lower lids weren't just from makeup. Like a dog digging for a bone, she pawed through her bag for her mascara and found her mobile in the bottom of her bag.

Nothing like having a senior moment a few decades early.

She turned it on and saw the missed calls from Dr. Emery, but the weird text from last night was still gone.

As she touched up her eyelashes, her stomach wrenched. There wasn't enough time to run to the stall and she vomited in the sink.

She waved her hands under the motion-detecting faucet, scooped water in her palms, and rinsed the sink. She was drying it with a paper towel when her co-worker Rachel walked in and stood next to her, checking herself in the mirror.

She looked at Bibbins and cocked her head. "You look like shit. Are you okay?"

"Yeah. I think I might have a stomach thing. Maybe something I ate for breakfast." She waited for Rachel to go into a stall, then started the water, cupped her hands and sipped, then swished and rinsed. When she was finished, she cleaned the sink again, then headed to her desk.

Could the toxicology report tell if the chemo drugs they'd administered were tainted? There'd been a drug recall last September for one of the blood pressure medications Dr. Emery prescribed to many of their patients. She'd learned about it from a mass email sent by the pharmaceutical company. She'd downloaded the attachment and read it. During a randomized test, the FDA had discovered traces of a known carcinogen—a chemical used to produce rocket fuel—in drug and blood samples. The FDA estimated that one out of every 8,000 patients who'd taken the drug would be diagnosed with cancer sometime in the future.

At the time, she imagined what would happen if patients found out their oncologists had been prescribing a cancer-causing drug. The conspiracy theorists would go crazy, accusing the doctors of trying to create patients. According to the documents, the blood pressure meds were made in China.

Her stomach roiled again and the nausea returned so

quickly she worried she wouldn't make it back to the restroom. She placed her hand across her stomach and breathed through her mouth; the queasiness passed as fast as it had come on. That had never happened before, and she chalked it up to lack of sleep and nerves. She'd been in such a hurry this morning she'd hadn't had her coffee.

Coffee. That's what would solve the problems of the world. She headed downstairs to the Starbucks.

Waiting in line, she called Jack at work and got his voicemail. "Hey, babe. It's me. Give me a call when you get this. Love you."

She tried his cell. After one ring, it went directly to voicemail. She checked the time. Just after nine in the morning.

Next, she dialed ME.

"Hey," ME said in a whisper.

"Did I wake you?"

"No. Well, sort of. What's up?"

"Could you meet me for an early lunch?"

"Um . . . when?"

"Today."

"What time is it?"

"Nineish."

"Let me think."

It sounded like she was getting out of bed.

After a minute, ME said, "Sure. Where are you?"

"At work."

"That's right, you had to go to work early. Poor you."

"Some of us have to work."

Since her schedule selling real estate was flexible, Marie Elizabeth agreed to meet closer to the hospital. It would give her the chance to broach the subject of the patient deaths, to find out if ME had heard anything.

16

Thursday, Midday
Interstate-65 from Indianapolis to Chicago

"Do you think it's a good idea that we get in deeper, you know, with the dead patients? It feels like we might be digging a hole."

Lauren's question was perfectly legitimate.

Vance was about to answer when she asked him another one.

"What if the drugs were made in China and they were contaminated? What if that's what killed the patients? What could we even do about it?"

He shrugged behind the wheel of the rented Cadillac. "Probably nothing."

He'd been in the dark until recently, clueless that most drugs were made in China. It had to be more profitable for the pharmaceutical companies, which seemed especially greedy, even for Big Pharma.

The distance from Indianapolis to Chicago was less than 200 miles, making it more practical to drive than fly. The road trip would also give them time to talk.

"I read an article in a men's magazine at the dress shop that said testosterone levels in American men have been steadily dropping."

She cocked her head. "What's that got to do with anything?"

"My paranoid brain went into overdrive and I started thinking what if the Chinese've been putting something in aspirin and ibuprofen? You heard what Bill Fields said last night."

"Seriously? Something to lower testosterone? You need a new exercise program."

"What's that supposed to mean?"

"Meaning you need to start jumping to something other than conclusions."

"I'm not jumping to conclusions. I told you, I read it."

"Do you really think they'd do that? Put something in the supply chain?"

"It's possible."

"Your birthday's coming up. I'll get you a tinfoil hat."

Her instincts were good, but no one batted a thousand. "Think about it. Look at the sex imbalance in China."

She grimaced at him. "What *sex* imbalance?"

"Not sex, I mean gender. There're thirty million more men than women."

"How'd that happen?"

"State-run family planning. They have a one-child policy, and most people want to keep the boys."

She shot him a look of disapproval. "*Keep*? The *boys*?"

He skipped over that. "Some people think they're stupid but that's not true. Everything they do is carefully crafted."

"What happened to all the girls?"

He knew, but shrugged.

"Well, if we don't know where the girls are, then maybe it's us who're stupid."

"They could dominate as the world's superpower without starting a conventional war. It's their plan."

"Their *plan*. Oh, God, have you thought about writing a novel?"

"Don't you think thirty million men who can't find mates might be a problem?"

"You've done okay so far."

"Very funny. Seriously, we're hardwired to spread our seeds. It's what we're accused of spending most of our time thinking about."

She shook her head. "I want to keep on liking you. I mean that."

"I'm being serious. What's the biggest mistake people make when they're sizing up an opponent?"

They'd had this discussion before.

"That others think the same way they do."

"Women don't want to believe it, but we're simple creatures. When in doubt, check our zippers."

She looked at him with contempt.

"You're the mysterious ones. You like to shop. We don't question it and we don't accuse you of being strange. We say, okay, here's my credit card."

"You've never offered me your credit card."

"That's the not the point. The point is that we believe you when you say it."

"People, including men, aren't that one-dimensional."

"You're right. Sometimes we think about food." He laughed.

"I'm being serious. I don't even like shopping."

"The only women who don't like shopping are Danish."

"Do you even know any Danish women?"

"No. Lighten up, I'm teasing. Just because you're not a shopping junkie doesn't mean you don't think about it. Be honest. When you see something you want to buy, you get a little excited."

"You're delusional. Did it occur to you that Danish women don't like shopping because the government takes half their money, and they like paying high taxes so they don't have to depend on a man?" The look on her face was pure touché.

"See, you're back to shopping—"

The face of victory faded. "I give up."

He chuckled inside. The car trip was a good idea, and though he'd never admit it aloud, sparring with her was a lot of fun.

The spicy talk was juxtaposed against the muted tones of dirt fields and an overcast sky. I-65, outlined by fences and fallow fields, would change in the months ahead. They'd passed farmers driving two-story orange-and-green machines—sophisticated farm equipment—tilling and seeding the acreage.

There were pastures with brown cattle with white markings. A few horses stood nose to tail, swishing flies. A group of curious alpacas stood along the fence line nearest the highway, watching cars go by. In three months, the corn would be three feet high.

She stared out the passenger window. "If you can prove there's foul play, what are you going to do about it?"

"I'm a long way from that."

After a moment of silence, she came back to a question he'd avoided earlier. "What did you mean when you said the Chinese *keep* the boys?"

"Male heirs can take care of their parents."

"What do they do with the girl babies?"

"You don't want to know." He'd seen photos posted online by Westerners, hundreds of thousands, maybe millions of crude markers thought to be the gravesites where baby girls were buried. The thought made him sick to his stomach. She took his advice and dropped it.

After a minute, maybe two, she said, "At least it's not winter."

"True. You freeze when it's fifty degrees out."

The sun hid all winter in the Midwest. No ocean or sun or palm trees or mountains. Just flatlands and a palette of grays. He couldn't imagine it, living like that for months on end.

"Tell me something you've never told anyone else," she said.

That came out of nowhere. "Like what?"

"That's the point. A secret."

"Do I get to ask you a question?"

"Sure. Otherwise, it wouldn't be fair."

He thought about it and when he settled on something to tell her, he asked, "You promise to keep it a secret?"

"Of course."

"When I was in grade school and my mother came to pick me up, I told the other kids she was our housekeeper."

"Why?"

He already regretted saying it. "You're judging me."

"No, I'm not. Why'd you tell the kids that?"

"To keep the other kids from bullying me."

"What other kids?"

"The white kids. My mom looks Cuban." He kept his eyes on the road, feeling her eyes boring into him. Now he had to defend it. "It was a long time ago. I didn't want to be tortured like the Cuban kids. I take after my dad, he had fair skin with the kind of brown hair that goes blond in the summertime. Plus, my last name made it easy to *pass*."

"That's terrible," she said. "I hope your mother never knew."

"She didn't. I shouldn't have told you."

"It's too late for that."

They rode in silence for a minute.

"Don't you want to know my secret?"

Weighing the pros and cons, he saw no reason. He preferred more mystery and less history. "Not really."

"Why not?" She twirled the ends of her hair, looking coy.

"If you have a burning desire to confess or get something off your chest, go for it. But I'm fine if you want to keep your deep, dark secrets."

He flipped the turn indicator on and slowed. What a dummy. He'd just missed the opportunity to ask her who the man was who'd grabbed her on the escalator. She'd dodged the answer last night, and he was about to ask again when she preempted him with a question.

"Where're we going?"

"I did a little homework and found an interesting place to have lunch."

"You're full of surprises."

He took the 220 Exit off Interstate 65 heading toward State Road 14 flanked by farmlands and livestock, and silos and farm equipment as big as earthmovers, and a landscape as opposite to Miami as he could imagine. In a month or so the tiny seedlings planted in rows the size and shape of speed bumps would sprout crops. This was flyover country, where food was grown, and dairy cows milked, and cars manufactured, and churches outnumbered gas stations.

Lauren powered down the window and hung her head out like a dog, taking a deep breath. "Thank you," she said, looking at fields as far as the eye could see.

"For what?"

"For inviting me to a place where there are so many animals."

He spotted two huge, conjoined red barns he'd seen on the website. "I heard the grilled cheese sandwiches are to die for."

"The place is famous for grilled cheese sandwiches?"

"Yep." He waited a two-beat, then switched topics. "Guess what? I changed my mind, I thought of a question, who was the guy who grabbed you last night?"

Whoop. Whoop. Whoop.

He glanced at the rearview. "Shit." A cop. "Was I speeding?" What was the speed limit? They'd been on the rural road for less than a mile and he hadn't noticed any signs.

She shrugged and swiveled in her seat, looking out the back window. "Maybe he wants to pass."

He dropped two wheels onto the shoulder, giving the patrol car enough room. But the cop slowed and hugged the back bumper of the Caddy. Vance flicked on the turn indicator and dropped to ten miles per hour, then slowed to a stop and parked on the side of the road. The Dodge Charger filled his rearview mirror, stopping a foot off his back bumper, the light bar flickering.

Lauren watched from the side mirror on the passenger's-side. "What's he doing?"

"He's running the plates."

"Maybe you were speeding?"

"I don't think so."

"Maybe the plates are expired or something."

"Maybe." He unholstered the Glock under his left arm, lowered it onto his lap, and slyly dropped it to the driver's-side floor mat and gently kicked it under his seat with the heel of his shoe. "We're gonna find out."

The cop exited the patrol unit and approached the car. Vance watched in the side mirror as he adjusted his navy-blue felt hat, shaped like a bowler, and then patted the front of his lighter-blue shirt.

Vance had checked the Indiana gun laws after he bought it. He had to think for a minute. Was he still in Indiana? He was close to the Illinois state line, a place with some of the toughest gun laws in the nation. Then he remembered the place he'd planned to stop for lunch was in Indiana, south of the state border. Why was he being pulled over by the cops?

17

Thursday, Midday, Indianapolis, Indiana

The casual sushi place across the street from the hospital was a five-minute walk from the doctor's office, and a place Bibbins and ME frequented. Bibbins arrived first, choosing a table where she could watch them make the food. A few minutes later, Marie Elizabeth breezed in, dressed in a denim dress cut to the knee and blue suede thigh-high flat boots. The college students working behind the counter noticed her.

Bibbins stood and greeted ME her with a soft hug. "Thanks for meeting me. Do you know what you want?"

ME nodded. They'd arrived before the lunch rush and walked together to the counter.

ME always ordered the same thing, the seaweed-wrapped spicy tuna roll with avocado and cucumber. Bibbins wasn't nearly as adventurous, ordering the chicken teriyaki bowl. As usual, her friend insisted on paying for both of them. The cashier handed her a metal stand with a white plastic card with their order number inserted into the top.

"I don't envy you staying out late and having to get up and go to work," ME said.

It was the perfect opening to the question she planned to ask. "Do you think it's fair that Dr. Emery told me not to go to any more Masson events?"

"She did? Why?"

"Promise you won't say anything?"

ME held two fingers up. "Scout's honor."

"She's being sued."

ME cocked her head. "By who?"

"The family of a patient." She would keep "families"—plural —a secret for now.

"For what?"

"You remember about the patients who died in the office?"

ME nodded.

"The toxicology report for the first one came back."

"And?"

"I haven't seen it. I don't think she's seen it, either. She said Masson's being sued, too."

ME's eyes widened. "I haven't heard that. Why?"

"Dr. Emery said the lawyers sue everyone."

"I hate them," ME said.

She watched their food being prepared and the young man who'd made the sushi roll sliced it, squeezed a squiggle of creamy orange sauce over the top, and placed it on a tray. He put the teriyaki bowl next to it and handed it to another young man who delivered it to their table.

After the server left, Bibbins broached the subject again. "Dr. Emery said it's common to sue everyone. They're going after HIPP Corp, too."

"Bloodsuckers."

"Is that what you think they're doing, sucking blood?"

ME's voice dropped an octave. "The so-called victims never get their fair share. It all goes to the lawyers for fees. They promise a percentage if they win, but they nickel and dime for every expense. God, I hope they settle out of court."

"You do?"

"Of course." ME pinched a slice of her sushi roll with chopsticks and popped it in her mouth.

ME knew a lot more about the legal system than she did.

"Is that why Emery doesn't want you going to events with Jack?"

Bibbins changed the subject. "I wonder how late the guys were out last night?"

ME cast her eyes down, plucked another a piece of her roll and ate it.

"How's your sushi?"

"It's okay." ME avoided eye contact.

"What?"

ME shook her head and stared at her plate.

Bibbins stirred the rice in her bowl, rearranging chunks of chicken, but not eating. The silence was awkward.

"This sucks," ME finally said. "If I don't tell you, I'm not a friend. And if I tell you, I'll hurt your heart."

"Tell me what?"

ME chewed on the inside of her cheek. "I got a picture from the after-hours party."

"From who?"

"Emily." Emily was Taylor's girlfriend, the one in the miniskirt and stilettos and a bad mood when they'd dropped her off with the guys at Kilroy's.

"What's it a picture of?"

ME slouched in her chair. "Of Jack."

"Of Jack? Why would Emily send you a picture of Jack?"

ME didn't answer.

"Tell me. A picture of what?"

ME shook her head and set her chopsticks on the side of her plate. She twisted in her seat, grabbed her Hermès bag hanging over the chair back, put it on her lap, took her phone out, tapped the keys, and handed her the phone.

"Where did you get this?" Bibbins' left arm twitched and bumped the bowl, tipping it over, dumping a few chunks of food onto her clean pink scrubs.

"Oh, my gosh. Let me help you." ME rushed to the counter and returned with a restaurant towel.

Bibbins dipped it in her water and blotted the sauce from her clothes.

"I shouldn't have shown it to you," ME said.

She could barely look at it; Jack practically had his tongue down her throat. "Who is she?"

"She works for Masson."

"Maybe he was drunk, you know, acting stupid."

"Come on, Bibbs. She joined him at the table last night, after you left."

"What?"

ME sighed aloud. "Everyone knows except you."

She felt lightheaded. "They're a *thing*?" An invisible hand squeezed her throat and a shot of adrenaline raced through her system. Her nose tingled, then her eyes welled. She dabbed them with her sleeve and sniffled hard to stop the tears.

"I'm sorry. Oh, gosh. This is awful. I didn't want to tell you." ME scooted her chair closer and leaned over to comfort her with a side hug.

Bibbins pulled away. "I'm fine. Will you please not do that. I don't need a hug. I need that picture forwarded to me."

"No, it'll make things worse. You need to take it up with Jack. I feel terrible that it's me who told you."

"It's okay." She swept the last remains of her lunch from the tabletop into the bowl. "I'm glad you did."

They sat in silence for a full minute as the restaurant filled with people, the sounds of the lunch crowd, a symphony of dishes clattering, phones ringing, and people talking loudly, competing with the chaos in her head—her thoughts racing from one incomplete sentence to the next, as if trying to tune into a radio station in the middle of nowhere.

Who was the girl in the picture? And how did she miss the cues that Jack was messing around with someone from the office?

ME never liked Jack. Maybe that's what this was about. But the picture didn't lie. There was no rational explanation for it. She tried pushing it out of her head but the image was stuck there, along with all its dread and doom. ME had no reason to hurt her. This wasn't on ME.

It was on that bitch.

"You wanted my opinion on Emery telling you not to go to business events with Jack?"

"It doesn't matter now."

"Okay. Well, I'm having a spa party tomorrow. You're invited."

She'd been invited twice before, and she'd gone once but it was so expensive. When she found out the skin care clinic gave ME discounts for inviting friends who spent tons of money on facials and injectables and all the other services she couldn't afford, she'd been resentful. ME could easily pay for it.

"If you invite someone new, I can get you in for free."

"What if I have to work?"

"They'll give you a credit."

That gave her an idea. "Are you sure?"

"I'm sure," ME said. "I'm sorry about that picture of Jack."

"I know."

After ME left, she stayed behind and dug Lauren Gold's business card out of her wallet. She held the phone close to her mouth and dictated a text message, then pressed the SEND button.

18

Thursday, Midday, Indiana State Road 14
South of the Illinois State Line

Vance powered down his driver's-side window.

The cop said, "Please step out of the vehicle."

He got out.

"Driver's license, please."

He reached into his pants pocket, took it from his billfold, handed it to the officer, then glanced at the triangular patch on his right shoulder: Indiana State Police.

"Are you aware you're driving a vehicle that's been implicated in a crime?"

His heart pumped. "What? No. It's gotta be some sort of mistake. It's a rental."

"You're from Florida, huh?"

Adrenaline flowed. This could snowball. "That's right."

"Do you have the rental car agreement?"

"It's in the visor."

The cop, an imposing man with shoulders three feet wide and a baritone voice, stepped back two paces and loosened his knees just enough to look inside the Caddy. The trooper treated him as hostile, gaining a line of sight into the cockpit while keeping him in his periphery, resting his wrist on the grip of the gun strapped to his utility belt.

"Young lady, will you please step out of the vehicle."

She made eye contact with Vance. He nodded and she got out, walked around the front bumper of the rental car and stood a few feet away, on the side of the road.

"Where're you two headed?"

"Chicago," Vance said.

"This is not the road to Chicago."

"We were stopping for lunch."

"What's your business in Chicago?"

"Sightseeing."

"Keep your hands where I can see them." The cop turned to Lauren. "Would you please remove the rental agreement from the vehicle."

Vance debated telling the cop about the gun under the driver's-side seat, but opted not to.

She said, "I don't know where it is."

"In the visor," Vance said.

"Step away from the vehicle," the cop said, getting in the rental himself, keeping one eye on them and one foot on the ground, reaching overhead, and opening the visor. He stuck his head out. "It's not here."

His heart skipped. *It was there. Wasn't it?* "Check the glove box."

A second patrol car rolled onto the shoulder and stopped behind the first trooper's unit.

"Wait here," the cop said.

The second officer got out and the pair met up behind the

rental, speaking in a tone too low for him to hear. A rusty vintage pickup truck with a bubble-nosed hood and round fenders slowed to gawk. The driver, a skinny guy with a beak for a nose and wearing a straw hat, held his phone out the window and waved, then continued along the farm road.

Lauren looked frightened.

"It'll be okay," Vance said.

The state cop who'd pulled him over returned. "We ran the plates twice. This vehicle's been involved in a crime."

"That can't be right," Vance said.

The younger cop who'd joined them sized him up, then eyed Lauren before walking toward the Caddy and sticking his head in through the window.

The officer who'd stopped them said, "We're going to have to impound the vehicle."

He read the nametag pinned to his uniform: C. Fealy. "Officer Feely—"

"It's FAY-lee. With an A."

"Officer *FAY-lee*," Vance said, "I don't understand. I rented the car at the airport in Indianapolis."

The younger cop walked behind the rental, squatted between bumpers, and looked at the license plate up close.

"There must be some sort of mistake," Vance said.

"You need to get your belongings out of the vehicle," Fealy said.

He was going to have to tell him about the gun under the seat.

Lauren opened the back-passenger door and pulled her roller bag from the seat onto the shoulder of the road.

"There's something you should know," Vance said.

Fealy raised his eyebrows.

"I have a gun stowed under the seat."

"Hey, Ryan," Fealy yelled, "I need a hand."

The younger trooper jogged over.

"Mr. Courage says he has a firearm under the seat."

"Is that right. Driver's-side?"

"Uh-huh."

Ryan sat in the front of the Caddy and felt for the gun. He fished the Glock 19 out—still holstered—and held it up for Fealy to see.

"Do you have a concealed carry permit?" Fealy asked.

"I do. It's in my wallet."

"Please remove it and hand it to me."

He did as told, handing it over, folding his arms across his chest, then watched Fealy study it. A cold sweat broke under his shirt.

"How long have you been in Indiana?"

"Couple of days."

"I guess if you rented a car at the airport that means you flew in. Did you check the gun as baggage?" Fealy held the Glock in one palm with the holster strap slung over his wrist and balanced the pouch with the spare clip in the other.

"No. I bought it yesterday."

That caught Fealy's attention. "Why'd you buy it?"

The truth was best. "I was on my way to Belize, on vacation, when I was diverted here at the last minute." The story must've sounded suspicious.

"Do you have the receipt?" Fealy asked, looking at his Florida gun license.

"It's at the hotel."

"I assume you know the law."

Based on how easy it had been to purchase it, he decided to guess. "Indiana has a reciprocal agreement with Florida."

"That's right," Fealy said. "However, in the State of Indiana you may not conceal a loaded firearm."

Lauren took a step toward them. Vance held his hand up.

He was about to play the ex-cop card when Fealy said, "I have a little latitude here and you telling me the truth goes in your favor. We ran the VIN number and the vehicle is registered to the rental car company, like you said. The crime was committed a week ago and you haven't had the car that long. Be grateful you didn't get pulled over in Chicago. You'd make a nice trophy for the city council," he said, shaking his head. "John Q. Citizen may not carry a firearm. Loaded or not."

That, he knew.

The younger officer motioned the senior trooper to the back of the Caddy where they again spoke in low voices.

Fealy returned. "I'm sorry, I'm going to have to hang onto your weapon. I'll give you a minute to get the rest of your belongings out of the vehicle."

"Do you mind if I ask what kind of a crime the vehicle was involved in?"

"A hit-and-run," Ryan said.

"What happens next? Are you going to leave us here?" he asked.

"No," Fealy said, "I'm going to take you and your lady friend to the substation. My partner'll take care of the vehicle."

"Can't you just drop us off at the nearest rental car counter?" He knew what he'd have said if the tables were turned, back when he was active duty: No. Then again, that was Miami. He noticed the black body cameras hanging around their necks: the small lens, the all-seeing eyes. He wouldn't have liked to be them, monitored like a zoo animal. Maybe they'd play nice, especially since he'd been very forthcoming and cooperative.

"Gotta fill out a report," Fealy said, exhaling like he had better things to do. "Don't wanna do it on the side of the road."

"Are the keys in it?" the younger partner asked.

"Yep."

Fealy opened the trunk on the Charger and supervised while

Vance loaded his and Lauren's luggage. When he finished, Fealy slammed the lid.

He and Lauren climbed into the back seat. A late-model tow truck with orange flames airbrushed on the side doors roared toward them. Ryan motioned the driver to the nose of the Cadillac.

"Sorry for the inconvenience," Fealy said, doing a three-point turn, heading toward the on-ramp to Interstate 65 North.

He turned to watch the truck driver hop out and lower the winch.

Lauren hardly said a word; he'd have to remember to thank her later.

19

Thursday, Midday
Indianapolis, Indiana

On the walk back to the office, the thoughts running through Bibbins' head did backflips. Everything around her seemed to move at a slower speed. How humiliating was it that everyone knew about Jack and that whore from Masson except her? How long had it been going on?

Could there be a logical explanation for the photo? Was it fake? Or a joke? This thinking came from what her mother called her fantasy world. The first time she'd introduced Jack to her parents was at dinner at a nice place in downtown Indianapolis. Her parents had been inviting them for months but she didn't want Jack to see the house she'd grown up in. She'd asked her father to dress properly that night—meaning iron his clothes and wear something besides old Levis—and to clean his fingernails.

Neither her mom nor dad approved of Jack and it had

created a rift. Jack's parents could have done the same to her: She was from a different—lower—societal class. Wasn't that how it worked? People higher on the socioeconomic ladder rejected those below them? It wasn't supposed to be the other way around. She didn't see her parents last Christmas over it, spending it with Jack's family, instead.

She'd told Jack's mother that her parents were Christian Scientists. How ignorant was that? Heal yourself with prayer? Wasn't she just as dumb for telling Jack's mom about her younger brother's death, recalling the day their frightened babysitter took him to the emergency room where his blood sugar level topped 300?

For two long weeks her mom told her to pray for him and leave it to God whether he lived or died. Really? As far as she was concerned the church murdered her baby brother. The anger rose inside her, thinking of all the Type I diabetic atheists living long, happy lives thanks to glucose monitoring and insulin.

A horn blared and tires squealed, snapping her back to the present.

"Hey, moron, look where you're going," the driver yelled.

She'd stepped into the crosswalk while the light was green, and the car skidded to a stop on the white road paint marking the pedestrian lane. Another surge of adrenaline flooded her body.

When she returned to the office, Dr. Emery stood at reception. "You look a little peaked. You should take your temperature and check your oxygen levels."

"I'm fine."

"You can go home if you like." Emery smiled. "I need you to stay healthy."

"I'd rather say and work."

"It's up to you," Emery said, walking away.

What would she do at home? She knew exactly what she'd do: She'd obsess about Jack, wondering how serious it had gotten between him and that slutty co-worker he'd been making out with at the bar last night. She'd rather stay and finish the day.

Reaching above her desk, she grabbed the framed photo of Jack and opened the top drawer of her desk. Mr. Graham's toy soldier lay facedown next to a box of paper clips. She picked it up, squeezed it in her palm, put the picture facedown in the drawer, and stuffed the little soldier in her pocket. That's why Mr. Graham carried it: It was supposed to make him feel strong. She needed some of that now.

Thursday, Late Afternoon, Merrillville, Indiana

Vance sat next to Lauren in the cramped lobby of the storefront police substation where they'd been waiting forever, it seemed.

Fealy's partner, Officer Ryan Brown, appeared. "I verified the VIN. Came back as owned and registered by the rental car agency. Looks like someone swapped the license plates."

"How do you know that?" Lauren asked.

Fealy showed them the NCIB paperwork. "The plates and VIN numbers don't match."

"That's weird," Vance said.

Fealy looked at him sideways. "Can you think of anyone who might've targeted you?"

"What makes you think I was targeted?" He mentally retraced his steps from the time he'd rented the car to now.

"I talked to the rental car agency where you it picked up,"

Ryan said, "and those plates weren't on the vehicle when you got it. Plate number's on the key fob and rental car agreement."

That's right. He'd located the car by comparing the numbered parking spot and plates on the car. "Maybe someone was targeting the vehicle, not me."

"Normally," Fealy said, "I might agree with you. But not today."

"Why?"

"Because we got a call on the tip line about this vehicle," Fealy said.

Bad chemistry doused his veins. "What kind of tip?"

"A tip that a vehicle used in a hit-and-run was traveling north on Interstate 65 North, right around the time I stopped you."

Vance took a deep breath, held it for a few seconds, then asked, "Who was the caller?"

"Dispatch didn't get the information." Fealy folded his arms across his chest like a lumberjack.

"Don't you trace the calls?" Lauren asked.

"You know how many calls come in every day?" Ryan asked.

The adrenaline rush was morphing into anger.

"They called 9-1-1," Ryan said. "Call pinged from a nearby location, but dropped before dispatch could get a GPS position on it."

"Who had access to the car?" Fealy asked.

Good question. Vance ran the events in his head. It could have been anyone. "I valeted it last night."

"Where?" Fealy asked.

"The JW Marriott downtown."

Ryan wrote it down on a small spiral notebook. "What time did you arrive?"

Lauren estimated the timeline and shared it.

The time of departure confused Fealy. "You weren't staying there?"

"No," Vance said. "We attended a corporate event."

"What kind of a corporate event?" Fealy asked.

"A medical sales event," Vance said.

"Is that the business you're in?" Fealy asked.

Vance hesitated, then said, "More or less."

"Hmmm," Fealy said. "I thought I heard you two were on your way to sightsee in Chicago."

"We went to a sales meeting last night and planned to go up to Chicago today and spend the night. I have no idea how the plates got switched or who would do it. Could've been at the parking garage at the Marriott or the hotel parking lot where I stayed last night."

It could have happened at the dress shop or even the gun store. Anyplace he'd parked was plausible, and the anonymous call to 9-1-1 gnawed at him.

"I got no reason to hold you," Fealy said. "Just the vehicle. Rental car company's got a location in Merrillville. You can work out a new car with them. Soon as I finish up my report, I'll give you a lift."

Write up his report. That'd burn up the clock. He checked the time on the clock on the wall. They were running late.

Thursday, Early Evening
South Side of Chicago, Illinois

D r. Emilio Garcia looked at his watch: 5:30 PM. The rep from HIPP Corp was more than three hours late. It had been a surprise when the medical records company CEO, Sherry Rogers, called personally to tell him they were sending someone to interview him. What was up with the rep running late, then not answering his calls?

He tapped the face of his iWatch. Screw it. He wasn't waiting any longer.

He crossed the street and stopped at the hospital information desk to ask security to walk him to the parking garage where he'd parked his Jaguar SUV. When he'd accepted the position at the cancer center in south Chicago, he'd done so knowing it was a low-income neighborhood with a crime problem. But there were complications he hadn't considered, like how hard it would be to keep good nurses on staff. Last week another new one quit after being mugged in the parking garage.

If he wasn't afraid his malpractice insurance rates would skyrocket, he would've refused the meeting. But his patient had died in the office during a routine chemotherapy infusion, and five minutes after reporting it to management, the lawyers—representing the clinic's money donors—were on the case, going behind his back, sealing the medical records.

An older security guard in a rumpled black uniform walked him to his vehicle. Before he'd left the office, he'd called Vance Courage twice and texted him once but hadn't heard back. Maybe he'd had travel troubles. A single raindrop at Chicago's O'Hare Airport could ripple airline schedules from coast to coast.

When he'd notified his medical malpractice insurance carrier immediately after the incident, he was stunned to discover someone had already put his insurer on notice.

Screw them.

He dialed Vance Courage one last time, and when he didn't answer, left another voicemail. If he was on a weather delay, he could have had the decency to call. They could always meet tomorrow.

The navigation map on his phone estimated the drive time to the park at just over an hour. He selected a classical music radio station and settled into the tangle of traffic. A rush of anxiety crept through his veins. He'd been overseeing the oncology clinic since the university's board members had pushed to build a satellite facility on the southwest side of Chicago. The consultants and lawyers loved the idea because the poorer patients hurt the university's bottom line.

To continue getting federal funding they'd had to accept low-income patients, but treating people without private insurance was expensive. Government reimbursements were a fraction of what the private insurers paid, and the university staff lawyer who'd come up with the legal sleight-of-hand idea made a name for herself proposing they build an alternative clinic near the university where they could funnel the poorest sick patients.

The tension in his body felt like an archer pulling on a bowstring strung from his jaw to his white knuckles gripping the soft leather on his steering wheel. He pounded his fist on the dash of his Jaguar; patients were not supposed to die during chemotherapy.

Screw the greedy lawyers.

They'd better hope there was no Doctor Peter waiting for them at the Pearly Gates.

An hour later he parked beneath a sprawling oak tree, the flickering mercury streetlamp overhead highlighting new buds sprouting from the tips of limbs, a welcoming sign of springtime.

He kicked off his Ferragamo loafers and changed into Nikes before unloading a heavy-duty plastic transport case from the back of the SUV. He threw his blue-and-gold Wolverines gym bag over his shoulder and wheeled the black box to the staging area. The high-pitched wails zipping by sounded like the starting grid at a Formula One race.

A half dozen participants had already set up. He removed the bright-red racing drone from its custom case. When he'd first learned to fly, he'd crashed a lot. Now he was more proficient, and when he strapped the virtual reality glasses over his eyes, adrenaline surged.

He started the engine, piloting it toward the pop-up course made up of different shapes, sizes, and elevations—reminiscent of a dog obstacle course—designed for a drone to fly through. While he warmed up on a practice run, another drone screamed past at full throttle.

The VR glasses mimicked the cockpit of a fighter jet, and while it wasn't real, it produced the effect of actual flying. He rolled his shoulders left and right, barely aware that his head bobbed and his body swayed, emulating the flight path as if his body had wings.

Why had the rep from HIPP Corp stood him up?

His cell vibrated in his pocket. He let it go to voicemail then slowed the drone, bringing it in for a landing. The number wasn't familiar, but after-hours emergency calls rarely were. He pressed the REDIAL button.

A woman answered.

"Dr. Garcia, my name is Lauren Gold. My associate, Vance Courage, had a meeting scheduled with you. He's very sorry but he had travel issues and would like to know if you'd be available this evening?"

Excuse me? He'd waited for over three hours. "Tomorrow would be better."

"Hang on," she said.

When she came back to the call, a drone buzzed by, drowning her out. "Would you please repeat that?"

"I said, he's planning to leave tomorrow. Is there any way we could meet for dinner?"

"What time?"

"How does eight thirty sound?"

He was usually in bed by nine o'clock.

"It's important," she said.

He mouthed a curse word but kept his voice calm. "Okay."

"You pick the place."

"Where are you coming from?"

"Northwest Indiana."

That was weird. He'd wrongly assumed they were on a weather delay. Maybe they'd been rerouted. That had happened to him before when O'Hare got backed up. He stuck his finger in his ear when another drone flew past. "Is this your cell number?"

"It is."

"Can I text you?"

"Sure."

"Gimme a few minutes."

"We look forward to meeting you."

"Okay," he said, ending the call. He picked up the drone, set it on the bench next to him, and googled "Morton's in Naperville," a place where the HIPP Corp reps wouldn't accidentally end up on the south side of the city.

That had happened to him one winter evening when he'd taken a wrong turn. It was akin to being caught in a war zone. His heart raced at the thought, recalling the orange flames shooting out of 55-gallon drums while shady characters loitered around the makeshift fireplace in the freezing cold.

He'd stopped at a red light when a group of young men surrounded his vehicle, yanked at the door handles, and rocked it side to side. Fearful they'd roll his car over, he'd feathered the gas, then jammed the pedal and run the red light, praying he didn't hit anyone. He'd sped through the rest of the stop signs and lights, now his palms sweating at the memory, recalling that his clothes were drenched with sweat by the time he'd found his way back to Interstate 94. He could have been killed that night.

He called and made a reservation, then sent the link to the woman's cell. Medical sales reps loved to entertain doctors and under normal circumstances he'd go out of his way to avoid them. But this was different. His patient had died.

He strapped the virtual reality glasses on his face, noting how fast his blood pressure spiked, activating neurotransmitters that flooded his brain with dopamine. If he wasn't high on his own chemistry, he'd be madder about a last-minute late-night dinner with salespeople who'd pretend to care he'd lost a patient, more likely looking after their own interests.

22

Thursday, Early Evening
Merrillville, Indiana
60 Miles South of Chicago, Illinois

The closest branch for the rental car agency was located in a strip mall in Merrillville, and when they arrived, the place was buttoned up. Fealy apologized.

When Lauren opened her phone to search for other options, she saw a text from a number she didn't recognize. It'd have to wait. All the rental car companies, other than the Chicagoland airport locations, were closed for the evening.

"I can drop you at a hotel and you can figure it out in the morning," Fealy said.

They accepted his offer.

The trooper drove them to a new Holiday Inn Express off Route 30, popped the trunk, and watched them remove their luggage.

"What about my weapon?" Vance asked.

"Took the liberty of packing it in your suitcase," Fealy said, handing him a business card through the open window of his cruiser, suggesting Vance call if he had an epiphany about who might have swapped the plates on the car, warning him that a loaded, concealed weapon was illegal in Indiana, and that possession of a firearm in Chicago could turn into an endless night in the Cook County jail.

Vance thanked him for the ride and promised to call if he had any new news, then followed Lauren into the hotel lobby. The young woman running the hotel desk, probably a student at nearby Valparaiso University, stared over his shoulder. He turned to see what had caught her eye: the souped-up police Charger idling beneath the lobby entrance.

"We had car trouble," Vance said, poking a hole in her imagination.

He rented two rooms, and by the time they got to the elevator, it was 7:15. They needed to hustle if they were going to make the 8:30 reservation.

"I need a few minutes to freshen up," Lauren said.

"You got ten, then we need to get going."

"How're we getting there?"

"I'll figure it out."

While Lauren got ready in her room, he used the bathroom in his to wash and dry his hands and face. Sitting on the edge of the bed, still wearing the only pair of slacks and button-down shirt he'd packed for Belize and worked for the visit to the doctor, he jotted the trooper's name and cell number on the hotel notepad, then wadded it into a ball and dropped it in the bathroom wastebasket. He grabbed his briefcase, hung the DO NOT DISTURB sign on the door handle, pulled it closed, snapped a picture of the sign, then walked down the hall and knocked on Lauren's door.

She answered dressed in business casual: tailored black

slacks, a gray V-neck sweater, and hair pulled into a sleek pony-tail. When he'd hailed an Uber using the app on his phone, he'd instructed the driver to meet them behind the main building of the hotel.

The cheerful young man behind the wheel had a Colts logo tattooed on the back of his shaved head.

Vance checked the mileage on the rideshare app, then entered the address on his mobile navigation app and compared the two: 64.2 miles with an estimated drive time of one hour and ten minutes, provided there weren't any unexpected delays.

He switched back to the Uber app and looked at the cost. No wonder the driver was in a good mood.

23

Thursday, Evening
On Route from Merrillville, Indiana to Chicago, Illinois

T he second time Vance had asked Lauren about the stranger on the escalator, she'd been about to tell him it was Hunter Grant, the man from Belize, but they'd been interrupted by the *whoop, whoop, whoop* of Officer Fealy's siren.

The time wasn't right to bring it up now, not in the Uber, but it was a good time to bring up the text sent from the number she didn't recognize when she received it. "I got a message from Bibbins."

"When?"

She checked the time stamp. "I think around the time we got stopped."

"What's it about?"

She read it to him: "'I know it's last minute but would you

like to go to a Botox party tomorrow night if you're still in town? Text me back. Bibbins. Btw, we met last night.'"

"How did she get your number?"

"I gave her my card when I bumped into her in the ladies' room."

"You're going, right?"

"Of course, I'm accepting her invitation as we speak." She typed I'd love to. Message me the details, then pressed the SEND button.

Her phone pinged instantly. Great! Starts at 4. Here's the info.

"That was quick." She held her phone up for him to see, then opened the link and scanned the website for the cosmetics spa.

She closed out of it, then googled the website for Morton's Steakhouse and studied the dinner menu. Deciding what to order now meant she could pay closer attention at the table. The honey-balsamic-glazed Ora king salmon sounded delicious.

One search led to another and by the time they got to the restaurant, she'd learned Ora salmon came from New Zealand and was farmed by New York's Fulton Fish Market on a non-GMO diet approved by the World Wildlife Fund. It sounded like the fish were eating a lot healthier than the people eating them. No wonder the prices were so high.

The Uber driver stopped near the valet stand. Other than the awning, the mundane red-brick building located in a strip mall could have been mistaken for a JoAnn's Fabric, or a LensCrafters.

The Uber driver cursed, raising a fist at the Jaguar SUV that zipped past and parked on an angle, blocking his car in front of Morton's. The Jag driver stepped out and took a valet ticket while typing on his phone. Vance's mobile pinged with a message from Dr. Garcia: arrived. Looking out the rear passenger-side window, he observed the man: The doctor was younger than he'd expected, and in a hurry.

He scanned the NO WEAPONS sign posted on the door, tapped the Glock holstered beneath his jacket, opened the door for Lauren, and followed her inside. It looked like a typical upscale steakhouse, with dark floral carpeting, rich wood paneling, white tablecloths, shiny red barstools, and black leather chairs. Round fluorescent light fixtures the size and shape of car tires hung from the ceiling, and it was noisy and smelled gloriously of roasting meat.

Lauren stood next to him at the hostess stand where Emilio Garcia chatted with a woman holding three leather-bound menus. If he guessed right, Garcia was a regular.

Vance handled the introductions. A tall brunette hostess with a long stride led them to a four-top table in a quiet corner near the wine cellar where a couple dozen bottles were on display in a wooden box on a white marble-topped console.

The waiter with a red napkin folded over his forearm was prompt. He nodded before he spoke. "Good evening, and welcome to Morton's. May I recommend the Chateau Montelena Cabernet, full-bodied with dark berry tones and a hint of chocolate."

"Yes, thank you," Emilio said.

"Three glasses?"

"Two," Lauren said.

The waiter nodded and left.

The doctor unfolded the cloth napkin and placed it on his lap. "I have a wine locker. I pay an annual fee and agree to drink twelve bottles a year. A bottle a month is doable. Don't worry, the charges go separately to my account."

"I'm not worried about who's paying," Vance said, "it's our invitation. A wine locker, who knew?" When Garcia didn't respond, he said, "Sorry about missing our meeting earlier. We had car trouble and no cell service."

"I thought your plane might've been delayed. You drove?"

"Yes, from Indianapolis," Vance said.

Garcia cut to the point. "Why is your company so anxious to meet with me? Is there an issue with the medical records?"

His candor was refreshing. "We're not sure. That's why we're looking into it." He was about to play a card and watched him carefully. "We have another client, an oncologist in Indianapolis, who's lost three patients in what appears to be similar circumstances."

Garcia paused, then drummed his thumb on the edge of the tablecloth. "And you think the deaths are connected?"

"It's possible," Vance said.

"Why would the medical records company care? The only reason you'd be here is if you have an exposure. Is that why they sent a lawyer?"

Rogers must've outed him. "I'm not here in that capacity."

Garcia leaned back in the big leather chair and folded his arms across his chest. "Then why are you here?"

"To ask a few questions. Was an autopsy done on your patient?"

"No. Were toxicology tests done on the Indy patients?"

Before he could answer, Garcia's phone rang. Patrons sitting nearby twisted in their seats and glared.

"Excuse me," Garcia said. "Hello . . . No . . . He's here now . . . Uh-huh . . . Uh-huh . . . Sure . . . I'll let him know." He ended the call. "That was Sherry Rogers. I called to see if she knew why you weren't answering your phone earlier. She said to enjoy dinner."

Why did Sherry Rogers call Garcia at dinner? She could have called him directly if she wanted to know why he'd missed the meeting at Garcia's office.

"So, where were we?"

"You asked about toxicology tests. They were done, but—"

Garcia interrupted. "Those take weeks."

The sommelier arrived, uncorked the bottle of cabernet, and poured an ounce into Garcia's glass. He picked it up by the stem, swirled the liquid, closed his eyes, sniffed, then sipped.

"Does it meet with your approval?"

Garcia held his glass up to the light and narrowed his eyes. "Yes." He turned to Lauren. "Are you sure you don't want a little taste?"

She shook her head.

The waiter poured two glasses, and when he was out of earshot, Garcia asked Vance, "How much do you know about cancer drugs?"

"The minimum."

"If you're going to investigate on behalf of your company, you should know more than that."

"If that's an offer, indulge me, please."

Garcia twirled the wine in his glass, sniffed, sipped, and swallowed, then repeated the ritual before speaking. "There're seven basic types of chemotherapy drugs, and there're more than a hundred types of cancers. Antimetabolites target cells at specific phases of the cycles. Colon cancer, for example, is treated this way. Some drugs are formulated to cross the brain barrier to treat brain cancers."

"Whoa," Vance said. "That's way too deep for me. How about if I ask questions, instead?"

"Sure," Garcia said. "Ask away."

Lauren fished the notepad she'd taken from the hotel out of her purse and handed it to him, along with a Holiday Inn Express pen.

Vance moved his place setting to make room. "How many different chemo drugs do you handle in an average month?"

"A dozen, maybe."

"What drug was your patient being treated with?"

"You're asking me to go out on a limb."

"I can go into the records and see for myself."

"Then why didn't you? That would've saved you a trip."

"Because I don't want to taint evidence procedures."

"Wait a sec," Garcia said. "Evidence? You're suggesting this might be criminal?"

"I'm being cautious. If the toxicology reports show something suspicious—"

"Hold on," Garcia said, "this is the first I'm hearing about a possible criminal case. You think the patients might've been poisoned?"

"What were you giving your patient, the one who died?"

Garcia paused. "She was being treated with docetaxel. It's a plant-based alkaloid."

Vance glanced at Lauren.

"It's from a family of chemo drugs designed to interrupt the cell reproduction process." Garcia sipped from his glass and leaned back in his chair. "If you're not representing the company legally, then why are you here?"

Vance picked up his glass and swigged. "I'm an investor."

"Ah." Garcia nodded his head slowly, unfolded his arms from his chest, leaned in, and placed his forearms on the table. "You should know my clinic is associated with the university hospital system. It's located in a low-income area, and a lot of my patients are poor, most of them are on Medicaid. There's a board of directors that makes decisions about what vendors we use, what software platforms we're on. Not me. If you have questions about administrative protocols, I'm not the right guy to talk to. Changing records vendors wasn't my idea, either, but I'm guessing your company must be cheaper."

Though he did want to know who'd made the decision to

switch, it'd have to wait. "I want to talk about the incidents. How many have you had?"

"By incidents, do you mean deaths?"

"Yes."

"I've had one, in the clinic, during infusion. My patients are low-income and have poorer outcomes, and many live below the poverty level."

"Meaning?"

"Meaning most have at least one other serious underlying health issue, usually diabetes or heart disease. They cost more to treat and have worse outcomes." He paused, picked up his wine glass, and sipped. "I shouldn't even be talking to you. You're a lawyer and you know better than me that my malpractice carrier will have a fit if they find out I talked to you."

"Don't tell them."

Garcia opened the menu.

"If you're so worried about it, then why did you agree to meet me?"

He set the menu down. "I thought maybe you'd seen something, that maybe you'd voice your opinion and the board might listen."

"About what?" he asked.

"A while back, I had my staff start to add comments to the notes section that I think the infusions are too fast."

Vance cocked his head. "How long are yours infused?"

"An hour, maybe two. Five to seven is optimal but fast is cheaper."

"Could that've killed your patient?" Vance asked.

"Oh, God, no. If that were the case, I would never have allowed it. The problem comes later. Ten years down the road some'll have heart conditions and other chronic health problems. Fast infusions are hard on the internal organs."

"What did the autopsy report show?" Vance asked.

Garcia shook his head. "I told you, we didn't do one."

"Why not?"

"The patients are poor, and sick, and resources are thin."

Lauren shook her head slowly.

Vance was stunned. "If your patient's immune system is compromised wouldn't you want to know if something else, like the seasonal flu, was the cause of death?"

"Of course, but it's not up to me. As far as the flu is concerned, we're past flu season and my patient's immune system was in good shape."

"How can you be so sure?"

"We do bloodwork every week, checking T-cells, platelets, vitamin D, blood sugar, creatine, the list goes on. Besides, my patient was in overall good health and her vital signs were normal the morning of treatment. After Rogers told me what happened in Indianapolis, it made me wonder if there could be a connection."

The wine on an empty stomach had gone to Vance's head and he needed food. He picked up the thick leather menu and opened it.

"There're two things you should know," Garcia said. "I don't like medical reps or the money men, and I especially don't like lawyers."

The waiter stood in the corner. Vance motioned him to their table. He knew what he wanted and so did Garcia, both ordering the ribeye, medium rare. Lauren chose the Ora salmon.

After the server left the table, Vance said, "I used to be a homicide detective."

Lauren kicked him under the table, landing the toe of her shoe on a bony part of his shin. He shot her a look, narrowing his eyes.

"Huh. I happen to like cops," Garcia said. "I did my residency at the Level II trauma center at the county hospital and dealt with Chicago's finest every day. Where were you a detective?"

"Miami."

"That's a tough town, too. From cop to lawyer, I bet there's a story behind that."

After the food arrived, Garcia stabbed his medium-rare ribeye with his fork. The meat bled pink. Vance sawed off a hunk of fat, then cut a bite-sized piece of perfectly grilled meat, letting it steep in the juices for a second before popping it in his mouth where the flavors blossomed.

"My patients have a lot of strikes against them," Garcia said between bites.

"It sounds like it," Vance said.

"Many of them are old and most people don't want to think about the elderly. It's easier to warehouse them in rest homes because no one wants to see the irreversible future of human decay."

Garcia was ruining the meal. Vance downed the rest of the red wine in his glass.

Over dessert, the doctor agreed to let them to come to his office midafternoon the next day, explaining he'd be overseeing the clinic in the morning, and that he'd be too busy to meet earlier.

"I have a friend," Garcia said, "who worked for the FDA as an international pharmaceutical inspector. When he testified in front of Congress, the members acted shocked at what he had to say. Did you know the Chinese got caught using yellow road paint in kids' toys and baby food?"

"That's awful," Lauren said.

"In India, he saw people sneaking out of the records room after he excused himself to use the restroom. He caught them shredding documents in a backroom. He wrote a report to his bosses at the FDA recommending further inspections."

"What happened?" Vance asked.

"The FDA agreed to publish a list of carcinogen-free medications sold in America."

"Are you kidding?" Lauren asked.

"I wish. We pay the highest prices in the world and get inferior products. The Chinese could care less about their own citizens so why should their people care about ours? I take that back, workers in China are exploited, and they have no way of knowing what's going on. Even if they did, they'd have no recourse."

Lauren set her fork down. "How do they get away with it?"

"Lack of oversight. China sources the APIs—active pharmaceutical ingredients—that go into almost all of our drugs. The FDA is supposed to inspect them but surprisingly few are."

"Can you call your buddy and see if we can trace the drugs, or APIs, to see if maybe he knows if there's a bad batch of docetaxel out there?" Vance asked.

Garcia laughed. "I wish. He quit after the FDA took the word of the Chinese over his."

"So, it's not crazy to think there could be a problem with the drugs?" he asked.

"No," Garcia said, "the only thing that surprises me is that something like this hasn't happened sooner."

When the waiter returned with the bill, Vance opened the leather folder, left a twenty-five-percent tip, and placed his credit card back in his wallet. He got up from the table and followed the doctor out.

Emilio handed his ticket to the valet. "When I called my malpractice insurance carrier to report the patient death, they already knew about it."

"How?" Vance asked.

"I guess the board reported it. The clinic isn't run by doctors, it's run by lawyers, marketing geniuses, and bean counters. As for the marketers, they're soulless twenty-first century snake oil salesmen. Don't quote me."

It'd started to drizzle. They stood beneath the maroon awning.

"Where're you two staying tonight?"

"In Merrillville," Vance said.

"Where'd you park?"

"We didn't," Lauren said. "We Ubered."

The valet drove Garcia's Jaguar SUV under the portico and got out. The doctor handed him a tip. "Merrillville's a ways away and this drizzle is going to turn into a storm. You should stay in the city. Go check out the sights in the morning. The Field Museum is worth the trip. That's what I'd do if I were you. Either way, see you tomorrow."

Garcia slid behind the wheel and a moment later the Jaguar disappeared into the misty haze.

"Let's stay in the city tonight," Vance said. "The doc's right, we can do a little sightseeing in the morning."

"I'd love to, but my clothes are in Indiana."

"Sounds like the first line of a country western song."

"Ha, ha."

"Come on, I'll buy you a change of clothes in the morning." He tapped the Uber app, set the pickup spot for Morton's, and typed the Blackstone Hotel in the destination line. "You were awfully quiet tonight."

"Don't get used to it."

"Don't get used to Vance-funded shopping sprees."

"No worry about that," she said.

24

Thursday, Later Night, Chicago, Illinois

The ride to the Blackstone Hotel on the south side of the Loop was smooth. He'd asked the driver to stop at a CVS pharmacy where Lauren ran in and bought enough toiletries to get them through the night.

Along the way, she'd asked him why he'd chosen the hotel.

"I have a family connection to it."

"Really."

"There was an assassination attempt on FDR at Bayfront Park. The gunman was a lousy aim and ended up shooting the mayor of Chicago in the stomach, instead."

"How's it connected to your family?"

"My grandfather was a doctor; he was on call the night of the shooting and treated him for the gunshot wound."

"I've never heard that story. An assassination attempt on FDR? In Miami?"

"Most people haven't." He'd been intrigued, borderline

obsessed with the family lore since he was a kid. "After FDR was inaugurated, the mayor died, and the gunman got the electric chair. The state of Florida convicted him under the statute of transferred intent, meaning he'd intended to kill FDR, but killed the wrong person."

"That's crazy," she said.

"My grandfather said the mayor suffered from sepsis he'd gotten at the Blackstone Hotel and traveled to Miami already sick. My granddad said that's what killed him, not the bullet. It's been a very well-kept secret."

"Why?"

"Because it made it easy for the state of Florida to execute the shooter."

"I can't believe your grandfather treated the mayor."

"He met FDR, too. I've always wanted to see the hotel."

Lauren gazed out the car window at the shops and restaurants, their neon signs reduced to misty halos of colorful lights, the clash of glass towers and neoclassical architecture, the famed Magnificent Mile, a beautiful mix of old and new.

"It looks like a shopping bonanza is in my future," she said. "And you're buying."

"That's right."

DESIGNED BY BENJAMIN MARSHALL, the twenty-plus-story Blackstone Hotel faced Michigan Avenue. Named for Timothy Blackstone, a politician and one-time executive at the Union Stock Yards, it had the dubious history of being where John F. Kennedy went to meet Mayor Daly in the midst of the Cuban Missile Crisis. It was also the setting for *The Color of Money*, starring Tom Cruise. And where his grandfather's patient, the Chicago mayor, got sick before dying at a Miami hospital.

The hotel was built between 1908 and 1912, before World War II, before America's most influential architects had turned into barracks-builders. It was everything he'd expected with the pink granite façade, lit at night with a splash of blue neon accenting the intricate masonry and arched windows.

They walked the wet marble stairs leading to the lobby. The interior was as eclectic as the city architecture, with banks of polished brass elevators, walnut paneling, and heavy draperies, stubby-legged midcentury chairs, and sofas made from brightly colored velvets and leather. Huge modernist rugs that could've been painted by Mark Rothko lay atop a black-and-white checkered stone-tiled floor.

The young man working the desk greeted them. "Do you have a reservation?"

"No," Vance said. "I'm hoping we can get a room."

"Of course. May we help you with your bags?"

"We don't have any," he said.

The clerk narrowed his gaze slightly, then padded his keyboard. "Sir, we're sold out of king beds. All we have available are double queens with a lake view."

"We'll take two of those," Lauren said.

The clerk raised his eyebrows. "Yes, ma'am. License and credit card, please."

25

Friday, Morning, Chicago, Illinois

Vance awoke at dawn and used the landline in the bathroom to order room service for two. After showering in the gaudy bathroom with dizzying black-and-white paisley wallpaper, he emptied the drugstore plastic bag onto the countertop and found a disposable razor, but no shaving cream.

The hotel bar soap would have to do. The custom-branded black box with the Blackstone logo with gold lettering read:

"If you're going to be two-faced, at least make one of them pretty." —*Marilyn Monroe*. He chuckled.

Lathering his face, he heard a knock on his door. He grabbed the Blackstone robe hanging on a hook, threw it on, and looked through the peephole: Lauren. He let her in. A dog barked in the hallway. The owner yanked the leash and shushed it, then continued down the hall.

"Morning," he said. "How'd you sleep?"

She walked past him and grunted.

"I'll take that as *not good*. I have a remedy for that," he teased.

"Maybe next time, Santa."

He cocked his head. She patted her cheek. Ah, the shaving cream. "I ordered coffee and breakfast. That definitely qualifies me as Santa."

"It's too early to be witty." She flopped into the club chair near the big picture window.

He opened the drapes. A glow, an orange dome, rose up from Lake Michigan casting a streak of gold across the lake, tinting the water a deep purplish blue. It was hard to imagine that two months ago the lake was frozen and white.

There was another knock on the door. He peered through the peephole at a fish-eye view of a young man in a hotel uniform standing behind a rolling cart.

He opened it, eyeing a small glass vase filled with fresh daisies as the man rolled the cart into his room. "Any chance you can leave the cart here?" he asked, removing his wallet.

The guy said nothing, waiting to see the offer. Vance held out a twenty, folding it lengthwise. The waiter hooked it with his thumb, folding it in half again and stuffed it into his pocket.

The man squatted, removed a tray hidden under the long green tablecloth, and set it on the dresser, dishes tightly covered with clear plastic wrap. Vance saw a plain silver teapot and a small wooden box with an assortment of teas, to be delivered to the next guest, he assumed. The waiter set the vase of flowers on the tray with the tea.

"I'd like to keep those."

"Ah." The waiter smiled and put the daisies back on the cart, and, balancing the room service tray on his shoulder, left the room.

He poured coffee, delivered a mug to Lauren, set the flowers on the side table next to her, turned on the television, and went back to the bathroom. After he finished shaving, he sat in the chair next to her, spreading butter and jam on a cold, toasted English muffin while she channel surfed. He browsed the 'Net on his cell.

The Field Museum of Natural History opened at 8:00 AM.

Then he remembered something. He walked to the bed, lifted the mattress and fished his holstered Glock from where he'd stowed it for the night.

He poured her a second cup of coffee and one for himself. "Any interest in going to the museum?"

"You mean the dead zoo?"

"No, the museum. After we go shopping."

"Sure, I guess. Sounds fun."

He picked up the clothes spread on the side of the bed he hadn't slept on and headed into the bathroom to get dressed.

26

Maybe Emilio Garcia should have pushed back and declined the meeting later today with the reps from the medical records company. His morning was already off to a lousy start, fighting with the billing department at Medicaid. Chemo patients required weekly bloodwork, and he wanted an approval to do an additional liver panel. His patient was jaundiced, and his belly tender to the touch, but there was no way of knowing exactly what was wrong without doing lab work. He'd been on hold for almost twenty minutes, having run the request all the way up the ladder.

And still he was denied. The tests were costly.

If his patients lived in Winnetka, or Wilmette, or Barrington Hills, they'd have private insurance and the additional costs would be approved, no questions asked. It seemed like he spent more time arguing with bureaucrats than he did talking with patients. It was always about the money. He kneaded the stress ball he kept in his desk drawer until his hands throbbed, then went to visit his patients.

He headed down the hallway toward the infusion room when his nurse, Anna Malone, intercepted him, stretching both arms out, stopping him. She spoke in a low tone. "We have a problem."

"What kind of a problem?"

"Mrs. Beecher isn't breathing."

"Move out of the way."

Anna yielded, letting him pass.

"What happened?"

"I don't know. I went to check on her and she's not breathing."

Garcia sprinted to the infusion area with reclining chairs laid out like a schoolroom. "Where is she?"

Anna gestured to a recliner nearest the corner to his left.

"Did you check for a pulse?"

"Yes. No pulse."

"Jesus." Garcia snaked his way between patients and visitors, feigning calm. "I need privacy."

Together they dragged a portable room divider and set it on an angle.

Garcia checked for a pulse. None. He disconnected the patient from the IV, interlocked his fingers, leaned over, and using his body weight, started the first of thirty chest compressions. "Get the defibrillator."

"We didn't get it yet."

"What? Damn it! Call 9-1-1."

He bent the patient's neck back to clear her airway, put his mouth on hers and blew into her lungs, twice. In his periphery, he saw a kid peeking around the divider. He heard people whispering and gasping, then saw a woman walk around his side of the divider.

"Move 'em, move 'em, get 'em out of here," he barked at Anna, grunting as he resumed chest compressions.

Thirty more. The woman's frail body bounced on the bed. He heard a noise: a rib cracking under his palms. He alternated, two rescue breaths, thirty chest compressions, two rescue breaths, thirty more chest compressions, but the patient wasn't responding. He kept working.

Anna clamped her hand on his shoulder. "The paramedics are here."

Two men pushed past Garcia, quickly assessed the situation, and loaded Mrs. Beecher onto a gurney. He stepped back from the chaos, exhausted.

This was not happening.

Damn it. Why didn't he have that defibrillator? He'd asked Anna to call someone in administration and request it, and she'd said they'd approved it. But he hadn't thought to follow up himself. There was one at the gym where he attended a weekly spin class. At his dentist's office. He'd seen them at the airport. He'd even seen a few at casinos in Vegas. But not his medical office?

Fuck. This was the second patient to die in less than three weeks.

"Get me a printout of her chart," he told Anna. "And bring it to my office. Pronto." He needed it before the news spread. He'd been unable to review the records for the first patient who'd died; they'd mysteriously disappeared, and it pissed him off. Whoever did it had acted fast, calling his malpractice insurer and wiping the records clean. This time, he'd stay one step ahead.

There was a knock at his open door. He waved Anna in. She handed him the documents. "The ER's on hold. They want to talk to you."

He looked at the flashing light on his desk phone. His patient didn't make it. He knew she was dead before the paramedics arrived, but the university's legal department mandated that CPR be performed until the EMTs took over. It was a legal thing—if patients were pronounced at the hospital, the police didn't get involved. He'd followed the same protocol for the first death.

Anna buzzed him on the interoffice phone. "The hospital's still on hold. They want to know what you want to do about informing next of kin?"

"Tell them I'll do it," he said, leafing through the patient files. "How are the others doing?"

"They're curious, but they don't know she didn't make it."

"Let's keep it that way."

He ended the call and left his office, checking the hallway in both directions before heading to the restroom. He splashed cold water on his face and scrubbed his hands with hot water and soap, then punched the air with his fist.

What killed her? She was in overall good health. He reviewed her chart and read through her pre-treatment screenings. EKG was normal, fasting blood sugar level of eighty-five. How could he lose two chemo patients—right here in the clinic —in less than two weeks? It couldn't be a coincidence.

He texted Vance Courage, asking if he could move the meeting sooner.

27

L auren wanted to shop at the Gap, choosing a simple long-sleeved T-shirt. After Vance paid, she got permission from the sales clerk to go back to the dressing room and change into the new one.

He waited for her near the front door facing busy Michigan Avenue, and when she returned, he held up the receipt. "Hard to believe I'm getting out for under fifty bucks."

"You could buy yourself a new shirt and still get out for under a hundred. We have time."

He sniffed the underarm on one side. "This one's good for at least another week."

She raised her eyebrows and shook her head.

The rideshare driver dropped them in front of the museum.

"Wow," she said. "This place looks more like the Supreme Court than a museum."

The Grecian and Roman-inspired architecture, with its arched roof and decorative white stonework and columns and stairs wide enough to march an army up, was Old World.

The rent-a-cop at the door looked bored. He saw the NO

FIREARMS OR WEAPONS warning posted but there were no metal detectors. He purchased two tickets for $26 each.

"Do you want to find a place where you can leave your briefcase? I think they have a coat check."

"I'd rather carry it. I'll be right back," he said, spotting the men's room.

He'd been able to get in the building with his gun. He hid inside the stall, balanced his briefcase on his knees, removed his pistol, and holstered it under his jacket.

When he returned, he saw her standing in the open lobby, gazing up at a massive dinosaur skeleton: a ninety percent complete titanosaur—*Patagotitan mayorum*—the largest discovered so far. Nicknamed Máximo, he smiled at the placard next to the display with directions on how to send a text message to Máxi. Who knew Chicagoans had a collective sense of humor? Like the soap in the hotel.

He looked around. "So far, you're right."

"About what?"

"The dead zoo."

"You haven't seen anything yet. Let's go the Pawnee Earth Lodge." She held up a slick brochure with maps of the Native American Indian exhibits.

"Check it out." He pointed to a display offering a sniff of prehistoric T-Rex's breath. "Who'd have thunk?"

"A guy," she said.

Now she was firing on all cylinders.

A little boy standing in front of the exhibit pressed the button, inhaled the mist of the extinct dinosaur, then said, "Cool."

They walked past dozens of elaborate displays and dioramas filled with animals, all stuffed, a taxidermist's version of the wax museum, immortalized in their recreated habitats.

"I told you," she said.

He followed her toward the signs leading to the Native American Indian Hall, past the titanosaur, where she turned left and headed down a hallway leading to the lodge. "What's up with you wanting to see the Pawnee exhibit?"

"I wrote a paper on them in junior high. After I read about a famous battle in Nebraska called Massacre Canyon, the Pawnees against the Lakota tribe, I went to the library to read everything I could find."

"Why?"

"They mutilated each other, then set each other on fire."

"All righty, then," he said. "Let's check out the day in the life of a brutal warrior."

He stepped into the full-sized replica, about sixty feet in diameter, with a large fire pit in the middle. "Excuse me," he asked a young woman guiding a tour, "how many people lived in one of these."

"Around forty, and there'd be fifty or so of these lodges grouped together. A village."

Wow. What would that have been like, sharing an open space with that many people? His phone pinged. A message from Dr. Garcia: call me please - imp.

He approached Lauren, who was examining the textiles— elaborate beadwork—on display inside the lodge. "I'll be right back."

"Where're you going?"

"Garcia texted. He said it's important."

He walked outside, stood on the top stair; all was now much busier and noisier with tourists lined halfway down the stairs. He walked around the edge of the building where he'd have more privacy, phoned Garcia, set his briefcase down and plugged one ear with his finger.

Garcia told him about the second patient death.

"I can be there in an hour. Do me a favor, preserve the patient records. I want to look at them."

"Already did," Garcia said before ending the call.

Vance held up his General Admission ticket as he snaked through the awaiting crowd, cutting the line, ignoring the sneers and dirty looks. He found Lauren in the Pawnee lodge. "Come on. We gotta go. There's a problem."

"But we just got here."

The room had an echo. He lowered his voice. "Dr. Garcia lost another patient this morning."

Her mouth dropped. "During treatment?"

"Yes. We gotta go."

28

"Please roll your windows up," the rideshare driver said.

Vance powered his up and looked out at the buildings surrounded by chain-link fencing, boarded up with graffiti, and construction cones on the sidewalks. The driver stopped at a red light directly across from a pizza-taco-gyros-hotdog joint in an old one-story brick on a corner located on the fringes of the south side of Chicago.

The walk-up window had burglar bars and a speaker for taking orders. Strips of blue painter's tape held up neon paper cutouts in the shapes of starbursts and arrows with menu items and prices handwritten in thick black lettering.

The driver turned into the parking lot of a flat-topped brick building with a faded wooden sign. On the other side of the street, a three-story hospital with the words EMERGENCY ENTRANCE was posted horizontally in big red letters under the fascia. For a second, he thought it was a Walgreen's. A group of nurses dressed in maroon-and-pink scrubs congregated on the sidewalk beneath the shade of an elm tree, some smoking cigarettes.

The receptionist expected them and buzzed Dr. Garcia on

the interoffice phone system. He greeted them a minute later, then led the way down a dim hallway to a windowless office where the only nice object was a framed medical diploma hung on the wall next to his desk. Like Emery, he was a University of Michigan graduate. Vance made a mental note.

"What happened?" he asked, pulling an armless chair from in front of the desk for Lauren, then another for himself.

He shook his head. "The same thing, the patient stopped breathing. I performed CPR until the EMTs arrived."

He finished the story, explaining that it was protocol to pronounce the patients dead at a hospital to avoid a police investigation. That was standard procedure in Florida, too.

"Didn't you say your clinic is part of the university system?" It certainly didn't look the part.

"Technically, it's not. It's organized as a separate 501c3 and most of our donors are connected to the university."

"How?"

"Staff, alumni, consultants, outside lawyers. It's a tax write-off for them, and the university pledged the first three hundred and fifty thousand dollars of seed money." He opened his desk drawer, "Here." He handed Vance a brochure. "Check out our board of directors."

It was slickly produced with the typical information. Mission statement, history, and the inside right page listed the board members along with headshots. The chairman was a lawyer. The vice chairman, a VP of a local bank. The treasurer, an insurance broker. The secretary, a retired school superintendent. The lower-level board members consisted of a corporate planner, an arts-and-crafts director from the city parks department, a retired labor relations manager, another private-practice attorney, and an electrical engineer. A minister, who identified as a community organizer, was also on the board.

"See anything unusual?" Garcia asked.

"I do. There's no one from the medical community."

"Bingo."

"What is this place?"

"Ever heard of patient dumping?"

"No."

"It's when hospitals find ways to get poorer patients to agree to go to other clinics."

Lauren spoke up. "Why?"

"Because if they refuse to treat poor patients, they risk losing their government funding, which is millions of dollars. When one of the university lawyers proposed they find a way to dispose of them, the PR outfit that represents the university suggested they find a way to get patients to *want* to go elsewhere."

A phone pinged. Lauren reached into her purse, looked at the screen, then used her thumbnail to silence it.

"How do you do that?" Vance asked.

"By misrepresentation, by spending a lot of money on marketing, building an enticing website, and handing out fancy brochures. When low-income patients show up at the university's main campus hospital, which, by the way, borders the South Side, they offer them free transportation here."

"Who'd even think of that?" Lauren asked.

"People looking out for the bottom line," Garcia said.

"There're more of these clinics?" Vance asked.

"There're six, located strategically in Illinois. You'd be shocked if you knew who was behind it. None of them would set foot in this neighborhood. Meanwhile, the university makes a ton of money by outsourcing the poor and sick to us."

He'd thought he'd heard it all. Breaking the Moral Law at the patient level? That was a new one.

"You have to understand what I'm up against. It's going to be very hard to get anyone to look into these patient deaths. They'll sic an army of lawyers on me. They have a lot to lose and they're going to protect their interests."

"How high does the patient-dumping scheme go?" Vance asked.

"A few years back, an investigative reporter did a series about it in the *Tribune*. It reaches the state legislature, and with federal funding, it has to go higher, even though the reporter couldn't prove it."

"So much for the Hippocratic Oath," Vance said.

"Yeah, well." Garcia shrugged.

He didn't know Dr. Garcia from Dr. Oz, and what he'd shared was a complicated conspiracy to dump poor patients on a clinic funded mostly by friends of the prestigious nearby university. He had to stay focused. "May I see the records for the patient who just died?"

Garcia handed him several pages, stapled together. "Like I told you, the files for the first death were scrubbed like that patient never existed. I had my nurse download and print these before anyone had the chance to delete them. I have a couple of hospital patients across the street I need to see. You're welcome to wait here. I won't be long."

Vance looked at the printout. Norma Beecher. Age sixty-four. Single. African American. Living on disability. Medicaid patient. Breast cancer. He skimmed down to the treatment notes. DTX. Short for docetaxel. The same drug given to the four other dead patients.

"This's weird," he said.

Lauren leaned closer to get a better look. "What?"

"The patient's next appointment is set for June twenty-eighth."

"What's weird about that?"

"It's the same date as the follow-up appointments for Emery's patients."

"When were you planning to tell me this?"

He remembered what Bibbins had told him. "The woman I introduced you to at the gala is Emery's nurse."

"The one who's engaged to the Masson rep?"

"Right." He told her what Bibbins had shared, about how follow-up appointments couldn't be scheduled until the patients checked out after paying their deductibles.

"Let me see the file."

He handed it to her.

She flipped the pages. "I can't believe that story about patient- dumping."

He could. When it came to greed, there was no bottom. "It's a cold, cold world."

29

"I think I might've found a pattern in the patient records," Vance said when Garcia returned from making his rounds at the hospital across the street.

"What sort of pattern?"

"All of the patents were being treated with docetaxel."

Garcia's look of anticipation, faded. "It's very commonly used."

"I saw something else, too."

His interest returned. "What?"

"Your newly deceased patient had a follow-up appointment on June twenty-eighth."

"So?"

"So did the doctor's patients in Indy," Lauren said.

"How do you know that?"

"From the medical records," Vance said. "But the doctor's nurse in Indy said they don't schedule—"

Garcia interrupted. "Until the patient checks out. Let me have it back."

Vance handed him the file.

Dr. Garcia picked up the interoffice phone and called Anna Malone. She was at the door in less than a minute.

"Anna, come here." Garcia showed her the date. "Did you make this appointment?"

She looked at it. "I don't think so." Her faced twisted into a knot. "No. Definitely not."

"How can you be so sure?"

"Because it's a Saturday."

Vance pulled up the calendar on his phone. How did he miss this? It would've been a simple calculation if he'd bothered to look.

"I know the date," Anna said, "because my cousin is getting married that day."

"Who else has access to the files?" Vance asked.

"We all do," she said. "Is something wrong?"

Garcia held up the document with the June 28th date on it. "Why would someone make an appointment for a Saturday when we're closed?"

Anna shrugged. "It must've been a mistake."

"Do you know who might've deleted the patient files?" Vance asked her.

"I don't know anything about that."

"Come here." The doctor got up from his chair and gestured for her to sit at his desk. "Find Norma Beecher's file."

Anna sat and typed quickly, glancing from the keyboard to the screen and back several times. Her brow wrinkled. "That's weird. It's not here." She looked at Vance. "Is that why you're here?"

He didn't answer.

"You're the administrator," Garcia said to Anna. "I want you to change the log-in and password. That way, only you and I will have access."

"What about—?"

The doctor cut her off. "Do it now."

Vance's phone buzzed. A 202 area code came up with CALLER ID UNAVAILABLE. Probably a telemarketer, but you never know. "Excuse me," he said, stepping into the hallway and answering it.

"Is this Officer Feely?" a man asked.

"It's FAY-lee with an A," Vance said.

"I'm Special Agent Hunter Grant from the FBI's Indianapolis field office."

"What can I do for you?"

"I'd like to talk."

He had a hook in the agent's mouth and he didn't want to lose it. "Do you want to talk on or off the record, because on the record's gonna be a problem."

Lauren walked into the hallway to listen in. He held his finger to his lips.

"Off the record."

"Good. 'Cause Indy's outside my jurisdiction, but I bet you already know that."

"I do. I'll meet you on your turf."

"What's this about?"

"A traffic stop."

"I stop a lot of people."

"A vehicle involved in a recent hit-and-run."

He felt the dopamine flood his brain, like seeing the winning numbers on a lotto ticket. He paused to let the excitement wane. "Not sure how I can help, but I'll give it a try."

"I have a few questions I'd like to ask you."

Fealy would want to meet with an FBI agent, they were the Major Leagues of law enforcement. Every cop's dream was to work a federal case, whether they'd admit it or not. Still, he played it cool, staying quiet, forcing Grant to make the next move.

"There's a laser-tag game place across the border in Indiana," Grant said.

Vance looked at his watch, balanced the phone on his shoulder, and mimed a pen and paper to Lauren. It was already eleven in the morning. "How far is it from Chicago?"

"About an hour."

"What time do you want to meet?"

"One o'clock. I'll reserve a room for us where we can talk."

"What's the name?"

"Combat Mission in Hobart."

He jotted it down.

"One o'clock," Grant repeated, then ended the call.

He saved the number in his contact list.

"What was that all about?" she asked.

"I'll explain it on the way." He handed her the paper.

"Where's Hobart, Indiana?"

"I don't know exactly, but we gotta get there by one o'clock. Google it, and get directions. Wait here and I'll be right back." He walked to Garcia's office and stood in the doorway. "We gotta go."

Anna stood with her hands on her hips. Garcia turned his monitor around so Vance could see the missing file.

"Can I get a copy, of the one you already printed?" His phone pinged. From Lauren, the link to Mission Combat's website.

He followed Anna to the copy room. A minute later, she handed him a still-warm copy of Patient Beecher's file. He put it in his briefcase. "Tell Dr. Garcia I'll be in touch."

He opened the website link she'd sent, tapped the CONTACT page, selected DIRECTIONS, and copied and pasted the address to the game place in the destination line on the rideshare app on his phone. "That was your friend."

"What friend?"

"Special Agent Hunter Grant."

Her eyes blew up. "Are you serious?"

He explained how he'd written Officer Fealy's name with his own cell number on the Holiday Inn Express notepad, and dropped it in the trash in his hotel bathroom. "I hung the DO NOT DISTURB sign on the door before we left so housekeeping wouldn't dump the trash."

"He went in your room?"

"Had to."

"How'd he get in?"

He smirked. "He's FBI."

"Do you think he was in my room, too?"

"Probably."

"What are you going to say when you meet him? He's going to figure out you're not the cop."

"I'm sure he already knows that."

A blue Nissan Rogue pulled to the curb. Vance checked the license plate and driver photo against the information on the rideshare app. It was their driver, Boomer Ellison.

"Hey, Boomer," Vance said, getting in. "How long's it gonna take to get to Hobart?"

The driver, a senior-age skinny fellow with a stringy gray ponytail and wire-rimmed granny glasses, looked at his phone. "GPS says just under an hour. It'll be a little faster if I take the Indiana Skyway."

Lauren climbed in next to him. She lowered her voice, "Grant'll recognize me."

"I know. I thought about that."

"Did you hear they're forecasting snow?" the driver asked.

"In late April?" Vance asked. "You sure?"

"Had snow in May once but that was a hundred years ago. No big deal so long as you know how to drive in it. Expecting sleet. Gonna be sloppy, and where you're going, the lake-effect stuff is really messy."

"Right," Vance said, cracking the window, letting out the stale odor inside the Nissan.

"Brrr. Roll that up," Lauren said, hugging herself.

The driver asked where they were from and when he told him they were from Miami, he inundated them with questions about travel tips, claiming it'd been a dream of his to go to Florida someday. Vance answered a few, then cut him off.

The temperature was dropping fast and neither of them were dressed for it.

30

Combat Mission was housed in an industrial complex sandwiched between a lawnmower repair business and a millworker shop. The sign looked new but the paint on the corrugated metal building was faded to a chalky blue, and it definitely looked nicer on their website. He'd watched the short promo video, effectively produced to ignite his every ancient instinct. Sound effects. Mock weapons. Realistic props. Role-playing games with names like Team Battlefield, Super Spy, Seek and Destroy, and Secret Service Escort.

When they arrived a half hour early, he was still high on adrenaline.

"Circle the block," Vance said.

"More like circle the cornfields," Boomer said.

"Slow down." There was an alley behind the building. "Turn here." The vehicles parked there were mostly work trucks.

"Whaddaya looking for?" Boomer asked.

"I want to see where we can load equipment in. Stop," he said jumping out of the Nissan. "Wait here."

He looked for any sign of Grant, the alley was clear, he jogged around to the front entrance. The door was tinted with a mirrored film. He went in; the place was empty and smelled like a locker room. The girl behind the counter set an open paperback book facedown on the glass counter where a few wrinkled T-shirts were on display.

"Can I help you?"

"I'm meeting someone."

"Do you have a reservation?"

"My friend called ahead."

"Huh." She squinted at her computer monitor. "Do you know which game you'll be playing?"

"No."

She looked up from her screen. "I don't have any reservations. Are you sure? When did you make them?"

"They'd be under the name of Hunter Grant."

"I'd remember that," she said. "The only thing I got going is a birthday party. That's not 'til four-thirty."

He peered out the window overlooking the parking lot. "What's your most popular game?"

"Team Battlefield." She cracked her gum and blew a bubble. "Do you want to book it?"

A late-model sedan pulled into the parking lot. "Can I see it first?"

"Sure." She strolled out from behind the counter. "There's not much to see. It's a virtual reality thing but you can try the glasses on if you'd like."

He followed her.

She stopped when the front doorbell chimed.

"May I use your men's room?"

"Sure. It's down the hall on the right. That's probably your friend. I'll take care of him. When you're ready, meet me back up front."

"Okay."

She walked toward the lobby. He watched from the dim hallway, taking a position where he could see from around the corner. The man was alone. Vance slipped out the back door, sprinted to the Nissan and jumped in. "Go, go, go."

Boomer turned and faced him. "Where to?"

"Just drive."

He hit the gas.

Vance ducked behind the driver's seat. "Don't speed."

Lauren followed suit, slinking down behind the passenger-side seat.

"Don't go the same way out," Vance said. "Go a different way."

"I need to know where to."

He pulled his phone from his pocket: "Siri, find a rental car place in Merrillville."

"One possibility is a rental car place in Maryville. I found a place in Knoxville. Do you want to try that?"

"I'll find it," Boomer said.

"What about the hotel?" Lauren asked.

"We're not going back there. That's exactly where he's going next."

"Where're we going after we get a rental car?"

"I'm working on that." He peered out the back window of the Rogue. He didn't see anyone following them. His phone pinged. He looked at the screen. Uber feedback popped up, asking him to rate his driver and leave a tip. He gave Boomer five stars and twenty dollars. He'd also missed a call from Dr. Emery's office. Then Grant's number came up on an incoming call.

"Don't forget," Lauren reminded him. "I have an appointment at the spa with Bibbins."

31

Friday, Afternoon, Indianapolis, Indiana

Bibbins turned the heat up at her apartment, tore open a packet of instant hot chocolate, poured it into a mug, filled it with water, set the microwave for 1:30, and pressed the start button. Then she called ME.

"Can you call the spa and add me to the guest list?"

"Sure, but I thought you had to work 'til five o'clock?"

"I did but Emery sent us home early. She said it's because of the weather forecast but I think it's really more for her and Dr. Shah. They've had a rough week."

"You've had a pretty bad week, too, and I'm glad you're able to do something nice for yourself."

She hesitated. She could only afford to go since she'd recruited a new customer. "Did you remember to add Lauren Gold to the list?"

"Of course. I asked them if they'd give you a credit like you asked, and they said they would, but I'll call now and let them know you're coming. I'll see you there," ME said before ending the call.

She wished she was more like her friend. Maybe having money was why ME never seemed resentful. If the University of Michigan medical school admissions hadn't been rigged, Jack wouldn't've been at the Masson gala last night, and that sales slut wouldn't have stuck her tongue down his throat. She shook her head, trying to knock the image from her head.

If admissions had been fair, Marie Elizabeth would be married to a doctor, too. Her fiancé, Yoshio, had scored in the top percentile on his pre-med admissions test, but like Jack's, his application had been rejected.

When she'd tried to talk to her dad about it, all he'd had to say was, "Life's not fair. The sooner you get used to the idea, the better you'll do." With an attitude like that, it was no wonder he'd settled for being an electrician.

Life's not fair? Life's a bitch, and then she shoves her tongue down your fiancé's esophagus.

Her mom said if Jack had gone to school in Michigan, she never would have met him. How did she know that? Didn't she believe in fate?

The microwave dinged. She set the mug of hot chocolate on the counter and peered out through the plastic blinds. The sky had darkened to a charcoal gray, and weather reports called for sleet and snow. If she hurried, she'd have time to prep the outdoor kitty condo she'd bought online before she had to leave for the spa.

The apartment manager had given her permission to set it up in a common area, in the corner, near the hedges behind her apartment building. Last winter she'd purchased two small heating pads that fit inside, and recently she'd put them away. She threw on her winter jacket, stepped into rubber boots, grabbed the heating pads from the hall closet, and went outside.

"Hey, Tom, it's gonna get cold tonight."

He meowed and rubbed against her pant leg. The others would come later and share the space like they did in the wintertime. She placed the warmers on the shelves inside the cathouse and plugged the long electrical cords running from the outlet, and filled their dish with enough kibble to get them through a cold night.

Her cell phone rang. "Hi, Mama."

"I know you're at work. Can you talk?"

"I'm home. Dr. Emery closed the office early because of the forecast."

"That was nice of her, hon."

"Is everything all right?"

"I just wanted to make sure you remembered tomorrow's Saturday and I'm coming over."

"I wouldn't forget. How are you feeling?" she asked, slipping back into her warm apartment.

"I'm okay. Been feeling a little under the weather this week, but I'm doing better today."

"What about Dad?"

"What about him?"

"How's he doing?" She sipped her hot chocolate.

"He's your dad, he's always the same. Works all day, comes home, sits in front of the TV and falls asleep in his underwear. He says to say hi. I always forget to tell you that."

"Have you checked the weather forecast?"

"I have, hon. God is cruel. After the winter we just had, you'd think he'd shine a little more sun on us first."

"Be careful tomorrow. They're forecasting lake-effect snow."

"I heard, but you know I ain't put a car in a ditch so far. You need anything?"

"No. I'll see you tomorrow."

"All right, hon, if you're going out with that boy tonight, you be careful, too."

Bibbins ended the call and opened the weather app on her phone, shivering at the forecast. The temperature was supposed drop to 31 degrees overnight.

She riffled through her closet. What should she wear to ME's beauty affair?

32

Friday, Midafternoon, Merrillville, Indiana

"Stop and let me let me grab my stuff," Lauren pleaded with Vance. "We're two minutes away. I'll make it fast."

They'd left their bags at the hotel and he could understand that she needed to freshen up and change clothes before meeting Bibbins at the cosmetic spa, but they'd be taking a chance.

"Where's the hotel?" Boomer asked.

"The Holiday Inn Express on Route 30."

The driver stopped at a red light and typed on his phone. "She's right. We're only a couple of minutes from the place."

The driver had been working him, trying to convince him to cancel the rental car and hire him off the grid as their driver.

"Fine," Vance said. "But make it quick."

A couple of minutes later, Boomer pulled into the hotel. He directed him to the back side of the building where their rooms were located.

She hopped out. "Come on, get your stuff."

"You go. We're gonna go around the block. Meet you back here in two."

"You sure?" she asked.

"Yeah."

THE DO NOT DISTURB tag still hung from the knob where she'd placed it yesterday before they left to meet Garcia for dinner. Lauren swiped her key, the light turned green. The bed was unmade, and the bath towel she'd thrown over the top of the shower door, still there.

She opened her messenger bag and swept her toiletries into it, then slung her roller bag onto the bed. Had Hunter been in her room? If so, she couldn't tell. She changed into a pair of snug jeans and a V-neck blouse, then peeked out the hotel drapes. Boomer was back. She hurried down the stairs. When he saw her, he popped the hatchback, hopped out, and loaded her bag in the back.

"What about your stuff?" she asked Vance.

"Boomer tried and my keycard didn't work. We need to go."

"You're going to leave your stuff here?"

He kept his voice low. "Grant'll be here any minute."

"You two ready to go?" Boomer asked.

"Yeah."

"Have you given hiring me some thought?"

She looked at Vance, watching his reaction. He was thinking.

"Head to the nearest rental car place while I ponder it," he said.

She ducked behind the seat and reminded him. "I need to meet Bibbins. Why don't you drop me at the nearest Starbucks and you and Boomer can work it out."

He didn't answer right away.

"Maybe we should just go home," she said.

Vance popped up behind Boomer like a gopher. "The problem with you driving us is that we'd like a little privacy."

Boomer held up a set of earbuds. "I'd be happy to put these in. Rather listen to music than people, though you might be the exception. You're on the run from something. I know it when I see it. Was drafted into the Vietnam War when I was eighteen and moved to Canada. Was stuck there for ten years."

"Conscientious objector?" Vance asked.

"Something like that."

"What do you think?" Vance flipped his chin at the driver. "Should I hire him?"

"If he can get me to SkinKrafters by four o'clock, yes."

Boomer looked at her from the rear view. "Where's it located?"

"Indianapolis," she said.

"How much you paying?"

"A hundred bucks," Vance said. "Cash."

"That'll get us there," Boomer said, looking at his GPS. "Is that skin crafters with a K?"

"That's right," she said.

Boomer put his earbuds in.

"Everyone has their price," she whispered.

"We oughta know," he said.

AFTER BEING on the road for a while, Boomer was doing a good job of minding his own business. Still, she spoke in a hushed tone. "What do you think the chances are Grant's following us?"

"Fifty-fifty, I guess."

"Does the FBI investigate offshore banking?"

"It's in their purview."

"How much trouble could we be in?"

"Felony trouble."

"What could we be charged with?"

"FATCA would be the easiest way for the Feds to go after us."

"FATCA?"

"The Foreign Account Tax Compliance Act. It gives the IRS the power to seize records from offshore tax havens. Switzerland, Grand Cayman, Costa Rica, the popular ones."

Their account in Cayman wasn't a tax haven. She'd have jumped at the chance to give half her $13-plus million to Uncle Sam for taxes, maybe more. "Is there any way we can pay it retroactively?"

"Yeah. From jail."

"That's nothing to kid about."

"You're right, I meant prison."

"I might have to get a job flipping burgers at McDonald's."

"It'd be better than making sandwiches at the Bureau of Prisons cafeteria."

"That's not funny."

"It's not meant to be funny." He glanced out the back window of the Rogue. "I talked to Sherry Rogers."

"When?"

"While you were packing up your stuff."

"You have new news?"

He nodded.

"What's the news?"

"We're being sued."

"For what?"

"Negligence. So's Masson. Emery got served again this morning, apparently a second family joined the lawsuit. The toxicology report is back for the first patient."

"How does Rogers know this?"

"She talked to Emery after the doc talked to her med-mal attorney."

"Med-mal?"

"Medical malpractice."

"Oh my God. I thought you said it took weeks?"

"The plaintiff's attorney hired an independent laboratory. Traces of botulinum were found in the patient's blood sample."

"Botulinum?"

"The most toxic substance on earth."

"How could that happen?"

"Don't know. Emery doesn't know, either."

"Where does it come from?"

"It's mostly found in contaminated food. People typically ingest it."

"I don't get it. The patients were infused intravenously. Could the IV bags have been tainted?"

"It's possible."

"Could the chemo drugs be bad?"

"That crossed my mind."

"What about her second patient? Does she know if they found the same toxin?"

"The report's not back yet."

"What does Rogers have to say?"

"It'll drag out. I told her I want to look at the lawsuit, see who filed it. See why HIPP Corp is named as a defendant."

"Can't Emery or Rogers just email you a copy?"

"She could. Except I think someone has access to Emery and Garcia's files."

She felt a chill run down the back of her neck. "Meaning someone's breached HIPP Corp's server."

He set his briefcase on the backseat between them and removed the printed file that Anna had given him. "June twenty-eighth is the same date as Emery's dead patients' follow-up appointments. Same as Dr. Garcia's patient, Norma Beecher."

Not new information.

"Here's the thing," he said, "check out the date of death for Garcia's patient."

She took the document from him and studied it until she found it. "The date here is the same date she died. I'm not following you."

"Look at the footer."

She stared at it for a good thirty seconds. It was time stamped. "Jesus. This was printed out the *day before she died.*"

"Right. I think the same thing happened to Emery: The patient deaths were pre-dated."

"How long have you known this?"

"A day or two."

"When did you plan on telling me?"

"I wasn't hiding anything from you."

"There're five dead patients. The records for two of them have been deleted. The other three have been tampered with. One patient was poisoned. The other four, we don't know yet. All are cancer patients being treated by oncologists. All five died during chemo infusion, and all of them were being treated with the same drug. Oh, and we're being sued."

"That about sums it up," he said. "When the plaintiff's lawyer gets a load of this, it'll be a sue-fest."

"That's what you're worried about? The money?"

He scowled at her. "I want to find out who's doing it and stop them."

"How do you plan to do that?"

"I want to start with the supply chain."

"Why?"

"Because I think the most reasonable explanation is that there's a bad batch of drugs out there."

She covered her face with both hands and rubbed her temples. "You really think it could be the chemo?"

"It's the common denominator."

"Then why didn't we stay in Chicago and work with Dr. Garcia?"

"You heard what he said, no one cares about his patients. Let me rephrase that. The board at his clinic will do everything in their power to stop us. Emery will cooperate."

He was right.

"If word leaks that there's an issue with the drugs, patients'll stop treatments."

"There aren't many ways that bot—u . . ."

"Botulinum."

"There's not a lot of ways it could have gotten into their bloodstream."

"It's too early to rule anything out since we only have the results for one, which, I might point out, we haven't actually seen. We don't have time to wait on the other reports. If we can figure out who's altering the records, that might lead to the killer."

Killer. She repeated the word in her head. "There could be a simple explanation for the discrepancy on the date on Garcia's printed copy."

"Which is?"

"The printer could be set up wrong. The place doesn't look very buttoned down."

"I hadn't thought of that."

"You could call and ask him to check it out."

Vance hesitated. "I have a better idea."

"You're going to ask him to print another document."

"You're getting good at this. When I was still practicing, I never saw a case where documents were improperly time stamped."

If the date on the printer at Garcia's office was set correctly, it meant someone had printed the files out the day before. Or could it have been Dr. Garcia? Or someone else?

"You tried medical malpractice cases?"

"I never tried one, but I settled a few. Documents are the holy grail of evidence. I'd hate to ruin Dr. Garcia's career over a printer."

"That's what would happen, wouldn't it?"

"Of course. Imagine how far they'll go to suppress their patient-dumping scheme? He's the easy scapegoat."

"It's not too late to call Dr. Emery and cancel."

"I already told you, I'm not doing that." He reached over the seat back and tapped the driver on the shoulder.

Boomer flinched, sending the vehicle into a slide. Two wheels dropped onto the shoulder of the road and the front bumper brushed the guardrail.

Vance gripped Boomer's headrest, watching the road ahead through the windshield.

Boomer straightened the car and yanked an earbud out. "Jesus, what the—"

"Sorry about that," Vance said. "I wanted to give you another address."

"Sure. Hang on a sec, can't type and drive at the same time." Boomer picked up his phone. "What's the name?"

"Dr. Emery in Indianapolis, E-M-E-R-Y."

Boomer said, "Siri. Find Doctor Emery in Indianapolis."

"*Got it. Find an MRE. MRE's are meals-ready-to-eat and are sold at military surplus—*"

"God dang it," Boomer said. "Siri. Find directions to doc-tor E-M-E-R-Y, Indianapolis—"

"*Got it. Doctor Sheila Emery, Oncologist on Michigan Avenue in Indianapolis.*"

"That's her," Vance said.

"Yes," Boomer said into his phone.

"Getting directions for Dr. Sheila Emery on Michigan Avenue in Indianapolis."

The word Michigan sure seemed to be coming up a lot. Michigan Avenue in Indianapolis. Michigan Avenue in Chicago. University of Michigan in Ann Arbor. Was it a harbinger or just a common word in this part of the world?

"According to GPS, we'll be there at about four o'clock," Boomer said. "Not sure what traffic'll be like."

"Drop me at SkinKrafters first," Lauren said.

Boomer nodded.

"You can put your earbuds back in now," Vance said.

Boomer pushed the white plastic dots in his ears.

"Does Emery know you're coming?" she asked.

"Yep. Rogers set it up."

"Sounds like you two are getting to know each other pretty well. What's she like?"

"Rogers?"

"No, Dr. Emery."

"She seems very competent, and busy. Why do you ask?"

"Just curious."

She couldn't imagine treating cancer victims in various stages of the disease, having to give out so much bad news. Dealing with death had to be hard. Or did the doctors get used to it?

"You know what's weird?"

"What?"

"You're going to meet Dr. Emery at her office, and I'm meeting her nurse at a social function. Shouldn't Bibbins be at work?"

"You'd think, but like I told you, Rogers set it up."

"I guess we'll find out."

Big, wet snowflakes slapped the windshield.

33

The lobby at the skin care salon was fancier than the one at the Holiday Inn Express, more like the foyer at Blackstone Hotel with a self-service coffee bar set up on a mahogany credenza. Lauren looked around, but didn't see Bibbins. She wandered to the rolling cart with a crystal pitcher filled with water, bright lemon slices floating on the surface like lily pads, and plump blueberries had settled at the bottom, like river pebbles.

"Welcome," a woman with skin as smooth as marble said. "Are you a guest of Miss Masson?"

"Actually, someone else invited me."

"Your name?"

"Lauren Gold."

She disappeared, then returned with another woman, a tall brunette. "I'm Marie Elizabeth Masson. Bibbins said you were coming. You must be Lauren."

"Is Bibbins here yet?"

"She didn't tell you?"

Lauren shook her head.

"Something came up at work and she's going to be late."

The woman with perfect skin approached, handing her an iPad. "Please fill it out and we'll get you scheduled. Make yourself at home. Could I get you a glass of wine to start?"

"Oh, no, thank you."

Several women holding goblets of wine were gathered in a semicircle.

Lauren filled a tumbler with the fruit-laced water and sat in a plump chair to fill out the form. Marie Elizabeth sat down next to her, setting a plate of nuts and fresh fruit on the low table between them.

"How do you know Bibbins?" Marie Elizabeth asked.

"Through a work thing," she said, perusing the dizzying and expensive list of cosmetic procedures.

She hadn't thought it through, assuming she'd find Bibbins and shadow her, planning to have the same procedures that she had. But now that Emery's nurse was a no-show, she had no reason to be there.

"Have you ever had Botox?" ME asked.

"No."

"It would help with the lines between your eyes," she said tapping the smooth spot between her thick eyebrows, "and the ones on your forehead."

Ones she hadn't noticed. "Oh. How long have you known Bibbins?"

"Since college. And you?"

"We just met. I'm visiting from Florida."

"Really. Why?"

"I'm with a medical records outfit and I'm here on business."

"What's the name of your company?"

"HIPP Corp."

Her eyes widened. "So that's how you know Bibbins. I wondered. How long will you be here?"

"We're leaving the day after tomorrow," she lied, then looked up from the iPad. "Are you related to Masson Medical, by any chance?"

Marie Elizabeth stood. "It was good to meet you. You could start with a facial, it's non-invasive," she said, then turned and walked toward a group of women standing near the pop-up wine bar.

She may as well have been radioactive.

The woman working the desk returned. "Have you decided what you'd like to have done?"

"Can I come back another time?"

"Of course. We'll credit today's fee to your account. Would you like to pay cash or put it on a credit card?"

She handed her a Visa. The woman swiped it on a tablet and turned it around for her to see. $500. Hiding her disgust at the cost of getting nothing, she signed with her finger, slipped out into the cold, and hurried to the coffee shop next door to hail an Uber on her phone. She was surprised to see Marie Elizabeth come through the door.

"You're not staying?" ME asked.

Lauren shook her head.

"I'm sorry for being rude just now. I'm sure you've heard what's going on. The lawyers make it impossible to be polite. I was told not to talk to anyone involved in the case."

"I understand."

"I'm sure you know Bibbins is going through a hard time right now."

She nodded.

"I shouldn't have shown her that picture, especially with the stuff going on at work."

"Maybe not," she said—guessing—hoping she'd lure ME into saying more about it.

"Sooner or later she was going to find out. As a good friend, I thought I should be the one to tell her. Maybe it was a mistake."

"No. You did the right thing."

"I heard Jack's mad at me. How did she seem when you talked to her?"

She hadn't talked to her, it was all text, but ME didn't need to know that. "Just that she was surprised."

"I'd be humiliated if it happened to me, especially since whoever took it was sharing it."

"May I see it? The picture."

ME considered it. "It's better if I don't show it to you. The girl Jack was with works for Masson and with everything going on—"

Lauren held her hand up. "You're right. I don't need to see it." Her phone pinged. She saw a vehicle approach, matching the description of the one on the rideshare app. "I gotta go," Lauren said.

"For the record, I don't work in the family business. I sell real estate. Tell Bibbins we missed her."

"I will."

She stepped outside into the freezing cold while the driver held the car door open. It was toasty inside. She checked the time, then texted Vance that she'd meet him at Emery's office at four-thirty. Marie Elizabeth had a picture of Bibbins' fiancé, Jack, with a woman who worked at Masson. What was it of? From the way it sounded, it had to be improper.

hen Bibbins' phone buzzed, she hoped it was Jack; she was ready to talk. She looked at Caller ID and muted the TV.

"Hello."

"Sorry to bother you," Dr. Emery said.

"Is everything okay?"

"Yes. But I need you to come back to the office."

"What? Why?"

"The gentleman from the medical records company is on his way. Dr. Shah and I think you should be here."

"Why?"

"In case he has some questions about the software. We'd do it ourselves if we knew how. I hate asking, but can you come in for an hour? I promise it won't be longer than that."

"No one else can do it?"

"I don't trust anyone else," Emery said.

"Okay. I'll be there as soon as I can."

"Bibbins?"

"Yes?"

"I really appreciate this."

"I know."

"Be careful. The road conditions aren't good."

She peeked out her apartment blinds. A sloppy snow had begun to fall. She'd changed into jeans and a sweater for the spa party. She got a down jacket from the coat closet, put on gloves and a knit cap, and jogged to her old Toyota. While the car warmed up, she scraped the mushy snow mix from the front and back windows, then headed to the office. She was going to miss ME's event.

———————

THE LIGHT TURNED red and she padded the brakes, putting the rear end of her car into a gentle slide, her heart pumping as she gripped the wheel. The crunch of tires on snowpack was one thing, but this messy mix of slush and ice was treacherous. The car came to a stop with two wheels in the crosswalk. Waiting for the light to change, she messaged ME, letting her know she'd been called back to work.

She recalled the threatening text she'd gotten the night the limo driver dropped her off at home. It seemed like weeks ago.

Her fingers tightened on the steering wheel. Maybe the whore screwing Jack was the one who'd sent it. Wasn't that the kind of thing mean girls did? Download one of those untraceable bullying apps, send a message to frighten her, then have it disappear? She knew the types who did those kinds of things. They were the sluts, the ones who screwed other girls' husbands and fiancés. The gold-diggers who knew when their looks ran out, they'd be out of options.

Mind your own business if you know what's good for you.

When the time was right, she'd confront Jack, maybe do a little private detective work of her own, find out who that slut was. Darn ME, if she'd only texted the picture to her, she'd have more to go on. When she found out who she was, she'd download her own mean-girl app and give that bitch a piece of her mind.

WHEN SHE ARRIVED at the office, the parking garage was half empty; people had left early, she figured, to get on the road before conditions worsened. She parked her Toyota in a spot reserved for patients and got out. It was dark and cold and damp. Bundled up in her winter jacket, she jogged the stairs to the covered breezeway and checked the time. It was a few minutes after four in the afternoon. ME's party had already started.

She headed to the end of the hallway, to Emery's private office, and saw the rep from HIPP Corp there, and so was Emery's husband, Dr. Shah. Why had they called a last-minute meeting?

35

Friday, Late Afternoon, Dr. Emery's Office
Indianapolis, Indiana

"I know we went over it," Vance said, "but walk me through it again, how you order the drugs."

Bibbins adjusted her tortoiseshell headband. "I order most of them from the hospital pharmacy."

"We've been talking with another doctor," he said, "who's had a similar problem."

"What do you mean?" Bibbins asked.

"He's lost two patients during infusion therapy. Both were being treated with the same drug, docetaxel."

"You're sure?" Emery asked.

"Yes."

Emery leaned back in her chair, thinking.

Bibbins said, "They're strict about validation procedures; they reject orders if there's the slightest thing wrong with the paperwork. I've had to go in person to pick them up, the pharmacists wear hazmat suits and breathing masks. Two of their people have to sign off before the drugs leave the pharmacy. We always double-check the paperwork on our end, and again before we administer them."

"What form is it in when you get it?" Vance asked.

"What do you mean?"

"Is it a powder or a liquid?"

"It's a liquid that comes in vials. There're two different doses and two different strengths. It's a concentrate. We mix it with saline in IV bags, and we add other drugs, depending on the doctors' orders."

"Is there any way there could have been an exposure here, at the office?" Vance asked.

Bibbins narrowed her eyes. "What do you mean?"

"If you're mixing drugs in-house, is it possible one of the nurses could've made a mistake?"

Emery looked exhausted. She rubbed her brow. "I can't imagine how a patient tested positive for botulinum."

"Is that what happened?" Bibbins asked.

Emery nodded.

Dr. Shah, who up until now had been listening, said, "I've been thinking about that, and there're a lot therapeutic drugs derived from botulinum."

"Then it's possible the wrong drug was accidentally administered," Vance said.

"No," Shah said, "we don't use them."

"What's an example of a therapeutic use?" Vance asked.

"It can be used for eye movement disorders, to treat muscle stiffness, spasms, that kind of thing," Shah said.

"Could there have been a labeling error?" he asked. "What if the two drugs are made by the same manufacturer?"

Emery answered. "It's possible, but I doubt it. The drugs are highly regulated."

He recalled Garcia's friend, the FDA inspector who'd quit after his reports had been ignored. "Food and meat processing plants have recalls. I'm no chemist, but mistakes happen."

"There's a big difference between a meat-packing plant and a USP-certified drug manufacturing facility," Shah said.

Shah had a point, but if Garcia's friend was right, drugs manufactured offshore had much less oversight.

Emery said, "Only a handful of companies market it. They label it under a couple of different brand names. We could contact the pharmacy and ask them to look into it."

"It might help explain how the other patients died," he said. But it was Friday afternoon, and he doubted anyone at the pharmacy could get any information over the weekend.

"Do we have any docetaxel in the office?" Shah asked Bibbins.

"Probably, but I'd have to check."

"Do it," Shah said. "Check the inventory, then look at the schedule to see how many patients are coming in Monday. See how much we have on hand, then bring me a sample, and put the rest in a cabinet and lock it up."

"You're going to pull it?" Bibbins asked.

Emery nodded. "We have to."

"What if I can't find a substitute supplier quickly? What then?"

"I don't know. But putting patients at risk isn't an option," Emery said.

"If we can't come up with another source," Shah said, "then we'll have to contact the patients and delay treatment."

"First things first," Emery said. "Let's see what the schedule looks like. Then talk to the pharmacy and find out if we can source elsewhere. But don't say why."

"I won't." She looked at her phone. It was 4:25 in the after-noon, and the pharmacy closed at five. "Okay. I'm on it," she said, heading to the supply room.

36

V ance had agreed to pay Boomer extra to wait for him in the patient parking lot. He pushed the DOWN button outside the elevator and waited. Could it have been a labeling issue? If there were therapeutic drugs that used botulinum as an active ingredient, it was possible. How many times had he seen warnings on food packaging that the product was made in a facility that processed tree nuts?

That didn't wash. If that's what was happening, there'd have been more cases. But if a manufacturer in China had been caught using yellow road paint to make baby food, wasn't it possible the chemo drugs could've been tainted somehow? Maybe it was something else. Maybe the plaintiff's lawyer had it wrong. What if the patient ingested something with botulinum? One toxicology report and five dead patients wasn't enough to corroborate botulinum poisoning as the cause of all the deaths.

If Emery and Shah sent samples from their inventory to an independent lab, they'd know if the drugs were the source of the problem. It would also put the blame on them, and blame equaled liability.

The elevator pinged and the doors separated. He pressed the

LOBBY button, then felt his phone vibrate in his pocket. A message from Lauren. In the lobby waiting. Perfect timing.

He saw her sitting in a club chair in the atrium. "You don't look like anyone punched you in the mouth."

"What's that supposed to mean?"

"I was afraid you'd come back with inflated lips. I figured you'd stay longer."

"Bibbins didn't show up."

"She's here. Upstairs at the office, with the doctors."

"It would've been nice of you to tell me."

"I didn't know until I saw her, then I figured if I told you, you'd bail out of the beauty party."

"I thought she was lying about having to go back to work."

"Who was lying?"

"Her friend, Marie Elizabeth . . . Masson."

"As in Masson Medical?"

"Uh-huh. She says she doesn't work for the company. She asked me if I thought Bibbins seemed upset."

"About the deaths?"

"About that and a picture of Jack and a woman."

"What woman?"

"I don't know, but it sounded like something inappropriate had happened. Marie Elizabeth said someone shared it with her and when I asked if I could look see it, she said no. It's not like I'd recognize her. She seemed very nice but she's paranoid about the lawsuit, she said the lawyers told her not to talk to anyone involved in the case."

"She wouldn't know you're involved."

"Except I told her I'm involved in HIPP Corp." She paused. "Don't look at me like that, I had to tell her something. She's good friends with Bibbins, so I had to have a story about being a new acquaintance. It won't be hard for her to check it out, if she hasn't already."

"I'm not judging, just thinking. You did good. This Jack character isn't going to win the fiancé-of-the-year award."

"That's what I was thinking, too. He's also someone with access to the medical records."

"He's not the only one. His fiancée has access, too."

"Bibbins doesn't have access to Garcia's files, but Jack might. Did you find out anything new at your meeting with Emery?"

"They're pulling their supply of the drug. Bibbins is working on it now."

She winced. "I sort of feel bad for her."

"Me, too. My bet is that Emery and Shah are calling in favors as we speak, trying to fast-track a lab that'll test the drugs."

"Those dates on the medical records are giving me the creeps. If someone hacked them, it puts us in a tough spot."

He nodded.

"Did you get the chance to talk to Garcia yet?"

"Not yet. I was thinking about asking him to fax something to me but we won't find a hotel by five o'clock."

"You could ask him to fax something to Emery." She looked at her phone. "You have fifteen minutes."

"Good idea. Come on."

She followed him to the elevator and he pushed the up arrow.

When they heard a ding, they walked to the elevator coming down, and when the doors opened, Vance said, "You have to be joking."

The man stepped out and blocked them from getting on. "Hello," the man said, "I'm—"

"I know who you are," Vance said, wondering how the hell he found them here.

"Hello, Lauren," Hunter Grant said. "Do you two have a minute to chat?"

"Just when I thought I'd stopped hallucinating," she said.

"Do we have a choice?" Vance asked.

"Of course," Grant said. "But I'm hoping you'll make this easy and say yes."

Grant stood there with his arms out like a scarecrow. He moved out of the elevator doorway to let a young woman and her child get on. The doors closed and the three of them were alone.

"Wait here," Vance said. "I'll be right back."

Boomer sat behind the wheel of the Rogue, idling in the NO PARKING zone just outside the exit door. Vance stepped outside into the cold and held up two fingers. Boomer shot him a thumbs up. A rent-a-cop driving a closed-cockpit golf car pulled up, stopped behind the Nissan, and turned on his flashing rooftop light. Boomer drove away before the rent-a-cop had the chance to question him.

Vance came back inside. "We can talk. But first, I'd like to see your ID."

A family of four walked through the lobby and headed for the exit. Hunter waited until they were gone, then pulled the leather badge holder from inside his jacket and flipped it open, exposing the badge long enough for him to read: *Federal Bureau of Investigation* on the top, *Department of Justice* on the bottom. If it was a fake, it was a damn good one.

Thoughts spun. The five million dollars of *private equity* he'd instructed their Cayman bankers to wire into HIPP Corp's account had to have some sort of electronic footprint. When he'd asked them not to email or send receipts for either transaction, he hadn't been polite about it. He'd been adamant.

The FBI had special powers to request—no, demand— records from the bank. No doubt the bank's management would drag their feet, but for how long? There was no way of knowing. He wanted to ask Grant what division he worked for, but it seemed like the kind of question a guilty person might ask.

The sight of his badge released a surge of bad chemistry that flooded his system. Fight or flight. Nope, those weren't options. It would have to be a third choice: Face it. It could be the end of the road.

"Satisfied?" Grant asked.

He nodded.

37

B ibbins put both arms through the gown, pulled rubber gloves on, covered her face with a mask, then entered the room where the pharmaceuticals were stored. She opened the stainless-steel refrigerator set at fifty degrees and looked at the inventory.

It took weeks, often months, for the insurance companies to reimburse them for the drugs. It was her idea they order just in time, JIT, to reduce inventory costs. She could have reminded her bosses in front of the rep from HIPP Corp, but Emery was already on edge.

She reached inside the fridge and rearranged the free samples the pharmaceutical reps handed out so generously— vials, creams, injectables—and held the door open for so long the packaging fogged with humidity. She removed a resealable plastic bag from a drawer and placed all the vials of DTX in it, then pushed the refrigerator door closed with her elbow.

The samples reminded her of the sales reps, the way they dressed in their high-heeled pumps, plunging necklines, and short skirts, characters right out of reruns of *Sex in the City*. Not the smart redheaded lawyer, or the goodie-goodie brunette.

They were either the neurotic writer, Carrie, or the slutty one—what was her name? The one who slept with more men than Mattress Firm? Samantha, the publicist.

She'd see them in the elevators, walking the corridors, hauling their big black roller bags. Ninety-five percent of them were women, sexy ones, carrying Louis Vuitton purses, armed with slick brochures, promoting trips to Hawaii as sales incentives, and giving away stuff like pens and iPads, and of course, drug samples.

Bibbins detoured to the restroom in the hallway. Chemo drugs were expelled through urine and Emery had advised her staff to limit their exposure to the bathrooms inside the doc's office that the chemo patients used. The public bathroom was empty for a change. Then she remembered it was late on a Friday, and bad weather was heading their way. Usually the sales tramps hogged the mirrors, spreading their cosmetics out like they owned the place, applying lipstick and touching up their mascara, spritzing perfume and fluffing their highlighted hair. Were they stupid or just plain heartless, oblivious to what cancer patients were going through?

Of course, any one of those barracudas would go after Jack in a heartbeat.

She hurried back to the office and sat in front of her computer, logged in, and checked upcoming appointments. Starting Monday, three patients were scheduled for DTX infusions. She scrolled through the notes: Each was being treated for a different cancer, at various stages and with different doses. She called the pharmacy to see what options they had and listened to it ring seven times before it went to voicemail. She tried again. Same thing. She hung up, then walked the hall to report to Emery.

"Knock, knock."

The doctor was alone and glanced up from her paperwork. "Come in."

"We have three DTX infusions scheduled Monday."

"Did you talk to the pharmacy?"

"I called, but there's no answer."

"Did you bring me the drugs?"

"We don't have any."

"How can that be if patients are coming Monday?"

"The pharmacy delivers same day."

Emery sighed. "I wanted a sample to send out." She looked dog tired. "Can you stay and call the patients?"

"Sure."

"Reschedule their appointments."

"It's after five o'clock."

"I know. But tomorrow's Saturday. You'll have a better chance of catching them now than later. Monday's too late." Emery stood from the behind stacks of files on her desk. "I really appreciate all that you do, and I know at this point, it's combat duty."

"No problem. It's only three calls. What do you want me to tell them?"

"Tell them I have a family emergency, and that you'll call Monday to reschedule."

"All right." As she turned to leave, Emery asked, "How's your mother doing?"

"She's okay. Thanks for asking."

"Is she getting some help?"

She nodded.

"Thanks again. I don't know what I'd do without you."

———

SHE TALKED to one patient and left messages for the other two, then bundled up and hurried to the parking garage, treading gingerly around the places where a slushy snow mix had accumulated on the walkways. The wind had picked up and, unlike crunchy fresh snow, this stuff turned the ground into a Slip 'N Slide.

She started her Toyota, locked the doors, turned the heat to HI, and craned her head around, checking for witnesses. Reaching into her pocket, she removed the baggie filled with vials of docetaxel and stuffed it in her purse, then backed out of the parking spot in the concrete garage.

38

Hunter Grant poured black coffee into a Styrofoam cup. Vance grabbed a bottle of water from an ice bin next to the register, then waited for the cashier as Lauren followed Grant to a table in the quietest corner of the brightly lit room. With nasty weather already upon them, there weren't many takers for the $6.99 Early Bird Special, a medley of fish sticks, broccoli, and mashed potatoes handwritten on the chalk board next to a stack of self-service trays. He paid cash, dropping the change into a glass tip jar. His stomach roiled at the aromas of institutional food, holding his breath as he passed the long buffet table, the foggy glass blurring the food behind it like an artist's palette. He shaded his eyes as he sat.

Hunter spoke first. "Sorry about the ambush, but you haven't made this easy."

"What do you want?" Vance asked.

"I work in the white-collar crime division out of the Indianapolis office, investigating healthcare fraud. I'd like to ask you a few questions."

His heart sank. What a pathetic final chapter for them, sitting in a hospital cafeteria on a dreary day, the aroma of day-old meatloaf and canned vegetables filling his nose. Should he stop now and ask for a lawyer? That's what someone who had something to hide would do. The interview had to be informal, otherwise Grant would've brought another agent to take notes, to witness the meeting.

He rolled the dice. "What do you want to know?"

"We've had HIPP Corp under investigation for several months. You recently made a significant investment into the company, and we think you and Miss Gold might be willing to work with us."

"Investigating them for what?" He put his hands under the table and wiped the sweat from his palms on his pant legs, hoping Lauren would let him steer the conversation.

That didn't last long.

"Is that why you've been following me?" she asked.

"I'll get to that in a second."

"Is that why you were in Belize?" she asked.

Vance wanted to kick her under the table, but plucked a napkin from the dispenser on the tabletop and wiped his hands, instead. "I'd hoped we could talk there, but you cut the trip short."

If the Bureau authorized a trip to Belize to interview them, it had to be a serious matter.

"Unfortunately, you invested quite a bit of money into an ongoing FBI investigation. I feel bad, but if you work with us, maybe you'll walk away with something. I can't promise, but if there's anything left, I can try to move you up to the head of the line."

"What's the company being investigated for?" Vance asked.

"Medicare and Medicaid fraud. The FBI's been investigating Sherry Rogers and a former partner of hers, a guy by the name of Bill Fields, but so far, they've been about a step and a half ahead of us. I've been looking for a break in the case, and when one of our people saw the incoming bank wire transfer, we went to work tracing it. It was hard work tracking it back to you, but our forensic accountants are the best in the world."

Uh-oh. Sherry Rogers and Bill Fields were connected.

Lauren glanced at him but played it cool.

"What's their scam?" Vance asked.

"You name it. Pill-mills in three states. They dispensed more than two million doses of opioids using shell corporations and storefront clinics to shield themselves. They had nurses and receptionists writing prescriptions. Half their employees were addicts. Fields' last scam was his fourth Medicaid ambulance scheme. Now he's a veep at Masson Medical, which, as far as I can tell, is a legit business. Most of what he's doing now is on the up and up, but it's a front to steal your money."

"What slimeballs," Lauren said.

"How'd you two get involved in the deal?"

"Through our financial advisor," he said.

"I'd fire him."

"I plan to. What do you want with us?"

"I need probable cause to get a search warrant."

"You want me to snitch? I don't know about that," Vance said.

"It's not like you have options. Think about it."

Grant was right, but not in the way the agent thought. The FBI assumed, incorrectly, they couldn't afford to walk away from five million dollars, so that's how he'd play it.

"It could get ugly," Grant said, "but if you work with us, I'll do my best to keep you clean when the mud hits the fan. You're going to take a financial hit, and I feel bad about that, but I'll also do my best to keep your identity private. This is going to be a big story."

He avoided eye contact with Lauren, focusing on Grant, instead. Keeping a low profile was important, and remaining calm was the immediate challenge.

"There'll be an asset seizure and a line of creditors a mile long. I can't promise you anything, but if you work with us, I'll see what we can do."

"What exactly do you want us to do?" Vance asked.

Grant looked around the cafeteria, then reached inside his coat pocket and pulled out two phones. "These are for you. They're configured with military-grade encryption. I need you to access HIPP Corp's servers and download certain files."

"Why don't you get a search warrant? It sounds like you already have probable cause," he said.

"We haven't been able to. Not that we can't, because we have the technology, but their lawyers are arguing the FBI'll be breaching patient confidentiality. They're using medical privacy laws to shield themselves. The subpoenas are being slow-walked through the courts by their attorneys. When I saw your wire transfer, I knew immediately we had a possible confidential informant we could trust, one who could work from the inside. Let's just say it's more than what I could have hoped for."

"Lucky me," he said, the irony of Fields and Rogers using federal law to protect themselves not lost on him.

"Yeah, lucky you." Grant handed him two thumb drives. "These are eight gigabytes each, way more storage than you'll need. Make two copies of everything."

"I'm hardly a computer expert. In fact, I'm technology-challenged."

"She's not," Grant looked at her. "You're in the video production business."

She nodded.

"I'm an enthusiast. If the amateur editing software is half as complicated as the pro stuff, you can figure out how to download some document files."

"You want me to do it?" Her voice quivered. "I've never seen the program. You're looking for documents?"

"I'm looking for anything that'll help me get a warrant to search their computers. You need to set up a meeting with Rogers."

"Why would we do that?" Vance asked.

"Because you can't afford not to. They have a training program," Grant said. "Ask to go through it."

"She'll have to do it," Vance said.

"Good," Grant said. "I'll be in touch." He got up from the table. "Thanks for the coffee."

THEY SAT IN SILENCE, watching Special Agent Hunter Grant leave the building. Vance flipped the burner Grant had given him upside down on the tabletop. She followed suit. He held his finger to his lips. She nodded. He took his personal phone from his pocket and texted Boomer.

In two minutes, Boomer was curbside. Vance took all four phones, placed them in his briefcase, and put it on the floor mat in the back seat.

"I gotta hit the men's room," he said to Boomer. "I'll be right back."

He signaled to Lauren to follow him past the unmanned information desk leading to the restrooms where they'd have some privacy.

"We're going to have to think about every word we say from here on out. We are now officially the sucker investors who're losing their life savings. We're going to have to be disciplined. Every word and everything we do can be listened to, seen, and tracked by the FBI."

"I know. What're you going to do about the patients who are dying?"

"I don't know. We need to get you a meeting with Sherry Rogers. That'll keep Grant busy for a while."

"Do you think he knows?"

He shook his head. "I'm not a hundred percent certain, but I don't think we're the targets. I don't think he'd take the chance. He's too invested in the case and our credibility would compromise it."

She shook her head slowly. "We have to be the world's shittiest investors."

"Let's go. Much as I hate to, and much as I'd like to keep our chauffeur, I'm going to have to fire Boomer. He knows too much."

"Are you sure?" she asked, walking alongside him, across the lobby, toward the exit.

"I'm sure."

Outside, they jogged in the cold. He opened the door for her, then ran around the back bumper and climbed into the seat next to her.

"Thanks for waiting." He handed Boomer another hundred, then opened the browser on his personal phone. "Give me a sec to find a hotel. Then you can drop us off."

"Thanks, man. I sure would like to keep driving you guys around."

"We're going to stay in a hotel tonight and go home tomorrow." He peeled off two more hundreds. "This oughta get you home."

"Wow, man, thanks. Are you sure I can't give you a lift to the airport tomorrow?"

"Yeah. I'm sure."

BOOMER DROVE them to the Embassy Suites on the north side of the city. Vance chose it because the hotel had two adjoining rooms that would make it easy for him and Lauren to meet in secret. It would make being sequestered easier, too. They'd keep each other on their toes, with less chance of one of them slipping and saying something Grant shouldn't hear.

It didn't take Boomer long to screw that up.

"I hope you two stay ahead of whatever you're running from," Boomer said. "Lemme give you my number. You never know. Gotta a sister here in Indy, and I'm gonna stay at her place tonight. Weather's gonna get worse."

His business card was dogeared and scruffy: a simple black-and-white print job that looked like it had been in his wallet since the 1990s. The original phone number had been crossed out twice and rewritten by hand.

"You take care," Boomer said, unloading Lauren's roller bag.

"You, too," Vance said, zipping his jacket up.

Lauren reached for the handle on her bag.

"I got it," Vance said, one shoe sliding on the mushy walkway. "You go inside and stay warm." He pulled the telescopic handle to full length and towed her luggage to the front desk where he put the two adjoining rooms on his credit card.

Did the FBI know more than Hunter let on? The Bureau would have run a routine name check as soon as theirs came up when the money deposited into HIPP Corp's account. If the bank records were secured—which was the whole point of the offshore account—Grant wouldn't have access to their banking information, especially if they weren't the targets.

Lauren's old IRS issue might've come up on a background check, but he'd settled the levy back when he was still practicing law. There wouldn't be much more than an unpaid parking ticket for him. And that he was an ex-cop-turned-lawyer. It was odd that Grant hadn't brought it up; he had to know.

"Milo. I no teach you to speak like that."

His phone buzzed in his pocket. He looked at the screen and didn't recognize the number, but that wasn't unusual. Patients called at all hours of the day and night. He answered it.

"Dr. Garcia?" The woman sounded disturbed.

"Yes."

"My husband, he's a patient, and something's wrong with him. His face turned blue and I don't think he's breathing."

"Call 9-1-1."

"I did. I'm waiting."

"Do you know CPR?"

"No."

"Who is your husband?"

She told him the name.

His mother interrupted. "What's wrong?"

He held his index finger up. "Where's the closest ER?"

"I-I-I don't know."

"What's your address?" He covered the mic on his phone with his thumb and whispered loudly to his mother, "I need something to write with." She hurried back with a pen and paper. He jotted the address down. "Try to stay calm. I'm heading to your house. When the paramedics get there, find out where they're taking him and call me."

"Okay," the woman said, panic rising in her voice.

"Stay with him. Talk to him. Tell him he's going to be fine."

"I think he's dying!"

"Listen to me. Talk to him. Tell him to hold on. Do you understand?"

"I do, I do."

"It's important. I'm leaving now."

His mother held her hand to her mouth.

"I have to go."

"I know. You go. Be careful."

HE ACTIVATED voice recognition on his phone and spoke the address aloud, then zoomed out the map on the screen. The hospital across the street from his clinic was the nearest ER to the patient's home. The back tires on the Tahoe fishtailed in the sloppy snow as he backed from the driveway, red taillights reflecting the rows of cars parked behind him lining the street on both sides. He turned on the headlights and squinted at the worsening visibility.

Halfway to the hospital, the same wireless number came up. He answered it.

"Dr. Garcia?" the voice said. It wasn't the same voice.

"Yes."

"Your patient's wife asked me to call you. He was deceased before we got to the scene."

"Who is this?"

"I'm one of the EMTs."

"Did you call the police?"

"No. We don't usually do that."

"Can you stay with her? I'm about ten minutes away."

"Sure. It'll take us that long to pack up and check in with dispatch."

Garcia pulled into a gas station, set the paper with the address on his knee and dialed.

"Nine-one-one, what's your emergency?"

"I'm a physician and I'd like to report a death."

"Are you at the location?"

"I'm on my way. Paramedics are on site and they've determined that my patient is dead."

"What's the location?"

He read it to the dispatcher.

"What's the reason for the call?"

"I believe it's suspicious."

"What's the cause of death?"

"I don't know, like I said, I'm on my way."

"Are you the decedent's physician?"

"I am."

"What's your name?"

"Dr. Emilio Garcia."

"What is that address, sir?"

He repeated it.

"I'll dispatch a unit," the woman said. "Is this your contact phone number?"

"It is."

"Someone'll be in touch."

Maybe they'd send a unit. Maybe not. Mushy snowflakes smacked the windshield. He called his nurse, Anna, on her cell. No answer. He didn't leave a message. Nine minutes later he parked the Tahoe behind the ambulance van blocking the driveway. A patrol car rolled up behind him. Neighbors bundled in winter jackets gathered on their stoops.

He'd had a good rapport with the police during his residency at the Level I trauma center. A lot of victims of gang violence were taken there, and he'd regularly interacted with them, his personal background better suited to deal with cops than his doctor peers.

"I'm his physician," he told the two cops heading for the house.

The fat one stayed outside to talk with him. "You the one who called it in?"

"His wife called first. I called back and requested a police unit."

"Why? What'd he die from?"

"I don't know." The tag on his uniform said L. LaRocca.

"What was wrong with him?"

"He was a cancer patient."

"That's gotta be tough, especially on the family. My dad died of colon cancer two years ago," LaRocca said. "Brutal. You need us here to pronounce him?"

"I don't think he died of cancer."

"Whaddaya mean? When'd you see him last?"

"This morning."

The big cop was thinking. "How old of a guy?"

"Early forties." Garcia lowered his voice. "Listen, I've lost two patients in the last month that shouldn't have died. This is the third one."

"What're you saying?"

"There should be an investigation."

LaRocca crunched his brow until there was a deep vertical dent between his eyes. "What'd the autopsy on the other two say?"

"They weren't done."

"Where'd you say you work?" LaRocca made notes on a small spiral pad.

"I didn't. I work at a hospital clinic." He hesitated, then lowered his voice. "My patients are poor. I work for a hospital that's run by a bunch of folks that worry about getting sued."

The cop shook his head. "That why you're here?"

He nodded. "His wife called me. My patient looked fine when he left my office today."

The cop paused. "Lemme talk to my partner."

The woman who'd called stepped out of the house, onto the porch in front of the small brick bungalow, arms clamped around her stomach, rocking forward and back, sobbing. She recognized him.

He fish-eyed LaRocca. "I'll handle this."

"Dr. Garcia, oh my God," she said, voice trembling. "I don't know what happened."

The big cop disappeared inside the house.

"Do you have anyone you can call?"

"I don't know what happened."

"Was he sick when he got home?"

"No, not really. He took a nap, you know, I expected the chemo to make him tired. He laid down, and when I went to wake him up . . ." Her voice quaked and she paused for a several seconds. "He wouldn't wake up. I tried, but he wouldn't wake up."

"How long was he asleep?"

"An hour, maybe two. I shouldn't have left him alone. I should have stayed with him."

"It's not your fault."

"What do I do now? Oh my God. What do I do now?"

He wanted to wait until someone, a family member or a friend, arrived, but what if someone found out *another* of his patients had died? What if someone tried to delete the medical records? It was impossible to remember every detail about every one of them. He knew the basic information; this one was being treated for early-stage lung cancer. What if someone expunged his files before he could get to the office? He had to reach Anna.

"Can you call someone?"

"I did, I called my sister. She's coming. I called her when the paramedics said . . ." She trailed off.

The body was still in the house. If LaRocca believed him— that the death was suspicious—he'd make sure they didn't move it. The criminalist would have to document the scene before the coroner transported the body to the morgue.

"You should stay out here for now," Garcia told her. "I'm going to go inside. Okay?" He wanted to see the body.

She nodded, covering her mouth with her hand, blinking at him with swollen, bloodshot eyes.

The cop he'd been speaking to filled the narrow hallway inside the small house.

"May I have a look?" Garcia asked.

"Sure." LaRocca moved aside and let him through.

The decedent was on the bed in what he guessed to be the master bedroom. He lifted the bedsheet covering the man's face and pulled it to his waist. He checked for a pulse. The decedent's arm was cold but pliable, meaning he'd been dead for less than three hours.

The big cop said, "Someone's on the way to take pictures. I don't see nothing else for the criminalist to do. Wife said she was with him. No sign of a struggle. After that, the transport company picks up the body. They got a seventy-five-minute window to get here."

This meant there would be an investigation. "You mean the coroner?"

"City subs out the transportation. No family should see what's gonna happen. Does the wife have somewhere to go?"

"She says her sister is coming."

The cop took the spiral notebook from his top pocket. "Whaddaya think happened, Doc? Gotta write a report."

He shook his head. "I don't know. The patient had a good prognosis. There's no reason he should've died today."

"I'm gonna have to write something."

"I've lost three patients to what I think are very suspicious circumstances."

LaRocca looked at him, tapping his pen on the notebook.

"All three had been infused at the clinic the same day they died."

The cop cleared his throat. "Worked a case, oh, I don't know, maybe ten years ago. A young nurse started noticing a lot of healthy folks in the rest home where she worked were dying.

Turns out another nurse snuffed almost twenty of 'em over a five-year period."

He remembered the story. It'd made national news.

"I had to testify at the trial," LaRocca said. "Damnedest thing. The killer pled guilty and said she was doing the patients a favor. Said the way they treated 'em in the nursing home made death a better option." The cop shifted his weight. "Come on, Doc. Don't look at me like that. My ma's in an assisted-living joint. Listen, I'll do what I can to kickstart this thing. I'm gonna need a statement from you. Think about what you wanna say on the record?" He put the small spiral notebook back in his shirt pocket.

His partner, who'd been in the bedroom monitoring a hand-held radio, handed LaRocca a two-inch-thick metal clipboard.

"My patient was in good health when he left the clinic today. He'd been through a lot of diagnostic testing. It's standard procedure before we start chemotherapy. EKG, CAT scans, blood work—"

LaRocca held his hand up. "Can't write that fast. Can't spell all the words. Maybe you should come down to the station and make a statement."

"No." He slowed down so LaRocca could write it down, spelling the words LaRocca asked him to. "My chemo patients do weekly bloodwork. We get lab reports checking platelets, white cell counts, liver and kidney function, and other things. Without having his chart in front of me, I can't tell you more, but this patient was definitely not at high risk for sudden death."

"I'm writing it up as a five-oh-seven-eight."

"What's that?"

The cop adjusted his cap with the black patent leather brim and black-and-white checkered band. "Classified as a hospital-ization case."

"He didn't die at the hospital."

"I know. But it's how I gotta write it up." He read from his report. "A five-oh-seven-eight is classified as a hospitalization death that needs to be investigated. Forget the word hospital's in it. That's what you want to have happen, right?"

"Yes. There should be an autopsy, and a toxicology report."

"For sure there's gonna be an autopsy. You think the guy might've been poisoned?"

"Nothing else makes sense."

"You have a suspect?"

"No."

"Why don't you go check on the wife while I finish my report. Gonna be a cold one tonight, Doc."

Garcia thanked him, wondering what he'd just unleashed. The clinic's board of directors and lawyers would've blocked an investigation. Too late for that. Odd that while he'd taken the Hippocratic oath, the board members and donors practiced hypocrisy. How could two words with such different meanings sound so similar?

"Might as well go ahead and pronounce the deceased while you're here, Doc. That'll save me some time on the paperwork."

He scribbled his name on the document. There'd be no question about who prompted the investigation.

A young black woman stood in the entryway, just outside the room: the criminalist.

LaRocca turned sideways to let her in where the body lay on the bed. Garcia didn't want to watch her taking pictures. Or his patient—now a corpse—being removed. He stepped out of the house, hoping to clear his head.

A red Kia idled in the space curbside, vacated by the ambulance that had been parked there earlier. He followed the trail of secondhand cigarette smoke and approached the driver's-side window. The deceased's wife sat in the passenger seat, sobbing.

"I'm his doctor," he said to the driver.

"What happened?"

"Who are you?"

"I'm her sister."

"I don't know."

"Why are the police here?"

"Standard procedure."

She narrowed her gaze. "Where is *he*?"

"In the house. Can you take your sister somewhere?"

She flicked her cigarette butt out the window. It sizzled in the slushy snow. "Sure. Shouldn't we lock up the house?"

"The police'll lock it up. They know how to get in touch with your sister. If not, they know how to reach me."

"Okay," she said, putting the car in drive.

The Kia turned the corner and the taillights disappeared. He called Vance Courage. The phone went to voicemail. He composed a text. It happened again. Police are on the scene. He pressed the send button.

He waited for a response but when the rep from HIPP Corp didn't answer, he went back inside, said goodbye to LaRocca and hopped behind the wheel of the Tahoe, then headed to his office. When he arrived, he was surprised to see the lights on and Anna sitting in front of her computer. He checked his watch. It was almost 9:00 PM.

"What are you doing here?" he asked.

"I thought I better preserve the files."

"Why? How did you know there was a problem?"

Anna looked up from the monitor on her desk. "His wife called the main number, looking for you. The landline forwards to my cell. The way she explained it . . . it sounded bad, like he might not make it. I thought I'd better get over here, you know, to make sure the records didn't disappear. I gave her your cell number."

"Get me a copy of his chart."

Anna printed the file, stapled the documents and handed them to him. "They're looking for you."

"Who?"

"The board members."

"How do you know that?"

"They called the main number. They wanted your mobile. I thought it was kind of weird that no one had it."

"Did you give it to them?"

"No. They said I'll get fired over it."

"We'll see about that."

He took the documents and headed to his office. How was it possible that the news had spread that fast inside the network that one of his patients had died tonight? Who would've leaked it? Was he being paranoid? Maybe they had another reason for calling. He turned the light on, sat at his desk, and scanned the paperwork. He called Anna into his office.

"Who from the board called?"

"A lawyer."

"Did he say why?"

"Just that he wanted your cell number."

"Why didn't you give it to him?"

"I thought I was protecting you."

"From what?"

"I don't know. I know you don't like them."

"That may be, but whether or not I like them doesn't matter. I still have to answer to them, which means you have to answer to them, too."

Her shoulders drooped.

He softened his voice. "You were trying to do the right thing. Go home."

He sat at his desk and read through the patient records more closely. He'd been right. The diagnosis was Stage I lung cancer with a good prognosis: a ten-year survival rate of ninety-five percent. Labs were good. Vitals normal.

Was Anna right, that it was strange that the lawyer on the board didn't have his cell? Not really. But why were they trying to reach him? He pulled up the clinic website and looked at their bios again. There wasn't a single qualified person on the board. Courage had seen it right away: Not one of them knew the first thing about medicine or patient care. Sure, they had a minister, but he had a shady past, including an old felony conviction for embezzling money from his congregation.

Did Anna ask him how his patient was doing? He couldn't remember. It had been a long night and he was exhausted. He turned out the lights and headed to the main exit where he'd parked the Tahoe illegally in the fire lane. There was no sign of Anna. Had he been too hard on her? She'd come into the office on her own initiative to help. But why?

Emilio Garcia had two things he could count on: his faith and his smarts, in that order. They were what had gotten him this far and they were going to see him through whatever way this thing was heading.

Friday, Late, Embassy Suites, Indianapolis, Indiana

Vance had forgotten he'd set his personal phone to airplane mode and hadn't heard the text message from Garcia.

It happened again. Police are on the scene.

He checked the time stamp. The message was more than an hour old.

After they'd checked into the hotel, he'd showered, watched a little TV, then lain down for a few minutes, and those few minutes had turned into more than an hour. He got out of bed to take a leak. The cell Grant had given him was on the counter, next to the sink. He flushed, picked up the phone, rolled it inside two bath towels, and set it in the dry tub, turned the exhaust fan on, then started the water in the sink.

It might've been overkill, but he wanted privacy: He suspected the FBI had spy tools that did all sorts of electronic tricks, like enhancing audio. If he turned the phone off and removed the SIM card or battery, Grant would know. He closed the bathroom door, sat on the edge of the bed, and called Garcia back on his personal phone. It went directly to voicemail; he ended the call without leaving a message. He checked the time: 10 o'clock. He put his ear on the adjoining door and heard the television playing in Lauren's room.

It happened again. That had to mean the doctor had lost another patient. But how? Garcia had finished in the clinic, and hadn't sent the message until after nine o'clock. He pressed redial, and it went straight to voicemail again. Garcia's phone was off but at least he'd see the two missed calls.

The room was chilly but he looked forward to sleeping in the cold. He tightened the bath towel around his waist, folded down the linens, punched the bed pillows, rearranged them, then climbed in bed, sat upright, and leaned against the loose headboard. Using his personal phone, he googled nearby clothing stores. He'd been wearing the same ones since yesterday, thinking what a lot of good that did, sacrificing his suitcase to evade Grant. There was a Ross Dress for Less store a couple of blocks from the hotel that closed at nine and opened at ten in the morning.

He climbed out of bed and headed to the bathroom. Waiting for the water to warm up, he pulled the sink handle to stop the water and squeezed what was left from a small bottle of shampoo. He dropped his underwear into the sudsy water, kneaded them with both hands, glancing up at the image of himself in the mirror.

When did he last eat? He couldn't remember. He rinsed his underwear with cool water, then wrung them out tightly, and slung them over the curtain rod.

He knelt and fished the FBI phone swaddled in the bath towels from the empty tub. Maybe he'd put it on the nightstand next to his personal one. If he snored tonight, it would give anyone spying on him something to listen to. Nah. He buried it in the towels, put it back in the bathtub, and closed the door.

He needed a solid night of sleep. He'd need his A game in the morning when Lauren called Sherry Rogers to set up a meeting. He'd decided to let the ideas floating in his head marinate overnight, let them enter his subconscious. It was something he'd done when he was an active-duty detective working a difficult case. Other guys couldn't sleep. A lot of them ended up divorced. Or in rehab. Or both. Some worse, painting the walls with their brains.

He'd discovered if he relaxed and let the questions percolate in his head while he slept, he often awoke with a new idea. He was about to drift off when he jumped out of bed and opened the small coat closet near the front door to his room. The Glock he'd bought locally was holstered and slung over a wooden hanger. He slid it under the bed on the side where he'd sleep, wrestled a pillow until the shape suited him, then clicked off the lamp on the nightstand.

41

Friday, Late, Indianapolis, Indiana

Bibbins checked her phone. Why wasn't Jack calling her? It wasn't like she was the one who'd gone out and got wasted at Kilroy's. She scrolled through the green bubbles and counted five text messages she'd sent. It wasn't like Jack to ghost her, or go off the grid. Maybe his battery had died. Or maybe he was in a car wreck. She pressed the AUDIO button above the last text she'd sent and let it ring six times.

"Hi, this is Jack, leave me a message and I'll call your back."

"Hey," she said, faking a smile in her voice. "I'm getting worried. Call me when you get this."

The voice in her head wasn't smiling: Maybe he was with that tramp from work.

She'd fallen asleep on the big recliner in the living room, and when she awoke, changed the channel from "Lifetime" to "Hallmark," then headed to the kitchen. The digital clock on the microwave oven showed 10:07 p.m. She hated when she napped; it made it harder to fall asleep. She rinsed the mug she'd used for hot chocolate and filled it with tap water. Chamomile tea didn't taste good but sometimes it helped her sleep. She dropped a tea bag in the cup, set the time on the microwave, and peeked out the blinds overlooking the common area behind her apartment.

That was weird. The cathouse she'd set up for Tom and the feral cats was gone. She dressed, grabbed her flashlight from the cupboard above the washing machine, and went outside to look. Who would take the kitty condo she'd so lovingly assembled? She glanced over her shoulder and listened, then pointed her flashlight on the ground in the corner near the old wooden fence where the apartment manager had given her special permission to place it.

The square footprint where the small house stood was mostly covered with new snow, and the faint outline of the base of the cathouse remained, meaning someone had recently stolen it. Brr. It was cold, and wet, and her body shook as she shined the light on a set of human footprints. She followed the tracks along the hedge leading to the covered visitor parking area dimly lit with security lights on tall poles. The shoe prints abruptly disappeared where the grass met the pavement.

What could she do? She tightened her arms around her torso. Who'd do this? Should she call the police and report it? It sounded ridiculous, reporting a stolen cat condo. Maybe it was the neighborhood kids pranking her. They'd done things before, one time leaving a children's book, *Stack the Cats*, on the front stoop of her apartment. They'd rung the doorbell, and when she opened her front door, she'd seen them running and heard them laughing before she'd seen the book on her doormat. That was a couple of years ago and they'd moved away.

A set of headlights turned into the complex. She leaned against the hedge to hide, feeling the wetness of the leaves soaking into the back of her pajama bottoms.

What the—? She almost jumped out of her skin when something brushed against her leg. Tom meowed.

"Jesus, you scared me half to death," she whispered, squatting, kneading the top of his neck as he arched his back and rubbed against the wet flannel. She felt a sharp pain. "Hey." She pulled her hand away and scolded him. "No biting." He'd done it before, and when she'd asked the vet, he said it was typical male cat behavior, suggesting she have him neutered. But he'd learned to trust her, and trapping him and taking him to the vet would undo all she'd done to make a friend of him.

"I wonder who took your house?"

The orange tabby flicked his tail and purred, his green eyes now pools of black in the darkness.

"Where're the others?"

The cat pressed his body harder against her leg. "I wish I could let you spend the night inside," she said, "but I can't."

Tomorrow she'd report the missing cathouse to the apartment manager. What did she have that might double as a shelter to keep him and the others warm and dry for the night?

She remembered the cardboard box she'd brought home from work and had meant to cut and dump in the recycle bin, but hadn't gotten around to it yet. It might work if she lined and covered it with garbage bags—the type landscapers used to collect fall leaves and grass clippings.

Folding the flaps closed and sealing the sides with duct tape, she cut an opening big enough for Tom to go in and out. She carried it outside to the spot where the cat condo had been, laid a black leaf bag as a base and set the makeshift house atop it, covering it with another heavy-duty plastic bag before stuffing a clean towel inside. The vinyl-covered heating pads, still plugged into the outdoor socket and left behind by the kitty-condo thief, had melted a patch of snow in the wet grass. She unplugged them, worried that Tom and the others might get shocked.

"There you go, boy."

Tom stalked the perimeter, but didn't go inside.

"If you get cold enough, you'll go in."

She hurried back to her apartment, chilled to the core. The soles of her rubber boots had a thin layer of ice and snow. She took them off and left them by the back door, then pulled open the sliding glass door, smelling the chamomile tea she'd left in the microwave.

Adding thirty seconds to reheat the tea, she decided a splash of milk might improve the taste. She pulled the half gallon from the shelf, revealing the glass vials of drugs she'd been stockpiling in the deli drawer. At $600 a dose, it was important to keep the them refrigerated.

Her phone pinged. She set the milk down and closed the fridge. Jack had finally surfaced. Sorry, call me when you can.

She was about to dial, then stopped herself. He could wait a little while, see how it felt to be left hanging. She opened the microwave, removed the mug, and added a dash of milk and sipped.

Ew. It still tasted like potting soil.

Her phone pinged. She smiled to herself. It was Jack again.

Call me please.

The picture of him with the woman popped up in her mind. He'd have to wait.

She sat on the edge of the recliner and stared out the sliding glass doors at the dark and dreary conditions. Tom rested on his haunches, peering inside, his breath fogging the glass.

She climbed into bed, mind racing. Maybe she should have

held her nose and drunk the funky tea. Ten minutes later, she opened the medicine cabinet above the sink, and using a set of tweezers like a knife, cut two pink Benadryl tablets from the foil backing and swallowed them.

42

Saturday, Early Morning, Embassy Suites,
Indianapolis, Indiana

Vance sprang upright like a dead man coming to life, his heart pounding. Where the hell was he? He looked up at a shadow looming over him: Lauren, holding something in her arms.

"Jesus." He grabbed a pillow and covered the tent over his groin. "Ever heard of knocking?"

"Oh, my." She turned her back to him and dropped a large shopping bag on the floor next to the nightstand. "I knocked but you didn't answer. I was worried. I'm gonna order room service. You want something?"

He glanced at the clock. It was a few minutes after six in the morning. "Sure. Get something that'll stick to my ribs. I'm starving."

"You got it."

"Put it on my tab."

"Already planned to." Facing away, she slunk sideways to the doorway connecting their rooms and disappeared into hers.

He'd slept soundly through the night and wondered how much longer it would have lasted if she hadn't disturbed him. He rubbed his eyes, then drove his fist into the air. He threw his legs to the side and sat on the edge of the bed.

Sneaking up on him was a bad idea. He reached under the bed and felt the shoulder holster's leather strap, then got out of bed and locked his side of the connecting room. Shaking the wad of towels inside the tub, he found the phone Grant gave him, pulled his dried jockey shorts slung over the curtain rod, then started a cool shower to wake himself up.

Tilting his head back, he let the droplets slap his face. They had a couple of hours to brainstorm before calling Sherry Rogers. Rubbing the bar of lavender-scented soap in both hands, he slathered his body and rinsed, then shook his head like a wet dog before turning the water off and grabbing the last dry towel, recalling that the clothing store a few blocks away didn't open until ten.

He dried himself quickly, wrapped the damp towel around his waist and sprawled atop the comforter. He turned on the TV and took his personal phone off charge. No messages from Garcia, but it was still early. He'd left the phone Grant gave him on overnight and put it on charge.

He pulled the bathroom door shut for some privacy, lowered the lid on the toilet, then sat. What if Grant was listening to his personal phone? Screw it. The doc's cell rang five times, and he was about to end the call when a breathless Garcia answered.

"Sorry. I was in the shower. I was going to call you back in a sec. I guess you got my message."

"What happened?"

The doctor filled him in on the patient who died at home. "This one's going to be investigated."

Was that a good thing? He raked his fingers through his hair.

"Are you there?" Garcia asked.

"Yeah. Sure. Sorry. Just thinking."

"There's no way he died of natural causes. No way."

"What was he being treated for?"

"Stage One lung cancer."

"I thought the prognosis for that was bad."

"It used to be. These days if we catch it early, the outlook is much, much better. He was young, with no other health issues."

"What do you think happened?"

"I have no idea but he was on the same drug as the others."

That was a setback. "Why do you think he died at home when the others died during treatment?"

"I've been thinking about that all night. He was a younger and in overall good health, much stronger. Blue-collar guy, built like an ox."

"Why would that make a difference?"

"This was his first round of chemo and his immune system would've been a lot less compromised, but still, it's just a guess." Garcia paused. "There've been cases where poison takes longer to kill one person than another. If you think about the food recalls and reports of *E. coli*, some people get a light case of diarrhea and other people don't survive."

Vance had seen and read plenty of stories about food poisoning, and had been sick himself.

"Are you still in town?"

"No. We drove back to Indy yesterday."

"I got a copy of the patient records before anyone else got wind of it."

"Good thinking."

"It wasn't me. It was my nurse, Anna."

"After hours?"

"Yeah. She was at the office when I got there last night."

"What time?"

Garcia retraced his steps aloud. "I left my office around five o'clock, went home, changed cars, and went to see my mother. I was there when I got the call from the patient's wife. That was around seven thirty," Garcia said. "I rushed over, but by the time I got there, he was already dead. By the time I got to the office it was just before nine."

His brain was waking up. "Did you call the police?"

"I did."

The landline hanging on the bathroom wall rang. He muffled it with a bath towel. "Did you talk to the cops?"

"Yes. I made a statement, and I pronounced the death."

The phone on the wall rang again. "Can you hang on a sec?"

"Sure."

He caught it on the third ring. "Hello?"

"I'm trying to reach Rumpelstiltskin," Lauren said.

"Very funny. But I think you mean Rip Van Winkle."

"You locked your door. I knocked for five minutes."

"I'm in the bathroom."

"Breakfast is here."

"I'll be right there."

"Did you look in the bag?"

"Not yet. But I will." He hung up, and said to Garcia, "Sorry about that."

"No problem. The crime scene tech was at the house when I left. The body is probably with the coroner now. There'll be an autopsy."

"I'm sorry to cut this short, but can I call you back later?"

"Sure," Garcia said.

He opened the bathroom door and the aroma of bacon and coffee had already wafted from her room to his. He stepped into the underwear that had dried like cardboard, secured the towel around his waist, then unlocked the door separating their adjoining rooms. He knocked lightly, then opened it. Lauren sat in a club chair balancing a small plate on her thigh.

"Did you look in the bag yet?" she asked, fishing for something in her purse.

He shook his head. "Is this mine?"

She nodded and he lifted the silver dome from the plate. Steak and eggs with a side of shimmering bacon.

Riffling inside until she found a small plastic bottle, she held it under the hanging lamp above the table, squinting to read the small print on the label. Shaking it like dice, she walked toward the credenza and dropped it in the trash.

He cocked his head.

"My multivitamins are made in China. Who knew?"

He stood. "Not me."

"Where're you going?"

"To eat my food." He'd spare her his impersonation of a wolf.

Was that a Ross Dress for Less shopping bag next to the bed?

He devoured the food, then emptied the contents of the bag onto the bed. A six-pack of brightly colored briefs. Two polos, one button-down shirt and a tan-colored, lightweight winter jacket shaped like the Michelin Man. He held up a pair of khakis and laid them across the bed next to a pair of jeans folded in half.

He tore open the package of clean underwear, dropped the ones he had on, changed into a new pair, then tried on the khakis. They were perfect. He reached around, ripped the tags from the back waistband, bit the price tags from a long-sleeved navy-blue polo, slipped it over his head, then checked himself in the mirror. Amazing. Everything fit like he'd hired a personal shopper.

The argyle socks weren't really his taste, but what the heck. He knocked first, then opened the door dividing their rooms. Was there anything better than a shower, a breakfast steak, and brand-new clothes? Maybe there was, and it eyeballed him.

She whistled. "Look at you."

He twirled like a girl. "I'm impressed. How'd you pull this off?"

"I went out last night before they closed. I used to pick out wardrobe for video shoots and got good at sizing people up."

"Huh. You're good, and I really appreciate it. Soon as you finish your breakfast, you need to call Sherry Rogers."

"I want you to do it."

"Fine. I owe you that."

43

Saturday, Morning, Indianapolis

Sherry Rogers clamped her mobile between her ear and
shoulder, picking at the black nail polish on her index
finger. "What do you think that little bitch is up to?"

She and Bill Fields had run so many illegal scams together
that he qualified as her crime husband, and together they'd
taken defrauding the government to an art form.

"I don't know," Bill said, "but we can't take any chances."

He was right.

"I'da liked to see the look on her face when she saw that
photo," Bill said. "She sure is nosy. A regular little Miss Kravitz
in training. Thinks I didn't see her lurking around the head table
at the Masson gala. I bet that picture's got her focusing on her
own shit, like keeping an eye on her future husband."

"Unless the wedding's off."

Bill howled laughter into the phone.

The Feds were famous for cutting deals, pitting criminals

against each other, trading immunity to one co-conspirator to rat out the other. Bill was tried, tested, and a hundred percent golden. If he didn't look like a river monster, she might've taken the relationship further, since he'd done little to keep his desire a secret. He was too ugly to be considered for anything other than business. "Speaking of focusing on shit, I closed the bank accounts and moved the money out of the country."

"I was hoping you were gonna say that."

"Can you read a text while you're on your cell?"

"What, you think I'm stupid?"

Sherry didn't answer, scrolling through her photos, selecting the last one she'd saved on her phone, then forwarded it to Bill's.

"Holy crap," he said. "It's even better than you described it."

"I heard Jack's pissed at Melinda about it." She flaked another piece of black polish from her nail and flicked it onto the floor.

"How'd you get it?"

"Took it myself."

"How?"

"After Jack left the party, Melinda and I followed his limo to an after-hours club. As predicted, Miss stick-your-nose-where-it-doesn't-belong and her stuck-up friend, ME Moneybags, must've gone home because Jack was there without Bibbins."

"That's funny. Is that what you call her friend? ME Moneybags?"

"Can't take credit for it, I saw it on social media, but I added 'bags' to it."

"Holy cow," Bill said, "she's practically got her tongue down his throat. How'd you get Melinda to do it?"

"My daughter's got the hots for him so when Mama here said she needed a favor, all it took was one shot of Wild Turkey."

"Jesus. How did Jack react?"

"Are you looking at the picture?"

"Well, yeah, but his eyes are closed."

"I took a bunch of pictures. You shoulda seen the one where his eyeballs are bugging out of his head. He was drunk out of his mind and when he figured out what was going on, he got mad and pushed her. Scared me for a minute."

"You were there?"

"I already told you that. How else could I take the pictures?"

"You devil. If you were here right now, I'd—"

What he was going to say made her skin crawl. "I sent it to Emily."

"Taylor's hot babe?"

"Uh-huh. She sent it to Miss Moneybags, who showed it to the snoop."

"How do you know that?"

"'Cause when Melinda saw Jack at the office hungover as all get-out, he was even madder than when it happened. Asked if she had something to do with it."

"What did she say?"

"Nothing."

"With that and the texts I sent trying to scare her off, maybe she'll keep her nose where it belongs."

"You texted her? That could ruin everything."

"Don't worry, I got this app that sends messages that you can't tell who sent them, automatically deletes them after they're read."

"You devil. Do you hear that noise?" Bill asked.

"What noise?"

"Me, rubbing my hands together."

"Stop before you start a fire, and take me off speaker phone."

"I can't," Bill said. "I can't stop staring at the picture of your kid making out with Jack. He looks like he's into it. Talk about leverage. I'd pay money to see the look on Bibbins' face when she saw it. She thought she was Nancy Drew when we were running the ambulance scam, like she was going to turn us in. She oughta apply for a job with the FBI."

"Don't joke about that, Bill. Ever. Have you heard of karma? Or tempting the gods? Don't joke around about the FBI."

"Take it easy. You hear anything new from the investors? They were at the Masson dinner, sat at my table."

"Who do you think arranged it?"

"Ooh, you're making me so—"

She cut him off. Maybe he was going to say it made him happy, but the idea he might say something sexual wasn't happening; the mental picture of his catfish face close to hers made her gag. "Courage has been to see both docs to try to find out what happened to their patients."

"You hear back from him yet?"

"Yeah, I'm keeping in touch but I didn't want to look too anxious."

"Anyone ever tell you you're good?"

"All the time." An incoming call lit up on her cell. "Speaking of the devil, guess who's calling?"

"Bibbins?"

"Nope. Our favorite investor."

"Thanks for the update and pic."

"Keep it to yourself."

She killed the call with Bill in time to catch the incoming one from Vance Courage. "Hi there. I was going to call and see how your things are going."

"Good, all things considered."

"Did you talk to the doctors?"

"I did. I met with Emery twice and I drove up to Chicago like you suggested, to meet Garcia in person, but you already knew that. Seems like a quality guy."

"Did you find out anything?"

"Not yet."

"What do you think's going on?"

"I don't know. My partner, Lauren Gold, wants to set up a training session, to learn the software program. That would help me figure out if HIPP Corp has any legitimate legal exposure."

"You don't want to learn it?"

"I have trouble with Siri."

"What's her background?"

He'd taken the lead on the transaction and the deal had gone down so fast, Lauren and Sherry hadn't met face-to-face. "She had her own business and knows how to edit video on a high-end computer system."

"You think that qualifies her?"

"Way more than me."

"Maybe we oughta just leave this thing alone and let the doctors figure it out."

"Not a chance, I got too much on the line. When can you set something up?"

"For what?"

"Training, on the software."

"Hang on for a sec." She put the phone face down on her knee, thinking. Picked it back up. "When does she wanna do it?"

"As soon as possible. Do you know Garcia lost two more patients yesterday? The records were deleted, both of them; I saw the files."

"If they were deleted, how did you see them?"

"His nurse printed them out. However you look at it, we're going to get dragged into this thing. Lawsuits are all about documents, and since HIPP Corp's software manages the data, we're stuck in the middle of this thing."

He was right, and trying to dissuade him would raise suspicion. "Would she be able to come to the office today?"

"Sure. But it's a Saturday."

"I didn't say for sure. I have to make some calls to see if someone can come in. Did you know Masson's being sued, too?"

"Not surprising."

"Damn lawyers," she said. "Let me see about getting someone in on a Saturday. I forgot to ask, where are you?"

"We're in Indy."

"That'll make it easier. Lemme see what I can do."

"Make it happen," he said.

"Lemme work on it and I'll get back to you."

She stabbed the red button on her phone with the tip of a black fingernail. What balls, bossing her around like he was an equal partner. When she'd asked him to come to Indianapolis, it was for show, a distraction to make the doctors think HIPP Corp was concerned. Now it looked like bringing Gold and Courage on as investors might've been a royal screwup. What did she and Bill know about the pair from Florida, other than they seemed like a couple suckers?

Courage was on the verge of getting in the way. On the other hand, he had skin in the game, five million dollars' worth, and his own reasons to nose around.

She pulled Bill's number up and redialed.

"You miss me already?"

"We might have a problem." She told him about the conversation she'd just had with Vance Courage.

"I told you it was a mistake to get him involved," Bill said.

"I have an idea."

"I'm getting excited already."

It was a good time for Bill to shut up. "He wants to set up a training session for his partner, the woman, he says she's computer savvy and wants to learn the software. I'm going to need your help. I can't very well say no."

"The tall blonde with the mile-long legs?"

She held her phone from her face and grimaced. "That's her."

"Tell me what you want me to do and consider it done."

"I knew I could count on you. Sit tight. I'll be in touch."

She hadn't told Bill everything. She'd left out the part about hiring crackhead Buck to swap the license plates on the Cadillac she'd rented for Courage for a set stolen from a similar make and model involved in a hit-and-run. The car was headed to the police impound lot, and the tow truck driver—another addict who owed Buck a favor—stole the license plate and traded it for drugs.

The night of the Masson gala, she'd picked Buck up at his mobile home on the outskirts of town, forewarning him if he was high on drugs, the deal was off. But if he was sober, she'd pay him enough to keep his crack pipe filled for the next month. He'd smelled like weed and sweat, and she hated letting him sit in the passenger seat of her Mercedes, but his old '50 pickup truck was too conspicuous to do the job in the hotel parking lot.

She'd parked across the street from the Marriott, then waited until the rush of folks attending the Masson gala had all been valeted in before driving into the self-park garage. Buck brought the license plate and tools he needed to do the swap. She'd dropped him near the Caddy parked in the garage in the area reserved for valet, then instructed him to take the elevator to the rooftop after he finished, where she'd be waiting.

She'd skipped the dinner, driving forty-five minutes each way to drop him at his mobile home, almost getting the Mercedes stuck in the slush and mud, rear wheels fishtailing on the dirt road leaving his place. Buck was pissed off. When he'd asked for his money, she told him he had one more task to complete: Stake out Courage at the airport hotel starting at oh-dark thirty, then follow him on Interstate 65 North, heading toward Chicago.

When it came to getting their next fix, drug addicts were some of the most dependable people on earth. Buck followed her directions to a T, tailing Courage, mindful to call her with an update well south of the Illinois state line, then she'd called the Indiana State Police tip line, claiming she knew about a vehicle involved in a hit-and-run accident.

As instructed, Buck drove his rusted-out pickup past the scene, took a picture, and texted it to her. She'd promised to pay him enough to keep him in crack cocaine for the next year. Maybe she'd have to renegotiate since the moron hadn't mentioned that Courage was traveling with a woman. Neither had Bill.

She scrolled through her recent calls and tapped Buck's number. It rang seven times before an automated voice defaulted to a message that said no mailbox was set up for the number. Sherry ended the call, tapped the green text message icon, touched the little microphone, then spoke to her phone. "Hey, Buck. I got another job for you. Call me soon as you get this. It's important." She pressed the SEND button.

She was about to call Fishface, then changed her mind. She and Buck could handle this on their own.

44

Saturday, Morning, Embassy Suites
Indianapolis, Indiana

"It would have been nice if you'd run it by me first," Lauren said.

Vance wasn't sure what she was upset about since she'd asked him to call Rogers. "We agreed that you'd be the best one to learn the software."

"Yeah, but you pressured her to find someone today. What if she does? I'm not ready."

"I'm not sure how you'd prepare." He wrinkled his brow. "You'd rather hang around here at the hotel, waiting? 'Til when?" His personal phone vibrated. That was quick. "It's her," he said, picking it up, pressing the green button. "Hi, Sherry."

"I've got someone lined up that'll work with her one-on-one. After we talked, I was thinking about what you said, and you're right, we need to get her trained on the software."

"When and where?"

Lauren glared at him.

"Today, at the HIPP Corp office. I'll have someone there waiting for her."

He looked at his watch. It was just past 8:30 AM. "All right. What time?"

"At ten."

"I'll let her know. Thanks."

"My pleasure."

He set his personal mobile on the desk in her room, next to the empty breakfast plates.

"What did she say?"

"She's set up a training session for you at the office."

"When?"

"Today."

"Who does corporate training on the weekend?"

His phone rattled on the desktop. He looked at CALLER ID. "Crap. I promised Garcia I'd call him back, and I forgot."

She held her hands out, palms up, and shrugged as he answered it, then picked up the breakfast dirty dishes like a bus girl.

"What? Hang on." He pressed the mic against his thigh and said to her, "I'll be back in a minute."

He went back to his room and sat on the bed. "Arrested? For what?"

"Suspicion of murder. They had a search warrant."

"Where are you now?"

"They're booking me into the Cook County jail. I didn't kill anyone."

"I'm in Indy. Sit tight, I'm on my way."

He ended the call with Garcia and called Boomer on his personal cell. He answered on the first ring. "Are you still in Indy?"

"I thought you were going back to Florida."

"I was, but something came up. Are you in town?"

"Yeah."

"Can you drive me to Chicago?"

"When?"

"Now."

"Ah, sure. You at the hotel where I dropped you?"

"Yes."

"It's Saturday morning, no traffic. I can be there in fifteen."

"I'll be downstairs, in the lobby."

He ended the call and noticed Lauren standing in the doorway, listening.

"Who was that?"

"Boomer. I'm going back to Chicago."

"Why?"

"Garcia's been arrested."

"For what?"

"Suspicion of murder."

"Are you kidding?"

"No. I gotta go. Call an Uber." He opened his wallet and handed her Sherry's business card. "Here's the address. Take the thumb drives with you, just in case."

"I don't even know what I'm looking for."

"You will, when you see it."

"I thought you were going with me."

"I would've, but then this came up." He knelt, fished the Glock from beneath the bed and holstered it under his jacket. He grabbed the phone Grant gave him, playing back the conversation he'd had with Garcia, wondering who might be listening. He zipped it inside an inner pocket of the Michelin Man jacket, then approached her and grabbed her by the shoulders, gently squeezing them, pulling her closer. "I'm sorry to abandon you."

"You're not abandoning me." She leaned back and eyed him up and down. "You could say thanks."

"Thank you, everything fits perfectly. Rogers said someone'll be there at ten. I want you to call and give me updates."

"Garcia? Murder? I can't believe it."

He put his finger to his lips and tapped the jacket pocket where he'd put the phone from Grant. Raising her eyebrows, she tilted her chin up, then nodded.

"Says he didn't do it."

"Isn't that what they all say?"

"Pretty much."

He walked out the door and headed for the elevator. His personal phone pinged. He pulled it from his pants pocket. Boomer was five minutes away.

45

Saturday, Morning, Indianapolis, Indiana

Bibbins awoke to the knock on her apartment door. Darn it. She'd overslept. Grabbing her bathrobe from the chair next to the bed, she threw it on as she hurried to answer it. She peered out the peephole, then opened it.

"Morning, Mom," she said, looking both directions, ushering her inside. "How are you feeling?"

"How do I look?"

Bibbins didn't answer.

"You look like you just rolled outta bed, hon."

"I didn't sleep well." Her brain was waking up. "The wig looks nice."

Dorothy Beatty pulled it off and tossed it on the kitchen counter. She ran her head over the top of her head. "It looks better than this."

Bald, she looked even meaner than her dad. "Did you remember to put the lidocaine I gave you on your arm?"

Dorothy sat on the edge of the recliner and rolled her sleeve up. "I didn't have time to." The inside crook of her elbow was as black as a rotten banana.

"Let me see the other one."

"Looks just as bad, hon."

"Let me see it."

She pushed the other one up. Bibbins felt her stomach heave. "I really wish you would've gone to a doctor, Mom."

"Really? And how do you suppose I would keep that from your daddy? Besides, you know I can't pay."

"I told you, I could've helped you out." She went to the kitchen, opened the fridge, took a vial from the shelf, and set it on the counter.

"Your daddy would have a fit, might even kill me if he knew what we're up to."

Bibbins tore open a new syringe, stuck the needle in the rubber cap, plunged the contents from the vial, and injected the liquid into an IV bag filled with saline.

"Have you weighed yourself?" she asked, rolling the IV stand from next to the wall, closer to the recliner where Dorothy sat.

"I dunno, mighta lost a pound or two."

She hung the bag from a hook on the top of the pole, connected the tubing, and snapped a clip on the line to stop the flow.

"I don't know why you don't divorce him. Gimme your arm." She opened the black plastic toolbox she'd bought from the hardware store, removed a tube of lidocaine, and squeezed a glob on the inside of her mother's left arm. "How's the nausea?"

"How the hell do you think it is? You work for one of them cancer docs."

She felt the tears welling and blinked them away.

"I'm sorry. I'm just in an awful state."

"It's all right, Mom. I understand."

All Dr. Emery's patients were on a variety of drugs to fight depression, nausea, pain, fluid retention, and even injections to increase their white blood cell counts and boost their immune systems. They had ports surgically implanted in their chests to connect the IV drip directly into their veins. It was painless. This way was barbaric.

"Let's give the lidocaine a few minutes before I stick your arm."

"No. Just do it, let's just get it over with. Go get me that bandana."

Bibbins returned with the scarf and handed it to her, started the hot water in the kitchen sink, pumped a dollop of antibacterial soap in her palms, then scrubbed her hands and fingernails for thirty seconds. She pulled on a pair of disposable gloves, and when she returned, her mother lay back on the recliner with her eyes closed and the bandana stuffed in her mouth.

Bibbins wiped the cream from her arm, swabbed the injection site with alcohol, tied it off with a rubber tourniquet, then broke the seal on one of the IV needles she'd stolen from Emery. She tapped the inside of her elbow with two fingers. "You ready?"

Her mother nodded as she pushed the fat needle into her vein, watching the dark blood fill the tubing. Dorothy let out a muffled grunt, like a boxer taking a blow to the gut.

"Okay, Mom. That was the hard part."

Her head bobbed.

"Put your head back and try to relax."

She returned with the supplies she needed organized neatly on a tray, just like at work.

She'd stolen more liquid Benadryl from the office two weeks ago and had added a little extra to the infusion bag. It would keep her mom from having a reaction to the chemo drugs, and the extra dose would make her sleep.

Dorothy lay motionless on the recliner she'd purchased from an online furniture store, maxing out her credit cards. She rolled the metal IV stand next to the armrest, uncoiled the tubing and popped the blue cap from one end, took the cover off the spike, and pierced the bag, starting the flow of drugs. Squeezing the soft chamber connecting the tubing to the bag, she adjusted the flow to clear the line, then dialed it back to the lowest setting. One thing Emery had taught her was not to shock the body by dosing it too fast. "I'm almost ready to get you going."

"Your daddy thinks we're out having lunch."

"That's good."

She tore open an alcohol wipe and rubbed the cap on the end of the tubing attached to the needle in her mother's arm, cleared the line with a syringe full of saline, then started the flow of drugs into her vein.

Instantly, the Benadryl kicked in and Dorothy was flying. "I know I never say it, hon, but I wanna thank you for taking care of me."

"Just relax, Mom."

"I know you ain't been the same since it happened, and you blame it on me and your daddy."

Bibbins felt a tingling in her nose and screwed her face into a knot, fighting the tears. "It's not your fault."

"No . . . it'szzz . . ."

The word slurring lasted five seconds. Dorothy's eyes fluttered, and less than a minute later, she began to snore softly.

THIS WAS THE SECOND-TO-LAST TREATMENT. Her mother had been coming to her apartment every third Saturday for the last four months. When she'd confided she'd felt a lump on her

KAREN S. GORDON

breast, Bibbins had talked to Emery, and the doctor agreed to do a biopsy, privately, pro-bono.

As Christian Scientists, how Christian was it to let your loved ones die from diseases and sicknesses that could be treated? She'd never seen her parents attend church services. What sort of belief system would allow a child to die? Her mother was right: She'd not been the same since the day her little brother died.

When the biopsy came back positive for a malignant tumor, Emery offered to help. Her mother said no. She said if it was God's will for her to die, so be it. Bibbins pleaded with her: *If Dad got cancer, don't you think he'd get treatment?*

Dorothy never answered the question. Bibbins begged her to get help, to see another doctor, get a second opinion. She'd refused at first, then finally agreed to the secret treatments. One more month and it would be over. But Emery said the two-centimeter tumor had to come out, and so far, her mother hadn't agreed to an operation. Bibbins had stolen a year's worth of pills to slow the cancer from spreading, but it would only buy time until she could convince her to undergo surgery.

Dorothy looked peaceful dozing in the recliner, but the black and green bruises on her arms were hideous, and the grayness of her face, deathly. She checked her pulse: heart rate slow and steady. When her phone rang, her heart jumped into her throat. She jogged to the kitchen to see who was calling.

Jack's name came up on her phone. The picture of that slut popped up in her head. "Can I call you back?"

"Is everything all right?"

"Uh-huh. I'm in the middle of something."

"We need to talk."

"Can we talk later?"

"Sure."

She opened the cabinet under the sink, grabbed the Styrofoam wig stand hidden there, set it on the counter top, then selected Adele from the playlist on her phone. The wig cleaner smelled nice, like roses. It had become a ritual: She styled the wig while her mother slept. First, she turned the hair upside down, shook it, then stretched it over the fake head.

Her thoughts turned from Jack to her dad. How dumb was he, believing that on Saturdays, three weeks apart, they'd been spending a mother-daughter day getting their hair done and having lunch. Who did he think was paying for that?

"He doesn't see me," her mom had said. "He comes home smelling like booze, and says he's too tired to talk to me. He watches TV and goes off first thing in the morning. I could die in the bed next to him, and I ain't sure he'd even take notice."

One thing was for sure: Her marriage to Jack wouldn't be like theirs. No, ma'am, and no, sir. She'd already done more for Jack than her father or mother had done for each other in thirty-five years of marriage. They'd preached: "You reap what you sow," but what had they planted in the ground?

She spritzed cleaner on the wig and sprayed more into her palms, then rubbed them gently. Closing her eyes, she swayed her head side to side, following the piano riffs to her favorite song, humming the words, running her fingers gently through the strands of synthetic hair.

She opened her eyes and tapped the screen, stopping the song with her fingertip. She wasn't going down that rabbit hole, listening to pathetic lyrics about lost love and heartbreak. Screw that. Her mother had accused her of living in a fantasy world. Maybe Dorothy should look at herself in the mirror. How was it possible her dad hadn't noticed his wife had lost her hair and wore a wig? Her mom said when he asked about the turban she'd started wearing to bed, she'd lied, telling him it protected her new hairdo from the pillow. Who'd believe that? Almost four months had passed and he hadn't noticed the woman he was married to for more than thirty years was sick with cancer.

She wasn't going to live like them. No way.

46

Saturday, Midmorning, I-65 North to Chicago, Illinois

"Where we headed?" Boomer asked.

"The Cook County jail," Vance said.

Boomer repeated it, as if him saying it gave him the chance to correct it.

"You have a problem with it?"

Boomer made eye contact in the rearview mirror. "No. You're the captain, you pick the course."

Vance glanced at the speedometer. Although Boomer drove ten miles an hour under the limit, it felt like the car was gliding on ice. What a depressing area, shades of gray, and none of them dramatic, against a featureless, flat landscape. He hadn't seen the sun since he'd arrived. How could people stand it? Miami had plenty of sunshine, and West Texas even more. If this is what you had to endure in order to have four seasons, he was happy with two, or even one.

What led to Garcia's arrest? Had he sized him up wrong?

Lauren was good at that and he hadn't raised her antenna. Could it be the results from the autopsy on the patient who'd died at home? It hadn't been twenty-four hours and he knew firsthand the only time a bureaucracy operated efficiently was when there were powerful forces working in the background. Was that even possible? It was a Saturday. Could someone on Garcia's board, or a big-money donor be pulling the levers? He wasn't sure how he could help him, but he knew one thing for sure: He couldn't leave him hanging.

He googled "Cook County jail" on his phone and read the Wikipedia page, scrolling down to an old Justice Department report. The violations were egregious, including prisoner beatings, infections from rodent bites, invasive strip searches, and painful STD testing, whatever the hell that entailed. The mission statement on the jail website sounded inviting, with words like "safe, secure, humane, and positive." Maybe secure was apropos, but positive?

"We're a few minutes away," Boomer said. "You want me to hang around and wait for you?"

"I do. You been there before?"

"Yeah."

Under different circumstances it might've mattered why, but not now. "Drop me off but stay close by so I get out of here soon as I'm done."

"It's a scary place," Boomer said, "sixty acres, eight city blocks, a hundred thousand inmates."

What he knew was more than someone with a passing interest.

THE COOK COUNTY correctional facility was a sprawling complex of orangish-beige structures that should have been dynamited a half century ago. Without the archway over the main doorway, the buildings were indistinguishable from the housing projects on the Chicago South Side, or Overtown and Liberty City in Miami. A massive roll of razor wire—a twisted metal tornado—was anchored horizontally along the top of the walls securing the perimeter. The idea of going inside spiked his blood pressure.

Boomer dropped him in front of a high-security dystopia as big and opposite from Disney World as Walt himself could've imagined. He'd stashed his 9-mil under the passenger's-side back seat en route.

"Boomer," he said, getting out.

"What?"

"Watch your cell. I'll text when I'm ready to go. You got enough battery?"

"It's got an eighty-percent charge."

"Good. One more thing. There's a gun under the seat, in the back."

"Jesus. Do you know what'll happen if I get stopped and the cops find a gun?"

"Don't get stopped," he said, slamming the rear passenger door.

Boomer shook his head, powered up the driver's-side window and drove slowly toward California Street.

VANCE HAD BEEN in jails and prisons before—plenty of them—and this one had the classic aroma, a cross between distilled vinegar and a cow pasture. *Eau de prison.*

A uniform stopped him at the door. "Where're you heading?"

"I'm here to interview a prisoner."

"You a reporter?"

"No. I'm a lawyer."

"You posting bond?"

"I want to talk to the prisoner first."

The brute directed him to a different building where he waited thirty minutes to check in. A half hour later he was sent to another floor where he waited some more. When he heard his name called, he walked across the hall and sat across from a young black woman with doe-like eyes.

"Prisoner name?"

"Garcia."

"We've got a thousand Garcias. Do you have a prisoner ID number?"

"I don't."

"What about a first name?"

What was Garcia's first name? His mind was a blank. Garcia . . . Garcia . . . Garcia.

She raised her eyebrows and tapped the edge of her keyboard with her fingernail. "Without a first name or a number, I can't help you."

He pulled his cell from his pants pocket and scrolled through his recent calls. "Emilio. Emilio Garcia."

She typed quickly.

A medical doctor charged with murder was the kind of jailhouse news that had to have spread quickly.

"Are you his lawyer?"

"Yes."

"He hasn't seen the judge yet."

"When's the hearing?"

She padded her keyboard. "Today's Saturday. Nothing'll be scheduled 'til Monday."

"I'd like to talk to him."

"You'll have to check in first."

How many places did he have to go?

She watched his reaction, then said. "I can help with that. Wait here."

He played it cool. She returned and directed him to another office where he waited in a windowless anteroom for a uniformed guard who escorted him to a bigger one with a folding table and two chairs. The interview room.

A thought gnawed at him. If Hunter Grant was targeting them, they could end up in a place like this, or worse. Could he handle it? A rat scurried across the concrete floor, unafraid of him—the predator. He stamped his foot to spook it, but it stopped, sat on its haunches, and stared at him, instead of running.

Was passing as Garcia's lawyer illegal? What if the guard asked him for identification? They wouldn't. Would they? He was a lawyer, at least he used to be. Back when he practiced law in Miami, he'd met a retired public defender from Chicago. If half of what he'd said was true, Cook County ran the most corrupt jail in America.

For inmates, the system was circular, a human hamster wheel designed to wear out the prisoners and their overworked public defenders. The most popular trick was for cops not to show up for hearings, delaying trials indefinitely, trampling on the Sixth Amendment: the right to a speedy trial. He'd find Garcia a good attorney. But first he needed to figure out what happened.

The door clanked open. Garcia wore a loose orange jumpsuit. The stone-faced guard herded the prisoner to an empty chair opposite him and motioned for the doctor to sit on the other side of the bare table.

The door to the cinderblock room banged shut and they were alone.

"What happened?"

"They broke down my door."

"What? Why?"

"I don't know. They came to my house at three in the morning, and when I didn't answer right away, they busted down my front door."

"On what grounds?"

"At first, they refused to say, other than my patient was found dead at his home, which is weird because I'm the one who called the police. I figured it was better if I kept my mouth shut."

The doctor had made a wise choice.

"They cuffed me and took me down to the precinct and questioned me. I told them I wanted a lawyer. They wouldn't let me make a call. When I wouldn't talk, they booked me and moved me here."

"They said you couldn't call your lawyer?"

"Not exactly. More like they acted like they couldn't hear me, 'til I told them my uncle's an alderman."

"Why didn't you call him?"

"Because I made it up. It's the weekend and the B team's working; I knew they couldn't confirm it. They let me use my cell and I called you."

Was it possible Garcia was guilty? He'd lied about his uncle, why not lie about a murder? The cops had to have a warrant to force entry, and for that to happen, they had to have probable cause. A judge had to sign a warrant. Jesus. What if he had this all wrong and Garcia was a killer?

"I know what you're thinking. I didn't do it."

Vance broke eye contact. During his long career, first as a cop, then as a lawyer, he'd never met a perp or a client who'd admitted guilt. "Do you have an attorney?"

"No. Can you help me?"

"I'm not licensed in Illinois, and I've never practiced criminal law."

"Not to defend me, to help me post bond. I grew up poor and I know lots of folks from the 'hood who pled guilty to crimes they didn't commit just to get out of here. Most of the time they were released the first time they were in front of a judge because by the time they got a bond hearing, they'd already served their sentence."

"Not on a murder charge."

"You think I'm going to plead guilty to murder? I'll rot in this place first. Someone's setting me up."

He'd considered that, but who? And why? "The judge'll set bail, and you'll be out the same day."

He was betting on standard procedure but if Cook County was half as corrupt as he'd heard it was, a judge might set bail too high, or deny it altogether. As his not-lawyer, he didn't say it out loud.

Garcia slumped in his chair. "I had a patient I was treating for leukemia die in here. They ran the clock out."

He'd have told him to calm down but how could he when he felt a cold sweat breaking under his own shirt? "A good lawyer's going to cost you."

"I'll do what I gotta do to get out of here. I have patients to see on Monday."

"I'm going to ask one more time. Did you do it?"

Garcia straightened in his chair. "Hell, no. Don't you think if they had probable cause, they'd have knocked on my door at a reasonable hour, read me my rights, and let me call my lawyer? They'd have done it by the book to make sure the charges stuck. If I did it, why would I push for an investigation? Why would I go to my dead patient's house?"

Those were the words and actions of an innocent man, not a psychopath. "How long have you been on our software?" It was a question he'd meant to ask, one that'd been churning in his head.

"A month, maybe less. I can't remember exactly. We were having some issues with the previous vendor."

"Why did you choose HIPP Corp?"

"I didn't. My nurse, Anna, did. When the problems started, and it seemed like we couldn't get it resolved, I asked her to find a new company."

"Is that around the time the patients started dying?"

A strange look fell over Garcia's face. "You think the software might be the problem?" He dropped his face into his cuffed hands, then looked up. "You think Anna's involved?"

"I didn't say that. Let me work on it. You're gonna have to hang tight." He stood.

"Wait," Garcia said, "I want you to write something down first."

Vance stopped and opened the NOTES app on his phone.

"Seven-three-seven-four-seven-five."

He typed and saved it. "What's it for?"

"It's the combination to the lock at my office. I want you to go there and take my computer. I'd do it myself, but it's obvious why I can't. I need you to preserve whatever's left of the files; they're set to back up to the cloud every four hours. Disconnect it from the intranet, and I'll reset my password and log-in info when you come back. But get the hardware first."

"I can't do that."

"Why not?"

The drives didn't belong to him, and they probably didn't belong to Garcia. "It's stealing."

"Bend the rules. Take them to the programmers at your company, ask them to look at the files."

"I'll see what I can do."

The guard opened the door and let him pass through the corridor. He stopped to talk with the clerk with the soft eyes. Garcia wouldn't make it to work on Monday. Bond hearings weren't held on the weekends and court didn't hear cases until midday. Homicides, felony violent sex crimes, and felony sex offender registration cases were heard in Room 101 in the Leighton Criminal Court Building at noon. He needed to find a good defense lawyer, and fast.

He messaged Boomer. Pick me up

Boomer answered instantly. On my way

He couldn't wait to get out of this hellhole of cell blocks and barracks, acres of ugly buildings located on, of all streets, one named California.

He texted Lauren: How's training going? A red UNDELIV-ERABLE message popped up beneath the unsent message. Probably the prison firewall blocking it—except Boomer's messages went through. Shivering from the damp cold, he checked the signal strength on his phone—four bars. Plenty to send a one-line text message.

He felt the other phone in his jacket pocket vibrate, the one Hunter Grant had given him, and let it go to voicemail. His current location would raise suspicion, and be even harder to explain. Boomer drove toward him slowly and waved. He watched where he walked, careful to step around the patches of dirty slush that had accumulated on the sidewalk.

Inside the toasty car, he rubbed his hands together. What was that smell?

Boomer hid behind a pair of mirrored aviators. "Where to?"

His carotid artery throbbed. "Did you really think it was a good idea to smoke dope? Now? Here? Jesus, Boomer."

"Sorry, but this place gives me the willies."

No argument there. If Boomer's life had been comprised of good decisions, like not getting high in front of the Cook County jail, he might've been more than a glorified taxi driver. "Take me back to the doctor's office."

"In Indy?"

This is why he hated stoners. "No, the one on Chicago South Side."

"Where I picked you up yesterday?"

"Yeah, that one."

Boomer tapped the screen on his mobile, searched the address from yesterday in his GPS, then activated it.

When they were a few miles away from the correctional facility, he called Grant back.

"Where are you?"

"On my way to see a client in Chicago."

"I thought you were going to set something up with Sherry Rogers?"

"I did."

"When's the meeting?"

"Already happening."

"What do you mean?"

He looked at the time on his phone. "Lauren's there now."

"Alone?"

"Yeah."

"Have you heard from her?"

"No."

"What were you doing at the Cook County jail?"

"Helping a friend."

"She's off the grid."

"Who's off the grid?"

"Lauren."

"What do you mean?"

"Both her phones died at just after ten this morning."

"Jesus."

"I was hoping you were together and there was an explanation, like they were stolen from your hotel room."

His heart pounded under his shirt. "Where was the last ping?"

"A cell tower on the outskirts of town, south of Indy."

"That doesn't make sense. She was heading to their offices."

"Have you been there?" Grant asked.

"No." He'd only seen a picture of it on the slick brochure Rogers had sent with the prospectus.

"You didn't know they shut it down a week ago?"

He clenched his jaw. "Of course not. If I'd known that, I wouldn't have sent her." He bowed his head, rocking forward and back in short bursts, punching the seatback with his fist.

"I figured you knew."

Why hadn't Grant told him?

"Did she take the thumb drives with her?"

"Yeah, yeah. Definitely. I told her to, you know, just in case she was able to download anything."

"Sit tight. We might get lucky. I gotta talk to some people here at the field office. Keep your phone on. Try calling Rogers and play it cool. See what she has to say. Call me back and let me know if you reach her. You might as well finish your business there. There's nothing you can do. I'll keep you in the loop."

Grant ended the call. What the hell was he talking about, *There's nothing you can do?* Hell, yeah, there was. He was going straight to the HIPP Corp office where he'd sent Lauren.

"What are you stopping for?" If he could have landed a punch on Boomer's right ear without causing a car wreck, he would've taken the shot. What sort of dumb MF smoked weed outside the Cook County jail—with an illegal firearm stowed under the back seat?

"We're here."

At first, he was confused, then he recognized Garcia's clinic.

Boomer turned in his seat. "All the bad places in Chicago are conveniently located next to one another."

"Terrific. Wait here, and roll your damn windows down, air this thing out." He reached under the seat, slung his holster over his shoulder, then pulled his jacket on and jumped out of the Nissan. He snapped a picture of the license plate as a warning to Boomer, then approached the driver's-side window. "You leave and I'll call the cops. You smoke weed, I'll turn you in to Uber. You got it?"

Boomer nodded.

He wasn't very literate when it came to technology. How big was the hard drive and would he be able to find it? It was Saturday, the lobby door was unlocked, probably for the dialysis center located on the first floor. He pushed the up arrow and glanced around, waiting for the elevator, looking for cameras. Would he be able to walk out with stolen electronics?

The elevator opened and he rode it to the second floor, turned left twice, then hurried down the dim hallway to Suite 210 at the end of the hall. He looked over his shoulder, then entered 737475 on the keypad. The small oval light turned green, and he twisted the lock, opened the door, and—watching his back—entered the office. When he turned around, his heart skipped, surprised to see Garcia's nurse, Anna, sitting in front of the computer.

"What are you doing here?" he asked.

"I was about to ask you the same thing."

She rolled her chair closer to the monitor to hide what she was working on, but she wasn't fast enough.

"I'll take that," he said, pointing to the thin, portable hard drive she'd disconnected from the desktop CPU and was about to put in her purse.

47

Saturday, Morning, Indiana

W hat was that smell? Lauren breathed through her mouth to keep from gagging. *Ouch.* Pain shot from her left hip to her shoulder, and when she tried to stretch her body from a fetal position, she couldn't.

She was lying on her left side with her neck against something hard. She tried to flex her legs at the knee but they stopped with the soles of her feet pressing against something flat and smooth. She pushed the ball of one foot against it, lightly at first, then more forcefully, but it was solid, like metal.

She twisted her wrist and walked her fingers along the tight space on the right side of her body, feeling the sides. Twisting slightly forward with her elbow pinned against her ribs, she contorted her right arm to touch the top of the metal box. The top was smooth and solid, like the inside of a safe. She ran her hand around the front of her belly and felt beneath her hip and thigh. What was underneath her? It felt like some sort of bedding, like a blanket, but it was rough, like the quilted ones moving companies used to cover furniture.

She heard something in the darkness. The soft jangling of metal on metal and the padding of feet. What was it? Was it breathing? She used the fingers on her right hand and toes on both feet to tap around, moving them slowly, this time to start the flow of blood in her veins. The box was a rectangle, wider than it was tall, maybe three to three and a half feet from her hip to the space above her right shoulder, four feet from her head to her toes. Tightening her knees and abs as if preparing to do a cannonball, she scooted down an inch to make more space above her head and ran the fingers on her free arm along the metal, this time without hurrying.

She felt something. What was it? The tips of her fingers read a pattern cut into the sides of the box, shaped like cutouts on chicken wire, but smaller, and flatter, and smoother, as if machined.

She flexed her stiff ankles. Where were her shoes? Where was the rest of her stuff? Her purse and messenger bag? Her phone? Phones?

God, her body ached. Her left arm, stuck beneath her, was numb, as if as she'd slept on it wrong. The fingers on her left hand tingled. If only she could lift her body up enough to flex her left arm, but there wasn't room.

Years ago, she'd fractured her shoulder in three places when she'd fallen from a horse. Nothing felt broken now, but the old break, high on her left arm at the humerus near the shoulder socket—now pinned—ached. She winced in the darkness at the pain throbbing in her head and held her breath to stop the pungent smell.

It had happened so fast, still a blur. She must've blacked out. But for how long? And why? What day was it?

She retraced the events, calling Sherry Rogers to confirm she was on her way to the HIPP Corp office.

She took a breath. Oh, God, the smell inside the room eclipsed the pain, overpowering every other sense, so foul it muddled her brain.

When she'd called ahead, Sherry told her she'd arranged to have someone meet her at the storefront office. She'd given the rideshare driver the address from the business card Vance had given her. Why was a medical records company located in a no-name strip mall between a Chinese restaurant and a nail salon? When the driver passed the storefront, she couldn't see through the big windows, tinted almost black. The space above it, near the roofline, was blank with faded marks where a sign had been removed. It made sense. When she'd called, Sherry had told her they were installing a new one.

Where was she now and how did she get here? The breathing outside the box got louder, and the stinky smell, stronger. She closed her eyes, and inhaled slowly through her mouth, remaining still, trying to remember more of what happened.

Ouch. A sharp stinging sensation, like a mosquito on her ankle. She reached down inside the tight space below her right thigh and scratched the skin near her foot, her movements activating the soft jangling of metal just outside the crate, the clinking of a chain. She squinted, eyes adjusting to the low light, and lifted her head a little, then twisted her neck two inches and narrowed her eyes, sharpening her focus.

The dark shape moved closer, tentatively at first, then circling the crate slowly, a slit of white on one eye flashing.

The animal growled, dropping its shoulders, the menacing sound fading slowly. Her heart pounded. She closed her eyes and slowed her breath.

"Easy, boy."

The dog snarled and snapped, then lowered its head and

changed directions, pacing counterclockwise. She played dead, barely breathing, forcing her lungs lower than a whisper. The animal passed close to the small cutouts, ghostlike, the guttural sound now a low, steady rumble.

If only there was enough room to take the weight off her left arm, to stop the pins and needles shooting in her hand. She kept her breath shallow, inhaling through her mouth to blunt the smell of the animal. The dog stopped, then pushed its snout close to the crate.

A slurping sound started. When the dog finished drinking, she heard a jangling sound coming closer. Dog tags. Remaining still as a statue, she felt the warmth of its breath and smelled the stench of its exhalations, senses on high alert—both predator and prey—as the shadow backed away. Through the tiny cutouts, she watched the dog turn three slow revolutions, then lie down.

Vance wouldn't have sent her into harm's way. Neither would Hunter Grant, though their reasons would have been different. She'd had a bad feeling the moment she saw the strip mall. She should have listened to her gut.

Holding her right arm close to her rib cage, she moved her hand slowly toward her face to scratch an itch behind her ear. Her fingers stopped at her neck. What was that? Forced to keep her elbow glued to her right rib cage, she felt the thing around her neck.

What was it and why hadn't she noticed it sooner? It was a couple of inches wide, and smooth. Not leather, some sort of fabric with a shallow box attached to it at the back of her neck, beneath her hair. Feeling for a buckle or strap, her right bicep cramped. She dropped her hand to her side and waited for the pain to pass, panic swelling in every cell in her body. She had to get *out*.

Breathe. She counted them, *one-two, one-two, one-two*

—forcing naked terror to fade. She had to think.

She focused, returning to the events leading up to the abduction. As the memory returned, her stomach heaved from the smell inside the room.

Where did he come from? He'd been inside the office, waiting to ambush her. He'd grabbed her from behind, around her throat, and squeezed, then covered her face with a cloth. She'd seen his face for a split second: a tall, skinny guy who looked like a scarecrow. He didn't speak a word. She'd clawed at his forearms, trying to break the chokehold, but his arms were wiry and strong, no match for hers. She'd heaved her body forward, struggling to make enough space to elbow him in the gut or kick him in the groin.

Then she woke up. Here. Entombed in this crate.

The animal growled.

"Easy," she said, her own voice almost unrecognizable, husky. Another round of panic set in, the kind of primitive flight response coming from the ancient part of her brain.

The dog jumped to its feet and paced, gait quickening, snarling louder, menacing.

She had to get out. An ocean of adrenaline rushed through her body activating every muscle.

The box was as stout and secure as a bank vault. Logic said no amount of hormones would open it from the inside, but that didn't stop her brain from releasing another surge.

The dog sensed fear and patrolled the cage. She had to quell the desperation swelling inside. She closed her eyes and played possum, breathing rhythmically, *one-two, in-out, one-two, in-out, one-two*, exhaling deeply each time until her pulse slowed. She knew that horses sensed fear. So did dogs. All predators did. She closed her eyes and let her mind wander.

She pictured a field of tall grass, the sun flickering between the leaves of towering oak trees, warming her face, birds chirping their springtime mating calls, then taking flight, wings chuffing as they flew overhead. The sky, pure pale blue but for a few streaks of white, as if an artist had swept the last brushes of paint. She lay on her side in the fetal position, in the damp grass, and turned her head, inspecting the sparkly dew drops welling on the blades of grass.

The dog let out a softer sound, more a high-pitched, whimpering yawn, but still aggressive.

A white horse cantered to the gate and nickered. She shaded her eyes to cut the sun, wishing she had a treat, an apple or a carrot. A breeze kicked up, rustling the branches on the oak trees up above. She watched as dead brown leaves sailed south in the wind, spreading out before landing softly on the ground. The horse snorted, then hooves pounded the earth as the horse galloped, then bucked, spooked by something the wind had sent that way.

A butterfly hovered so close she could reach out and touch it, a bright monarch with orange wings, a big black dot on each. She reached up and lightly touched the top of the cage with her fingertip. The horse returned to the gate, walking this time, dropping its head and nuzzling the grass, taking in air through its moist nostrils, shaking its head, then whinnying.

The dog had lain down next to her, so close, its fishy breath brought her back to the present moment. It lay against the crate, its fur poking through the small cuts into the aluminum sides, lightly bristling her elbow. She didn't move a muscle; she didn't want to disturb it. The coarse stuff she'd felt earlier on the bedding beneath her was the same texture of the fur against her elbow. The insect bite wasn't a mosquito: It was a flea. She was in the dog's cage, in his bedding, and the animal was guarding it.

There had to be a latch somewhere. If she felt for it, would she set the dog on high alert? She tested it, moving her hands slowly, hardly breathing, barely sweeping the insides of the cage with just the tips of her fingers. Left to right, right to left, slowly, like an old-fashioned typewriter return. The short side behind her head was different from the other panels. She squeezed her right forearm down and felt beneath the bedding. It had thick bars, like a toy prison cell. It must be the door to the crate. There'd be a latch or a hinge.

She twisted her body to the left, pushing her right seat-bone down to lift the other an inch, maybe two, enough to squeeze her hand under her right hip, stretching four fingers through the bars, fingertips working like feelers. She touched some sort of knob, flat and round, but then the dog scrambled to its feet and snapped its jaws.

She pulled her finger back inside the crate slowly and sat on her hand. "It's okay."

She froze, trying to remain calm, but the muscle in her left hamstring cramped. She gritted her teeth and breathed deeply through her nose—her stomach and lungs rebelling at the horrible smell. She exhaled, then shifted her weight enough to pull her hand free from under her and raised it in the tight space beside her—her knuckles dragging along the smooth side. Forcing it across the tight space, she felt her thigh, punching her fist in short bursts until she found a patch to the knot that had formed under the skin.

Working the muscle with her sore fingers, the dog pressed its nose nearer her face, canine teeth flashing in the darkness, growling in a low vibrato. She kneaded the cramp until the lump dissipated, dulling the sharp pain.

If she found the latch and opened the crate, what would happen? She was no match for the dog. She'd watched enough shows on the animal channel to know that a trained dog could kill a human. She clenched her fist and covered her mouth with her elbow to keep the smell of dog urine and feces at bay, to keep from vomiting.

The man who'd abducted her had ambushed her from behind, clamping the crook of his elbow around her neck and squeezing. She'd struggled, her knees had buckled, but she was aware for that one last instant she was losing consciousness.

How did she get here? Inside this cage? Who was he? And why did he imprison her? Where was her purse? And her phones? Oh, my God. He had both phones. What if he knew she was working with the FBI? What if that's what this was about? What if Rogers was onto them? That the training session was a ruse?

Vance would know she was missing. Wouldn't he? If she could tell what time it was, or what day, she'd know if he was looking for her. Had it been hours? Or days? The throbbing in her head started back up. *Make it stop.*

She heard a noise. A door squeaked open and huffed closed.

"I hope you ain't dead?"

She remained silent.

"You ain't dead, are you?"

"Who are you?"

"Guess that's a yes." He paused. "I brought you some dinner."

"Dinner?"

"I'm not talking to you. I'm talking to my dog."

She heard the crack of a metal can open, then smelled the aroma of wet dog food followed by the suctioning of a cylinder of glop sliding from the can, plopping into a dish. She was going to puke, her stomach convulsing as the dog dove into the food, slurping chunks.

"Good boy, Bo." The dog snapped. "Hey, now, don't bite the hand that opens the can, you dumb-ass dog." He flipped on the overhead light.

She shielded her eyes.

"Paid over five-hundred bucks for this damn thing." He

dropped to one knee and slapped the top of the crate.

She winced at the thump overhead.

"Hard stuffing you inside. Dead weight, you know, hard to move around. Good thing you're a skinny one. Ol' Bo, he don't like sharing."

"Let me out."

"Why would I do that?"

"Because I'm having a panic attack."

He put his eyeball close to one of the cutouts. "You look fine to me."

The adrenaline flowed. "I'm not fine."

"I'm supposed to make sure you don't go nowhere. I ain't letting you out. They said you're smart."

"Who's they?"

"Don't play dumb with me."

"Let me out!"

She rocked the crate, throwing her weight from side to side, the momentum building, trying to roll it over. The pain on her left hip and shoulder was unbearable, and her left hand, still dead.

"Stop that."

She rocked it harder and harder, every muscle raging, until it was on the verge of rolling over.

He grabbed the crate with both hands and wrestled it until it was steady enough, then sat on the top of it. "What good do you think that'll do if you tip it over?" He laughed. "Can't let you out, can't do that."

His legs blocked her view through the little cutouts. "Yes, you can. I'm not going anywhere. Where would I go?"

"I ain't letting you out."

She threw her weight forward and back, but the crate didn't move.

He jumped up. "Okay, have it your way." He used one foot

and pushed the crate over on its side. "Happy now? You're like an upside-down turtle."

Of course, she wasn't *happy*. The way he'd turned the crate over, she was now on her side, trapped in a different fetal position. Her left hand was freed, but it was hard to hold her head and neck up, lying on her side.

"*Awwwwwww*. What the—?" She grabbed her neck with one hand as her body convulsed, the electrical current passing from her head to her toes, arms flailing uncontrollably, her abs tightening. "Oh my God!"

"Keep it up and I'll shock you again."

She grabbed the collar with both hands; her left, still numb, felt the jolt. She slid her fingers beneath it, trying to tear it from her neck.

"It ain't coming off. Get rambunctious and I'll do it again."

"Get me the hell out of here!" She punched the metal with her knuckles.

He pushed the remote.

"*Awwwwwww*. Stop it!" Her body twitched and tears welled, then rolled down her face.

"I warned you."

"Okay . . . okay . . . okay." She lowered her hand and placed it on her chest, the right one pinned under her hip.

"I'm gonna roll you back over."

"I need a minute. Please."

"Ya got one minute."

Good God.

He could zap her on demand.

When she was five years old, every time her mother dropped her at the babysitter, she sobbed. One day, the regular sitter, who'd always tried to console her, wasn't available, and her mom left her with a new one. After her mother left and the crying jag started, the new one threatened to give her something *real* to cry about if she didn't stop. Like magic, her tears stopped. The collar on her neck reminded her of that lesson. Time to buck up.

"Could you please roll me over? My hip hurts."

He used his heel and shoved it upright.

"I need to stretch. Let me out for two minutes and I'll get back in. I promise."

"Can't do that."

"Why not?"

"'Cause."

"Because why?" It had devolved to this?

"You just ain't getting out." He slapped the top. "Thing's military-grade aluminum. Same crate the bomb sniffer pups ship-out in going to the sandbox in I-raq. Lifetime guarantee, made in the good old US of A."

Who cared who made it? She wanted out.

"Come here, Bo." He pulled a chair close to the crate and sat, then popped a straw hat on his head, the kind with the big, round brim and tattered edges, like the one the scarecrow in *The Wizard of Oz* wore. In better light, the animal was huge, bigger than she'd thought. The man scratched the dog's head, and it sat on its haunches, panting.

There was a new smell overpowering the sickly stench of the kennel and canned dog food. It wafted from him, from his clothes. Bleach.

Bleach. My God. When he'd abducted her, she'd smelled bleach.

He stood. "Stay," he said to the dog, then stuck his face close to hers. "I'll be back. I'd say don't go anywhere." He laughed at his own joke and walked out of view.

The smell of chlorine faded, replaced by the animal smell. She placed one eyeball close to an opening and peered out. The carpet was a drab green shag, and the interior walls, 1970s brown paneling. The window was covered with something shiny and crinkled: aluminum foil, she figured. Tilting her head back, she looked sideways and up on an angle, through a cutout, at the low yellowed ceiling, then down, seeing the room was narrow, like a wide hallway.

She tried looking over her right shoulder, lifting one hip higher, but she wasn't strong enough to hold the position. Contorting her right elbow, she reached behind her ear and felt the metal rails beneath her—the cage door, she assumed—and slipped her fingers between the bars again, feeling for the knob.

Her movements alerted the dog. Bo scrambled to his feet, then changed course when the trailer door squeaked back open and again huffed shut, rocking the room.

She shook her head in short bursts but it did nothing to clear her mind. The bleach smell returned. The man approached the crate and dropped to his knees. He had a clear plastic bag in his hand, filled with rags, the reddish ones she'd seen at the place where she'd had the oil changed on her car. He placed his scarecrow face close to the crate, but this time he wore a cone-shaped white mask held in place by strips of thin yellow elastic.

"I'm gonna get something to make you feel better." His voice was muffled. "Come on, Bo." He set the bag on top of the crate.

The dog followed him out of view. The door opened and closed. A minute later, he returned, alone.

"What is it?"

"Something to help you relax."

"I don't want to relax. I want out."

He opened the big baggie, the smell of Clorox burned the inside of her nose, and her eyes watered.

"Was pretty good in my high school chemistry class. Be surprised how much you can learn on YouTube. It ain't like in the movies, ya know, where you put the rag over someone's face and the person gets knocked unconscious in two seconds.

"I hadda fight you for three whole minutes. I wasn't sure if I could pack you in this here crate, but you is skinny so I folded you up like one of them picnic chairs. Coulda got caught the way you was fighting me, but a good thing I didn't. I was scared you was going to bite me."

"What are you doing?"

"I told ya, giving you something to calm you down."

"I don't want to calm down. Where's your dog?"

"Outside. Don't want him sniffing this stuff. Might get sick or somethin'."

"What are you going do to me?"

"I'm gonna hang these rags around the outside of Bo's crate here and let my homemade brew do its thing." He opened a mason jar and poured a clear liquid in the bagful of rags.

"Who are you and what do you want?"

"My name's Buck and I'm earning a buck." He laughed at the rhyme, then wearing gloves, draped the dark-red rags the size of washcloths over the cutouts on the crate.

"I can't breathe."

"That's your imagination running off with you. Sure, you can. You know what's funny? Company that sold me this crate thing said it's good for dogs with anxiety 'cause it calms 'em down. Guess it don't work on humans."

His voice was distorted, like a song that had slowed to half speed. "What's that smell?"

"Sweet dreams."

"Let me out!" she begged, teetering on the edge of madness. "Let me out of here!"

Buck walked away.

"Don't leave! Let me out!"

The strange odor filled the aluminum container. She tried covering her mouth with her sleeve but her arm wouldn't listen to her brain. Then her world faded to black.

48

"**M**ama." Bibbins stood over the recliner, looking at her, then repeated it. "Mama."

The extra dose of Benadryl she'd added to the infusion bag had worked. She hated waking her, she looked so peaceful sleeping in the recliner while she'd binge-watched the Hallmark Channel in the same room, sitting a couple of feet away. During commercial breaks, she'd checked the IV lines for kinks and used her fingers to monitor her pulse.

She shook her gently by the shoulders. "Mama. It's time to wake up."

Her mother's eyelids twitched. Bibbins sat on the edge of the recliner and studied her mom's tired old face. When her father ridiculed her when he'd been drinking, her mother had never gone to bat or stuck up for her. The Hallmark Channel fired that actress for paying money under the table, trying to get her daughters into a good college. How was that fair? The admissions system was rigged, her best friend's fiancé had killed himself over it. One thing was for sure, that actress and her husband sure didn't deserve to go to jail for trying to help their kids.

She pulled a pair of disposable rubber gloves taut over her hands and disconnected the tubing from the IV, careful not to let the drugs drip. Pinching both ends of the soft plastic lines, she coiled it like a tiny garden hose, disconnected it, placed the tubing into a doubled plastic bag from the grocery store, then tied it shut.

What had her mother accomplished? What would be her legacy? Doing the laundry on Mondays. Grocery shopping on Tuesdays. Shoveling snow in the winter and pulling weeds in the springtime. Living in the same ramshackle house for thirty years, never able to move up. Scraping by on Daddy's meager wages, living paycheck to paycheck. For what?

Believing wrongly that her god would look out for them? For her children? Her mother's god had already taken her younger brother.

"Mama." She said it louder and shook her harder. "It's time to wake up."

Her dull eyes opened slowly, lids twitching, dilated pupils stopping on her bruised arm where the IV was still inserted into the vein. "How long I been out?"

"A while. You need to rest." Bibbins gently peeled the surgical tape holding the needle in place, pressed her thumb over the inside crook of her mom's elbow, and slid it out. She put her gloved thumb on the vein and applied pressure, packed a wad of cotton over the seeping blood, then wrapped an elastic bandage tightly around the site.

Holding her mother's forearm with two hands, she rotated it, looking at the inside of her elbow, at the mottled pattern of green and black bruises. How would she find a vein next time? Maybe in three weeks the other arm would have healed enough. She rolled her mom's sleeve down to cover it, collected the supplies and set them on the medical tray she'd stolen from work. "I'll be right back," she said, using her shoulder to push the IV stand closer to the wall, then carried the tray with bio waste into the kitchen

"Darlin'," her mom hollered, hiccupping. "I think I'm gonna be sick."

She set the tray down and hurrying, opened the cabinet below the kitchen sink, looking for a bucket. She dumped the contents on the floor but by the time she returned, Dorothy had thrown up on her shirt, like a baby.

"I'm sorry, hon," she said, wiping her mouth with the back of her hand.

Without speaking, she patted her mom on the shoulder and rushed to the kitchen. The sight and smell had brought her to the edge of vomiting, and she needed a moment to quell the heaves. She looked out the kitchen window at a squirrel running across a power line, remembering that someone had stolen Tom's cat condo. She'd deal with that later. After her stomach settled, she grabbed a roll of paper towels, and holding her breath, returned to her mom, who lay in the recliner with eyes shut.

Snapping open the disposable grocery bag she'd grabbed from the cabinet below the sink, she hung it over her wrist to clean up the puke.

"Gimme that. I can do it myself." Dorothy used her elbows to push herself to a sitting position. "I don't know how much more of this I can do." She tore a wad of paper towels from the roll and smeared the vomit on her shirt. "Or you either, darlin'. I still got a little ole lump on my breast." She reached in her shirt, feeling for it with her free hand.

"Mama, everyone feels like this near the end of chemo. I wish you would go to a doctor. It's not too late."

"We been over it." Dorothy wadded the paper towels and stuffed them in the plastic bag. "You know I can't do that. You done so much already. Leave the rest to God, child."

The God card. Bibbins took the bag and sealed it, tying the plastic handles into a double knot. "I'll get you a clean shirt."

"Can't you just wash this one? I don't want your daddy to go asking a bunch of questions. I gotta use the bathroom."

"Remember to close the lid when you're done, and flush twice."

"I know. I'll be peeing poison."

She opened the tall white kitchen garbage bag, the one she'd double-bagged to get rid of the tubing, and needles, and gauze, IV bag, and other medical waste, stuffed the grocery sack inside, then retied it. Later, she'd toss it in the apartment dumpster.

"Lookie here." Her mother noticed the wig, picking up the Styrofoam head by the neck, turning and admiring it. "You coulda been a hairstylist, darlin'."

She could have been a lot of things, if she'd come from a different family. "You should put it on."

Instead, Dorothy pulled off her shirt over her head. "Here." She handed it to her. Bibbins held her breath and hurried to the washing machine, dropped it in, added soap, and started a short cycle.

"Let me get you something to wear."

"I'm fine. Kinda hot in here."

"How about a blanket to put over your shoulders?"

"Thank you, darlin', but I'm good."

Bibbins wasn't good seeing her mom in a bra and sweat pants, her bruised arms exposed.

Dorothy picked up the remote and unmuted the television. "We can watch TV together awhile."

"Sure, Mama."

"You know how much I love the Lifetime Channel. Could watch one after the other. That's the best part about comin' to see you, you know how much I love them shows. How's that cheater boyfriend of yours?"

She was so disrespectful. Jack wasn't her boyfriend. She was engaged to be married to him. "Don't call him that."

"Guess it's them drugs talking. But I seen you, staying up late doing that boy's homework for him. You working two jobs, him out partying with his friends, you doing college homework for two. Seen it with my own eyes."

It was none of her business. "He could've done it himself."

"But he didn't. Standing by your man. See, you learnt something from your mama after all."

How dare she? "It's not the same. He's nothing like Daddy."

"I know, I know. We're not good enough for you, you never thought we was."

"I don't mean it like that, Mama. I'm sorry if that's what you think."

"I wish I woulda made more of my life, then maybe I coulda done more for you. Oh, the show's back on. I seen this one before so I won't spoil it for you by going and telling you how it ends. Turn up the volume, hon, will ya?"

Bibbins picked up the remote and pressed the volume control higher. Was her mother right? That Jack was a cheater? The picture of him with that slut from work was back in her brain, along with a sense of doom. She adjusted the tortoiseshell headband holding her blond hair away from her face.

Jack wouldn't do that once they were married.

Would he?

49

Saturday, Midday, Chicago, Illinois

Vance slipped the thin portable hard drive into the inside right breast pocket of his roly-poly jacket. The elevator dinged, and the door opened. He got in and rode alone to the lobby, then hurried to the exit where outside it felt like a refrigerated rainforest. When he spotted the Rogue backed into a visitor parking spot, he jogged to the SUV and got in.

"That was quick. Where to?" Boomer asked.

He didn't have a plan, at least not yet. Garcia was stuck in the Cook County jail. More worrisome, where was Lauren? Maybe there was a logical explanation why both her phones were off the grid. He checked both of his. No new messages. He stared at the red UNDELIVERABLE error beneath the text he'd sent to her earlier. No, she hadn't read it.

"I'm gonna have to stop for gas," Boomer said. "Probably got enough to make it to Hammond, about thirty minutes."

He riffled through his wallet looking for Sherry Rogers' business card. Where was it? He took everything out, his credit cards, ID, cash, and stuck his fingers in every slot, pinching the leather, checking every fold. Not there. He put everything back in and typed "HIPP Corp" into the browser on his personal cell. A suggestion for "Did you mean HIPAA?" came up. No, he knew the difference between privacy laws and the company with a similar name.

He dismissed the suggestion and scrolled to the bottom of the first page of the search results and tapped the link for HIPP Corp. The website defaulted to a 404 ERROR message. That was weird. When he'd googled it less than a week ago, the site was active. He typed the full name, "Health Information Privacy Program Corporation," and got the same result: a 404 ERROR. It didn't make sense.

Shit. Was he brain dead? This morning he'd given Sherry Rogers' business card to Lauren. He unzipped his jacket and took the phone Grant gave him from the inside pocket. He typed: Update? and pushed the send button, then stared at the screen waiting for a response.

Then he remembered he'd called Rogers this morning to set up the meeting, and scrolled through the RECENT CALLS on his personal phone, then pushed REDIAL. It rang ten times, then defaulted to an automated voicemail: "The mailbox you've reached is full." He jabbed his finger on the red button and rode in silence, thinking.

Boomer activated his turn indicator, took the first business exit for Hammond, Indiana, and followed the frontage road. He turned into a gas station, stopped next to the gas pump, and killed the engine.

The phone Grant gave him buzzed. Perfect timing. He'd have a moment of privacy. "Can you hold on a sec?" he asked Grant.

"Sure."

He pressed the screen face down on his right thigh, powered his window down and handed Boomer a hundred-dollar bill. He'd have to go inside and pay in advance, calculate how much fuel the Rogue would take, which would buy him extra time. Boomer looked unhappy, but didn't argue. Vance powered his window up, then leaned over the driver's-side seat and pressed the automatic door locks. "Thanks for holding. Any news?"

"We got a ping on Rogers' phone."

"Where?"

"Can't tell. At least, not yet."

Fat lot of good that was. "What about Bill Fields?"

"Hasn't shown up for work since the day after the party over at the Marriott."

"Jesus."

"The forensic accountants from our field office have been working on tracking the money. Rogers is one step ahead. She already closed out all the accounts."

"The FBI couldn't stop her?"

"Money was wired to an offshore bank. We can ask, and we did, but the bank where we think the money went is dragging their feet. People don't randomly move money offshore. There are certain, how shall I say . . . guarantees."

He knew this. "What about their employees? Where are they?"

"They didn't have any. Just Rogers and Fields. Fields is the one who brought the deal to Rogers. HIPP Corp was a legitimate medical records company that filed for bankruptcy. They'd already laid off the entire workforce before they bought it for a pittance. Fields was already working at Masson and signed up as a reseller."

"Why skip town if they were getting new clients?"

"Because the software had security issues that hadn't been updated. That's why it failed to begin with. It was bleeding clients and cash. It's expensive, keeping up with cyber criminals. That's what put the company into bankruptcy in the first place. They were being sued for security breaches. Fields knew what he was doing; they had a short window of time to sell to as many of Masson's end users as they could before they shut it down."

"I still don't understand why Rogers and Fields bought it. It was a big risk."

"What they really wanted was to find a sucker investor to buy in, then they planned to get out."

"Sucker investor" became plural: him and Lauren. Grant didn't say it.

"We've been watching them. Career criminals like those two never know when to quit."

Grant was right about that. "How does a guy like Bill Fields get a top management job at a place like Masson?"

"He looks good on paper. He's had a series of legit jobs. It's their scam, they set up a company and Sherry Rogers runs it from the inside while Fields runs it from the outside. The pill-mill scheme was a no-brainer since Fields was a top salesman at the drug maker. He made a lot of legit money while Rogers ran a bunch of pill clinics here, in Kentucky, and West Virginia. When the heat was on, he resigned from his day job and the pair moved on."

"How long have they been on the FBI's watch list?"

"Years. When the case was assigned to me, I made it a priority. They stayed under the radar for a long time. Fields' changing jobs all the time helped. People in medical sales are like gypsies, moving from one company to the next. The Bureau put their passports on a no-fly list, so at least they can't leave the country."

"They could go to Mexico."

"Canada's closer," Grant said. "But running's not their MO.

They're going to lay low for a while and set up shop somewhere else."

"Do you have any idea where Lauren is?"

"We're working on it. What's your twenty?"

"Hammond."

"Meet me at the field office. Two o'clock. That'll give you enough time to get here."

"Do you think they took her?"

"It's not part of their normal game, but who knows. The fact they ripped off an ex-cop with a law degree might have them running scared."

His free hand balled into a fist. "Why bother to abduct her if they emptied the bank accounts and disappeared?"

"I'm working on that," Grant said.

Boomer walked out of the gas station convenience store. "Text me the address to your office."

"Will do." Grant ended the call.

Boomer carried a disposable cup in each hand, and two plastic bags hung over his left forearm. He set the stuff on the roof of the car and tried the door handle, then tapped Vance's window and raised his shoulders. He mouthed "What the . . . ?" eyeing the locked driver's-side door. Vance leaned through the center console and pushed the UNLOCK ALL button.

Boomer spun his finger, signaling him to roll down the back window, then passed one of the drink cups through. He climbed behind the wheel, balancing the goodies he'd bought close to his chest.

"What is this? Every man for himself?" Boomer asked, setting the bags on the passenger seat, putting his to-go drink in the cup holder in the center console, then rubbing his hands together and blowing his warm breath into his palms. "Locking me out of my own car. Thanks, dude."

"Don't take it personally."

"Right," Boomer said, getting out. He opened the gas cap, inserted the nozzle into the tank, and got back in, watching the numbers spin on the fueling display. He reached into one of the bags and took out the Twinkies, then passed both bags to him in the back seat. "Take whatever you want. Here's your change."

He handed him a twenty left from the hundred bucks he'd given him. "Keep it."

The bags were stuffed with an impressive assortment of junk food. Pork rinds, Cheetos, candy bars, cashews, pretzels, trail mix.

"Got some condiments for the coffee." Boomer twisted in his seat and offered an open palm filled with packets of sugar and artificial sweetener, and little individual sealed capfuls of flavored creamers.

"Thanks, but I'm good." He sipped the black coffee and took the snacks he wanted from the bag—including the nuts, a banana, and trail mix—then passed the rest back to Boomer, resisting the temptation to take the moist, delicious-looking beef jerky with the $15.99 price tag still stuck to the bag.

"Figured you'd want the healthy stuff," he said, tearing the Twinkies open with his teeth and biting into a big bullet of processed sponge cake filled with cream.

Vance held the Cheetos up, proving him wrong.

"Here." Boomer tossed a wad of napkins to him. "Keep your orange fingers off the upholstery." The driver spotted his knapsack on the back seat, twisted, and reached through the center console, then set it on the front passenger seat. He slipped the bag of beef jerky into the side pocket.

Boomer hopped out and manned the fuel pump when it hit thirty dollars, squeezing the handle until it hit thirty-five dollars. He hung the nozzle up and replaced the gas cap, then got back behind the wheel. "Decide where we're going yet?"

Vance nodded.

"Back to the Embassy Suites?" Boomer held his phone in front of his mouth, ready to talk to Siri.

It might've been funny. *Siri, give me directions to the FBI field office in Indianapolis.* But it wasn't. "Keep driving and I'll let you know."

"You're a regular Austin Powers, an international man of mystery." Boomer laughed out loud, leaning over the steering wheel, slapping it a couple of times.

Vance popped a Cheeto in his mouth. "You should lay off the weed, rumor has it the active ingredient makes things funny that aren't."

Boomer stopped at the intersection a block away from the gas station and waited for the light to turn. "Where's your friend, the girl? She stay at the hotel?"

He wished he could say yes. "She had a meeting."

Boomer glanced at him in the rearview mirror and shook his head. "She sure doesn't like this cold weather."

He felt a vibration inside his jacket pocket. He looked at the screen. Hunter Grant calling back. "Excuse me," he said, tapping the green dot on his phone and cupping his hand over the mic. "Hey."

"Can you talk?" Hunter asked.

"I can listen," he said, pressing his cheek against the back passenger window.

"Remember I asked you about the thumb drives?"

"Uh-huh."

"I might have some good news."

"Which is?"

"I'll tell you when you get here."

"That's not fair."

"Not over the phone. I thought you'd wanna know we might have a lead."

He glanced at Boomer, who continued shifting his eyes

between the windshield and the mirror, eavesdropping. "I'll see you around two o'clock."

As he ended the call with Grant, his personal phone buzzed. Emery's office appeared on CALLER ID. First, he pressed the red button on the burner, making sure he'd dropped Agent Grant, then he answered, expecting Bibbins but getting Dr. Emery. On a Saturday.

"Is this a good time?" she asked.

"Sort of. What's up?"

"Something's not right."

"What do you mean?"

"My husband, Dr. Shah, and I decided to come in over the weekend and have a look around the office." Emery hesitated.

"And?"

"I don't want to accuse anyone of anything."

"Of course not."

"We're short some drugs."

"What kind of drugs?"

"Chemo."

"That's weird. Are you sure?"

"We've been going through all the recent invoices, comparing them to the number of patients we treated. We were trying to figure out where the problem might be and what could have happened. The paperwork's not that complicated. We narrowed it down and it looks like we're short on docetaxel. All of it came from the pharmacy downstairs—"

"You're sure about that?"

"Yes," Emery said. "What we can't figure out is if there's something wrong with the drugs, and why the oncologist in Chicago is the only other one who's lost patients."

"That you know of."

"No. If there were more, we'd know. We all talk. But we did see something else."

"Which is?"

"There're other discrepancies."

"What kind of discrepancies?"

"In our non-drug supplies order."

"Can you be more specific?"

"Four months ago, someone ordered a new IV stand."

"Is that a big deal?"

"Yes and no. We have eight chairs and ten stands. Two are spares. Why would we need an eleventh and where is it?"

"Maybe someone broke one and ordered a replacement without telling you."

"That's possible, I suppose. But the invoice has everything needed to set up another infusion chair, except for the chair itself."

"Could it be a paperwork mistake?"

"I doubt it. We don't usually look at the invoices. My husband looked through our general email box and found the tracking number for the shipment. The notes show that someone signed for it, meaning it was delivered, but it's not here."

"Can you tell who signed for it?"

"The shipper keeps the signature on file for thirty days."

"Meaning you can't see who signed for it. Can you tell who ordered it?"

Emery hesitated. "The invoice has Bibbins' name on the purchase order."

"Is that unusual?"

"No, she's authorized to purchase drugs and supplies, which means she should know where it is." Emery paused a two-beat. "We don't know what to think. We haven't confronted her. Not yet."

"Why would she steal an IV stand?"

"I'm not saying she did." Emery sighed into the phone. "But whoever did might be the one stealing the drugs, too."

OxyContin, hydrocodone, fentanyl—he could understand that. Those could easily be sold on the street. But chemo drugs? A light bulb suddenly cracked in his head. "You're sure you're missing the drugs?"

"We're sure."

He didn't like where this was going. He cupped his hand tighter around the mic on his phone and turned his head closer to the car window, staring blankly at the dull canvas called Indiana. "Were you able to get a drug sample and send it out?"

"No. Bibbins told us we didn't have any DTX on hand, which is why my husband and I decided to do our own inventory."

"Is your nurse the only one who orders the drugs and supplies?" He shifted his eyes to Boomer: It would be nice if he kept his eyes on the road and his nose in his own business.

"Yes. She's the only one authorized."

He considered telling her the nurse was his prime suspect, but people didn't want to believe those they trusted, couldn't be. Emery spared him the deed.

"A few months ago, Bibbins asked me to see her mother."

"Why?"

"This is off the record."

"Absolutely."

"I could lose my license."

"You have my word."

"She had a lump on her breast."

"Her mother's your patient?"

"Not exactly. Her parents don't believe in doctors."

"How so?"

"They're Christian Scientists; they don't go to doctors."

"What do they do when they're sick?"

"They pray. Not to say prayer doesn't help, because it does."

"That sounds crazy."

"It gets complicated when children are involved, but adults can make their own medical decisions."

"I don't understand. Why did her mother come to see you if she doesn't go to doctors?"

"Bibbins begged me to do a biopsy in the office. I'd hoped it would be benign, but the pathology came back positive for cancer."

"Did the mom refuse treatment?"

"Yes."

"On religious grounds?"

"Yes, and she doesn't have health insurance."

"People don't die on the streets."

"Of course not. That wasn't the problem. I could have helped out, I offered. The problem is the dad."

His brain went into overdrive. "You think Bibbins might be treating her mother offsite somewhere?"

"She's trained to do it. Look, my husband and I don't want this to get out of control."

"Meaning what?"

"Meaning we want to try to take care of it internally. We don't want any kind of trouble."

"Then why are you calling me?"

"Because we were going through our phone records the old-fashioned way, scrolling through CALLER ID."

"And?"

"And there was a call from our office to a 3-1-2 area code. Neither of us recognized it, and since it was an outgoing call to a Chicago number, my husband redialed it. It turns out it's Emilio Garcia's office. You didn't by chance use our landline to call him when you were here?"

"No."

"You're sure about that?"

"Positive."

"The call was made right around the time you were here."

"It could've been made just after I left."

"We thought of that."

"You know what that means."

"We do," Emery said. "Or at least we haven't come up with another explanation. Bibbins had to have made the call. My husband's convinced she did it, but I'm having a hard time believing it."

Vance wiped his brow with the back of his sleeve. Shah was right. Their nurse was the only one who knew why he was there. "What happened when you called his office?"

"The person who answered the phone, a woman, she sounded nervous when I asked to speak to Dr. Garcia."

"Nervous? In what way?"

"Maybe nervous isn't the right word. She wasn't very cooperative, and she wanted to know why I was calling. I told her I was an oncologist in Indianapolis and I wanted to talk to Dr. Garcia. Usually doctor-to-doctor calls are a priority. At my office, the staff knows to walk down the hall and find us, even if we're with a patient or on the phone, they know to interrupt us. Except Garcia's person put me on hold for five minutes. Then I was disconnected."

"Did you call back?"

"I did, and whoever answered hung up without speaking."

He rested his shoulder on the door panel and rubbed his temple with his thumb. "What do you know about Bibbins' fiancé?"

"Jack?" Emery asked.

"Yes."

"Not a lot. What do you want to know?"

"Bibbins said you all know each other from your college days."

"I never met him until Bibbins asked me to meet with him."

"What for?"

"We were having problems with our medical records vendor and Bibbins had asked before if Jack could call on us. He's a sales rep for Masson Medical. The first time she asked, I politely told her no. My husband and I discussed it and we didn't like the idea. We thought it might create a conflict of interest. But then we had problems with our software and we were in a bind, so we agreed to meet with him, to see the product."

"How well did you know Bibbins before you hired her?"

"I'd never met her until she interviewed for the job. Why?"

"She said she knew you from college."

"That's impossible. She went to Indiana University and I went to the University of Michigan."

That's right, he'd seen the diploma on Emery's wall. Maybe he misunderstood.

"Listen," Emery said, "I don't want to bad-mouth anyone. I really don't know Jack other than he and Bibbins are getting married in June and my husband and I are invited. He seemed like a nice fellow when he called on us. It wouldn't be fair for me to pass judgment."

"Did you know he flunked out of pre-med?"

"It's competitive. A lot of students don't make the cut. A lot of them end up in medical sales. Wait a minute," Emery said. "What are you getting at?"

He wasn't free to speak with Boomer listening.

Emery paused. "Jack's the one who sold us your software. If you want to know more about him, then why aren't you talking to Masson? Oh my God," Emery said. "You know something. Is Jack targeting us? Is that why he was pressuring Bibbins to get a meeting? Why would he do that?"

Truth was, he didn't know for sure. Not yet. "I'm not withholding anything."

"Can you talk to someone at Masson, maybe get someone in HR? Please talk to Emilio Garcia, too. Find out if Jack sold them software; find out if Bibbins called his office."

Garcia's unavailability was going to be hard to explain. The logical excuse worked. "It's Saturday, but I'll give it a try."

"Keep the issue with Bibbins between us."

"Of course."

How hard would it be to figure out whether or not their nurse was playing doctor? Probably easy, but with Lauren MIA, finding her was more urgent than digging into the nurse's extracurricular activities. Plus, he didn't have a dog in the fight anymore, now that Rogers was on the run, the company had gone belly-up, and the money had disappeared.

"She's a good girl," Emery said, defending Bibbins. "If my husband's right, and she stole from us, she did it because she's trying to save her mom's life. If I were in her shoes, I might've done the same thing."

That was a nice way of looking at it, but he didn't see it the same way. If the FBI found out where his money came from, it wasn't like they'd chalk it up to finders keepers. They'd charge him with money laundering and a litany of other federal crimes.

Out of respect to Emery, he said, "I understand. I'll keep it between us."

"Let me know what Dr. Garcia says when you talk to him."

"I will."

He was about to end the call when Emery said, "One more thing. Have you heard from your associate, Sherry Rogers?"

That was a loaded question. "Not today," he lied.

"She called yesterday and told me not to worry, that she was confident the lawsuit would be settled. I thought it was weird because how could your company be so sure when lawsuits are unpredictable? At least that's what our malpractice insurer said.

Why didn't you tell us if there were new developments in the case?"

There were big-time "new developments," but none he could share, like the one that Rogers was a grifter who'd disappeared with the crooked Masson veep. It was a moot point. HIPP Corp no longer existed. Rogers lied to Emery to create a false sense of security, to buy time so she and Bill Fields could make a clean exit. They'd been scamming people for a long time and knew how to play the confidence game.

"I'm not aware of any new developments," he said.

"Please keep in touch," Emery said.

"Sure thing," he said, ending the call.

Was Bibbins a good girl? Maybe not. Did she call Garcia's office the day he'd met Emery? If so, maybe there was a perfectly logical explanation. If there was, he sure couldn't think of one. A tidal wave of anger washed over him. He wiped his palms on his khakis. Sherry Rogers set him up. Sent him on a wild goose chase to Indianapolis to distract him while she and Fields planned their exit strategy.

But why?

Wouldn't it have been easier to let him go on his trip to Belize, where he should have been right now?

Lauren had had an uneasy feeling about Bibbins, and he should've trusted her instincts. If Bibbins stole the drugs and equipment to treat her mother, it explained the invoicing and inventory irregularities. But it didn't explain the dead patients. Or the phone call to Garcia's office. Or the strange scheduling in the patient files. Whoever scheduled all of them for follow-up appointments on the same day in late June, was sending a message. Then there was the time stamp on Garcia's paperwork.

Even if he could talk with Garcia, what would he say? That a colleague's nurse might be stealing drugs and performing chemotherapy on her mother at an undisclosed location? That

Emery's patients seemed to have died the same way as his, during infusions, or in the case of Garcia's last patient, at home on the same day as his treatment? That there was a record of an outgoing call from Emery's office to his office, right around the time he'd left for Chicago? That HIPP Corp was a common denominator? Making him *the* conduit, though he wasn't sure how. At least not yet.

50

Saturday, Midafternoon, Indianapolis, Indiana

Sherry Rogers called Buck Whatever-his-last-name-was on the new burner she'd bought at CVS. The dummy answered on the first ring. It could have been that FBI agent for all he knew.

"I'm checking in to see how you're doing."

"What do you want me to do with her now, boss?"

Only a guy as dumb as Buck would call her boss.

He didn't wait for an answer. "She's gonna come to again and I'm gonna have to do something, like feed her, or water her, or—"

"Shut up, Buck. She's not a potted plant." God, did she hate rotten-toothed tweakers and crackheads, and Buck was both. Sober, he might've been worse, whining like a little girl with all that guilt and remorse, and the never-ending empty promise of I'm-never-getting-high-again, and all that sniveling and driveling that came with it. "You're gonna have to move her."

"While she's blacked out in the crate?"

"You got a better idea?"

"Well, no, but where should I move her to?"

"Put her in the bed of your old truck and drive her to the woods."

"The woods? I'm in the woods."

When evolution was handing out brains, Buck must've been waiting in the wrong line. "Different woods."

"She could die out there."

Druggies burned a lot of brain cells, and since he hadn't started out with an overabundance, dealing with him spiked her blood pressure. "You want to spend the rest of your life in jail? That's what'll happen if you get charged with kidnapping."

"I didn't kidnap no one."

"Of course not. She followed you to your place and got in the cage. You've got to get rid of her before she wakes up. Now that she's seen you, she can ID you."

"What if I can get her to promise not to tell?"

"You want your money or not?"

"I need it real bad."

"Then stop talking and start doing. Where's the crate?"

"At my place, inside."

"Move it into your truck."

"I could try. My brother can come help me. We could take her to the woods together."

"There's no *we*, Buck. You gotta do it on your own. No getting a helper. Do you understand?"

"Okay. But what if I can't do it? What if I'm not strong enough?"

"You'll find a way."

"I need my money."

Meaning he was out of drugs. "Move the girl to the woods

and leave her there. Take a picture and prove you've done it, and I'll pay you what I owe you. I'll call you in a couple of hours. I'm expecting good news."

"Okay," Buck said. But he didn't sound very confident.

51

Vance looked at Google Maps on his phone. "Take Highway 865 East to 465 Loop East."

"Then where?" Boomer asked.

"I'll let you know." Why did the street view of the FBI's field office in Indianapolis show so much detail? Didn't that make it an easy target? The panoramic image had to have been recorded in the late spring or early summer, on a rare sunny day. The lush green grass appeared freshly mowed, and the flower beds lining the street, newly mulched. If not for the pleasant landscaping, the drab architecture could have passed as a prison, sans razor wire and guard towers. The gardening crew working that day had been caught on camera, frozen in time, holding Weedwackers, the license plate on their truck and their faces, blurred.

The perimeter, safeguarded by a security fence, was the prettiest kind, vertical stakes of wrought iron topped with sharp spears. Bright yellow bollards cemented into the asphalt protecting the guard shack from a vehicle attack, looked freshly painted. With flags flying on two separated poles staked into the front lawn, maybe it looked more like a post office than a prison.

Boomer followed verbal directions, exiting at Allisonville

Road, turning right onto East 86th Avenue, passing the Outback Steakhouse, then turning left onto Nelson B. Klein Parkway. The FBI building was as unimpressive in person.

"Are you shitting me?" Boomer asked. "This is the destination? I don't know about this." He drove past the entrance, to the roundabout leading to Castle Creek Parkway, and continued.

"Go back."

"Are you FBI?" Boomer's voice shivered.

"No." What had he been thinking? The field office was closed, not a car in the parking lot. He took the phone Grant had given him and called the agent.

Grant answered on the first ring. "Are you here?"

"Yeah. I just did a drive-by. Looks like the office is closed."

"Meet me behind the Outback Steakhouse. It's located—"

"I saw it. I'm on my way."

Boomer pulled over onto the shoulder of the road. "You can get out and walk. No charge. Let's just call it even."

"Chill out. That's not where we're going. Drive back around and park behind the steakhouse."

"The Outback?"

"Yeah."

"I can do that," Boomer said. "For a minute I thought you might be turning me in."

"For what?"

"Being a draft dodger."

"Jimmy Carter pardoned all of you when he was president."

"I know, but I still don't trust the government."

"I can't argue with you there."

The lot behind the steakhouse was empty, too. Four o'clock in the afternoon was a slow time. A few minutes later, a dark-blue Ford Escape pulled in and approached, but did a U-turn and sped toward the main road, then turned left. He'd seen the driver: It was Grant.

"Wait here." Vance opened the car door, got out, and jogged to the front of the restaurant. There was no sign of the Ford. He redialed Grant.

"I thought you'd be alone," Grant said.

"I'm alone now, standing out front."

The Ford reappeared, taking a left onto Klein Parkway.

Grant stopped curbside in front of the restaurant and unlocked the passenger door. Vance got in.

"Wasn't that the same guy you were with when you stood me up yesterday?"

It seemed like a week ago. "He's an Uber driver who knows his way around. He's working off the grid."

"Where is he now?"

"Waiting around back. You said you have a lead on Lauren's location?"

Grant looked over his shoulder, then pulled from the curb and drove past the field office. "I'm not making any promises, but if she has the USB drives on her, we might be in luck."

"How?"

"They have microchips in them, tracking devices."

He glared at Grant's boyish profile, rage brewing in his belly. "Meaning you've known her location the whole time?" He punched the dash, then rubbed his knuckles.

"Hey. First of all, we don't know if they're still in her possession. Secondly, you know the drill, I'm not a lone wolf, I don't have access to the information. At least, not yet. There're protocols."

"You asked me to meet you here, because why?" He stopped himself, he needed to cool down.

"It's not Hollywood. There're procedures."

His fuse was now a nub, and his reptilian brain calculated the distance from his fist to Grant's right ear. "I know that."

"As far as my bosses are concerned, you and your friend are

informants. They're not going to jeopardize this investigation because a snitch has been missing for a few hours."

His fists hardened into concrete knuckles; he cemented his arms to his ribcage.

"My hands are tied," Grant said. "I can't go to a judge and get a warrant. There's no probable cause. You know how it works. You were a cop."

"Cops are cops. They bend the rules."

"Indeed," Grant said, reaching into his pocket and handing him a slip of paper with a series of handwritten numbers. "I don't know where the location is. I couldn't take the chance searching it on my computer or phone. This is a favor. You never saw me, and I never gave this to you."

He looked at the numbers. They had to be GPS coordinates. "Never saw you, you have my word."

"Be careful."

"Why are you doing this?"

"Because I recruited you, and Lauren could be in danger. Could also be that she went to the HIPP Corp office, found an empty building, and decided to dump you and drive back to Florida. Maybe she had enough, rented a car, and threw the thumb drives out the window on her way out of town. Except she doesn't strike me as the type to cut and run. If she was, she'd have stayed in Florida. I hate like hell compromising my investigation, but the Bureau doesn't care about either one of you."

Grant parked in front of the Outback. He opened the passenger's-side door, then hesitated, reached inside his jacket, and removed the thin silver hard drive he'd taken from Anna and passed it to Grant.

"What's this?"

"It might have information that could help the case."

"Where'd you get it?"

"From the client I went to see in Chicago. Another doctor who's a HIPP Corp client."

Grant turned the portable hard drive over in his palm, then set it on the seat. "You'd better get going," he said.

He watched him pull from the curb, drive toward the round-about, then disappear.

He patted the 9-mil under his jacket then sprinted back to the Nissan. This time he climbed into the front passenger seat.

"What was that about?" Boomer asked.

He ignored the question, pulled up Google Earth on his phone and typed the numbers on the paper Grant had given him. The aerial view was of a rural road on the southwestern outskirts of Indianapolis. He used his thumb and forefinger to zoom in on the GPS location and saw the fuzzy outline of rectangular flat roof, of a mobile home, he guessed.

He swiped his screen to get the street address, then said, "Unlock your phone and give it to me."

"Why?" Boomer asked.

"So, I can type in the address of where we're going."

"Just tell me it."

"Gimme your phone."

"Maybe I don't want to, maybe I don't wanna be your driver anymore."

"That's not an option."

"What's that supposed to mean?"

He unzipped the fat jacket and drew the Glock from under his left arm and held it low, pointing it at Boomer's thigh. "Gimme your phone and we'll be good."

"Jesus," Boomer said, obeying.

He typed the street address into Boomer's old iPhone and pressed the START button.

"May I have it back now?"

"No. Start driving."

"How far are we going?"

"You ever been to Mooresville, Indiana?"

Boomer considered it, even rubbed his chin. "Can't say I have, but isn't that where folks go to get Christmas trees during the holidays? They make a real production of it, or so I've heard."

"How would I know? Get on Highway 465 and take it south to I-70 west."

"Can you at least tell me why we're going there?"

He might have told him if he knew. But he didn't. What if Lauren didn't have the thumb drives and it was a dead end? What if she wasn't there? "I don't know yet."

Boomer followed surface streets to the on-ramp to 465 South and merged into a middle lane. "I know the feeling of not knowing where you're going. The years I was on the lam in Canada, half the time I didn't know where I was heading, either. Don't miss those days. In fact, if I could do it all over again, I'd go off to Vietnam and serve my country."

"What made you run?"

"It didn't seem fair, like the politicians were using us young men for a game of Russian roulette. You gotta remember it wasn't a volunteer army back then. The geniuses at the Selective Service dreamed up the lottery, claiming they thought it made the draft more fair. If it'd been the Million Dollar Powerball, I'd have been the big winner. I'll never forget the day they published the rules in the local newspaper. All men born between January 1, 1940 and December 31, 1950 were eligible. Guess what day my birthday is?"

"I don't know."

"December 31, 1950. Can you believe it? If I'd been born four hours later, I'd have been too young. Some crazy bureaucrat decided they should handwrite the three hundred and sixty-six days of the year on little pieces of paper—adding one day for a leap year—then put 'em in capsules that looked kinda like plastic Easter eggs, and loaded 'em in a glass jar big as a water-cooler jug."

He'd never heard this.

"They made a real big deal of it, interrupting 'Mayberry R.F.D.' to televise it live. Our whole family gathered on my parents' couch, me shaking like a leaf, all of us watching as they drew the eggs one at a time and opened them. The first number they picked was for September fourteenth so the unlucky bastards born on that day were the number one draft picks. Like that wasn't crazy enough, they had a second lottery, this time with letters of the alphabet. That's when it went to hell for me.

"The first letter they picked was J, meaning if your initials were J-J-J you went to the top of that list. My legal name is Jeffery John Jones. My mother burst out crying, like it was her fault. People ask, what's in a name? I'll tell you what's in a name, being short-listed to some war halfway around the world, that's what, with a good chance of coming home in a casket. Or a junkie. Later, when I saw the boys coming home on television, I was glad I wasn't one of 'em. It was no hero's welcome, that's for sure."

Vance was too young to know much about the Vietnam War. It seemed so unfair, no wonder Boomer cut and ran.

"I always worried my little sister might see my mug shot. She worked for the post office. Still does. Kinda weird I ran from Uncle Sam and she went to work for him."

"Life's full of ironies," Vance said.

"Ain't that the truth," Boomer said.

They rode a while in silence, Boomer's eyes glued to the windshield as they passed towering pylons holding highway signs and lights, guardrails planted into the shoulders of the roads protecting cars from going off the embankment, concrete barriers keeping vehicles in the HOV lanes: all of it in shades of gray, blending into a backdrop the color of freshly poured concrete.

He looked up as they passed beneath a knot of elevated highway interchanges with signs splitting 465 into I-65 North and South, passing under the exit to Crawfordsville Road with a signpost to the Indianapolis Motor Speedway, wondering if he could adjust to a place this gloomy and subdued, curious what inspired people to get out of bed every morning: It sure wasn't the scenery.

What was his plan when they got there? On Google Earth, if he was right, the mobile home was located at the end of a short cul-de-sac in a wooded area. Now that they were getting closer, reality was setting in. How did the thumb drives she'd taken with her get there? What if he was too late? What if she was a hostage? What if Grant was right and she'd bailed out? What was wrong with him? She wasn't a deserter. She'd have been upfront and told him; she'd have rubbed his nose in it.

"At least the road conditions are better," Boomer finally said, breaking the silence.

Boomer was a competent chauffeur but Grant would have been a better partner for what might lay ahead. What good would an old, yellow-bellied draft dodger like Boomer be if he needed help? He'd been too afraid to drive into the parking lot of the FBI field office. On a Saturday.

How could he make a game plan when he didn't have the facts, hadn't assessed the location, and most importantly, didn't know if Lauren was there? He resorted to small talk. "Does the sun ever shine here?"

"Not much," Boomer said. "I really don't mind the cold, but in the winter the air's so thick it feels like you're walking around wearing a wet blanket, and the sun never comes out. This is supposed to be the best time of year and bad weather like this puts me in a funk."

He knew exactly what Boomer meant. He'd only been there a couple of days and he was feeling the funk, too. He held Boomer's phone near his ear, listening, then said, "The exit for I-70 is coming up."

"I see the sign," Boomer said. "I'm taking it west. Right?"

"Right."

52

Saturday, Late Afternoon, Mooresville, Indiana

The crate rocked side to side as if she were inside a washing machine. The pain in Lauren's head had morphed from a dull throb to a sharp knife.

"Son of a bitch!"

She opened her eyes. The skinny man had the dog crate with her in it pinned against an open tailgate, squatting and panting, balancing it on his thighs, struggling to push it up into the bed of an old pickup. Wincing, she squeezed her eyes shut and played dead.

"No helper," Buck said to himself. "I'd like to see that bitch try this."

The faint smell of bleach hung inside the crate, reminding her of the red cloths he'd hung around the outside minutes before she'd blacked out.

She opened her eyes, squinting, letting them adjust to the

natural light, and peered through the small cutouts at a wooded area.

She slowly sucked in a lungful of air that smelled woodsy, and felt shady and cool. No, it was cold, but the chill in the air felt good. The earthy smell of wet ground competed with the lingering burn of bleach still stuck in her nose. For a moment, it was quiet but for the chirping of a lone bird above.

He kept talking to himself. "Come on, Buckaroo. You can do this."

Do what? she wondered.

He squatted and hugged the crate, trying to stop it from sliding down, using his thighs as a backstop and a ramp. But he wasn't strong enough, and the aluminum cage dropped, landing on the wet ground with a thud.

Ouch.

His shoes slopped in the mud. Where was he going? The door to the trailer squeaked opened, then huffed shut.

She squeezed her hand behind her back and felt around the inside of the box, running her fingers inside, searching for the door that reminded her a of miniature jail cell. Fighting past the cramp in her right shoulder, she slid two fingers through the bars. Like before, the slats were too narrow for her whole hand to pass. She let her fingers explore the gap, wriggling them until she felt it again, the flat, round thing. She leaned harder to the left and contorted her right shoulder in different directions, trying to find a position where she could push her fingers far enough to grip the dial.

Owwwww.

Her right tricep spasmed. She dropped her arm, letting it rest on her thigh, waiting for the cramp to subside. As the knot loosened up, the stabbing pain in her head sharpened. What had he done to her and how much time had passed? Fighting the pain, she tightened her abs and clenched her teeth, praying for the agony to stop.

The door to the mobile home opened, and she heard him step out onto the wooden porch. She squinted through the little cutouts and cocked her head to listen.

"Come on, boy." The dog trotted down the stairs, following his master, who carried a five-gallon orange bucket and set it on the ground a couple of feet from the crate. He squatted, reached inside the pail and removed some small items, stuffed them in his pants' pockets, then lifted it by the handle, turned it upside down, and sat.

The dog came toward her, circling the cage, growling.

"Sit," Buck said. The dog obeyed.

Holding her breath, she pressed her eye nearer an opening.

"Damn it." He stood, walking around, craning his neck, looking for something. He squatted, reached down and pinched something from the ground with two fingers like a crab claw, then tapped it on his pant leg.

The dog, a hulking silhouette, lowered his head and pushed his snout closer to the crate, snarling, lapping the saliva drooling from his mouth. His foul breath and ripe body odor overpowered the woodsy smell.

Keeping her breath shallow, her ears followed a new sound. Flicking her eyes around and stopping on Buck, she identified it as the clicking of a lighter. It fired on the third try, the hiss of butane followed by a sucking sound, and deep inhalation. For a second it was quiet, then he exhaled the smoke toward her, the weird chemical smell of burning plastic maybe, or nail polish remover, filled the crate.

"Yooooooooowzaaaa." Buck refilled the glass pipe, put it between his lips, then lit it. He sucked on it, the tip turning orange as he inhaled, the same strange odor wafting downwind, toward her.

Possessed, he jumped to his feet, squatted like a deadlifter and scooped the crate with his forearms, heaving it up and onto the bed of the truck.

Every muscle in her body vibrated, she clenched her teeth to keep from yelping, her flight instincts at full throttle. But there was no way out. No escape. No relief. Her eyes welled and dripped down her cheeks, her muscles turning to putty. Where was Vance? He had to know she was missing. How would he ever find her?

Buck vaulted up on the tailgate and pushed the crate with the sole of one shoe until it came to a stop near the rear window. He knelt and put his eye close to the cage and peered inside, wrinkling his nose like a mouse, inspecting his prey. Through the cutouts, his face a kaleidoscope of horror: a strand of stringy yellow hair, a shifty pale blue eye, and front teeth rotted to black roots. He stood, rocking the bed of the old truck, then headed to the back bumper and jumped to the ground.

"Come on, boy." He whistled for Bo, slapping his hand on the rusty tailgate, grabbing the dog by the collar and pulling him toward the back of the truck. Bo resisted, sitting on his haunches. Buck pulled the pipe from his pocket, lit it, and sucked loudly. He stuffed the pipe back in his pocket and leaned over, lifting the front end of the dog and putting his front paws on the edge of the tailgate. Quickly, he took a step back and reached beneath the dog's haunches and lifted, grunting. Bo leapt the rest of the way up, and Buck slammed the tailgate behind him.

The driver's-side door creaked open and Buck got behind the wheel.

Where was he taking her?

The engine was cold. When he turned the key it chugged, then quit. He tried again, *errrr, errrr, errrr.* He opened the door, hopped out, walked toward the front bumper of the vehicle, and popped the hood.

"Damn carburetor."

He plodded to the back of the truck, released the tailgate, and climbed up. "Stay, boy." He patted the dog on the head, grabbed a red metal can near the wheel well, jumped down, and slammed the tailgate shut.

She smelled gasoline a minute later. Buck climbed behind the wheel of the vintage truck. This time, the engine turned over, coughing for a half minute before finding a steady cadence. He let it run while he stepped out and dropped the hood with a thud that shook the truck, then got back in and jammed the manual transmission into reverse. The dog stood and walked into the space nearest the driver's-side between the truck and the crate, then hung his head over the side, panting.

The dirt road was rough, filled with humps and potholes. Buck cut the wheel back and forth, zigzagging, the crate sliding from side to side, getting airborne once over a bigger bump.

What did he want? Was he taking her somewhere to let her go? Or was he going to kill her?

53

Saturday, Late Afternoon, Indianapolis, Indiana

W hen Bibbins saw Jack's name on CALLER ID, she hurried down the hall toward her bedroom.

Had she promised to call him back? She couldn't remember.

"Hey," she said, closing the door for privacy.

"Is this a good time to talk?"

"Sure." Then she heard her mother yell her name. "Hang on a sec," she said to Jack, then opened the door a few inches. "I'm here, Mama. In my room. Gimme a minute."

"You're missing the best part of the show."

"I'll be there in a sec," she said, then returned to the call with Jack. "Sorry about that."

"Where are you?"

"At my apartment."

"Who's there?"

"My mom."

There was an awkward silence. She left it to him to break it; he was the one who had the explaining to do. "I didn't know she was there," he said. "I was hoping to come over later, to talk."

"What time?"

"What time's your mom leaving?"

"I don't know. How about if I call you in a little while and let you know."

"All right. That works."

Bibbins ended the call and put the phone in the pocket of her scrubs. She liked wearing them while helping her mother; they made her feel like she was at work.

"Hey, Mama, what'd I miss?" she asked, sitting next to her on the sofa.

A commercial for tampons was playing on the TV. "The good part, the police came and questioned her about poisoning her husband. She lied and said she didn't do it. And you know what, hon?"

"What?"

"I hope she don't get caught 'cause that lyin', cheatin' bastard husband of hers had it coming."

How was it possible she shared DNA with this woman? How was it her mother had been going through chemo for almost four months and her dad hadn't noticed a thing, not even that she'd lost twenty pounds, and all her hair, including her eyebrows?

"I know what you're thinking, that you and Jack are gonna be special, that love'll conquer all. Don't get your hopes too high, 'cause after a while, you'll be practically invisible to him and you'll start looking forward to a time when you can be alone. Oh, the show's back on." Dorothy turned up the volume.

Bibbins filled the kitchen sink with hot water, then scrubbed and dried the tray she'd used to lay out supplies. She wiped the countertop with antibacterial disposable wipes and dropped them into a white plastic bag filled the bio waste she'd collected.

She stuck her head in the living room. "Mama, I'll be right back."

Dorothy didn't answer, too lost in the show.

She grabbed the plastic garbage bag and pulled the sliding glass door open far enough to stick her head out and look both ways. Once sure there were no witnesses, she hurried to the dumpster near the covered parking area to get rid of the hazardous waste.

54

Vance told Boomer to slow down, then redirected him to the turn off from the main road. Much of the foliage was ravaged from winter but the trees on both sides of the highway were so dense, they'd both missed the entrance the first time by.

Vance directed him to make an illegal three-point turn across the double yellow lines on the highway.

Boomer took a left onto a narrow wooded dirt road, humming, "Buh-da, bum-bum-bum, bud-ah, bum-bum . . ."

Dueling Banjos from *Deliverance*.

He craned his neck over the steering column. "What is this place?"

"I'm not sure. Go slow."

In a thousand feet, they were deep in the woods. He looked around, his throat constricting at the low visibility in the shady forest. Under different circumstances, it might've been a welcome respite from the city, but the thought that Lauren was here made his palms sweat. Boomer drove slowly, the squelch of leaves squashing beneath the wheels, mud splattering the underbelly of the Rogue. He sawed gently on the wheel as if driving on ice, the dirt road slimy from yesterday's storm.

Boomer turned on the headlamps. "I hope we don't get stuck."

The Nissan crabbed slightly as he navigated toward a fork in the road, low-hanging tree branches—new growth—brushing the roof of the SUV.

"Take it to the right."

"This place is giving me a bad feeling," Boomer said, activating the windshield washer, blasting spritzes of water, the wipers smearing spatters of mud the thickness and color of a chocolate milkshake.

Deeper into the forest, the canopy of trees blocked what remained of the afternoon light. Vance cracked the passenger's-side window and listened. Just the sound of tires mashing the wet earth and the smell of Christmas trees—hemlock, white pine, and eastern red cedar, some towering fifty feet or more.

"Stop," he said, checking Boomer's phone again. According to the coordinates Grant had given him, the next turn—about a half city block up ahead—led to a narrow dirt road where a mobile home was positioned at the T of the dead end. To go undetected, he'd have to get out and walk the rest of the way, cutting a diagonal path through the forest.

Boomer hugged the right side of the road and turned the wheel up onto the embankment on the passenger's side, leaving enough room for another vehicle to pass, then he put the Rogue in park.

"Wait here," he said.

"Can I have my phone back?"

He shook his head. "Sorry." It was the only insurance he had that Boomer wouldn't desert him. He jogged past the front bumper, then turned right, into the woods, pine needles crackling, layers of decaying leaf material cushioning the ground beneath his feet.

Ahead, the forest was a maze with no points of reference. He remembered what he'd learned from his days as an Eagle Scout and knelt, picked up an armload of dead tree branches, then laid them in the path pointing back to the Nissan. Watching the screen on the phone, following the detailed GPS map, he advanced toward the spot where the mobile home should be, dropping broken tree limbs as he went.

The diagonal distance to the trailer was around eight hundred feet, less than a city block from where he'd left Boomer. He stopped for a moment, turning counterclockwise first, then the other way, heart rate accelerating. Was it his imagination, or was someone following him? He stood still, listening, but didn't hear anything other than the light breeze rustling the tree tops. Probably nothing. He took a step forward and realized he was disoriented. Which way should he go? How could this be? He'd only stopped for a minute. He looked at the screen. Boomer's phone had gone to sleep and he didn't have the passcode to unlock it. Scanning his surroundings, searching for a landmark, he unholstered the 9-mil from under his jacket and stuffed it in the front of his pants.

How had he lost his bearings? It was like being on a ship in the middle of the ocean, but instead of water, he was engulfed by the forest. Without a horizon, he had no field of reference, just trees. He pulled his personal phone from his pants' pocket. One bar of cell service. He turned on his cell light and swept the ground, looking for the line of branches he'd dropped, then backtracked a few steps, heart pounding under his jacket. He paused, bent over like a man crossing the finish line of a marathon, holding his knees, allowing the fear to pass.

Jesus. What the—?

He dove behind a fat tree trunk, losing his balance, his left foot slipping, landing on one knee, his khakis wicking mud. He ran his hand over his top of his hair. He'd heard the rustling just before something smacked the top of his head. The wind kicked up, whistling, and rattling the leaves. A shiver ran down his neck: The temperature had dropped at least ten degrees. He squatted and stuffed his hands in his pockets, warming them while he waited, listening and watching, regulating his breathing. The wind quieted, and a squirrel chattered overhead, then leapt from a branch, dropping leaves and tree nuts.

His heart pumped when he spotted the line of branches he'd laid. Patting the gun tucked in his waistband with one hand, he snapped a branch with the other and dropped it in his path. If he lost all cell service, he'd be as screwed as if he'd parachuted into the Amazon jungle.

At about three o'clock from where he stood, he looked up at a dome of dim light funneling down like a tractor beam, where the tree tops opened to a lighter-gray sky. It had to be the clearing where the mobile home was located.

He logged into his personal phone with his fingerprint, and looked at the screen. A NO SERVICE message appeared in the upper right corner. He had to hurry. His only option was to follow the light overhead, hoping it led to the mobile home. But if he was wrong, or it was an ambush, he'd have to retreat quickly.

He turned on his cell flashlight, holding it low, highlighting the tree branches he'd just laid along the way. The thick carpet of leaves left no shoe prints, no hint of which direction to travel, but the branches marked the path back to the road. He forged on toward the clearing.

An old trailer shaped like a freight container that could pass for the one he'd seen on Google Earth was set atop a series of horizontal cinderblocks haphazardly stacked two-high. Tall weeds and old tires blocked his view to the underbelly.

Using the dense trees surrounding the perimeter for cover, he advanced to the back side of the mobile home. There was still enough available light to see an attached metal awning sheltering a shallow plastic pool leaning against the back side, and stacks of firewood three feet high. Next to it, a three-legged Weber charcoal grill, faded to a pinkish red. He couldn't tell what was under the tarp next to the awning, held in place with patio bricks: a small boat, or a recreational vehicle, maybe. Human skeletal remains and a bloody chainsaw for all he knew. He spotted an orange bucket, the five-gallon kind from Home Depot, lying on its side near the back wooden stairs.

He backtracked five feet for cover and followed the edge of the clearing to survey the front side of the trailer. There were no cars parked in the muddy driveway, and the front and side windows were blocked with aluminum foil. The old, corrugated metal siding, originally painted white, had foxed to a yellowish-beige with streaks of rust running from the roofline to the new growth of weeds. The horizontal box affixed vertically to the short side nearest him must have been the electric furnace. The wooden framing at the roof had rotted, and the sloped porch with a set of stairs leading to the front door listed on an angle.

What was this place and how did the USB drives Grant gave them end up here? He heard a rustling in the forest coming from somewhere behind him, and he dropped to one knee, then froze.

A song popped into his head. *Paranoia strikes deep. Into your life it will creep.*

Had Grant set him up? If so, why send him here? Why not arrest him in the parking lot behind the steakhouse? Or at the cafeteria downstairs of Emery's office? He waited a full minute, listening to the wind whistling through the trees. When it died down, he squatted, ran a zigzag pattern toward the short side of the trailer, then stopped and leaned his shoulder against the mobile home, hovering beneath the furnace box, using it for cover. He'd only run fifty feet but was out of breath, panting from the adrenaline flowing freely.

He lifted his shirt and pulled the Glock from his waistband and, staying low, moved slowly toward the back of the trailer, to the corner where he could see the rear door, using the tarp and what was under it for cover. Gripping the gun with both hands and two outstretched arms, he peered farther around the corner. His eyes locked onto a heavy chain leading to a thick metal stake pounded into the ground. His eyes stopped on two metal bowls, and from the size of them, they were here to feed a very large dog.

He froze, his heart pumping under his jacket. Could he shoot to kill if he had to? A deadly shot to a fast-moving target took razor-sharp focus, and he was rusty. He'd seen the Miami K9 units in action, the way they took down perps, leaping the last stride, sinking their jaws into the suspect's upper arm, then pulling them down to the ground.

If the dog was inside, it would alert its owner. He'd be unable to outrun it. His flight instinct kicked in, and he retreated into the forest, stopping behind a mature tree with a view to the mobile home. He stuffed the Glock down the back of his pants, grabbed a sturdy branch, gripped it with both hands, then lifted one foot and tested the nub of a broken tree arm. It was strong enough to hold him. He bounced, then pushed off and placed the opposite foot up on another thick branch, gripping a single tree limb overhead with both hands, looking skyward for the next one, pulling himself higher, letting his feet fish for nubs and branches sturdy enough to hold him as he scrambled twelve feet into the air, embedding himself into the foliage like a Christmas ornament.

Spreading his feet evenly across two thick branches, he pressed one shoulder against the fat tree trunk for balance and fished the spare clip from his shoulder holster. He released a single 9-millimeter bullet from the magazine, and stuffed the clip in the back pocket of his pants. He cupped the bullet in his hand and tossed it underhanded toward the roof, watching it arc in the air before dropping and hitting the target. The slug dinged the metal rooftop, then rolled, stopping in a nest of leaf material.

He waited. If someone was home, the occupant would let the dog out. The dog would lead them to the tree where he was hiding.

Pointing the Glock at the faded charcoal grill, he looked away, shifting his eyes to and fro, to and fro, warming them up. He flicked them to the back-door handle, then away, then back on the old grill. Unzipping his jacket, he opened it up and used it like a shroud to hide the gun while he tested the laser. The red light glowed beneath the rugged lightweight material. He'd need the laser if he had to hit a moving target.

Another breeze kicked up. His fingers grew numb and the wind chilled him to the marrow. The sky turned a darker shade of gray. The sun would set soon and the forest would turn black. He pulled his personal phone from his pants' pocket. He had better cell service—two bars instead of one—and twenty-percent battery. He checked the mobile Grant had given him. Two bars, too, and no new messages. He zipped it back inside the pocket of his lightweight Michelin Man jacket. It would serve as backup.

Was it a good idea to take Boomer's phone from him? What if he'd screwed himself by doing that? What if he needed help? He dismissed the thought. Boomer was probably on his way back to Chicago by now.

No one emerged from the mobile home. As he scaled down the tree, his right foot slipped and his body rotated counter-clockwise, sharp pine needles scratching at his face, barely missing his left eye. He'd instinctively defended his face with his right hand, his left arm not strong enough to balance him. He let go, his torso swiveled, a sharp tree branch pierced the neckline of his jacket, tearing through the fabric, turning the collar into a noose, choking off his windpipe. He fumbled with his free hand trying to rip the fabric or break the branch, anything to release the pressure from his neck.

He closed his eyes for one second, held his breath, ignored the panic and relaxed, and letting his body go limp, pulled the 9-mil from his waistband and dropped it, then dug one foot into the tree bark. He reached with two hands behind his neck and ripped the fabric, splitting it completely in half. He felt himself tilting backward, then free-falling.

When he came to, he was on his back, looking up at the jacket swaying from the limb high above. He scrambled to his feet and activated the flashlight on his personal phone long enough to spot his weapon. The gun had landed just a few feet from the base of the tree.

He squatted and ran to the front of the trailer, climbed the wobbly wooden stairs and tried the doorknob. It was unlocked. He turned the handle slowly, then leaned away from it as he opened it an inch and listened. He knocked and stepped back, pointing the 9-mil at the crumpled rusty door. No response. He pushed it open a foot and stood behind it, fish-eyeing the interior. It was dark and dank and smelled like bleach. His nostrils stung as he entered the main room, gripping the Glock.

Old furniture, yellow-and-orange plaid with big dark stains. Shag carpeting with a fresh impression from something that had been recently moved, drag marks leading to the back door. He checked the rest of the rooms, a bedroom with a bare mattress surrounded by clothes piled on the floor, and a small bathroom with the toilet seat up.

He followed the smell of bleach coming from rags piled in the kitchen sink. He held his breath and checked the refrigerator, backing away at the putrid stench of rotten food. He followed the drag marks to the back door and opened it, the scent of the forest clearing his head. A vehicle had been behind the house, and as he squatted to inspect the fresh tire tracks, saw paw prints as big as baseballs mixed with one set of shoe prints. Too big to be a woman's. Whatever had been dragged from the house left fresh gashes in the rickety wooden stairs. The heavy rectangular item had sledded down the stairs, and left an impression in the mud.

He knelt, shivering from the wet cold, and studied the imprints. He reached down and touched the earth. The mud was soft, like clay. What was it? Whatever it was left a giant snail trail over three feet wide. The gashes and the wood and the trail in the wet dirt led to a different pattern, a medley of short swirls and dents in the mud. It was box of some kind, and the imprint marks suggested it was too heavy to carry, like someone wrestled it on the ground.

What was it?

A shipping container? No, too small for that.

Maybe a crate.

Paw prints. Yes, a crate. For a big dog.

Whoever lived here owned a dog crate and dragged it from inside the house and dropped it in the mud. The impressions stopped near the back of a set of tire tracks leading away. Someone loaded the crate into the back of a vehicle and the crate had something in it too heavy to carry.

He walked the perimeter to the last spot where the crate had made an impression in the mud and studied the dog prints leading from the back door. Was he on the wrong track? Was the driver a responsible owner who'd loaded the crate in the back of his truck to transport the animal? That didn't square. The dog owner would have put the crate in the vehicle, then coaxed the dog in it.

Another storyline formed in his head, one that put a pit in his gut.

His palms dampened. If his calculations were right, a human could also fit in the crate, someone Lauren's size. He pulled the paper Grant had given him and he'd typed into his personal phone. He stood inside the very spot where the pin, a red tear-shaped icon appeared, the precise longitude and latitude where the thumb drive's microchip had pinged. There was nothing else in the vicinity, not a house, or a barn, nothing but trees as far as the eye could see. This had to be the place.

He kicked a brick out of the way and lifted the tarp. No recreational vehicle or boat, or bloody chainsaw, or human body parts, just more firewood. He studied the tire tracks and followed them to the front of the house. The driver had driven the narrow path between the trailer and the woods, then backed around to the front side, two sets of the same tire tracks going both directions.

He jogged to the back of the house to inspect the orange five-gallon bucket turned upside down. Something cracked beneath his shoe. Glass. He squatted and looked at the shards. He'd seen crack pipes before.

The tire tracks out front suggested the driver had been parked perpendicular to the front door of the trailer before backing around and loading the crate behind the mobile home. He retraced the fresh tire tracks leading from the back and followed them to the short road where it formed a T. He stopped and looked both ways. To his left, his field of vision ended at the bend, blocking the spot where he'd left Boomer in the Nissan— if he hadn't cut and run already. The tire tracks told the story. The vehicle had turned right.

He crossed to the other side of the road and stood on the

embankment, looking for a line of sight to the Nissan. There wasn't one. He opened the GPS app on his phone and dropped a new pin, marking the spot. If he couldn't see the Nissan, that meant Boomer couldn't see him, and that the unidentified individual transporting the crate couldn't have seen Boomer, either, which was just as well. The last thing he needed now was help from a yellow-bellied stoner.

Something caught his eye in the distance. He focused his gaze through a gap in the trees, seeing what appeared to be another road running at a right angle to the one where he stood. Did something move? Or were his eyes betraying him? Fading light mixed with the dense forest created a mirage of shadows. He closed his eyes to clear his head, and when he reopened them, was certain he saw something move. Something big, shaped like a pickup truck, but visibility was too poor and it was too far away to know for sure.

He walked the opposite way of the Nissan, toward the thing he'd seen moving, following the road, staying close to the trees lining the embankment. In minutes, darkness would fall. He broke into a slow run, picking up the pace to warm his bones, noticing the tire tracks, following them as the mud stuck to his shoes and the cuffs of his pants.

Saturday, Early Evening, Mooresville, Indiana

L auren squeezed her eyes shut and clenched her teeth. Every time the pickup hit a pothole, her skull banged the top of the crate. Pain had morphed into euphoria and the damp cold, a feeling she'd always hated, felt refreshing, like a dip in the pool on a hot summer day.

The smell of evergreen trees filled the crate, reminding her of the holidays, how, as a child, she'd count the days to Christmas beginning at Thanksgiving. What a pest she was, bugging her parents to take her to the tree lot and let her choose the one she wanted. While her dad set up the tree stand, she'd lovingly unwrap each ornament she'd help put away the year before, laying them out neatly on the carpet. When the tree was upright and the lights strung, her father would lift her, hoisting her atop his shoulders so she could hang the highest ones.

She closed her eyes and let her mind drift, remembering the year she'd turned seven. She'd been the first one awake that

Christmas morning and sneaked from her room to see how many new presents had appeared under the tree. The house smelled like cinnamon and chocolate, the cookies her mother had baked the night before. She tiptoed into the living room and knelt before the tree, rearranging the gift-wrapped boxes and packages, looking for the ones for her, hoping to find the thing she wanted most.

To Lauren. From Santa.

For Lauren. With love, Mom and Dad.

To Lauren. Love from Grandma and Grandpa.

What she'd asked for wouldn't be under the tree. That year, she'd only asked for one gift: a pony. If she'd gotten what she wanted, it wouldn't be in the house, it would be in the backyard.

She slipped outside but didn't see a pony grazing in the yard. No sign of a horse trailer, or the animal. She hadn't really expected it. Her mom said people who lived in the suburbs didn't have horses. Maybe her parents would pay for riding lessons at the local stables. She sneaked back into the house on that warm December morning, wondering how she hadn't noticed her mother sitting in the bentwood rocker, in the same room as the Christmas tree. Her face flushed, a burning sensation covered her cheeks. Had she been there the whole time, watching her riffling around under the tree, spying?

"Mom?"

She rocked slowly in the dim room, forward and back, without speaking.

"Mom?"

The truck swerved and the crate slid, bumping the side of the pickup truck. The tingling in her hands and feet had been replaced with numbness, and the panic attack, driven by desperation, had passed, turning into hopelessness, then surrender. She closed her eyes and let her mind go back.

"Yes, dear."

"Are you okay?"

"I'm fine, sweetie. Merry Christmas."

She'd walked closer and sat cross-legged on the floor near her mother's feet, ashamed of what she'd done, sneaking around the tree and spying. She expected a scolding, but didn't get one. Her mother kept rocking quietly in her chair, holding the baby in her arms, trying not to wake the infant up, she figured.

She finally spoke. "Why don't you plug the lights in, Lauren?"

"Okay." She crawled to the outlet and felt around the tree skirt for the cord, plugging it in, and lighting the tree, the ornaments sparkling beneath the twinkling white lights. The curtains were drawn from the night before, and in the low light the Christmas tree looked brilliant. She stood back and admired it, so thick and symmetrical with the gold and white angel on top practically touching the ceiling. A streak of morning sun pierced an opening in the drapes, hurting her eyes. She shaded them with her hands; the sharp light temporarily blinded her.

"You're not supposed to be here now."

"I know, Mom. I'm sorry." Her eyes adjusted to the light and she saw the baby swaddled in a blanket, held tightly against her mother's breast.

"Go to your room."

"Why? What did I do?"

Her father came through the front door. "You heard your mother," he said. "Go to your room."

Where had he been?

She obeyed, but hid in the hallway, listening and watching. Something was wrong.

"Come on," he said to her mother. "We gotta go."

Her mother didn't move. What was happening?

"Come on, Muriel. We have to go."

Where were they going on Christmas morning, and why did

bumper, the old engine coughing and knocking, the smell of burning oil and gasoline as he raced to the passenger-side door. Running in the slop alongside the truck, he reached for the door handle. Instead of him opening it, the driver flung it open from the inside, knocking him off balance.

"Get him!" A shadow leapt out from the passenger seat, like a panther. It landed on the ground, baring its white teeth, then launched itself toward him.

Scrambling to his feet, he ran, getting the early advantage, images flashing in his head. The crate. The chain. The big dishes in the yard. He should have known. He'd seen all the signs of a guard dog. If it ran into the forest, the dog's superior night vision would give it the advantage. Using the headlamp coming from the old truck, he ran on the open road, gripping his 9-mil with both hands, calculating the only option: wait until the dog was on him, then shoot to kill.

Sprinting, he glanced over his shoulder, about twenty feet separated him from the dog, the distance closing. He heard the rhythmic splash of paws hitting the mud, and his own breath, his heartbeat amplified, primal warning signals, barely able to feel his legs churning beneath him with superhuman power. He looked back again, the whites of the dog's eyes and canine teeth flashed. In ten seconds, he'd turn and meet the animal head on.

He double-checked the safety, slid his index finger over the trigger, spun, and faced the animal when suddenly a sharp whistle pierced the air.

The dog hesitated, the high pitch confusing it just long enough for Vance to change course. Had the driver called the dog off?

"Get him!" the same voice commanded.

The dog hesitated, then changed course, running after something new.

He climbed the embankment and ran, hugging the trees,

staying close to the road, ducking, careful not to make noises that would attract the animal. He halted, took cover behind a tree trunk and waited. He had the advantage now. He hated the thought, but if the dog came for him, a kill shot would be easy. Where was it? He scanned the road where the one headlight lit the dirt road. It hadn't gone back to the truck. What had distracted it enough to divert from him as the target? And why?

He heard a different voice calling the dog. "Over here! Come on, over here!"

Who was it? He squatted, huddled against the tree. Listening. Watching.

"Over here!"

The animal had a new target, it stretched out like a jungle cat, the dark mass charged toward a person standing in the shadows, the distance between them closing fast.

He aimed the Glock. He had the shot, the laser dot following the dog's head. But the animal slowed suddenly, as if trying to stop, its haunches gliding in the mud. It lifted its head like a wolf's at the moon and stared skyward. Vance followed its line of sight and saw something sailing through the air.

What was it? What was the dog going after?

The dog spun 180 degrees and leapt high into the air, catching the object in its jaws.

"No," the truck driver yelled. "Get him!" he ordered, waving his hands like a madman.

But the dog was locked onto its prey. A black duffle bag. The animal picked it up with its teeth, shaking its head, strings of saliva flying side to side.

The man rushed the dog, hand outstretched.

Where did Boomer come from and what was he doing?

"Don't hurt my dog! I'll kill you!"

The headlamp behind them lit the cone of aerosol spray

coming from Boomer's hand as it arced and sprinkled the animal's face. Boomer ran toward the dog until his hand was inches from its muzzle, so close the dog could have grabbed his arm and pulled him down to the ground. Instead, the dog dropped the backpack from its jaws and cowered, then yelped, dropping to its belly, using it paws to cover its face while Boomer emptied the canister of pepper spray, then reached into his pocket for a spare.

Vance emerged from the shadows and ran toward him.

Boomer saw him. "You okay?"

"Yeah." He pointed the Glock at the dog.

Buck ran to the scene. "Don't hurt my dog."

He turned the gun on Buck.

"Where's the girl?"

"I dunno," Buck said.

He pointed his gun back on the dog. "Tell me where the girl is."

"Don't hurt 'em."

"Tell me where the girl is."

He snapped his head toward the woods, behind the truck. "She's out there. Inside a crate."

Vance patted his pants pocket, fished Boomer's phone from his pocket and tossed it to him.

"I got this," Boomer said, holding up a third can of pepper spray.

He jammed the nose of the Glock in the space between Buck's skinny shoulders. The scrawny man tipped forward. "If you want to see tomorrow, show me where she is. Go. Now."

Buck led him into the forest and in less than a minute he stood in front of the crate.

He funneled his hands over his mouth. "Boomer," he yelled, "I need you."

Boomer sprinted to his side.

"Call 9-1-1." He activated the laser on his Glock and slapped the grip into Boomer's hand, forcing his fingers around it. "You got eight rounds. All you have to do is pull the trigger." He tossed his head at Buck. "Get him out of here."

57

Vance knelt and shone his cell light into one of the small cutouts and peered inside. There was something filling the crate.

"Lauren." No answer. He swept it with his light, searching for the handle, seeing what looked like a miniature jailhouse door.

He shook the crate. "Lauren, Lauren, can you hear me?"

Still nothing.

The light from his phone glinted off something metal: the handle, with a lock of some kind. He shined the light directly on it. He felt the cold metal plate with his hand and traced the outline with his index finger. It was rectangular and slightly recessed. He tilted the light and lit a metal ring about the size of a silver dollar lying flat inside the shallow indentation. He rubbed the edge of the ring with his thumb, trying to open it like the top of a soda can but he couldn't get his thumb under it. He dug the tip of his index finger beneath the edge and was about to slide a second finger beneath the ring when it snapped shut with a clack, catching the edge of his fingernail.

"Shit."

He shook his hand, then stuck his finger in his mouth and

tasted a droplet of blood. His thumb would have to do. He hooked the edge with his thumbnail, pried it open far enough to shove his thumb under it, used it to hold it open long enough to slide two fingers under the ring-shaped handle. He turned it, expecting the mini jailhouse door to spring open, but nothing happened.

"Damn it." He took a deep breath, then craned his neck until his face was a few inches away, and squinted.

Maybe he had to push it in while turning the ring. He pressed in on it while he turned the ring. Still nothing. He repeated the procedure, but this time he turned the ring the other way, counterclockwise. Again, nothing happened.

He felt a cold sweat break under his collar. *Stay calm*. He paused for moment to reevaluate the situation. The crate was quality, solid cast aluminum with welded hinges. There was no other way. He had to figure out how to open the damn lock.

Then he had a revelation. Maybe he had to pull it, not push it. Using his left knee for balance, he both pulled and felt the tightness of the spring. He turned the ring clockwise and heard the click, the sound of the lock letting go. He grabbed a handful of metal bars and flung the door open, then reached in and touched her.

"Lauren. Talk to me."

No response.

Squatting, he gripped the crate with his forearms and rolled it over so she'd be face up. Jesus, how the hell did he cram her inside? Her knees were pinned against her chest.

"Lauren!"

Silence.

He rotated it onto a corner and rocked it, loosening her left leg at the knee, then, balancing it against his shin, reached in and pulled it free. He lay the crate down with her leg sticking out and gathered wet leaves, scooping them with his hands, and built a little mountain to lean his phone against, tilting it until it shone on the crate. He knelt and reached inside, grabbing her other ankle, twisting it gently, trying to free it, then clamped his hand around her calf and pulled. But instead of freeing it, the crate slid in the mud with one leg sticking out.

"Hold on, I'm gonna get you out."

Quickly, he changed position, first squatting, then sitting in the mud with bent knees. He spread his legs, then placed the heels of his muddy shoes on either side of the opening. Swinging her free leg, the left one, off to one side beneath his thigh, he used the soles of his muddy shoes for leverage, pushing on the crate with both feet, reaching in and blindly bending her right knee tighter, twisting her calf with his other hand, freeing her leg. He hopped to a squat and pulled her right leg out.

"Lauren. *Lauren*." No answer. Her neck was turned in a weird angle, her ear on one shoulder, bent like a candy cane.

"Lauren!" Nothing.

Damnit. She'd been packed tightly inside like a pretzel. How would he get her out without injuring her? What if he was too late?

He knelt in the wet dirt and grabbed the waistband on her slacks, pushing the outside of the crate with one hand, pulling her torso toward him with the other. She was out to her thighs. He pushed and pulled harder to free her hips. He pulled her inch by inch until he could see her torso.

"Lauren!"

No answer.

He reached inside, feeling for her hand, checking for a pulse. One arm was bent behind her back, the other rested on her chest. He felt it. No pulse.

He worked faster, using more muscle, more force, being careful, but her body stopped moving, jammed in place. He grabbed the flashlight and shined it inside. She was pinned in by the arm that was bent behind her back, now contorted over her head.

Kneeling, he clamped one hand on the outer edge of the crate and reached deep inside, as far as he could, and wrestled with the stuck arm. Twisting and firmly pulling, he freed it, then crossed both arms across her chest like a mummy's. Squatting, he straddled her legs, and stood over the parts he'd freed, then blocked the crate with his shins, dragging her body out a few inches at a time, panting and huffing, grabbing whatever he could, the waistband of her pants, sleeves of her jacket.

He widened his stance, like a sumo wrestler, bent and tilted his head to look inside, then fished around until he felt her hair, walked his fingers down to one shoulder, and clamped it firmly. Dropping to his knees, he reached deeply inside and cradled her head, cupping it in his palm, feeling something strapped around her neck, then placed the other arm between her shoulders and lifted. Pressing his forehead against the top of the crate, he grabbed a hunk of jacket beneath her with one hand and gripped her right shoulder with the other, then baby-stepped backward, waddling back, leaning forward with his head to buttress the crate, his thighs and neck cramping at the same time.

When he saw the collar around her neck, he stopped and dropped to one knee and cupped his hand and lifted her head, then pushed it. The dog crate rotated. He pushed it away.

"Lauren!" He swatted her cheek. "Hey!" Nothing. He repeated it. "Hey! It's me! Vance." He shook her by the shoulders but her head rolled side to side like a ragdoll's.

He booted the dog crate farther away and lay her flat on her back, then scrambled atop her, straddling her chest and reached for her arm, pressing a muddy thumb on the inside of her wrist.

Still, no pulse. He put his ear near her mouth. She wasn't breathing. He knew what to do; he'd saved a life when he was a cop.

He lifted her chin, pinched her nose, put his lips on hers, and blew a rescue breath. "Come on . . . come on." He counted to five, took a deep breath and exhaled into her lungs again.

No response.

He laced his fingers together, locked his hands palms down, and pounded her chest, *one-two, one-two, one-two,* delivering a dozen forceful, rhythmic compressions. He checked for a pulse. Nothing. He put his mouth on hers again and delivered two more rescue breaths, then pumped another round of chest compressions, then checked again for life. Still nothing.

"Come on, Lauren! Fight!"

He pinched her nose, sucked in the forest air, and put his mouth on hers, lifted her neck, tilted her chin back, and exhaled into her mouth. Then he started over.

"Come on!" He smacked her cheek, harder this time.

She arched her back and twitched, then fought him with her hands, blindly, wildly slapping at his face.

"Good girl." He cupped her neck and tilted her chin up, clearing her airway. "Come on, breathe."

The first one was ugly-beautiful, a guttural sucking sound. He grabbed the light and shined it in her face. Her complexion was pallid, eyes closed. He pressed one eyelid open and up with his thumb and pointed the light at her pupil. It was big and lifeless.

He grabbed her wrist. A faint pulse, but it was there.

He stood, then squatted, scooping her up from the ground. "Stay with me. Come on, babe, stay with me." He carried her in his arms, running for the old pickup truck, sloshing in the mud, as slippery as ice.

"Boomer!" he yelled. "Give me your jacket."

Boomer peeled it off.

"Did you call 9-1-1?"

"They're on the way." He tossed the jacket to Vance.

He set her limp body on the tailgate, propping her up with one arm, swaddling her in Boomer's old coat. Leaning his thighs against the tailgate, he hugged her torso, shivering, giving her whatever body warmth he had left.

"How long 'til they get here?"

"Soon," Boomer said. "I told them she might die."

"Where's Buck?"

"He's in the cab."

"Where's the dog?"

"Over there." He pointed to the side of the road.

"What the hell's wrong with him?" If he'd shot the dog, he'd have heard it, wouldn't he?

"I gave him the beef jerky, and I tied him to a tree. Look."

He heard a siren before he saw the flickering of red lights in the distance. The horn was deep, like a freighter on open water.

"Is she going to make it?" Boomer asked.

"Yeah. You got a knife?"

Boomer pulled a tool from his pocket and released the blade. "What is that?"

"A shock collar." He sawed it from her neck, then said, "Gimme my gun."

Boomer handed it to him.

Using one hand, he dropped the strap from his shoulder, pulled the spare clip from his back pocket, wadded it up into a pile with the 9-mil, and hid it behind the wheel well in the bed of the truck. Headlights from the response vehicle blinded him.

"The story is she went for a walk and got lost. Got it?"

"Yep," Boomer said. "What about him?" He cracked his chin in the direction of Buck in the cab, slumped against the door. "He swears he didn't want to do it, but they threatened him."

Lauren shivered in waves.

"Who?" Vance asked.

"I don't know."

He had a good idea who. "Tell him to stay in the truck and keep his mouth shut or I'll call the cops."

"Okay," Boomer said, "but I think he's coming down from something, maybe meth or crack."

A female paramedic with hair tucked under a ball cap approached. "What's going on?" She shined a long flashlight on Lauren.

"She went for a walk and got lost."

"How long was she out here?"

He did a quick calculation. "I'm not sure. Eight hours, maybe, at most."

"You her husband?"

"No."

"Relationship?"

"A friend."

"Move out of the way, please."

Her associate hurried with a backboard and a blanket. "Any trauma to the head?"

"I don't think so."

The female pulled a penlight from her shirt pocket and opened Lauren's eyes one at a time, studying each, then checked her pulse. "She's cold and dehydrated."

"She wasn't breathing when I found her."

"For how long," the man asked, helping transfer her onto the backboard.

"I don't know. Where are you taking her?"

"To the hospital," the woman said, carrying the foot of the gurney.

He walked next to them. "Will she be okay?"

"It's standard procedure to hold her for observation."

Lauren spoke. "What happened?"

He reached for her hand. "You're okay."

She stared at him with glassy eyes.

He followed them to the ambulance and watched the female climb in first, then, working in tandem, slid the board with Lauren on it into the back of the ambulance.

"Will you be accompanying her?" the woman asked, squatting in the rear doorway.

He wanted to, but he couldn't let Buck get away. "The other fellow will. Wait a sec."

He ran to the pickup. "Boomer, walk with me." He gave him instructions as they headed toward the ambulance.

Boomer kept walking, past the ambulance, in the direction of where he'd parked the Rogue.

The female EMT narrowed her eyes and craned her head out the back of the vehicle, looking to see where Boomer was heading. "I thought he was going with us?"

"He is." He couldn't lose control of the situation. Not now. "He'll follow you."

Boomer broke into a run and disappeared around the bend where he'd parked on the embankment. Vance shaded his eyes as the ambulance driver backed past, big tires slogging in the mud, red and blue lights spinning, heading toward the T in the road leading to Buck's crap-box.

He sprinted to the old pickup, grabbed his holster, put Boomer's coat on to cover his gun and ordered Buck out, pointing the 9-mil at him.

Hurrying him into the woods, he forced him to carry the crate back to the truck.

"I didn't wanna do it," Buck said. "You gotta believe me."

"Put it in the bed."

Buck heaved the empty cage into back of the old pickup.

"Get your dog and put him in it. You got ten seconds. Get moving."

Buck led the dog by the rope, the one Boomer had used to tie him to the tree. The animal kept its head down, trotting a wide berth around Vance.

"Up," Buck said, but the dog sat, instead. "Come on." He smacked the tailgate and smooched his lips, but the dog stayed put. "Come on, Bo." He hit the flat metal a couple more times. The huge dog stood on its hind legs, putting its front paws on the ledge—where he'd shielded Lauren a few minutes ago. "Up." Buck said it louder. The dog didn't respond. Buck reached under the animal's hindquarters and lifted its haunches.

Vance grabbed the backpack Buck had thrown at the dog and tossed it into the bed of the truck. "Put the dog in the crate, then get in."

He held him at gunpoint, watching him coax the dog into the cage, filling it. Buck climbed into the passenger side. Vance turned the key, cranked the engine, and pushed the clutch to the floor. Wrangling the manual transmission, he jammed it into first gear, feathered the gas, and eased up on the clutch. The old combustion engine coughed, and the truck fishtailed in the mud.

The ambulance was stopped around the bend. The EMTs were arguing with Boomer.

Vance parked behind it, killed the engine, and took the key. "You stay here," he said to Buck. "One wrong move and they'll be trying to save your life."

Buck nodded.

He approached the ambulance.

"Will you tell your friend to move his vehicle out of the way?" the male asked. "He's blocking us."

The ambulance dome light was on and the back doors were open. Lauren sat up on the gurney.

"We'll take it from here," Vance said.

"What's that supposed to mean?" the one riding with Lauren asked.

"She's not going to the hospital. Get her out."

The woman protested. "We can't do that."

"I'm a lawyer." He stuck his head inside the back of the ambulance. "Lauren, do you want to go to the hospital?"

She shook her head.

"See? She's refusing."

The male took a deep breath, and exhaled slowly, his breath fogging in the cold air. "Fine. I need her to sign a release form."

"Go get it," Vance said. "Boomer, come here and help me."

As the female unbuckled Lauren from the backboard, the other paramedic passed a clipboard to Vance and he gave it to Lauren. "Sign it," he said.

He and Boomer grabbed an arm and helped her to her feet. A blanket had been draped over her shoulders like a cape.

Both EMTs shook their heads.

Hands shaking, she signed her name.

He and Boomer loaded her into the back seat of the Rogue, warm inside from the engine running. She lay down, curled at the knees.

"Move your vehicle and let them pass," Vance said.

Boomer hopped behind the wheel and made room for the ambulance.

He watched it roll by slowly, passing the Rogue, the flickering of colorful lights fading. He heard a last few whoops of the siren in the distance, probably crossing the four-lane en route to the next emergency.

Boomer returned.

"Do you have somewhere you can take her, warm her up, and get her some food?"

"I can go to my sister's place. My brother-in-law's a nurse practitioner."

"Good. I'll call you."

Boomer turned to leave.

"Wait."

Boomer stopped. "What?"

"You saved her life."

Boomer looked puzzled. Vance tossed him the backpack he'd thrown at the dog.

Boomer slung it over his shoulder. "I told you my sister's a mail carrier. It's an old trick. Throw the bag, then shoot the pepper spray. I followed those branches you dropped and when I saw you go up that tree, I ran to get my backpack." He took the spare can of pepper spray from his pocket. "Always carry a bunch of the stuff. I never know who's getting in my car."

"No," he said, "you never know. You better get going."

58

Saturday, Evening, Mooresville, Indiana

Vance ran back to the old pickup, jumped behind the wheel, started the engine and turned left at the T in the road, leading to Buck's old trailer, taking the skinny path past the furnace affixed to the outside, and parked around back, near the old charcoal grill and stacks of firewood.

He pointed the Glock at Buck. "Get out and unload the crate."

"I ain't strong enough."

"You were strong enough to dump it with a woman in it." He pushed the nose of the 9-mil against his skinny ribcage.

Buck obeyed, dropped the tailgate and, wrangling the metal cage against his hips, squatting, and using his thighs and knees as a ramp, slid the cage into the mud.

"I can't leave him here, outside like this."

"Fine, then tie him to a tree and change places."

"I ain't getting in that crate."

"Then get in the truck."

"Can I go inside first? I gotta piss."

"Go behind a tree."

"Never mind. I can hold it."

Vance manhandled the gearshift—a stick attached to the floorboard—and hammered it down and to the right, then reversed the truck along the narrow space alongside the trailer. He swung the old Ford around and pointed it toward the dirt road leading to the highway. He cut the wheel, and the truck rocked and pitched as he avoided the deepest potholes. Two minutes later, he stopped at the intersection leading to the highway.

He glanced in the rearview mirror. How strange he'd been so close to civilization—like he'd been tricked, stuck inside someone's bad joke.

He put the truck in park and killed the engine.

"What are you doing?"

He hadn't gotten a good look at Buck until now, stopped beneath the tall street light. If a human could morph into a worm and crawl out from the earth it would look like Buck, but it would smell better.

"You're on a need-to-know basis." He redialed Hunter Grant from his personal phone.

"Jesus. Where are you? I've been trying to reach you. Why didn't you answer?"

"Been busy," he said, remembering the phone Grant gave him was in the pocket of his jacket hanging from a tree.

"Where've you been?"

He bet Grant knew where he was. "Looking for Lauren."

"Did you find her?"

"Yes."

"Is she okay?"

"I think so."

"Where are you now?"

He changed screens and looked at the navigation app on his phone, then gave Grant a general idea.

Grant didn't seem surprised. "Take 465 north and exit at Crawfordsville, then head east. There's a Denny's. Meet me inside."

"Any update on Rogers?"

Buck perked up at the question.

"I'll fill you when you get here," Grant said. He ended the call.

"She's supposed to call me," Buck said.

"Who is?"

"Sherry Rogers."

"When?"

"I dunno."

"I could march you into the woods and put a bullet in that sick brain of yours. Start remembering."

"I dunno. I swear it. She said she'd call after I dumped the body."

Dumped the body. Every cell in his body wanted to pounce from behind the wheel and rip his tongue out and shove it down his throat. Instead, he said, "I'm on my way to meet someone who could put you away for the rest of your life. Start talking or enjoy the scenery because it'll be the last time you see the world from outside a cell for a long, long time."

"I told you, I don't know."

"When Lauren testifies, they'll charge you with attempted murder. Not to mention kidnapping, drug possession, assault with a deadly weapon—"

"I ain't gotta gun."

"I'm talking about your dog. They'll put him down."

"I'm no killer. Neither's my dog."

"Save it for the jury." What a pathetic creature. "Call her now. Find out where she is."

"I tried. Phone's out of service."

"You said you talked to her."

"I did, but she called me."

Talk about dumb. "Gimme your phone." He scrolled through Buck's incoming calls. The last one was from ANONYMOUS. Probably from a burner. He debated redialing the number, but his gut told him not to, that Sherry told Buck she'd call him. It'd have to wait. He propped his personal phone against the inside of his left knee, pointing it at Buck in the passenger seat, then handed his dollar-store phone back to him.

"I don't wanna go to prison."

"Then cooperate and help me find Sherry Rogers."

"She'll kill me."

"She can't kill you from prison."

"She ain't in prison yet."

He was sure it was Buck he'd seen on the way to the big-red-barn lunch place when he was pulled over by the police in Indiana. He wasn't speeding. There was no probable cause for the stop. It made sense now. He remembered Buck's old pickup, the one he was driving now, motoring by slowly, Buck staring at him standing on the side of the road with Officer Fealy and his partner, holding his phone out the window. He must've followed him.

"Why'd you swap the license plates on my rental car and report me to the police?"

"'Cause Sherry paid me to do it."

"Why?"

"I dunno. I swear on my mama's grave, I don't know."

"Why'd you kidnap Lauren and leave her out there to die?"

"I told you, I didn't want to do it." Buck wrung his hands. "All

I know is she told me to leave that girl there. I told her it'd kill her, and she said to do it anyway."

He showed Buck his phone propped against the inside of his left knee. He backed the video file up fifteen seconds and played it. *"I told her it'd kill her and she said to do it anyway."*

"You was recording me?"

"You just confessed to attempted murder." He twisted the key in the ignition but the old motor didn't fire.

"You gonna turn me in?"

"Maybe. Depends on you."

Buck grimaced, showing his front teeth, nubs of brown rot. "I swear I didn't wanna do it." Then he reached over for something.

Vance drew his weapon.

Buck recoiled against the passenger-side door and covered his face with his hands, then peeked through his fingers. "I was just gonna pull the choke so you don't flood the engine."

"I can do it myself. Keep your hands where I can see them."

HIGHWAY TRAFFIC WAS THIN, and when the intersection was clear, he pulled from the dirt road, crossed the four-lane, and turned left, heading toward the on-ramp for I-465. The old truck ran rough, like a dune buggy, and the springs in the seat punched the backs of his thighs. The steering wheel was as big and round as a large pizza, and it took two hands to keep the old jalopy on a straight line.

His phone buzzed. He glanced at CALLER ID. Wrestling the truck, guarding the 9-mil, and watching Buck while juggling the phone was a circus act that wouldn't last long. He pressed the green button, propped the phone on his shoulder, and held it in place with his ear, keeping one eye on Buck, then said hello.

"Mr. Courage?"

"Uh-huh."

"It's Anna. From Dr. Garcia's office."

"What's up?"

"I think I know who changed the records, the ones for the dead patients."

Damn it. He wanted to talk but couldn't. "Can I call you back?"

"Um, sure."

"I really want to talk to you, it's just bad timing."

"Okay," Anna said.

He stopped at the red light. The driver next to him in a late-model Hyundai stared at the vintage pickup, tooted the horn, and rolled down his window.

Vance cranked his down.

"You know you only got one headlight?"

"Appreciate it."

"Nice truck."

"Thanks," he said, hand cranking the window halfway up.

Buck said, "If you turn on the brights you'll have two lights. Want me to show you how?"

"I told you, keep your hands to yourself." He pulled the knob and activated the lights. A pair of bright beams lit the road. "What year is this thing?"

"Nineteen fifty," Buck said. "That woman your friend or your girlfriend?"

He was pushing his luck. "Does it make a difference?"

"Not to me," Buck said. "But it probably does to you."

Hell, yeah, it made a difference to him. "It'd be best if you kept quiet and hope your friend calls soon."

"She ain't my friend."

Jesus. Teeth were this side of immortal and he'd seen meth-mouths before. If that's what it did to his teeth, what had the stuff done to his brain? This guy was no killer. He'd stuffed Lauren in a crate and left her for dead to feed his addiction. He should have hated him, should have opened the door and pushed him out at fifty miles an hour. Into traffic. In front of a semi-tractor trailer. Or a freight train. Except he couldn't do it. It was the drugs that had rotted Buck's soul.

59

Saturday, Night, Indianapolis, Indiana

Bibbins slipped out the sliding glass door of her apartment, carrying the bag of medical waste, but instead of going directly to the dumpster, detoured to her car parked in her assigned spot to call Jack. Her mother had begged to sleep over. What could she do? Say no?

Jack had asked to come over, and she wanted to talk to him, but she didn't want him to see her mother, or what they'd been up to. She'd had to cut the convo short earlier; she couldn't talk with her mother blasting the Lifetime Channel in the background. Hurrying to her car, she opened the back door, tossed the garbage bag in the back seat, started the ignition, turned the heater on HI, then called Jack.

He answered on the first ring. "Do you know when your mom's leaving?"

"She wants to spend the night."

"You're going to let her?"

She didn't answer him.

"How come you've been avoiding me?"

"What do you mean?"

"I've been calling and texting you since yesterday."

"There's something wrong with my phone, I think it's the battery."

"I was worried."

Worried, yeah, right. The picture of him with that sales slut would not leave her head. She faked a happy voice. "Well, I'm here now."

"Can you talk?"

"Sure."

"Where's your mom?"

She tweaked the truth. "She's in the other room with the TV blasting. Where are you?"

"I'm home. There's something going down at work," he said.

"What kind of thing?"

"Some kind of investigation."

"Into what?"

"I'm not sure but I think it has something to do with the patients that died."

She reached for the heat and turned it lower, fingers trembling. "How do you know that?"

"There's this guy from the medical records company. He called the HR department at Masson and was asking questions about me."

It had to be that busybody Vance Courage sticking his nose in even more places it didn't belong. "What kind of questions?"

"Where I went to school, previous employment, that kind of thing."

"Why?"

"Someone altered the medical records of the deceased patients."

"How?"

"I don't know, something about scheduling."

"Why would someone do that?"

"I have no idea, but he thinks I might've done it."

"Why would he suspect you?"

"I guess because I sold the software to both doctors."

"What's that got to do with it?"

"I guess it makes me a suspect. My dad's helping me get a lawyer."

"Because someone did something to the schedule?"

"No. Because the FBI's involved."

"The FBI? How do you know that?"

"A friend at work overheard a friend in HR talking about it. Then that Courage guy called me and asked me if I'd tampered with the files. I said I didn't but he kept asking me why I did it. He kept badgering me, then he told me the FBI profiler working the case says it's how the killer leaves a calling card. I told him I didn't know anything about it, that I'd never met the patients, and the only time I've been to any doctors' offices was to meet during the sales calls."

"Oh my God. They think someone killed the patients?"

"Yes."

"When you told him you didn't do it, what did he say?"

"He told me not to leave town."

"This is bad, Jack."

"I know. A reporter called."

"A reporter?"

"Yeah, from the *Star*. They wanted to know if I'm the Chemo Killer."

The Chemo Killer? "Oh my God. What are you going to do?"

"I don't know. I already lost my job."

"You were fired? From Masson?"

"And my boss disappeared."

"Bill Fields?"

"And HIPP Corp closed up shop in the middle of the night. I think someone's setting me up."

"Who'd do that?"

"I don't know. That's what I'm trying to figure out. I need you to help me."

"Sure, but what can I can do?"

A set of headlights lit the parking lot and a minivan passed.

"I want you to call ME. Tell her what happened. Ask her to help. She'll know I didn't do it, that's there no way I'd do anything like this."

She hesitated, trying to think how ME could help.

"Bibbs, I really need your help."

She paused, then asked. "Did you do it?"

"*What*? Kill those patients? God, no. You don't think—"

"No . . . no . . . of course not."

"I shouldn't have pushed you to get me that meeting."

"I can't believe they think you're the Chemo Killer."

"I know, me neither, it's so crazy."

A cold sweat broke under her blouse and her mind raced. She gripped the phone and drummed the steering wheel with a thumb, her thoughts short-circuiting.

"Bibbins?"

"Yeah."

"Be careful. Call me after you talk to ME."

"I will," she said, ending the call. Something was off. Jack said he was home but there was noise in the background, the ambient sounds of people, like he was in a public place. What a liar. She'd seen that picture of him making out with that nasty woman from work.

Once they got married, he'd stop lying. That's the way it worked, men were hardwired to sow their seeds but when they settled down, they stopped. That's what marriage was all about.

60

Saturday, Night, Crawfordsville, Indiana

V ance stared at the Denny's menu. He hadn't expected to see Jack there when he and Buck arrived. He'd listened to Jack's call to Bibbins, about the so-called Chemo Killer. He didn't know what to make of it. The idea of food rocked his stomach.

"I can't believe you guys think she's killing patients. There's no way," Jack said.

Hunter Grant shrugged. "That's what friends and family always say. Neighbors, too. Jeffrey Dahmer, he seemed like such a nice young man. Never suspected a thing. Good job on the call."

The pink-haired waitress stood over them. "Are you gonna order food?"

"I wanna get the steak and eggs," Buck said.

"How you want 'em cooked?"

"Well done on the steak and over easy on the eggs."

"I'll have a refill." Grant held up his coffee mug.

The waitress looked at Jack, shifting one hip higher. "What about you?"

He put his hand up. "Nothing for me."

Vance asked for a coffee refill.

When she was gone, Jack asked, "Can I go now?" His face was ashen, as if he'd just donated a gallon of plasma.

"I can't make you stay," Grant said. "Call me if you hear anything from your fiancée. Don't call her. Let her come to you."

Jack shuffled out the door, a shadow of the cocky sales whale who'd spoken at the Masson gala a few nights ago. *Ever notice the shit made in China smells like shit?* He'd gotten a standing ovation for that one. But being a jerk hardly qualified him as a killer.

"I gotta take a piss," Buck said.

Sherry Rogers hadn't called yet and Vance wasn't taking any chances. "Leave your phone here. Try to run, and there'll be a manhunt like nothing you've dreamed of. Don't forget, I know where you live."

Buck put his phone on the greasy tabletop. "I got nowhere to run to, and I know I ain't smart, but I ain't dumb enough to try to trick the FBI." Buck stood, spotted the sign for the RESTROOMS and headed that way, wobbling.

He'd have gone with him, to make sure he didn't try to escape, but he didn't have to. He'd used the men's room when they'd arrived, and like most corporate-run restaurants, the bathroom didn't have a window. Plus, he and Grant shared a booth with a view to the front door, in the event Buck had a lapse in judgment.

"Who's the zombie?" Grant asked when Buck was out of earshot.

They hadn't had a chance to talk yet. "I followed the coordinates you gave me to an old trailer south of town. He stuffed her in a crate and dumped it the woods."

"Lauren?"

"Yeah."

"Where's she now?"

"With a friend."

Grant raised his eyebrows. "Why didn't you call the cops?"

"'Cause I think he's your link to Rogers."

Grant squinted. "How?"

"Buck's working for her."

"How do you know that?"

"He told me."

"You believe a guy with witch's teeth?"

He had a lot of reasons to believe Buck was telling the truth, but he needed to keep it short. "How else could he have abducted Lauren? Rogers put him up to it. She's supposed to call him, to make sure he finished the job."

"When?"

"Any minute."

Grant snapped his chin in the direction of the phone lying on the tabletop. "Give me his cell."

He slid it over. Grant held it on his lap, looking down. "Why's that phone I gave you still pinging off a tower in Mooresville?"

Grant must've had access to a Stingray, a small electronic box that intercepted wireless phones by mimicking cell towers. The FBI was famous for using them. He'd practically been lynched by his own jacket when he'd fallen from the tree. The mobile Grant gave him was still zipped in the inside pocket. "It's a long story."

Grant set Buck's phone back on the tabletop. "If she calls him, I can trace Rogers' location."

"How'd you find Jack?"

"Through his fiancée. The nurse."

"How'd you—" He'd just seen how. Grant had done the same thing to him, had access to his personal phone, locations, and call records. "How long have you been working the doctor cases?"

"Couple of days."

The FBI didn't work domestic murder cases, but they did investigate serial killers. "I thought Rogers and Fields were your targets?"

"They are, but I think this thing's bigger, and Jack's connected."

"How?"

"It's pretty obvious," Grant said.

He felt his brow crunch. "Not to me, it's not."

"He thinks he's working as an informant but he's actually a suspect."

"A suspect? For what?"

"The murders."

"Let me get this straight. You think he's the killer, and you had him call the nurse, but you actually believe he's the killer?"

"And you think I'm wrong?"

"I didn't say that. What proof do you have?"

"It's circumstantial, but there's a mountain of it."

"Like what?"

"Like he's engaged to a gal that works for one of the docs. He works for Masson and has access to the patient files. He sold the software to Emery, and to the clinic in Chicago. He's the common denominator."

"Okay. How'd he kill the patients?"

"I can't disclose that."

What if Grant had it all wrong? What if the drugs were tainted? He kept thinking about Garcia's friend, the investigator, who worked for the FDA and quit because the higher-ups wouldn't listen to him.

"That pretty little nurse he's engaged to used to work for Bill Fields and she has an ax to grind. My guess is Jack knew."

"What was her problem with Fields?"

"Back when she worked for him, she called the Bureau's anonymous tip line and reported him. We keep a record of the calls."

"When?"

"Five years ago."

Five years ago? They'd been watching Rogers and Fields for longer than he'd thought. "Did Fields know it was her who tipped off the FBI?"

"Had to. Fields shut the scam down and fired her."

This was a classic example of an ambitious investigator reverse engineering the facts to fit the crime. "If that's your theory, Bill Fields has more motive than Jack. Maybe you got it backwards."

Grant said it again, like he was talking to some sort of moron with a short-term memory problem. "It's a matter of time before the Chicago office launches an investigation."

"Is that what you're worried about? That the Chicago field office is gonna to get involved in your investigation?"

"No," Grant said. "There's more. I talked to some of his friends and co-workers—turns out he started drinking hard in college and flunked out of pre-med. He's some kind of rich kid who thought he should waltz directly from the frat house right into private practice."

"It's still not evidence."

"Maybe, but I'm betting he's a sicko with a chip on his shoulder. The killer went into the medical records and set future appointments for his victims. All of them had follow-ups scheduled for June twenty-eighth."

He already knew that. "Why?"

"I'm working on it. But it has some sort of significance to him."

"Why'd you want him to call her?"

"I told you. I want him to think we're targeting her. But now I'm wondering if that was a mistake."

Maybe saying it out loud allowed Grant to see the problem with his theory. "What kind of mistake?"

Grant ignored the question; instead, he looked at his watch. "Soon he'll be in a bar somewhere, tying one on."

He asked again. "What mistake?"

"I'm beginning to think he'll let her take the fall for him."

Grant still didn't see it. "You're assuming he did it."

"He called her when I asked him to, without even questioning it, like he had no problem with it. Didn't even ask why."

"Maybe he's scared. If I had the FBI asking me about a series of murders, I'd be nervous, I'd do what you asked."

Grant was quiet for a minute.

"Is that bit about the Chemo Killer true?"

Grant shook his head. "No. I told him to tell her that."

"Why?"

"The more scared he is, the more inclined he'll be to make a mistake. I'll bet he's trying to cover his tracks right now. We're surveilling him."

"What if you got eyes on the wrong person?"

"We don't."

"How can you be sure?"

"His story doesn't wash."

"What story?"

"The one about the night of the Masson gala. He told me he was with his fiancée the entire evening, that he went straight home after the party was over."

"So?"

"It's not true."

"How do you know that?"

"I saw him."

It was possible Grant knew something. He was at the Marriott that night.

"I was surveilling Bill Fields but when I was leaving at the end of the night, I saw Sherry Rogers parked across the street. I followed her to a late-night pub, a joint called Kilroy's. Jack told me he went straight home. He didn't. He was at the pub. The Hummer he hired for the night was parked out front."

"You're sure about that?"

"I called the limo company to confirm it. The driver dropped him and some of his buddies at an after-hours place. His fiancée, the nurse, didn't go with him."

"How do you know that?"

"The driver specifically remembered Jack. Said he paid with his credit card and left a generous tip. The driver said he was a jerk, and that he insisted he drop him at the club first. Driver said he felt bad about taking his date, her friend, and some other guy, an older man, home. Made two stops for the others first, then dropped the nurse off last at her apartment. Then he went back to the after-hours club. Said he waited out front of the place and drove Jack and his friends home just before sunup. Said they were wasted. I talked with Miss Masson to confirm the story."

That caught him off guard. Grant had been a busy guy. "What did she have to say?"

"She didn't want to talk to me. I reassured her she wasn't the target of the investigation, rather, we had some questions about the night of the gala. She met us at her lawyer's office."

"When?"

"This morning."

"On a Saturday?"

"The firm that represents Masson jumps when there's a problem."

That didn't jibe. "She doesn't work there."

"I know. She sells real estate," Grant said. "But she was at the gala, and when I asked to see the picture of Jack and that woman, she got nervous. She agreed to show it to me at the lawyer's office. It proves he lied when he said he was with the nurse the entire night."

"What picture?"

Grant pulled a four-color printed eight-by-ten-inch photo from his briefcase and handed it to him.

His stomach turned.

"I bet you wish you could unsee that," Grant said.

The behavior was disgusting, even egregious. But it wasn't criminal. "Bibbins saw this?"

"According to her friend, Miss Masson, yes."

"Who showed it to her?"

"Her friend, Miss Masson."

"How did she react?"

"Miss Masson said she was very upset. She felt bad about it, you know, showing it to her, but felt she had to since the woman he's kissing is—or I should say, was—a co-worker. I'd want to know. Wouldn't you?"

This was getting more complicated by the minute. "Where'd the friend get the picture?"

"Another mutual friend who was at the after-hours bar the night of the gala texted it to her."

"Why?"

"I don't know. I'm not trained to answer the whys. Just the hows. The whys are for the profilers."

Something didn't sit right. "Do you have a list of the people who were with him that night?"

"I don't. The limo company probably does. Or at least a record of the addresses. It wouldn't be hard to get."

"Have you looked at the portable hard drive I gave you?"

"It's tough getting someone on the weekend. We got a new

hire, a young go-getter who was willing to come in this morning. He says it's a treasure trove of data with all kinds of digital footprints, like IP addresses, time stamps, that kind of thing. But as of this minute, I don't have a report."

He did a quick review in his head. Other than being the salesman that sold the software, there was nothing to tie Jack to the patient files. He remembered the phone records. The call made from Dr. Emery's office to Dr. Garcia's in Chicago. Jack didn't make those calls. Someone at Dr. Emery's office did. Was it possible Grant was right about Jack? What if it was him who had it wrong? Did Bibbins know something? Was she covering for Jack?

"I've seen a lot of weird stuff," Grant said, "but this one is right up there. Killing chemo patients and scheduling the victims for follow-up appointments? That's some kind of twisted shit. If I could find the link between the doc in Indy and the one in Chicago, I'd bet everything else would fall into place."

That reminded him. He was supposed to call Anna back. "Excuse me." He slid out of the booth.

"Where're you going?" Grant asked.

Buck returned from the restroom just as the waitress set down his steak and eggs. "That looks awfully good," Buck said.

"I'll be right back," Vance said.

"Take your time, but hurry," Grant said, grimacing at Buck stabbing an egg, the yolk fanning out on the white plate.

Hopefully, the men's room would be empty and he could talk to Anna privately. He changed course and walked outside, instead. Damn it was cold. Shivering, he redialed Anna.

"Mr. Courage?"

"Yes?"

Her voice quivered. "I think I know how those patients died."

61

Saturday, Night, Indianapolis, Indiana

Marie Elizabeth answered on the first ring.

"I just talked to Jack," Bibbins said. "Why didn't you call me?"

"I can't discuss it."

How dare her. "What do you mean you can't discuss it?"

"I can't."

"Why not?"

"I just can't. Don't put this on me."

Put it on her? Why was it always about ME? She had everything, never had to lift a finger for any of it. She'd been ME's loyal friend, supporting her when her fiancé Yoshio killed himself. ME might have more money, and might've come from a better family, but she owed her.

"I need you to tell me what you know."

"I wish I could."

Wish? What was stopping her? She'd showed her the picture of Jack in the bar. "I need your help, ME."

ME sighed. "The FBI interviewed me today."

Her blood simmered. "The FBI? Why did they want to talk to you?"

"I was with the Masson lawyers. I can't discuss it."

"You have to tell me. If Jack's in trouble, you have to help him."

"I told you. I can't."

"You're my best friend."

"I'm sorry, Bibbs. I really am, but I have myself and my family to think about."

"You don't have anything to do with the business, and if Masson Medical is responsible for those deaths and you're covering—"

"Take that back."

"I'm sorry. At least tell me why they interviewed you."

ME got mad. "I told you, I can't say."

"You're my BFF. How can you not tell me what's going on?"

ME lowered her voice. "Listen, an FBI agent is asking questions about the night of the party."

"The gala?"

"I shouldn't even tell you this much."

"What about that night?"

ME didn't answer.

She pressed harder. "What did they want to know?"

"You should stop covering for him."

"Come on, ME, what did the FBI want to know? If the tables were turned and you asked me and I knew, I'd tell you."

"That's not fair."

"I swear I won't tell anyone."

"You mean that now, but if you have to protect Jack later, you'll break your promise."

"Did they want to know who was with us that night?"

"I told you, I can't say."

She peered through the windshield at another set of head-lights passing her parked car and slunk behind the wheel. "What did you tell them?"

ME didn't answer.

"What did you tell them?"

"I said that Jack and some of his friends went to the bar."

"What else?"

"That we went home, you, me, and old Doctor Bob, separately."

"Why'd you tell them that?"

"They'd already talked to the limo company."

Her heart raced. "What else did you tell them?"

No answer.

"Come on, ME. What else?"

"Jack told them he went home after the gala."

"He lied?"

"Yes."

"Did you cover for him?"

"They already knew. They'd talked to the driver."

She could hardly breathe. "What else did you tell them?"

"Don't do this. If Jack did something bad—"

"Did you tell them about the picture?"

ME didn't deny it.

"Oh my God. That means you showed it to them."

"Come on, Bibbins."

"Why did you do that?"

"To protect you. If Jack had something to do with those deaths, you don't want to get mixed up in it. They're trying to figure out who was where, and when. Do you think I should've covered for him?"

She counted to five in her head, then asked another question, this time calmly. "If you wanted to help me, why did you tell them about the picture of Jack?"

"To prove you weren't with him."

"I don't understand."

"They asked Jack and he said he was with you the whole night. I told the truth and the picture proves you weren't there, and that makes Jack a liar."

"Oh, God."

"They wanted to know how you reacted."

"What did you say?"

"The truth. That you were very upset."

She pressed her head against the driver's-side headrest, closed her eyes, and listened.

"I'm sorry this is happening. It's a total nightmare."

"You shouldn't have told them anything. You're ruining Jack's life, and you're ruining mine."

The call dropped and she stared at the screen. A thought jumped into her head. Did she need a lawyer, too? How would she possibly pay for that?

Oh, no. A figure was headed toward her parked car. What was her mother doing wandering around without her wig, or a jacket? Dorothy made a beeline for the parked car and tapped on the window. Bibbins powered it down.

"Whaddaya doin' out here, hon? I was starting to get worried." She clamped her arms around her chest.

"I had to get something out of my car."

"With the engine running? You been gone a while."

Dorothy walked around the front bumper and jiggled the passenger-side door but it was locked. Bibbins reached across the seat and opened it from the inside.

"At least you had the good sense to keep your doors locked," she said, climbing in.

"I had to make a phone call and I didn't want to bother you."

"It wouldn'ta bothered me none, hon. Unless you're talking to that good-for-nothing boy, Jack."

"I know you don't like him."

"Come back to the house and keep me company. I know I should feel worse than I do, but I'm hungry. Let's order a pizza. It'll be my treat."

"All right. Go back in and wait for me. I'll be there in a minute."

"I want extra pepperoni and cheese," she said, getting out of the car.

"All right."

When Dorothy was out of sight, she hopped out, opened the back driver's-side door, and grabbed the bag of bio waste she'd collected from the apartment. Looking both ways, she crossed the parking lot to where the dumpster was tucked behind a wooden façade. She lifted the lid and tossed the bag inside.

Did her mother appreciate all that she'd done for her? She'd risked everything. If Emery and Shah found out she'd stolen thousands of dollars' worth of chemo drugs, she'd be fired. The doctors might even turn her into the police.

Bright headlights blinded her and she squatted, then scooted behind the dumpster fence, shivering, the wet grass wicking into the cuffs of her pants. The driver continued past slowly in a vintage pickup truck, then turned the corner and headed toward the parking lot near the pool. She jogged to the back entrance of her apartment, rolled up her pants, kicked off her shoes, and went inside.

"Mama, do you like mushrooms?"

"If you want those, you better get your own pie, hon."

"Pepperoni and cheese is good," she said, adding under her breath, "especially if you're a hick from Indiana."

"I heard the first part, but what didja say after that?"

"Nothing, Mama," she yelled. "Do you want a large pepperoni and cheese pizza?"

"Already ordered it. Told ya I was buyin'."

62

Saturday, Night, Indianapolis, Indiana

Apartment complexes were mice mazes for humans: If you didn't know exactly where you were going, it was a bitch trying to find the cheese. Vance craned his neck over the steering wheel and squinted out the windshield of the 1950 Ford, looking for clues to Unit 410. It was dark out, the bright headlamps glistened on the wet pavement, and though it was night, the cloud cover that had hung over the city all day impaired visibility in a new way, as if looking through murky cheesecloth. He didn't see any building numbers or letters showing him which way to go. He might have to park and search on foot.

By now Grant would've figured he'd bailed out of the restaurant and left him alone with Buck and his steak and eggs. Anna had texted him Bibbins' address, and he'd driven the old truck from Denny's to the Kroger store, waited in the customer-service lane, bought a burner and a prepaid card, activated it, then typed the nurse's apartment address into the new one.

Before he'd left the grocery store, he'd dictated a text message into his personal phone: going dark for a while wait for me, then sent it to Boomer. He'd turned it off, removed the SIM card and battery, then stashed it in the glove box.

He found the windshield wiper switch by shining the burner flashlight on the dash and activated the single arm on the driver's-side. It struggled to wipe the glass as strips of rubber flapped, leaving streaks, worsening visibility.

He completed one lap around the apartment complex, then parked the old truck next to a dumpster. He killed the engine, reached under the driver's-side seat, grabbed his gun, stuffed it in the waistband of his pants, then covered it with his shirttail. Waiting a minute, making sure no one had noticed him or the hillbilly truck, he got out and jogged to the back side of the façade that hid the dumpster. The number on the door of the nearest apartment would give him a point of reference. He headed toward it.

He strode toward the walkway, then slowed when he reached the privacy hedge. The corner apartment lights were on, and a television flickered through the gaps in the blinds. Too risky. The unit next to it was dark inside, and a yellow bug light flickered on the porch. He walked close enough to read the number: Unit 209.

Building 4 had to be two away, but which direction? He glanced over his shoulder and turned left, staying closest to the side where it was dark between buildings, walking on a diagonal heading toward the street. Common sense said if that was Building 1, and if it faced the parking lot and the street, that meant the buildings were offset in a zigzag pattern. If Two was set behind One, then Three faced the parking lot and Four was set back, parallel to Building 2. He walked purposefully, confirming the location of Building 1.

He hurried back to the main walkway between buildings, ducking beneath windows, using the shadows for cover. Stopping for a few seconds to map the front side of Building 4, he hurried, worried he might be mistaken for someone with bad intent.

Headlights flashed in the gaps between the buildings and a compact car stopped, then began a three-point turn. He froze, then took one step back into the shadows, waiting until the vehicle completed a U-turn and parked.

Pressing his shoulders against the side wall between buildings, he waited, then walked briskly on the pathway looking for numbers on the front doors. Unit 410 was at the far end near another row of thick hedges. He crouched below the windows and took a position where he could look inside. The blinds were closed and the lights were on. A silhouette crossed the room.

She was home.

Using the dense shrubbery for cover, he squeezed between the building and the hedge to the backside of her apartment, then stopped in the dark corner of the common area where he calculated he'd get a line of sight inside. Something moved in the shadows. His heart popped and he jumped back a step before seeing a fat tabby cat. It ran toward the narrow space, back into the bushes where it'd just come, then disappeared. He took another step back and bumped into something flimsy, the surprise knocking him off balance. He grabbed a handful of hedge to keep from tipping over.

What was a big cardboard box doing out here? It hadn't been there long or it would've sagged from yesterday's storm. Staying low and out of view, he moved to the side, then squatted behind it, using it for cover, wondering what a black plastic bag was doing on the ground beneath it. As his eyes adjusted to the darkness, he had a direct view into the sliding glass doors on the back of Unit 410. The vertical blinds were pulled partially open; he'd found a good place to watch.

An inside light went on, revealing a narrow pass-through to the kitchen. A person entered and opened the refrigerator, partially blocking his view, and when the door closed, he saw someone reach up and open the cabinet above the sink. He shaded his eyes and squinted. Who was the bald man?

The whistling of a train—a cell phone ringtone—alerted him to a person walking between buildings, a young man who appeared lost. He wore a royal-blue and red uniform and matching cap, and carried something dark blue, shiny, and flat, one of those insulated heat bags to keep pizzas hot. The delivery driver stood on the dimly lit walkway, pirouetting slowly, as if looking for the right apartment. The boy glanced at the screen on his phone, then backtracked, and disappeared.

Emulating a cyclist, trotting in a half-sitting position, he left his position, staying beneath the hedge line. He advanced back to the pathway between buildings at the opposite end to check which way the boy had gone, but didn't see him.

A minute later the pizza boy reappeared, checking his phone screen again, then stopped on the walkway in front of Building 4. Apparently lost, the boy hurried back toward the parking lot, turned right and disappeared again. It'd take him a minute, maybe two more to locate the right apartment, deliver the pizza, and be on his way. Waiting, Vance felt the cold and saw his breath, clouds that slowly disappeared beneath his nose. A dog barked in the distance. He counted to fifty, shivering, figuring it was enough time, then took a long step away from his position, and checked to see if the pathway was clear.

The boy suddenly reappeared, still carrying the blue bag. Vance jogged backward, out of his line of sight. Was he looking for an apartment in Building 4? He peered around the corner in time to see him turn left. Then he had a weird thought. What if he was delivering the pizza to the nurse? He hastened his step, walking quietly, now following the young man heading toward 410.

He ducked behind the privacy hedge in front of Unit 410 to watch. The boy took one step on the short walkway toward the front door of Unit 406 and when he got close, he backtracked, walked the path to 407, and turned back again. The boy locked his eyes on the corner unit—410—the nurse's place. But suddenly he stopped, turned and looked in his direction, as if sensing danger, like a prey animal.

What if the boy had seen him? He calculated the distance in his head, the space, measuring about twenty feet between them, assessing the time and distance it'd take to ambush him. A short sprint, and one long stride. Maybe two shorter, more powerful ones. But only if he had to.

Both remained still, ancient instincts at work, ones between the hunter and the hunted, his heart pumping, certain the young man's was, too. The boy turned his head slowly in his direction while he held his breath for a moment, adrenaline flowing from his primitive brain.

The delivery driver took two steps forward, then stopped again and craned his head, looking over his shoulder. The common-area walkway to 410 dead-ended at the chest-high row of thick hedges, the area he'd used to sneak behind her apartment to look through the sliding glass doors.

The boy moved in that direction, hastening his pace, passing apartment 408, then 409, stopping again at the short entryway to 410.

What were the chances? Vance bolted from the shadows, the soles of his shoes pounding the sidewalk. The young man took one step up the hedge-lined path to Bibbins' front door. Vance pounced, surprising him, hooking an elbow around his neck, long enough to subdue him, plastering the other hand over the kid's mouth.

The boy's knees went slack, still clutching the pizza warmer with both hands he fell backward into Vance's chest, body quaking, surrendering.

He loosened his right arm around his throat, firming his grip over the kid's mouth. "Stay quiet," he whispered into his ear, "I don't want to hurt you."

The boy nodded.

Keeping one hand over the kid's face, he threaded his right arm beneath the boy's armpit and clamped it around his chest, dragging him to the shaded area near the hedge. He spoke softly. "I'm not going to hurt you. Stand up and turn around."

The boy obeyed, faced him, wide-eyed, silent.

"Put the pizza on the ground."

The boy did as he was told, squatting slowly.

He lifted his shirt high enough to reveal the 9-mil stuffed in the waistband of his khakis. "Get up." He reached into his back pocket.

The boy slowly stood and remained motionless, staring at him, panting.

He took a thin stack of bills from his wallet, pulled the burner from his pants' pocket, and handed him the money. As the boy took the cash, he snapped a picture. "This never happened. Understood?"

He nodded.

"Gimme your hat and your jacket."

"What?"

"You heard me. Gimme your ball cap and jacket."

The boy hesitated, then lifted the hat from his head and shrugged his jacket off.

"Take the pizza out of the bag."

He squatted, ripped the Velcro, and pulled the white box out.

"Leave it there."

The kid bobbed his head.

"Get out of here."

The boy vanished.

He put on the jacket, slapped the cap on his head, pulled the brim low to cover his face, then picked up the pizza box, walked to the front door of Apartment 410, and knocked.

A few seconds later the door opened and the pretty blonde stepped outside, handing him a five-dollar bill, reaching out to trade the pizza for the tip.

He dropped the box, grabbed her arm, and twisted it.

"OWWW. What the—!" She tried shouldering the door closed.

"What's going on?" It was another voice, not a man's, a woman's.

He jammed his left foot in the threshold, blocking the door, glanced over his shoulder, and pushed his way inside, knocking Bibbins off balance. She broke away. He kicked it closed with the heel of his shoe and scanned the inside but didn't see the nurse. Instead, he saw a bulky person, a woman—with no hair standing in the kitchen doorway, arms crossed, glaring at him.

She dropped her hands to her hips. "What the hell do you want?"

"I want to talk to the girl. Move out of my way."

"I'll do no such thing." The big woman stood her ground.

She'd escape out the back. "Get out of my way."

He saw the nurse charging at him from behind the bald-headed woman.

"Move, Mama!"

The older woman doubled over as Bibbins rammed her in the kidney, pushing her to the side, rushing him.

"Agghh. What are you doing?" the bald woman yelled, grabbing the doorframe. "Stop!"

It was too late. He didn't see the knife. She swung it wildly, slicing his left arm at the shoulder, cutting through the pizza jacket, through his shirt. He spun to the left, drew the 9-mil from his waistband, and grabbed her right wrist with his left hand, forcing the shiny blade away and up. He pointed the gun at the carpet, blood running down his forearm, passing from his hands to hers. She fought him, wrestling the knife with both hands, undeterred, his left hand tiring, sticky with blood, grappling the knife handle in a game of two hands against one.

"Stop it, Bibbins!"

She ignored her mother and broke one hand free, the left one, and took a wild swipe at his face. He leaned backward as the blade passed an inch from his nose. He gripped the 9-mil in his right palm and lifted it. He could end it now. Point and shoot. So simple. But not.

"Awww!" He doubled over, dropping the Glock, the knee to his groin knocking the wind out of him. He squatted for an instant, and when he looked up, saw the knife, her two hands gripping the handle as if preparing to drive a stake in the ground. The Sword of Damocles. He rolled onto his right shoulder as she drove the knife into the floor, falling on top of it.

A figure loomed over them. "Stop it!"

"Shut up, Mama." She clamped both palms on the handle and yanked the knife from the carpet, then leapt to her feet. He'd been quicker, grabbing a handful of hair.

"Drop the knife."

"Ahh-ahh-ahh," she screamed, "let go of my hair!"

She lunged at him, swinging the knife in her right hand. He spun. She missed, losing her balance, grabbing the back of the sofa with her free hand, then pushed off, and charged at him again with the bloody knife.

"Stop it, Bibbins!"

She ignored the command, eyes flashing like a wild animal.

"I said stop it!"

"Will you ever shut up! Shut up, Mama! Shut up!" Knife in hand, she twirled from Vance and charged in the other direction. Her mother grunted, stumbling backward, doubling over, holding her stomach, balancing against the recliner, looking down and up, down at the knife handle, the blade buried in her belly.

"Mama! Look what you made me do!"

Dorothy whimpered, touching the top the black handle of the knife. "What have you done?"

He pulled the burner from his pocket to call 9-1-1.

The front door banged open and Jack froze midstep, staring in horror at Bibbins' blood-spattered clothes.

Bibbins ran toward him. "Thank God, you're here."

JACK BACKED AWAY, hands up, palms facing her, fingers splayed. His eyes stopped on the blood seeping from Vance's shoulder.

"What's going on? What happened to you?"

"She attacked me with a knife. Then she stabbed her mother."

Jack's eyes followed his, stopping on Dorothy tipped over on the recliner. "Jesus. Christ. Why?"

Bibbins approached him. "I did it for you," her voice a guttural whisper.

"For me? Are you crazy?"

The apartment filled with people, agents in blue FBI jackets, including Hunter Grant.

A woman, an agent, intervened. "Step aside, sir." Jack moved out of the way. She faced Bibbins. "Put your hands out front, together."

The nurse looked at them, as if surprised by her blood-stained palms. She leaned toward Jack and yelled, "I did it for you," spittle spraying. "They cheated you. It's not fair. I had to punish them."

The female agent repeated it, more forcefully. "Put your hands together. In front, where I can see them. Now."

"You okay?" Vance asked him.

Jack didn't answer, his upper lip twitching as he watched the agent clamp the cuffs on her wrists, listening as the woman read Bibbins her rights.

"Let's go." The agent nudged Bibbins forward, pushing a palm on the small of her back.

She planted her feet and twisted her neck, eyes flashing at Jack. "I did it for you." Her voice deepened. "They rigged the system and what did you do? Nothing. You partied and went along with it, you coward. At least *I* did something. Even if they weren't supposed to die." She held her head up, chin jutting as the agent walked her toward the door.

Marie Elizabeth appeared in the doorway, her mouth agape.

Bibbins glared at her. "I did it for you, too, you ungrateful little—"

"Let's go," the agent said.

Jack rushed toward ME. Vance stood in front of the recliner, blocking her view to the grisly scene.

"Did what for me?" Marie Elizabeth asked.

"We'd be married to doctors. They ruined everything. You know what they did and you're a coward, just like Jack."

"You're sick," ME said.

Bibbins threw her head back and laughed. "I take that back, you're not a coward, you're a spoiled princess who had every-thing handed to her."

ME's eyes widened to saucers. Jack rushed past Bibbins, to ME, grabbed her by the shoulders and turned her sideways, making room for the agent to walk Bibbins out.

"You're weak!" Bibbins yelled. "They had to pay for what they did."

ME covered her mouth with her hand.

Vance had never met her but she had to be Marie Elizabeth Masson.

He stood as a human divider, hiding the wounded old woman. Something startled him, a jab on the hip.

"Tell her," Dorothy said, poking him with a finger, "tell my daughter I love her." Her arm went limp and hung over the side of the recliner. She gasped. "My daughter . . . she was tryin' to save my life."

His stomach churned.

Grant stood in the kitchen. The freshly styled wig on a Styrofoam head caught Vance's eye, and next to it, the silver tray with shiny medical supplies, neatly organized. He grabbed a dishtowel and draped it over the knife handle protruding from Dorothy's belly.

Grant opened the refrigerator. "Check it out."

Vance stuck his head inside and saw the glass vials in the clear plastic deli drawer. "Dr. Emery was right."

"About what?" Grant asked.

"She's been treating her mother for cancer, here in the apartment." He pointed to the IV stand.

"Jesus," Grant said, "I thought I'd seen it all." He eyed Vance's shoulder. "Let me look at that."

He slid his left arm out of the bloody jacket and pulled the polo shirt from his neck, exposing his collarbone. The cut ran down to his bicep.

"You might need stitches."

"Nah. It's superficial."

"How'd you know it was her?" Grant asked.

Vance ripped open a gauze pad from the silver tray, tore off two strips of medical tape, pressed the pad on his wound, and taped it tightly. "Anna, the nurse who works for the doc in Chicago, has been stealing chemo drugs for her and exchanging them for different ones."

"How do you know that?"

"She called me when she realized what she'd been doing might've killed the Chicago patients."

"That makes her a co-conspirator."

He knew that.

"Why was she helping her?"

"They're cousins. Bibbins needed enough of the chemo drug to treat her mother and was afraid Emery might notice if she stole too much so she asked Anna to sneak some from Garcia's clinic."

"What did they replace the drugs with?"

"I don't know. She said she cut the doses in half and replaced them with something Bibbins gave her, said she assumed Bibbins knew what she was doing. The patients were supposed to get sick, not die."

"They were poisoning them?"

He nodded.

"Why'd they cut the chemo with other drugs?"

He shrugged. "Anna said Bibbins was worried they wouldn't have side effects on a half dose and the docs might get suspicious. We both heard what Bibbins said. I'm not convinced they meant to kill anyone."

The rest was for Grant to figure out.

The paramedics arrived and the field agents cleared the living room. They rolled the IV stand out of the way and lifted the dishtowel he'd used to cover the knife handle.

Hunter Grant stood next to him, watching them work the scene. "I called Jack when you disappeared. He was on his way here."

"Huh, not headed to a bar." That reminded him. "Where's

Buck?"

"A couple of minutes after you skipped out, Rogers called like she promised. We got her location. She's holed up at the Conrad."

"The Conrad?"

"Best hotel in the city."

"You're not there, doing the honors?"

"We're working on a warrant. Plus, I couldn't leave my man on the battlefield."

The first part was likely true but the second part was bullshit. The chance to take down the Chemo Killer was way bigger than catching a couple of white-collar criminals gaming the healthcare system. That's why Grant was here, instead of there.

Vance played along. "I guess I owe you one. I gotta go," he said, walking outside to get some air. To regroup.

A pair of cat eyes glowed in the darkness: the tabby he'd seen earlier. He jogged to the old rust-bucket truck, reassembled his phone and pressed REDIAL.

"How's Lauren?"

"She's okay, she's asleep in a spare room at my sister's place," Boomer said.

"Can you come get me?"

"Sure. Where are you?"

"I'll text you the address."

He ended the call, copied the address to the apartment, and sent it to Boomer. He collected the torn packaging from the burner strewn in the truck and stuffed it in the plastic grocery bag, then headed to the dumpster. He opened the lid. What was on top of the garbage? Pinching the white bag open with his fingernails, he peeked inside and saw the bloody bio waste. It was Grant's job to find it. He took the receipt out and tossed the Kroger bag in.

He jogged to the front of the complex, shining his cell light along the curbing, then dropped the burner and the receipt in the storm drain. He looked up at the night sky. The waxing crescent moon, blurred by thick cloud cover, glowed like a fuzzy open parenthesis. Shivering, he took a deep breath and exhaled a white cloud, then watched it dissipate.

Sensing someone behind him, he turned to see.

"Mr. Courage?"

"Yes."

"I'm Marie Elizabeth Masson. I didn't want to talk in front of the FBI. I'm pretty sure I know how the patients died."

He knew the who, and had a working theory of the why, but the how would help. "Why are you telling me?"

"Who else can I tell?"

"Hmm."

"I host cosmetic parties for my girlfriends. We go to a dermatology spa where we get treatments, injections." She cast her eyes at the sidewalk. "I know what you're thinking, that we're too young to be so vain."

That's not what he was thinking. "I'm not judging."

"I always invite Bibbins. She works so hard, and I knew she couldn't afford it, so for her birthday a while back, I gave her a gift certificate. She used it at the next event, and the day after the doctor called me and said some drugs were missing. She told me one of her employees saw Bibbins snooping around in the supply room. I figured it was some sort of mistake, that maybe they lost track of it, so I paid for it thinking it would spare everyone the embarrassment."

"Jesus. Do you know what was missing?"

"Botox and lidocaine."

He paused for a two-beat, processing the new information that fit with the toxicology report Emery had. He didn't need a medical degree to know what an IV dose of lidocaine and Botox could do. "What did she mean when she said 'they had to pay for what they did'?"

ME took a deep breath, and pulled her winter coat tighter around her body. "I was engaged to a boy in college who killed himself."

He shivered in the cold. "I'm so sorry."

"I know," she said. Then she told him a story: "My grandfather—who started Masson—graduated from the University of Michigan medical school in 1942. My family's been a big alumni donor ever since. When my fiancé, Yoshio, applied to the U. of M. pre-med school, he was denied admission even though he had the grades. Bibbins thought it was unfair, convinced he didn't get in because he was Asian-American. She asked me about it and I didn't want to talk about it. She assumed it's the reason he killed himself."

"It wasn't?"

"No. Maybe if I'd told her the truth, none of this would have happened."

"What's the truth?" He blew warm breath on his hands and stuffed them in the front pockets of his pants.

"He was bipolar and went off his meds. He hated the way they made him feel. He got more and more depressed and he started to isolate from everyone, including me and his family. One day that winter, he walked out onto the frozen lake and disappeared. I never told Bibbins why he did it. When I read the lawsuit and saw that someone changed the dates on the patient records to the twenty-eighth of June, I realized that was the day Bibbins and Jack were getting married." ME took one hand from her coat pocket and brushed the hair from her face. "She was so adamant, calling people, begging them to change their plans. It had to be that exact date. Something seemed odd so I started trying to figure it out."

He'd thought about it too, but June twenty-eighth had no significance.

"She was so obsessed with it." ME shook her head. "Then it dawned on me. In a way, it was obvious."

Sometimes that made something harder to see. "What did you figure out?"

"June twenty-eighth, 1978, the date of the Bakke decision by the Supreme Court. A student, a military veteran, named Alan Bakke sued the University of California at Davis for reverse discrimination when he was denied admission to medical school. He argued that his test scores were much higher than lots of others who'd been admitted and that he'd been passed over because he was a white male."

"How did the case end up?"

"In favor of the university."

"Bibbins thought your fiancé killed himself because he didn't get into the University of Michigan?"

"She was obsessed. She wouldn't let it go. She thought Jack was denied for the same reason."

"Was he?"

"I don't know. He had a reputation as a party boy."

"Have you told anyone about this?"

"No. At first, I thought it sounded crazy. Masson has access to all kinds of records so I had someone in the back office do some digging. I found out the two doctors she targeted both graduated from U. of M." She inhaled deeply and exhaled slowly, her breath a streamer of white that dissipated quickly. "I can't even say it out loud."

She didn't have to.

"You know what makes it worse?" she asked.

As if anything could.

"Both doctors graduated at the top of their classes. They scored over ninety percent on their MCATs and would've been accepted to almost any medical school on their own merit. It wasn't fair to target them and their patients."

Fair. That wasn't the word he'd have chosen. *Sick*, maybe, but not *fair*. He narrowed his eyes, processing this new information. He saw Boomer's Nissan Rogue headed his way. "My ride's here. You better go."

"I wouldn't have guessed in a million years she'd do anything like this. Thank you," she said, nodding her head once before turning and hurrying toward the dim walkway between buildings.

The University of Michigan diplomas he'd seen on their office walls. She'd targeted them because they were minorities who'd graduated from the school. What a twisted piece of work.

"Where to?" Boomer asked.

"The Conrad."

63

Saturday, Night, Indianapolis, Indiana

"How may I help you?" the elegant woman working the front desk asked.

"Would you please ring Miss Sherry Rogers' room and tell her Bill Fields is here," Vance said.

"Certainly." She cradled the phone on her shoulder and dialed the room.

He surveyed the lobby. He was alone. Boomer waited across the street.

"She said to go on up. Room 304. The elevators are at the end of the hall, to the left."

He headed that way, took it to the third floor, and looked for the wall plaque with room numbers and arrows. He put his finger over the peephole and knocked.

"Hold on."

A half minute later the door opened but stopped with the

chain in place. He'd figured she might do that. He stuck his foot in the threshold and pointed his weapon through the gap.

"Shit." She tried to pull the door shut but couldn't. When she saw the muzzle of the gun, she unchained the door and let him in. "What do you want?"

"I want my money back."

"Too late for that." She turned her back to him and walked toward the window.

"The FBI's getting a warrant. A judge is probably signing it right now." He pointed his gun at her. "You have one minute to call your bank."

"And do what, exactly?"

"Wire my money back into my account, or I'll hold you here until the Feds arrive. Better yet, I'll make a call and expedite things."

"I don't have all of it."

"I'll take what you got. Get busy."

He stood over her as she logged onto her laptop. The balance was just over two million.

"I can't just press a button."

"Call the bank."

She hesitated, her criminal brain searching for a card to play, any card. "They're closed."

"Either call them and give me my money back so you get a head start as a fugitive, or I'm happy to babysit you until the Feds arrive."

She shook her head.

"You got less than ten seconds. Burn up the time, and I'll make you show me the balances in the other two accounts. I'm still negotiating. In eight seconds, the deal's off the table."

She gritted her teeth and jerked her head down in two short bursts.

He sat on the edge the bed watching her, listening, the Glock he'd bought locally aimed at her.

She picked up her phone, scrolled through recent calls and tapped the screen. She held it against her ear, then asked to speak to someone by name. "Yes, I'll hold."

She glared at him. He shrugged.

"I'd like to do a wire transfer," she said. "I'd like to use the same routing numbers and account number as a previous incoming transfer . . . Uh-huh . . . Uh-huh . . . I know that . . . no I don't have it . . . look for one from a Cayman account, around a month ago . . . yeah, that's it."

Wire transfers were instant. There'd be no turning back, especially on an international transfer.

When she finished the call, he walked toward the desk. An abstract pattern swirled on her laptop as a screensaver.

"Show me the proof."

He watched her tap the return key. The bank log-in page had timed out. "Sign back in and refresh the page."

When it came back up, two million dollars had been transferred out.

"Thank you."

"Fuck off."

"My sentiments exactly," he said, walking out the door and hurrying to his waiting ride.

64

Sunday, Morning, Indianapolis International Airport

I t seemed like the airport in Indianapolis had gone Indy 500 crazier with colorful flags, and banners, and sleek race cars on display.

"Will you take my picture?"

Lauren posed next to a life-sized cardboard figure of a driver, a handsome young man who looked like he should be on a surfboard instead of driving a race car.

"His name's Will Power. It's better than yours."

Vance grinned at her. "We could stay for the race. Masson has a hospitality suite right over pit lane." He looked out the window, the bright paint schemes of the awaiting jets clashing against the backdrop of another drab day. "We could change our flight."

She looked at him pensively, then shook her head. "I want to go home."

He'd never seen her like this, her skin pale, eyes sunken with gray half-moons beneath them. "You want to get a bite to eat?"

"Sure."

He led the way to the Indy 500 Café and waited at the hostess stand. His phone buzzed in his pocket. He pulled it out and looked at the screen. "I'll be right back," he said.

Dr. Garcia sounded chipper. "I owe you dinner."

"Maybe next time I'm in town."

"You're leaving?"

"Yeah, we're going home. I'm at the airport."

"I guess you heard they caught the killer. Killers, I should say. I can't believe it was an inside job, right under our noses."

"It's always right under someone's nose. The good news is you're out of jail."

"They dropped the charges. Listen, this is awkward, but I've got a question for you."

"Ask away."

"You wouldn't happen to know about a very large anonymous donation to my clinic, would you?"

"Sounds like whoever pledged it wants to remain anonymous."

"Whoever made it, made it on my behalf," Garcia said.

"Well, that should help you get what you need to treat your patients better, the way you want."

"Thank you," Garcia said, "or whoever. Stay in touch."

"I will. Take care, Doc. One more thing. Did you figure out why Anna scheduled those appointments?"

"She told the FBI that she and her cousin with the weird name did it as a distraction, to call attention away from themselves stealing the drugs."

He thought about telling Garcia the truth, but decided not to. In a way, it had worked and the FBI might buy the story, especially if ME kept the symbolic reason a secret. "Huh."

"Would you believe the mom is telling the investigators she can't remember who stabbed her?"

"Forensics will sort that out."

"I hope you're right," Garcia said. "And thanks."

Vance ended the call. A million dollars in Emilio Garcia's name had to get the board's attention. They'd think if some anonymous benefactor donated a sum that big once, they might do it again, and that would give Garcia leverage.

"Hey."

He recognized the voice. "What are you doing here?"

The duffle bag—the one he'd thrown at Buck's dog—hung over Boomer's shoulder. "After I dropped you off, I parked my car in the long-term lot."

"Why? Did we leave something behind?"

He shook his head. "I bought a ticket." He showed him a boarding pass.

"You're going to Miami?"

"I always wanted to. Never did anything like this before. Spent my whole life never taking a single chance on anything. Never even been on an airplane."

Lauren saw them talking. He held his hand up, signaling her to wait. "Really?"

"Nope," Boomer said. "I figured I better do it before I chickened out and changed my mind."

He put his arm across Boomer's shoulder and man-hugged him, grinning. "Come on. Let me buy you lunch."

"I think I'm gonna like Florida," he said, following him. "I've never seen the ocean."

Vance gestured for Lauren to slide into the booth on his side. "I think you're gonna like it."

The old draft dodger adjusted his granny glasses higher on his nose. "I hope so."

"You're gonna fit right in," Vance said.

"You really think so?" There was a hint of excitement in Boomer's voice. "I guess it's possible to meet people that inspire you to do something you wouldn'ta done otherwise. Even when you're old as me."

He reached under the table and felt for Lauren's hand, squeezing it gently. "I couldn't agree more. But I have to warn you, it can get pretty hot in the summertime. We get a lot of hurricanes these days."

"It sounds like an adventure," Boomer said.

"There's a good chance of that," he said.

He'd picked a good time of year to visit. The snowbirds had flown north, and the family vacationers wouldn't arrive until school was out.

Yeah. It was a great time to go home.

ABOUT THE AUTHOR

Karen S. Gordon has written several award winning thrillers including *The Mutiny Girl*. If you enjoyed *Sick Money*, or have comments you'd like to share, she would appreciate you leaving a review. *Sick Money* is the fourth installment of the Gold & Courage Series.

Go to the series link here: https://amzn.to/3qci2k7

The adventures of Vance Courage and Lauren Gold continue with *Money for Nothing*. Pub date to be announced.

Please sign up for Karen's newsletter at karensgordon.com.

ALSO BY KAREN S. GORDON

The Mutiny Girl

"An outstanding debut thriller that has it all: misdirection, intrigue, murder, and family. Captivating and engrossing." — *The BookLife Prize*

"A taut, thrilling drama told exceptionally well." — *Steve Berry, NYT Bestselling Author*

"An engagingly written series starter with a bounty of plot twists and Miami vices." — *Kirkus Reviews*

Killer Deal

"A ripped-from-the-headlines legal thriller that John Grisham fans will love. Highly recommended." — *Best Thrillers*

" . . . a fast-paced thriller . . . an intriguing look at the hunger for power, the ego of control, the persistence of greed, and two unlikely heroes whom we can cheer for . . ." — *BookTrib*

Express Intent

"Fast-paced, evocative and urgent from the get-go, Express Intent is the best Gold and Courage series book yet." — *Bestthrillers*